Lilith smiled, and it was a cruel expression stippled in moonlight and shadows.

"I told you that she would be trouble. Better to leave her now. Or kill her."

The thought had crossed Warren's mind. Violent solutions to problems tended to be normal for him these days. Before the Hellgate had opened and the demons had arrived, that had never been the case. He'd run from every fight he'd ever faced. As a result, he'd been taken advantage of by nearly everyone he'd trusted.

"There's something out here," Warren said.

"How do you know?"

"Because I feel it." Warren lifted his metal hand. "In here."

Naomi started to say something, then she glanced at the hand and closed her mouth. He'd already proven that he was much more adept at the arcane forces the demons wielded. Now that he had a new hand, his power had taken on new turns that he hadn't had access to before.

"All right," she said finally. She pulled her long coat more firmly around her. "But I hope we find it soon."

Another of the zombies dropped into one of the unseen bog holes barely covered by ice. The sharp *crack* sounded just before the zombie plunged into the black water. This one didn't come back.

Only a little farther on, gray smoke plumed against the dark, star-filled sky. The feeling that pulled Warren lay in that direction as well.

Lilith walked beside him again. "You'll want to hurry," she stated calmly. "You're being followed."

HELLGATE LONDON®

BOOK THREE OF THREE
COVENANT

MEL ODOM

POCKET STAR BOOKS
New York London Toronto Sydney

Pocket Star Books
A Division of Simon & Schuster, Inc.
1230 Avenue of the Americas
New York, NY 10020

This book is a work of fiction. Names, characters, places, and incidents either are products of the author's imagination or are used fictitiously. Any resemblance to actual events or locales or persons, living or dead, is entirely coincidental.

First Pocket Star Books paperback edition September 2008

POCKET STAR and colophon are registered trademarks of Simon & Schuster, Inc.

For information about special discounts for bulk purchases, please contact Simon & Schuster Special Sales at 1-800-456-6798 or business@simonandschuster.com.

Cover art by Blur Studio

Manufactured in the United States of America

10 9 8 7 6 5 4 3 2 1

ISBN-13: 978-1-4165-2581-3
ISBN-10:   1-4165-2581-5

*For Dr. Gary Wade, who keeps my
world clear and in focus*

ACKNOWLEDGMENTS

Thanks to Bill Roper and the Flagship team for bringing a great game into the world and letting me play in it. And to Marco Palmieri, the editor who made it all work.

HELLGATE
LONDON®

COVENANT

PROLOGUE

T his is madness, Emily. You've got to come away
from here before it's too late. The demons aren't
your friends. They'll *never* be your friends." Rob
Houghton pleaded with his sister, but he knew she wasn't
listening to him. She was listening to that inner voice she
claimed to be attuned to these days.

The Burn, the strange power that came from the Hellgate that had opened by St. Paul's, hadn't made it this far
outside London yet. But everyone knew it was coming.
Demons occasionally prowled the forests and screamed
through the skies of the outlying areas.

As the Burn crept outward, it terraformed the land,
rendering it into a hellish landscape that only the demons
thrived on. No one in the scientific think tank that Rob
had worked in until the demons arrived on All Hallow's
Eve had been satisfied with what they believed the Burn
to be.

Some believed the Burn was changing the land into a
proper environment for the demons, but that was refuted
when it was pointed out that the malevolent creatures
handled themselves quite well under regular planetary

conditions. Others believed that the demons weren't causing the change at all; rather, it was their presence in the world that left a cancerous boil on the earth.

Rob's own beliefs held that the Burn was simply another weapon in the arsenal the demons had. By unleashing the Burn, the demons destroyed potable water and vegetation, all things livestock and wildlife needed to survive. He was convinced that it was supposed to eliminate the natural food chains the world supported.

To the south, he could see London. He thought he could almost see the Hellgate, the interdimensional portal that allowed the demons free egress into the world. He could definitely see the ever-circling dark clouds filled with ominous green lighting that hung low over the metropolitan area.

Chipping Ongar was a small town outside Greater London. Rob's mother had grown up there before she'd gone off to university to meet their father. As children, Rob and Emily had visited their grandparents there often. They'd maintained a small farm outside the city. When the horror swept over London, Rob had found his sister in all the confusion at the university and gotten her out of the city.

They'd lived on their grandparents' farm since the invasion. Their grandparents were long dead. Their parents had never made it out of London.

For a time, Rob had believed that they could wait it out. That had been over four years ago, and there was no relief in sight.

Even worse, Emily had fallen prey to the twisted mystics that had risen up to embrace the demons and their arcane powers.

"Emily," Rob called again.

She turned toward him and he could scarce bear her gaze. When he'd taken her from university, she'd been twenty, not truly innocent anymore—because college served to wear some innocence away—but not worldly, either.

She was petite and slender, possessing a boyish shape made popular by modeling agencies, Hollywood, and adverts. Her natural red hair was cropped even with her jaw, parted in the middle, and she'd had ash-gray eyes.

Rob was bundled up in the winter's cold. A thick parka with hood, thick gloves, and insulated coveralls barely kept him warm as the wind cut into him. Gusts carried new-fallen, powdery snow up in what looked like sugar confection whirlwinds. The white powder gleamed in the cracks of bark on the tree trunks. Cold moonlight beamed down through the skeletal branches.

Despite the bone-aching cold, Emily only wore what amounted to a halter top and hip-hugger shorts. She went without shoes even though the snow reached her mid-shin. They were clothes probably every university girl had hidden away from her parents and older brothers.

Now, though, Emily embraced her sexuality. She claimed that clothing interfered with her ties to the arcane forces that the presence of the demons had loosed in the world.

Rob didn't believe her. He was a scientist. He believed in things that could be weighed and measured. Magic was something for role-playing games.

Not all of the Cabalists, as they called themselves—and Rob called them cultists—had the same control over their bodies. Plenty of them that Rob had seen wore winter clothing.

"Rob," she said in that eerie voice she'd developed. "You shouldn't be here."

"Neither should you," Rob countered. He watched the shadows closely. The demons liked shadows because they could use them to hide in.

"You're cold," Emily said. "You should get back to the house."

"Not without you."

Quietly, her face serene, she turned her gaze back to the full moon. "It's not going to be safe out here for you."

"Then it won't be safe for you, either."

"I'll be fine."

Rob shook his head vehemently. "I'm not leaving without you, Em."

"All right," she told him, and sounded just for a moment like the little sister he'd pulled from university four years ago. "Follow if you must, but run if there's any trouble." She started walking.

"Trouble?" Rob made himself follow. "What trouble?"

Emily didn't answer. She strode through the snow as if it weren't there. Her exposed skin turned blue-green, and Rob noticed that it suddenly looked *scaled* in the moonlight. He'd seen the effect on other occasions, but never was it so pronounced as tonight.

Several of the cultists had taken to grafting the parts of slain demons onto their bodies. They claimed that the demon parts helped them amplify their powers. Rob didn't think that was true. As a geneticist, he didn't know how that could be true. The recipient of a transplanted organ didn't suddenly experience a DNA change. And that was the comparison the cultists offered. Except their change was on an arcane level, not a genetic one.

"There will be trouble," Emily stated.

Unconsciously, Rob shoved his hand into his coat pocket and felt for the massive Webley .455 revolver his grandfather had prized. Until he'd left London, he'd never touched a firearm. Now he not only knew how to use them, but he'd practiced till he was proficient with the Webley.

"Then you shouldn't go," Rob protested.

"I have to."

"Why? Who said?"

"I said."

Startled, Rob pulled the Webley from his coat pocket and took aim. Even with gloves on, the pistol was so big it accommodated the gloves easily. He aimed at the shadow next to a bare elm tree.

"Who are you?" Rob demanded.

"It's Seeker Orrus," Emily said. "The one I came to meet. Put away your weapon, Rob. It's not needed here. You're among friends."

Rob kept his weapon where it was. It suited him there. And he definitely wasn't among any friends that he recognized.

Seeker Orrus remained by the tree and surveyed Rob from under hooded eyes. He was tall and lean to the point of emaciation even in the winter clothing he had on. His head looked heavy for his thin shoulders. He leaned on a tall staff.

"You have nothing to fear from me," Orrus said.

"I'm safeguarding my sister," Rob replied.

The tall, thin man barked laughter. "Your sister is far more capable of protecting herself than you are."

"On that we disagree."

"It doesn't matter," Orrus said. "She's here because I asked her to be."

"Why?"

Orrus lurched out from the tree. Evidently he'd suffered an injury in the past that left him at least partially crippled. When the moonlight stripped the shadows from the man's long face, Rob thought he was going to be sick.

The cultist had braided small demons' horns from the bridge of his nose all the way to the base of his skull. Weird tattoos in a half-dozen colors covered his shaved scalp. One of his eyes was yellow and far too large for his head. Ridged scar tissue around the eye socket showed where someone had removed bone and tissue to make it fit. Two more horns, these downturned, jutted from either side of his chin. His breath leaked away from him in a slow pour of gray fog.

"Because she has done something no one else in our sept has been able to do," Orrus declared. "She's touched the mind of a demon."

Rob kept his pistol pointed at the man. "I don't know what kind of tripe you've been filling my sister's head with, but—"

"This isn't their doing," Emily said. "I truly have touched the mind of a demon. I called Seeker Orrus here tonight to help me work through this."

"Work through what?" The pistol had grown heavy at the end of Rob's arm. His hand shook and his shoulder ached from the weight of it.

"I dream of the demon," Emily said in a quiet voice. "I dream of the demon every night." For the first time in months or years, she looked distraught. "I can't tell you what it's like, Rob, but I've got to gain control of this . . . or it's going to destroy me."

Pain tightened Rob's throat. "What you need is to get out of here. If you get out of here, Emily—"

"I will only dream of the demon somewhere else," she interrupted. "Seeker Orrus believes he can help me."

Rob hesitated, but he didn't shift the pistol aim from the cultist.

"Please," Emily whispered. "Rob, permit me this. I can't bear this much longer." Fear showed in her eyes along with the pain. "I can't do this on my own."

"I can help her," Orrus said. "You can't."

Knowing he was defeated, Rob lowered the pistol, but he didn't put it back in his pocket. "What are you going to do?" With his surrender, the wind suddenly seemed colder.

"I'm going to help her break the link," Orrus said.

"Then get it done."

The cultists' choice to remain in the open surprised Rob. The arrival of seven more members of Orrus's group joining them in the moonlight under the bare branches of the trees also surprised him. Tiny snowflakes fell.

Two of the new arrivals, both male, didn't wear any more clothes than Emily did. The flesh of both of them looked like it was covered with scales as well.

At Orrus's bidding, Emily sat cross-legged on the ground. The cultist leader squatted in front of her.

As he watched, Rob wondered again at how much all life had changed since the arrival of the demons. Their metropolitan lives—his job at the R&D department at Gardner's Genetics—was gone. His kid sister had gone from a literature nut studying the works of Neil Gaiman and Ian Rankin to some kind of weird sorceress.

The thing was, Emily was a sorceress. Rob had seen her work magic: move things with her mind, summon fire from nowhere, and read minds with uncanny accuracy. He'd learned to be afraid of her, and he regretted that because he'd felt certain she'd sensed that about him.

What Rob hated most was the helplessness he now felt. When they'd first left the city, they'd both foraged for things to eat. Then, slowly but surely, she'd developed her own interests with the cultists. Even after arguments about it, something they'd never done before, she hadn't given up her studies of the old books that the cultists had let her borrow to make her own copies.

But he wouldn't leave her. He'd made that promise to himself when he'd gotten her out of the city and they'd both lived.

Orrus took an object from his robe and put it on the ground between Emily and himself. It looked like a jade figurine of a lighthouse.

"This is my foci," the cultist said in a soft, soothing voice. "Through it, I will access your thoughts and bring more control over them to you."

"Yes." Emily sat in a lotus position. Her hands were upraised on her knees.

"Stare at it," Orrus crooned. "Stare at the foci and feel the dream within you. Unleash its power. You don't even have to provide energy to feed the dream."

Rob thought the man's words were worthless. It was just noise to make himself feel important.

"Feed the dream to my foci," Orrus said. "I'll help you contain and bring it forth. We'll see your dream together. Then we'll conquer it and build safeguards for you."

The jade lighthouse glowed. The lambent green barely showed against the white field of snow.

"People have dreamed of demons before," Orrus said. "Many times. There's always a great deal of energy expended to do something like this. Always, unless the dreamer gets the upper hand, the energy only flows one way."

Rob barely restrained his anger. He couldn't believe Emily bought into all of this. *But the powers are real, aren't they? It isn't all crap.* But if she hadn't been messing about with those arcane forces, she wouldn't have been in the shape she was currently in.

"That's it," Orrus said. "Only a little more."

The jade lighthouse suddenly glowed as bright as a star. Snow around it started to melt, and it sank a couple of inches. The heat was intense enough that the figurine melted the snow for several inches in any one direction.

The hairs on the back of Rob's neck stood up. His stomach turned sour. This didn't need to happen. Emily already believed too much in the power of the demons.

"Reach for the dream," Orrus said. "Bring it forward."

A green, smoky incandescence drifted up from the jade lighthouse. Figures writhed within the two-foot-wide smoke cloud.

"How many do you see?" Orrus asked gently.

"Two," Emily said. "The demon and the woman he has taken for his own."

"How do you know this?"

"Because I can hear bits and pieces of their conversations."

"Concentrate harder," the cultist said. "I'll help you."

As he stared at the smoke and the figures within it, Rob discovered he was able to see as well. The green smoke cleared and became sharper all at the same time. Unbidden, he stepped forward toward Emily.

"Don't touch her," Orrus said.

Angered, Rob stared at the cultist.

"If you touch her at this point, you could cost your sister her life," Orrus told him. "Is that what you want?"

"No."

"Then listen to me. This is very dangerous work. For both of us." Orrus focused on the glowing lighthouse. Despite the cold air that blew snow around him, sweat covered the cultist's forehead. "Emily."

"Yes."

"Do you know where you are?"

Emily hesitated. She frowned a little, and Rob was instantly reminded of the little girl his sister had one day been.

"Underground," she answered.

"Underground where?"

"I don't know."

"What are you doing there?"

"Searching for something."

"What?" Orrus remained patient.

"I don't know."

"Does the demon know you're there?"

"No," Emily said. "I don't think so."

"You must be aware. Don't ever lose sight of the demon's attention. We must always know."

"All right."

Rob watched as the lighthouse grew even brighter. The heat reduced the snow around the figurine to a silver puddle. As he watched the smoke, Rob felt himself drawn into it.

Rob guessed that he must have blinked, because when he opened his eyes again, he stood in an underground cavern. When he'd been a child out on his grandparents' farm, he'd found caves to crawl into. They'd been little holes in hillsides. Formed by shifting rock or from the efforts of other kids in the past, they'd become insect infested and had held curious artifacts from earlier visitations by other children.

He and Emily had joked that they'd been hobbit holes. They'd made up all kinds of delightful adventures of quests and all manner of dangerous foes they encountered. But those holes had only gone back into the hillsides a few feet.

They'd been nothing like the great space he now found

himself in. The walls, the floor, and the ceiling thirty or forty feet above him were all solid stone. Rob didn't know how he was able to see in the darkness, but he could.

It's a trick, he thought. *Orrus has managed to hypnotize me.* He tried to rouse himself but couldn't. He remained stuck in the dream and in the cavern.

"Where are you?" Orrus's voice seemed to come from the air around Rob.

"I don't know," Emily repeated.

Rob turned to his right and found her there. She stood, her scaled skin glowing incandescently in the darkness. He wondered if that was how he could see in the pitch black of the cave, and if that was how he could see. When he looked at his own body, Rob found that he glowed as well.

"Are you alone?" Orrus asked.

"Rob is with me."

Consternation tightened the cultist's voice. "He should not be there with you, Emily."

"I'm scared."

"You're above fear."

"Not now. Now I'm afraid."

Rob looked around, but Orrus was not there with them.

"Emily, you shouldn't have him there with you."

"I want him with me."

"You shouldn't—"

"No," Emily said, shaking her head. "Rob is going to be here."

"I'm going to be here," Rob said. At least there, however they had gotten there, he could protect her. "Shove off and leave her alone, old man."

"You don't know what you're doing, or what you're risking," Orrus said.

"I know you may be risking my sister's life, and I may be the only one here who cares about that fact," Rob growled. "Deal with it."

"Emily, look around," Orrus said. "Do you see the demon?"

"No."

"Look for it. I can pull you back when you need to come out."

Rob reached for his sister and closed his hand over her cold, scaly flesh. "Em, we shouldn't be here."

She looked up at him. Pain and fear were writ upon her features. "I have to find a way to stop this, Rob. The nightmares are growing worse. I . . . I see what the demon does. I saw it tear a hand from a man's arm and give it to a woman. I have to know what the demon is and what it wants." She paused. "Please."

He relented, hurt to see his sister in such a bad way. The heavy weight of the pistol in his pocket reassured him a little. "All right, Em. We'll have a go at this." He drew the pistol.

"Look around," Orrus said. "The demon has to be there somewhere. We need to know where you are. And we need to know what the demon seeks."

"All right." Emily looked around the barren earth, then pointed to the left, up an incline toward another tunnel. "That way."

Rob trailed his sister through the underground chamber, quickly realizing it was even more vast than he'd first thought. He also understood that they were lost. There were no markings of any kind.

"Now down," Emily said, turning and jogging to the right.

Rob followed her but lost his footing and skidded

down the steep incline the last twenty feet. Bruised and battered, he heaved himself to his feet and struggled to get his breath back.

"Are you all right?" Emily asked.

"I'm fine." Rob blew out a breath. "It was just steeper than it looked."

"I know. Everything looks different here." Emily took off again.

Doggedly, Rob followed. He didn't know how far they'd come. "I think I know where we are, Em."

"Where?" She paused and searched in all directions again. She looked frantic.

"If we haven't left London"—*And when did you ever think you'd say something like that?* Rob asked himself— "then we have to be under it."

"So?"

"Londinium. That's where we have to be."

Londinium was believed to be the ancient Roman city built on the north side of the River Thames. Rob had been fascinated by the archeological finds during the recent excavations. Just before the demons had arrived, archeologists had found a whole new section of the ancient city beneath the ruins of the aboveground sections.

Emily led the way through a twisting tunnel. This one held writing.

"Em, wait." Rob turned to the wall, once more amazed at how well he could see.

"I'm letting you borrow my sight," Emily said as she rejoined him. "That's how you're able to see in the dark."

Rob looked at her. "You can see in the dark?"

"Yes," she answered as if that were nothing.

Of course, seeing her pull fire from thin air was even more impressive. Rob didn't pursue that line of thinking because it only made his scientifically trained mind hurt.

Then again, the whole idea of demons did as well. Thinking of them as aliens from another dimension was only slightly easier because there were problems with that, too.

"Do you see the writing?" Rob pointed at the wall.

"Can you read it?" she asked.

"It's Latin. Of course I can read it." Rob studied the words. "This is called the Passage to the Land of the Dead."

"Not exactly cheery, is it?"

Rob was sorry he'd drawn her attention to it. "No, it isn't."

"At least we won't find Gollum down here," she said brightly, and for a moment she was like the old Emily that Rob remembered. "Let's hurry on, then. The sooner we're done with this, the sooner we can be home." She gave his hand a squeeze, then continued in the direction she was headed.

Only a few moments later, Rob discovered why the tunnel had been called the Passage to the Land of the Dead. Once they left the tunnel, they came out into a cavern filled with crypts. A small lake filled the center of it.

Gaping holes covered the surrounding walls. All of them held moldering skeletons. Some of the skeletons wore textile clothing, but others wore primitive armor. Many of them had bronze shields and weapons lying next to them.

"This place is an archeologist's dream." Rob walked over to one of the crypts, knelt down, and studied the skeleton and the weapons he found there.

"I don't like it here."

Hearing the anxiety in his sister's voice, Rob looked up. "It's all right, Em. These blokes are all done for."

"They say the dead walk in London these days." Emily

wrapped her arms around herself as if she were suddenly chilled.

Rob had heard those stories, too. They'd been told by those who had fled from the city later: that the demons, at least some of them, had the power to draw the dead from the graves and even reanimate those that had fallen in combat. He didn't know if it was true, but he had no reason to disbelieve it.

He stood and went to his sister. "We're all right." He embraced her briefly, but it was awkward because he felt the strength of her. Since she'd started changing, she'd also gotten a lot stronger than he was.

She looked at him. "I had to do this, Rob. I had to."

He knew then that she must have read his thought, or maybe only guessed at them. "Shhhhh. Don't. There's no need to talk about this now."

"You wouldn't change," she told him. "Even after the Cabalists told us about the power that was out there we could use. You didn't believe them. I had to. One of us had to change so we would be safe."

Rob didn't know what to say.

"Even if you had changed," she said, and stroked his cheek with her rough hand, "you wouldn't have been as strong as me." She smiled a little. "This is what I was born for, Rob. I can master the demons' power. And I will."

With a shiver, Rob stepped back from her. He couldn't help feeling that he wished he could leave her. No matter what, he felt certain she would never again be the sister he'd known.

A hurt look filled her face.

Rob cursed himself for a fool, knowing if she could have read the other thoughts, she could have read that as well. He tried to think of something to say, but the words didn't come quickly enough. She turned and was gone.

He followed her around the lake in the center of the cavern. Only then did he realize why the archeologists hadn't found the chamber. Once the Burn had started, it had affected the River Thames as well. The river was down a lot from its normal depth. In fact, it was down so much that instead of emptying out into the North Sea, it was now often fed by that great body of water. The resulting mix of salt and fresh water had rendered the river water undrinkable most of the time. The survivors in London were dependent on wells and rainwater.

But the drain on the river had also uncovered the cavern. The lake wasn't a lake. It was merely the residue of what had once filled the cavern.

Emily stopped abruptly and allowed Rob to catch up to her. A light glowed in the distance and reflected from the lake. The incandescent glow floated in the air and revealed two improbable figures.

Rob had never before seen a demon in the flesh. During the mad rush from London, he'd headed straightaway to his grandparents' farm with Emily in tow. Later, while purchasing petrol for his car, he'd seen television footage of the monsters rampaging round St. Paul and Central London.

The demon had to have stood at least eight feet tall, and that was before the two horns on his savage forehead added another foot in height. Scars mottled his face, making his features even harsher. He was as muscled as a power-lifter, but his body was covered in red scales that looked as if they were on fire. Blue-green armor made of what looked like some kind of giant lizard scales covered his chest, arms, and thighs. He carried a huge obsidian trident in one hand and a sword scabbarded on his hip.

The woman with him was another cultist. She wore horns as well, and some kind of chitinous armor that covered her breasts and hips. Dark canvas trousers covered her lower body. Four horns jutted from her head, curling around from the back of her skull to almost make a protective cage for her face. She'd defiled her body, filling all of her skin that Rob could see with tattoos. Curved bone stuck out from her right forearm. The right hand was different than the left. It looked silvery-gray as it flashed in the incandescent light.

The woman prowled through the crypts, making short work of them as she reached in and dumped bones and rotting cloth or armor to the ground. Metal clanked as it struck the stone.

"That's the demon I keep seeing in my dreams," Emily whispered.

Those aren't dreams, Rob told himself. *Those are nightmares.* He knew from the news footage he had scene, as well as the live reports from reporters in the streets, that the demon wasn't as big as many of them were. But there was something inherently evil about this one.

"Show him to me," Orrus ordered.

The cultist kept searching through the crypts.

"Find it," the demon growled. "It has to be there somewhere. The Romans brought it here, then abandoned it because they thought it was cursed."

The cultist suddenly froze, then withdrew with a gladius in her hand. "This?" she asked, holding the short sword out to the demon. "Is this it?"

The demon stretched forth his hand. Whirling purple embers leaped from the sword before he touched it. "Yes."

Rob recognized the sword immediately. It was only two feet in length, but Roman soldiers had used the gladius to bring the world to its knees during their heyday. The capulus, the hilt of the gladius, was ornate, a mixture of inlaid ivory, lapis lazuli, and obsidian. Whoever had carried it had to have been an officer or a personage of importance.

Emily put her two forefingers and thumbs together to form a triangle. She peered through it at the two creatures—Rob didn't want to call the woman human—in front of them.

The demon turned with the quickness of a cat. Its malevolent gaze came to a rest on Emily.

"Who are you?" the demon demanded.

For just a moment, Rob froze. Then he grabbed Emily's arm and dragged her into motion. "Run! Now! Run!" He pulled her along beside him as he headed back the way they'd come.

They were never going to make it, though. The demon swirled his obsidian trident in the air and pointed it at them. Immediately a wavering blur took shape between them and quickly caught up to Rob and Emily. Rob saw it coming and didn't know what to do.

Then the force hit them and it felt like every bone in Rob's body shattered. He tried to scream, but there wasn't enough breath left in his lungs for that.

Just as everything was about to go black, the world suddenly turned white again. Rob spun head over heels and smashed to the snow-covered ground. He rolled uncontrollably, then fetched up against a pine tree. Dazed, he watched Emily appear from nowhere right after him.

The lighthouse sat in the pool of melted snow and continued shining like a beacon. The green light strobed the black night.

Rob gasped for breath and pushed himself to his feet. Body filled with aches and pains, he lurched toward Emily. He felt frozen where the snow caked to his body.

"What have you done?" Orrus climbed his staff and stood on his two bad legs.

"We didn't do anything, you stupid git," Rob snarled. "The demon saw us and hit us with some kind of energy." He couldn't bring himself to say "magical spell."

Emily rolled easily to her feet, as if she hadn't been blown across twenty yards of landscape. She shook herself, and the snow fell away as if it had somehow been statically discharged.

"The demon saw you?" Orrus demanded.

Rob whirled on the man, intending to curse him out. But Emily answered in a calm tone before he could get started.

"Yes," she said. "The demon saw us."

"Who was it?" Orrus asked.

"It wasn't handing out bloody introductions," Rob said. He turned to Emily. "It's time we got out of this. We've overstayed whatever safety margin we had." They were lucky to get four good years out of the old farm.

"I don't know who it was," Emily said. "He wasn't in any of the books of demons I'm familiar with."

"This is bad." Orrus shook his head. "Did the demon mark you?"

"I don't think so."

"Em," Rob pleaded. "We don't have time to stand here playing Twenty Questions with this sod."

Emily glanced at him. "Everything we learn about the demons matters, Rob. We can control them. We can harness the powers they wield and make this world a better place. We can fight back and triumph over them. If only we learn what they know."

"No," Rob said. "They've got you believing this, but it's not true. You can't possibly learn to do the things those creatures can do. You saw the police and the military get torn to shreds on the day the demons invaded."

"They weren't prepared," Emily said calmly. "We will be."

"You can't prepare for something like this. It's not possible."

"It is possible—"

A keening shrill occupied the forest without warning. Rob clamped his hands over his ears and tried to track the sound. It hurt so badly that his ears pulsed. Finally he realized that the sound came from the jade lighthouse.

Orrus noticed it too and stepped back with a wary look. He mouthed some words and threw a hand out at the lighthouse. A shimmering burst of energy skated over the lighthouse, but it shook even harder and finally exploded in a pistol crack. Jade fragments ricocheted off the trees and branches.

Suddenly, in the next moment, the demon they'd seen down in the cavern was among them. It snarled in rage, something undoubtedly in its own tongue.

The other cultists turned and fled back into the trees. Orrus tried to flee as well, but the demon pierced the old man's chest with the thrown trident. Orrus kicked and flailed, but the trident kept him pinned to the snow-covered ground. Then he was still, facedown for all to see. Blood leaked from his body and spread across the snow.

Rob grabbed Emily again. The demon turned toward her and threw out its hand. A wave of shimmering force spread outward and overtook Emily.

Emily suddenly locked up as though seized. She jerked in an invisible grip. Rob felt the tingle of electricity shudder through his hand. Then his grip on her was forced off and he was thrown to the ground. He tried to recover, but his muscles wouldn't respond.

Helplessly, Rob watched as Emily stood straight and tall. Then she floated a few inches off the ground. She stood as still and as frozen as a statue, clearly held by some force. Her eyes wept crimson tears. It took Rob a moment to realize that that liquid was blood.

Then Emily's head exploded.

Almost out of his mind with fright, Rob pushed himself up and ran for the brush. He didn't know if he was going to make it.

ONE

Shadows meant safety. At least, shadows meant safety most of the time. They didn't offer shelter or a defensive position if those shadows were trying to eat someone hiding within them. And when someone hiding within them attacked, the shadows lost all effect.

Leah Creasey worked to think only good thoughts about what she was about to do. Thinking that she might die at any given moment wasn't conducive to stealth. At the moment, stealth was her greatest ally.

She eased through the alley in southeast London's Greenwich Peninsula. Not much of the metropolis existed here that the demons didn't control. However, most humans stayed out of the area these days and the demons didn't have anyone to hunt. Since they lived to hunt, most of them had gone where the hunting was better.

For the moment, the area wasn't as heavily patrolled as it had been in the past. From personal experience, Leah knew that the demons lived to hunt. They didn't like pulling guard duty or anything that didn't allow them to unleash their blood frenzy.

Halfway down the alley, Leah found a fire escape that zigzagged down the thirty-four-story building. She wore the lightweight black nanoflex aug-suit, built to boost a human's strength and speed. It covered her from head to toe.

Her headpiece was reinforced to provide protection

from bullets that caught her at an angle and didn't strike her dead-on. These days it also served to keep demons' claws from slicing off her face. It was also filled with a communications array and vision-enhancement programming. She carried a backpack that held additional munitions, meals, and other supplies. The heavy Poseidon sniper rifle across her back felt familiar and reassuring.

"Blue Scout, this is Base," a woman's voice said. Commander Jane Hargrove called the shots on the night's operation. "Are you in position?"

"I will be." Leah jumped up ten feet easily with the +Flex nanowire that ran throughout the suit. The suit was cutting-edge, ahead of anything else that had been reached inside the military.

Only Leah knew that the suits, while serviceable and as good as anything she'd ever used in clandestine ops, were no match for the sheer onslaught and defensive capability of Templar armor. After all, the Templar designer of the suits had given the schematics to the military. That secretive order had kept the best for themselves. She didn't blame them. With the enemies they'd planned on facing, they'd needed an edge.

Leah caught hold of the ladder and pulled herself up easily. The suit augmented her strength and speed, putting her far ahead of the abilities of Olympic champions. Almost effortlessly, she ran up thirty-three flights of stairs in the darkness. All power to Central London had been lost when the Hellgate opened at St. Paul's.

At the rooftop, she slid the Poseidon from her back and crawled onto the roof. The LiquidBalance soles of her boots, kneepads, and elbow pads protected her from the rough roofing material and kept her movements soundless. The nonorganic, frictionless liquid didn't deaden her sense of touch, though. She felt the surface, but she didn't suffer injury.

Leah lay prone on her stomach and stared at the dome-shaped white building below. Londoners simply called it the O_2. Originally, it had been called the Millennium Dome and had been built to celebrate London's third millennium. Unfortunately, it hadn't proved to be the cash cow investors had thought it would be. The enterprise had since been renovated into an entertainment center that housed shops and a sports arena.

The white dome had been constructed of polytetrafluoroethylene, a synthetic fluoropolymer that was lighter than the air trapped inside the dome. A network of support cables held it in place. Now, though, several holes gaped in the material and it looked like a battered wasp's nest.

The look suited. From what Hargrove's intel officers had discovered, several Darkspawn had taken up residence there and converted the dome into a weapons manufacturing plant.

Leah and her group intended to cripple the demons' operation.

If they could. At best, it would be a holding maneuver.

"Blue Scout," Hargrove called again. Irritation edged the commander's words. Or it might have been fear. Even after four years of fighting the demons, the fear didn't go away.

"I'm here." Leah leaned her cheek against the Poseidon's buttstock. The electronic connection juiced immediately, and the rifle's telescopic sights fed directly into her right monocular. Her left eye still swept the streets below. Mentally, through years of training, she switched from left eye to right eye without closing either of them.

"All right," Hargrove said, "send in the drones."

Leah put a hand to the side of her helmet and clicked the

control pad. The vision in her left eye changed slightly as it acquired a greenish cast. DRONE/BOT TRACKING ENABLED tracked across the upper left of her vision. She needed to be able to identify friendlies down in the battlezone.

Almost immediately, dozens of green lights lifted from the surrounding neighborhood. All of them were bots and drones created by Agency tech. Before the demonic invasion, several of the designs had only been computer plans or prototypes. Now the Agency readily produced them. They just couldn't get manufactured quickly enough.

Some of the bots flew through the air like miniature airplanes, while others sped across the rock-strewn terrain with oversized tires, like ATVs. It looked like the attack of children's toys.

Except that no child's toy was ever as lethal as the bots. They were equipped with heavy weapons—HARP rifles, flamethrowers, grenade launchers, and other munitions— and operated on the run by the cyber kill squads within the group.

Leah intended to pick off targets that showed up. She forced her breath out, relaxing into that state of near hypnosis she'd learned when she'd first trained as a sniper.

The first wave of bots painted enemy targets with infrared beams. Drones followed immediately behind and opened fire on the designated targets.

With calm detachment, Leah picked up on the infrared targeting beams and tracked one to her first target. No one knew how many Darkspawn worked within the wrecked dome. In bygone days, thousands of humans had shopped and watched sporting events there.

At first glance, the Darkspawn looked like starfish. They had pointed, conical heads, gray-green skin, and multiple eyes on their flat faces. They stood on massive, three-toed lizard's claws that could rip and destroy.

Leah's finger curled round the Poseidon's trigger naturally. Certain of the target, she pulled through the trigger and rode out the recoil. A beam of energy—something the techsmiths had designated "spectral" because it interrupted the electromagnetic and electrical fields of a human and a demon—blasted out for just a moment.

The Darkspawn staggered back. Leah shot it again and watched it fall back once more. The demon never recovered this time. One of the tracked drones locked on to it and spewed Greek Fire over it. The flames sucked the demon down and he rolled across the ground in an effort to put them out. Then it collapsed.

Leah moved on to the next target, a Darkspawn Scout. The designations had come down through informants the commander had among the Cabalists. They'd agreed with the information Leah had gotten from the Templar histories Simon Cross had let her have access to.

She pulled the trigger again and again, riding out the recoil and staying locked to the target. Other buildings held other snipers.

All of them, Leah knew, lived on borrowed time. She looked for the next target as the last one crumpled to the ground and lay still.

"C'mon, baby," Engineer Third Class Geoffrey Baker pleaded. "Get up. Get moving. Don't just lie there and wait to be destroyed."

Through the connection to his drone and bots inside the O_2 building, Baker saw his battle drone kicking its legs futilely as it tried to stand.

"C'mon. You're hurt, but you're not dead yet." Baker took cover behind an overturned car. Rust framed the rents and tears in the metal. The rust went against Baker's training, and he resisted the impulse—even while fighting for his life—to buff the orange cancer from the metal.

He tabbed the controller sheathing his right forearm. The fingers of his left hand danced across the touchscreen as he utilized the drone's onboard self-repair programming. The drone worked around some shorted circuits, but any substantial damage required attention back in the labs.

Arc-flare from a NanoDyne Shockstorm flared uncomfortably close. Baker instinctively dived away from it and took cover in another position as he brought up the F-S Rail Gun he carried in his right hand.

The electrical energy used by the Shockstorm lifted the Darkspawn out of the darkness as it reached for Baker. The sharp claws sliced within inches of his face.

Terrified even after four years of fighting the demons, Baker brought the Rail Gun up and fired only because he'd been trained to. That was why, his instructor had told him repeatedly, they trained.

The Rail Gun exploded and jumped in Baker's hand. The depleted uranium bullets tracked across the demon's hide and opened craters. Vile purple blood leaked out of the wounds. Instantly the smell of corruption rose up stronger than the stench of ozone from the Shockstorm.

The demon fell back. The rounds amputated one of its feet.

"Hey Baker," the black-suited agent behind the young engineer said, "good thinking shooting his foot off like that. Makes it bloody hard for him to stand up."

"I didn't—" Baker tried to say *mean to,* but he never got the chance. The agent patted him on the shoulder and moved to a new position.

Calming himself, Baker turned his attention back to the drone inside the O_2. The recircuiting had been finished.

Watching from the "eyes" of one of the inhibitor bots he controlled, Baker saw the drone right itself.

From the "waist" up, the drone looked vaguely human. The head that rotated 360 degrees; eyes that saw under low-light conditions, thermal, and infrared; and two arms that held an XMS10 Jackhammer shotgun. The lower part of the drone consisted of a tracked assembly.

The drone pushed up with its arms till it once more sat on the tracks. A Darkspawn attacked at once, firing energy bolts from a weapon Baker couldn't quite identify. There were just too many demon weapons to know at the time, and they continued building new ones.

The energy bolts rocked the drone backward. Through the sim-link connecting him to the drone, Baker ordered the drone to get up and get moving. Locked into the viewpoint of one of his inhibitor bots, Baker watched as the drone pushed with both hands and righted itself.

"There you go," Baker told himself. A wave of relief washed through him. He commanded the inhibitor bot to spin and look around.

Although the bots were equipped with F-S Nitesite, the interior of the dome's interior held impossible darkness. The bot barely saw fifteen feet in the blackness. Thankfully, Baker had also equipped them with sonar. When he switched over to that, his monocular filled with the flat images of the milling demons.

He commanded the drone to fire at will.

The drone opened up at once. Even though he was too far away from the strange happenings, Baker searched the area. It was too much to hope for one of the Named Demons to be in charge of the manufacturing plant.

As the bot jostled about the building's interior, a laser tracking signal suddenly painted the Darkspawn less than twenty feet away. *Okay, let's bring him down.*

The inhibitor bot was designed to slow down the demon's moves. They didn't offer heavy weapons like those carried by the drones, but they carried a sonic and microwave array guaranteed to throw off most demons with nausea and blurred vision. The effects were also painful.

The Darkspawn raised its weapon, then got hit full force by the inhibitors. The creature lurched to the side and barely caught itself in time to stay upright.

Baker's fingers glided across the touchpad without looking at it. He saw the drone through another inhibitor's lenses as it brought up the Jackhammer, fitted the heavy shotgun to its shoulder, and fired. The drone worked the slide, ejected the spent cartridge, and seated another one. It fired again.

The shotgun pellets were soft metal, designed to shatter after sinking into an opponent's flesh. Half of the pellets contained Greek Fire. The other half held plastic explosives treated to react with liquid. As soon as an enemy's blood touched the broken pellets, they exploded.

Fire spewed from the massive wounds in the demon's chest, then its chest came apart as the explosives kicked in. Almost hollowed out by the blasts, the Darkspawn toppled backward and crashed to the floor in a loose-limbed sprawl.

Baker sent his bots and drone deeper into the dome. He was concentrating so fiercely on what they were seeing that he didn't notice he was no longer alone until it was too late.

Feeling eyes on him, Baker turned to his right, toward his monocled side where his peripheral vision was limited. The Blade Minion standing there grinned at Baker. The thing stood seven feet tall, broad across the head and shoulders, and covered with a dark green carapace that made it look like an insect. Spikes jutted out from its massive forearms.

Baker tried to bring up the Rail Gun, but he knew it was already too late. The Blade Minion stabbed him through the armor he wore and pierced his heart. Judging from the way the demon's fist snugged up against his chest, Baker knew that several inches of the spike jutted out his back.

He tried to breathe and failed. His drone and bots became unresponsive, trapped in the middle of the war zone. Desperate, he tried to bring them to him. They came, but they'd never make it in time. Something that reached out of the darkness crushed one of the bots.

Baker felt the bot go off-line as his own life faded. He tried again to breathe and failed once more; now he felt his lungs filling up with blood.

Where's my cover?

Someone was supposed to be watching over him. His knees folded under him, and his vision tightened to one small dot. The last thing he saw, though, was the Blade Minion's head going to pieces as one of the snipers found the demon too late.

TWO

Zombies, Warren Schimmer thought irritably, *are difficult to control outside of the city.* He glanced back at the pack of forty strong that he controlled. At least back in the city they tended to march more or less together because the narrow streets kept them together.

Warren hated where they were now. He'd not been out of London much, and never to Kent. They were deep in it now, following the River Rother toward Romney Marsh. The stench of the salt marshes thickened the air and made them almost unbearable.

Few trees grew in the area, though there were stubborn clumps of oak and alder. All of it was snow-covered at the moment. The pristine whiteness made the land appear innocent and hid the treacherous bogs and pits that filled the countryside.

Warren kept his little group of undead well away from the main road, though he kept the road and the River Rother in sight. People still lived out this way in rather rough means. The demons hadn't quite spread this far yet.

If the survivors from the city or the farm people that lived out here saw him with the zombies, Warren knew he'd find no friends among them. Most likely, they would kill him on sight.

He pulled his cloak more tightly around him. Despite the fact that London was demon-infested, he appreciated the warmth that he found in the city. He'd trade it for the cold any day.

Except that the Burn killed the land and drained the River Thames.

Resolutely, Warren marched on. What he looked for, whatever it was, wasn't much farther away now. He kept moving his feet, and listening to the frozen grass and brush rustle and snap under his boots.

"Maybe we should stop somewhere for tonight," Naomi said.

She was a constant companion of his these days. When he'd first met her four years ago, she'd known more than him about arcane forces. But after he'd bonded with Merihim—taken hostage would have been a more apt description—Warren had become the master and she became the student.

She was a couple of years older than he was. Petite, full-figured, and beautiful, Naomi turned men's heads. She was the kind of woman that Warren would never have had a chance at back when the world was normal. There had been a few perks with the arrival of evil.

Tattoos and piercings covered her body. Two short, curved horns stood out on her forehead. As a Cabalist, she embraced the demon's ways and tried to emulate their look.

Warren didn't want that. When he'd first encountered Merihim, the demon had blasted Warren and burned him significantly. His normally ebony skin had become mottled and grotesque. He'd lost hair and gained lots of scar tissue. Now all of that was gone. Courtesy of the demanding voice that usually dwelt within his mind.

But he had a hand back. The Templar Simon Cross had taken his flesh and blood hand from him. Merihim had given him one of his own, and the demon flesh had changed his body, remade it to be a proper vessel to the hand. Even now that Merihim's hand was gone, taken back by the demon, Warren remained changed.

The voice had also given him another hand. This one hung at his side and was a thing of alien beauty rather than one of horror. Made of silver, the prosthesis looked like something a clockmaker might design. Tiny gears and braided cables filled it. Magic existed in the hand, though. It moved as easily and flexibly as Warren's old hand. Most amazing of all, he could touch and feel things.

"Did you hear me?" Naomi asked. "I wanted to know if we could stop for the night."

"No," Warren replied. He knew that was impossible. The voice in his head had told him he couldn't stop until he'd found what she'd sent him for. "We press on."

"I'm cold."

Although he understood her discomfort, Warren couldn't help his bad attitude. He wasn't any happier about what he was having to do, either. He wanted the warmth of a fire and a good book.

Instead, he marched a group of zombies he'd raised as personal guards deep into the briny quagmire under a quarter-moon and a sky full of bright stars. Stealth was possible at night in the city, but not out here.

Not only that, but he nursed a deep anger toward Naomi. When he'd had his hand taken from him, she'd stayed at his side long enough to make sure he was as well cared for as she could manage, then she'd fled. She'd only returned to him a few weeks ago when she'd discovered him searching the city. She'd asked him where he'd gotten his new hand. He hadn't seen fit to tell her.

"The zombies are losing us again." Naomi sounded as petulant as a child.

"I know." Warren stopped at the top of a promontory and glanced back. He had started with sixty zombies, all pulled from graves inside London at the beginning of his long trek. Now he had less than forty.

He'd robbed one of the older graves. The most recent interment there had been over eighty years ago. It had been a potter's field, a place where the unknown and indigent had been buried. No mortician had pumped them full of preservatives. These had rotted down to bone, wisps of hair, and leathery flesh. Over the course of the past few years, Warren had learned that zombies like that were more durable than those contaminated by formaldehyde and other chemicals.

"Come," he ordered. He didn't just speak. He pushed the command out to the zombies with the arcane energy he harnessed.

The zombies stopped what they were doing and turned toward him. The moonlight and starlight showed the gaping holes of their eye sockets and broken-toothed mouths. In that moment, they reminded Warren of a television special about prairie dogs he'd seen. The zombies had that same frozen attentiveness.

A moment later, they approached him. Several came out of the trees and the tall reeds that almost masked their presence. Snow flurries eddied about them as they stirred the white powder from the brush.

Marching zombies in wide open spaces was a lot like herding cats, Warren couldn't help thinking.

"You should have waited to summon an army," the quiet, melodious voice inside his head told him. "As I suggested."

Warren didn't argue. His exception to her plans had been obvious the moment he'd ordered the corpses from their graves back in London. He wasn't as completely within her power as he'd been in Merihim's. He didn't flaunt that lack, though.

Her name was Lilith. She claimed to be Adam's second wife. Mythologies mentioned her, and many of them claimed that she was the mother of demons, of vampires, and the dark things that hunted in the night.

Warren didn't know all of her story. He'd inadvertently found her in an arcane book Merihim had ordered him to steal. The demon had forgotten about it, and Lilith took the credit for that. She was powerful, she'd told Warren, but she wasn't ready to take on Merihim. Not yet.

The thought of fighting Merihim when the demon had easily twice bested him left Warren sickened and hammered by anxiety attacks. But even though he didn't do everything exactly the way Lilith wanted, he knew he didn't want to step completely away from her. He needed her protection.

When the last of the zombies joined the group standing at the base of the promontory, Warren pointed at three of them.

"Lead," he commanded.

The three zombies fell out of the pack and marched toward Romney Marsh again. One of them promptly disappeared into the deep salt bogs that plagued the countryside. A moment later the zombie crawled back out of the muck. Not all of them reappeared from the bottomless bogs.

Warren waited a moment and followed, stepping in the footprints left by the zombies that didn't sink. The snow continued to fall and swirl around them.

Naomi fell into step beside him. Warren felt her presence and her mood weigh heavily on him. After all this time, it was easy to read the woman.

"You haven't told me what we're out here looking for," Naomi said.

"No."

Naomi loosed a sigh of disgust that turned gray in the cold wind. "We're out in the middle of nowhere. It's not like I can tell anyone."

Warren looked at her and thought again that bringing her was a problem.

"She's going to be trouble," Lilith said. In an eddy of snowflakes, she was suddenly there walking beside Warren. She was taller than Naomi, almost as tall as Warren. Her milk-white complexion caused her to blend into the snow, and it almost made her black eyes and long black hair stand out. She wore a long, flowing dress with deep cleavage and wide sleeves. The cutting wind bothered neither her clothing nor her hair.

Naomi couldn't see her because she wasn't there. Not in physical form, at least. She manifested so that Warren saw her, but no one else. Warren still wasn't sure if that resulted from the book or the silver hand.

"Warren," Naomi said. "Did you hear me?"

"You shouldn't have brought her," Lilith went on.

"I heard you," Warren said, and the answer sufficed for both women. Neither was happy with his response.

"If you're not going to trust me, why did you bring me?"

"I brought you because I felt I needed you."

"For what?"

"I don't know."

"This is bloody asinine."

Lilith smiled, and moonlight and shadows stippled the cruel expression. "I told you that she would be trouble. Better to leave her now. Or kill her."

The thought had crossed Warren's mind. Violent solutions to problems tended to be normal for him these days. Before the Hellgate's opening and the arrival of the demons, that had never been the case. He'd run from every fight he'd ever faced. As a result, nearly everyone he'd trusted had taken advantage of him.

"This is not asinine," Warren said. But he felt it was because Lilith hadn't told him what they'd come this far for, either. She'd only told him that he needed to come. "There's something out here."

"How do you know?"

"Because I feel it." Warren lifted his metal hand. "In here."

Naomi started to say something, then she glanced at the hand and closed her mouth. He'd already proved much more adept at the arcane forces the demons wielded than her. Now that he had a new hand, his power had taken on new turns that he hadn't had access to before.

"All right," she said finally. She pulled her long coat more firmly around her. "But I hope we find it soon."

Another of the zombies dropped into one of the unseen bog holes barely covered by ice. The sharp *crack* sounded just before the zombie plunged into the black water. This one didn't come back.

Only a little farther on, gray smoke plumed against the dark, star-filled sky. The feeling that pulled Warren lay in that direction as well.

Lilith walked beside him again. "You'll want to hurry," she stated calmly. "You're being followed."

THREE

S imon Cross hated what he was about to do. The whole performance was unfair. His victim—and he saw no other term that fit—didn't have a chance. The only good thing about it was that death would come quickly.

It's meat, he told himself. *You've got to make meat for the others. They're depending on you.*

The doe stood less than five feet away. She scraped at the snow with one delicate hoof till she exposed a few tufts of grass that weren't quite dead. The earth didn't die immediately after the coming of winter. It wavered and clung to life.

Other deer dotted the hillside. They worked the ground with their hooves and muzzles as well. Several of the does were heavy with fauns that would be born in the spring. That, at least, was promising.

Provided we don't eat this herd into extinction, Simon amended.

That was a very real threat with the way things were going these past few months. The hydroponics systems back at the redoubt that he'd chosen as their fortress weren't keeping up with the demand of the burgeoning numbers of people living there. Enlarging the redoubt and building more hydroponics tanks took time and materials.

One of the main problems was that the population at the shelter continued to grow. In addition to survivors

whom the Templar were still bringing out of the wreckage of London and the suburbs, babies were being born.
Simon couldn't believe that anyone would have children
given the threat of the demons in the world. But it happened.

Focus, he told himself.

The doe ate the tender shoots.

For a time after he'd left London and the Templar life-
style because he'd lost faith in the existence of demons,
he'd been a guide in South Africa. He had learned to track
and hunt animals. That had been an honorable profession.
His skills as a Templar had made the vocation a natural fit
for him.

Primarily, though, he'd guided people who'd only
wanted to record video of the animals. His fellow guide,
Saundra McIntyre, hadn't liked killing. He'd liked Saundra enough, and the money had been good enough, that
he hadn't often pursued trophy-hunting guide work.

But then the animals he'd sometimes hunted had had
an even chance against him. His strength, speed, and instincts had been matched up with theirs. He hadn't taken
any part in the "canned" hunts that went on there. Hunting animals that had been fed and trained to live in certain
areas wasn't hunting. Those animals had been slaugh-
tered.

They were taken for trophies, Simon reminded himself.
*These aren't going to be trophies. These are going to feed
people.*

He knew his argument was right, and the necessity was
there. But it still didn't feel good to do what he was about
to do. Even worse, he believed this kind of "hunting"
brought only disgrace to the armor he wore.

Dressed in the dark blue and silver Templar palladium
shell, Simon knew he could weather a direct hit from a

main battle tank's long gun. With his strength and speed augmented, he was superhuman, stronger and faster than anything the deer had ever before faced.

Except demons, Simon reminded himself. *If they've been preyed upon by demons, they've seen creatures far worse than me.*

"Simon," Nathan Singh called over the suit's comm.

"Here," Simon replied.

"Are we going to do this, mate?" Nathan Singh was one of the other Templar currently involved with the hunt. "Not that I'm in any hurry to start the carnage of *When Humans Attack,* but waiting around isn't going to make it any easier."

Simon took a deep breath. "I know."

"Then let's be about it and get on home."

Home.

Simon heard that term resonate in his mind. It was a good thought, but he didn't even dream about that anymore. All real possibility of the world going back to anything normal was certainly past the end of his years.

"All right," Simon said. "Count them down as we take them. Only as many as we need. The killing stops when we reach our quota."

Grimly, he hefted the short sword in his right hand. He wore his Templar blade down his back. He wouldn't defile it on hunting the deer. Nor would the other Templar. They'd all forged plain, steel blades, good quality, but not blessed as their righteous weapons were.

"Do it." Simon shifted into motion. He streaked for the nearest doe, one of those they'd marked from the herd. She never heard him coming. His sword pierced her side and split her heart before she knew death was on her. He yanked his sword from her body as her legs buckled and she fell.

Fast as he'd been, Danielle counted her kill before his. "One," she said.

"Two," Simon echoed.

"Three," Boyd Lister said.

And Nathan, almost on Boyd's heels, breathed, "Four."

By that time the deer herd broke into a run. They flitted and bounded across the snow-covered terrain. Muscles bunched and exploded into motion as the deer fled for their lives.

The "hunting" continued unabated, as did the relentless countdown.

In less than three minutes, it was over. Feeling sickened and disgusted, Simon watched the herd race to safety. They headed south and west of London. Everything that wanted to live these days headed in that direction.

Inside the armor, Simon had a full 360-degree view of the nearby terrain. He saw the corpses of the deer lying behind him. The kill zone, according to the measurements provided by the suit's onboard AI, was less than a quarter mile long.

Simon tried to tell himself that it wasn't seventeen deer that lay dead on the ground. It was over a ton of red meat that people back at the shelter needed.

He leaned down and grabbed a handful of snow to clean the sword blade. Crimson slush dripped to the ground, but gradually the sword was clean. He sheathed it along his leg and reached down for the carcass of his last victim. Slinging the deer's body over his shoulder, hardly noticing over three hundred pounds of deer, he walked back to the center of the kill zone.

They strung the deer up from trees, and the bodies hung there like obscene fruit. All of the Templar knew how to kill demons. They'd been trained to do that from the day they'd taken their first few steps. But few of them had known how to field dress a kill. Simon had had to teach most of them.

Danielle and three others stood guard while Simon, Nathan, and the other four Templar gutted the deer. Simon worked quickly. Steaming entrails piled at his feet.

"Warning," the onboard AI gently interrupted. "Perimeter invasion imminent."

Simon shifted his attention to the HUD and studied the approaching shapes. They were long and lean. Before the demons had invaded the world, he felt certain he would have known what they were immediately. Now there were too many opportunities for him to be wrong. Even four years into the invasion, they hadn't managed to identify all of the demons because new ones kept arriving.

"Identify invaders," Simon instructed.

"*Canis lupus*," the female AI voice responded.

"Wolves," Danielle said.

Simon watched the shapes come closer to the Templar. Normal wolves couldn't offer a threat. Their claws and teeth would never penetrate the armor. But creatures didn't always remain the same after the demons were through with them. The shambling corpses that crawled from graveyards to attack proved that.

Nathan stood nearby in his dark gray armor trimmed in red. At five feet eleven, he was six inches shorter than Simon and considerably lighter because he wasn't as broad in the shoulders. He wore a gunfighter mustache, had short-cropped black hair, and had the tattoo of a dragon from shoulder to elbow on his left arm.

"Think they'll attack?" Nathan asked. His faceplate remained impenetrable and blood-red, so dark in the moonlight that only red highlights now and again hinted at the color.

"No," Simon answered quietly. Their voices couldn't be heard outside the suits, so the wolves wouldn't know for certain that they were human. "They're just hungry. Maybe curious."

"It'll be better if they don't attack. I don't feel like killing anything else." Nathan's voice sounded hollow. Patches of dried blood stood out on the armor.

Simon silently agreed and turned his attention back to the next deer. He used a short knife to open its belly. "According to the sec stats, the wolf population in the area has increased since the time we moved into the redoubt. The jury's still out on whether they're increasing through reproduction or being crowded into the region by the expansion of the Burn."

"Does growth of the wolf population mean anything?"

"There was a time back in the early part of this century that the gray wolf had to be reintroduced into Europe. Civilization had almost rendered them extinct."

"But the predator population is growing again."

"In just four years since the Hellgate opened," Simon agreed. "Things are going to be even more different a short time from now. If the deer population thins, the wolves may decide that human flesh is tasty." He concentrated on his blade and tried not to think about the ramification of what he was talking about. "If they do, it's going to be even harder for escapees from London and the suburbs to survive out here. But—given the paradigm we're seeing here—I'm wondering if that increase is everywhere."

"You're wondering that if the predators here—the natural predators—are increasing in numbers, then what does it mean for the rest of the world?"

"Something like that," Simon admitted.

"Maybe you should hope that the wolves develop a taste for demon flesh."

"I am. I just don't see it happening. I think the wolves and other predators like them may become more of a threat outside the Burn. We're not exactly the dominant species on this planet anymore."

Although they hadn't gotten any news in years, Simon knew that other Hellgates had opened around the world.

"You win a war one battle at a time," Nathan said.

"I know. We just need an edge. Something that puts us on a more equal footing with the demons for a while."

"Professor Macomber is still translating the Goetia manuscript. He and the other members of the geek squad seem to think they'll come up with something."

Professor Archibald Xavier Macomber was a specialist in dead languages. He'd also become something of demonologist as a result. Until the Hellgate had opened, he'd been a prisoner in an insane asylum in Paris. When those people had been released, they'd been turned out into the streets or killed outright.

Macomber had been one of the lucky few.

Someone connected to Leah Creasey had negotiated delivering Macomber to Simon. The professor had known Simon's father, Thomas Cross, and about the Templar Order enough to know that no one there could turn away from the fight. For a time, Terrence Booth—the present High Seat of the House of Rorke among the Templar still living in the Underground—had taken Macomber prisoner. Simon had been forced to try to get Macomber back, and in doing so had gone head-to-head against Templar that he should have been treating as his brothers.

Macomber had reputedly found information in the ancient Goetia manuscript, written by King Solomon, that detailed how to build arcane and scientific defenses against the demons. In all the annals of the Templar, there had never been mention of such a thing.

Simon dared not get his hopes up too high regarding those defensive fields, but it was hard not to wish for the knowledge to exist. There were too many men, women, and children who depended on him. He couldn't fail them.

"Let's get back to work," Simon said finally. "Danielle and the others will watch over us."

"Maybe the wolves will be patient and wait for the left-overs."

Simon hoped so. He turned back to the deer he worked on. His knife blade slid easily through the flesh, and he focused on his work.

"Simon," Danielle called softly.

"Yes."

"We've got trouble."

"What?"

"We've identified a small group of Ravagers coming from the east."

FOUR

Leah sighted the Poseidon in on the Blade Minion that was only now yanking its spikes from the young engineer's corpse. She had no doubt that Baker was dead. If he wasn't at this minute, he would be before someone could get to him.

And the demons would get to him before any of the team did.

Calm down. Do your job, she told herself.

You got him killed. You took your eye off him long enough for that demon to get him.

The crosshairs wavered over the Blade Minion's chest.

People die in this business. Leah's first handler had told her that the first day she'd met him. *People die in this business. It's what you hire on to do. Whether for patriotism or money, and for your sake I hope it's both, people die. Hopefully you'll help us keep the balance sheets in order.*

That day they'd just gotten the body of an agent back. Her handler—he'd been code-named Winder and she'd never found out his real name or anything about him—had shown her the young man's body. He'd been brutally tortured for weeks. At the end, he'd been decapitated.

The exfiltration team wasn't able to save this poor bloke, Winder said. *They certainly weren't able to pull his body back into any condition we can allow his poor mum to see. But one thing they were able to do before they brought him home.*

Leah had waited. She'd been scared to death and mad and sickened all at the same time. She didn't know how she was supposed to act, and Winder had given her no clue.

Before they left that despicable little African nation, Winder had said, *they balanced the sheets. That tinpot warlord is wormfood now.* He stared at the young man's body. *Sometimes in this business, that's all that you can hope for: that someone will balance the books for you when you're taken from the board due to your own bad luck or inadequacies.*

Leah had stood silently there and stared at the body.

Go on and tell yourself that this will never happen to you, Winder said. *Tell yourself that you're that good or that lucky. Maybe you'll even believe it. At least for a while. But some night, whether in the safety of your own bed or in some transient hotel where you're hiding out under another name and risking all you've got on an op you don't fully under-stand, you'll realize that this will happen to you.*

Leah had tried to wall herself off from the sensory over-load of the dead body. In addition to the horrific sight, the smell of death crowded the small coroner's room.

He's going to be quietly buried, Winder said. *No glorious homecoming for him. And do you know why?*

Shaking a little, Leah had shaken her head.

Because MI-6 can't claim him, Winder had said. *The Queen has to disavow him. His mum won't even know how he got himself terminated. And isn't that a lovely word for it? "Terminated"?*

Leah had said no, that it wasn't.

Winder had laughed. *Maybe you'll make a good agent then, missy. You don't come in here singing "God Save the Queen" and spouting patriotic nonsense, maybe you'll live longer.* He sighed. *This boy, he got sent to his death. Given an impossible mission. But it pulled his killer out into the open so the exfiltration team could take out the target.*

That thought had horrified Leah.

Winder must have seen her reaction on her face at the time. She hadn't learned to hide them so well back then. Now, she felt certain, he would never have known how his announcement struck her.

Then Winder had laughed at her. *Don't take it so bloody personal. He was doing his job. That's all anyone ever asks of you here. Only sometimes they ask you to die. Not a very pretty thought, is it?*

No, Leah had answered.

Well, that's what you're signing on for. Winder had patted the cheek of the amputated head. *He was a good boy. Never asked any questions. He did everything right. Even died right. You can't ask anything more than that.* He'd paused and looked at her, still smiling incongruously. *And do you want to know who was callous enough to send this poor sod off to die so painfully for his country?*

Leah hadn't been able to answer.

Do you know what kind of person it would take to do something so bloody awful? Winder had asked.

No, she'd said.

Me, he'd told her in that same soft voice. *I sent him off to be tortured and finally executed by the cold-blooded bastard that did for him. Just so we could flush out the warlord that was our real target. What do you think about that?*

Leah had gotten sick then. Winder had directed her over to a basin and she'd purged. When she'd finished throwing up, he'd washed her face with a warm cloth. The reflection of the dead agent had been in the mirror above the sink.

And if it comes time to do it, Winder had said softly, *I'll send you to die, too. Don't you ever think I won't. Every time*

I send you out the door, you have to realize that you might not be coming back. Knowing that is the first thing that's going to help you stay alive.

Four months later, Winder was gone. No one had ever said what happened to him. Leah had asked once, and she'd been told that the question wasn't allowed. She hadn't asked again.

Leah pushed the bitter memories away. She'd known what she'd signed on for. She just hadn't ever expected demons to be involved. Her imagination had only limited her to terrorists and enemies of state.

And the young agent had known what he'd signed on for as well.

She raised the Poseidon's crosshairs from the Blade Minion's chest to its horrid face.

Don't try to be a hotshot, her range instructor had always taught her. *Aim for the center of the body mass. Head shots are for American cowboys and trick shooters. You're neither. You're a killer, and you're going to be the best killer I can make you.*

Leah squeezed the trigger. The sniper rifle recoiled as it launched the bolt of spectral energy. The Blade Minion jerked sideways as the energy struck it in the temple. Visible damage through the sniper scope was limited to charred and bloody flesh. It didn't show the havoc created throughout the demon's central nervous system.

When the rifle's sights were centered again, Leah pulled the trigger through once more. This time the demon's head imploded. The creature dropped to its knees, then fell forward across the body of the young agent.

Leah took a deep breath and cleansed her mind. She couldn't control all of the events taking place on the playing board. Too many moves were beyond her. In the overall scheme of things, she—like the young agent—was just a small cog.

"Blue Team and Red Team," Commander Hargrove called over the comm, "signal readiness."

The loose translation of that, Leah said, *is to signal to let everyone know you're alive.* "Blue Scout ready," she whispered just loud enough for the subvocal mic in her mask to pick up.

As she watched, the battlezone shifted. Several of the blue and red lights on the map open to her view winked out. She guessed that their casualties had run close to a quarter of their number so far.

"Courier remains viable," Commander Hargrove announced. "We are still a go on this op."

"Affirmative," Leah answered, knowing that the commander's comm team would still expect a response. "Blue Scout is a go." She continued firing as she found targets.

"Prepare for delivery," Hargrove ordered.

"Affirmative." Leah locked on another target and fired again. A Darkspawn demon dropped in its tracks.

"Blue Scout," a man's voice called. "This is Firefox Courier."

"Ping Firefox Courier," Leah said. Immediately a four-man group lit up on her computer-generated field of vision.

Firefox Courier was second in the line of explosives experts. There were four groups in all. Each group carried satchel charges designed to take out the demonic weapons plant.

"What can I do for you, Firefox Courier?" Leah asked.

"We're pinned down by sniper fire. You're the closest countersniper we have."

Leah shifted her attention to the buildings around the O_2. She tracked enemy fire back to five snipers. The blazing light from the demons' weapons made finding them easy.

"Firefox Courier, Blue Scout confirms five snipers," Leah said.

"Five sounds about right."

"Are you intact?" Leah focused on the closest sniper in one of the nearby buildings.

"We've got wounded," the Firefox Courier officer replied, "but we're still up and about."

"I'll see if I can make some room for you."

"Awfully generous of you."

Leah focused on the Darkspawn sniper, got the creature's timing as it leaned forward again to fire, then squeezed the trigger. She aimed for center mass and saw the demon spin sideways. Before it could recover, she shot it in the head. The demon went still and slumped to the floor.

The second and third Darkspawn snipers went down just as quickly, and without knowing they were being fired on till it was too late. When Leah locked on to the fourth sniper's position, she discovered the demon had cut and run. Ignoring him for the moment, she moved on to the fifth sniper's position.

This time as she locked on, she saw the demon sniper had also locked on to her. The Darkspawn sniper's head was squarely behind the heavy rifle it held. Knowing she was at most a heartbeat away from death, Leah locked on to the demon's sniper scope and squeezed the trigger just as *something* whizzed within inches of her head.

The Darkspawn's sniper scope went to pieces, and its head snapped backward. The demon slumped without a sound. Electrical energy slammed into the corner of the rooftop only a couple of feet from Leah's position. She ducked back, tracked the shot mentally, and knew that the sniper she'd passed on earlier was back in the game.

After three rolls, Leah spread her elbows and came to a stop in the prone position. The Poseidon speared before her, and she moved the rifle into line with the Darkspawn.

On the ground, Firefox Courier was already on the move. The men and women of the unit stayed low as they raced for the O_2. All of them wore heavier armor over the blacksuits and carried satchel charges filled with arcane-charged plastic explosives.

Leah found the final sniper as the Darkspawn swung back into position around a window frame. She aimed for center mass, not trying to do anything more than hit the target, and squeezed the trigger.

The first charge knocked the Darkspawn backward, sending its weapon flying as it flailed its arms and tried to stay upright. The second charge turned its chest into a pulped mess of shattered bones and ripped organs.

"Good shooting, Blue Scout."

"Thank you." Leah looked for additional targets around the explosives team. From the corner of her eye, she caught sight of the shadow coasting across the rooftop toward her. She rolled again and heard the Blood Angel's shriek as it tried for her. Then the demon's heavy claws thudded against the rooftop and left gouges.

Get up! Leah shoved herself to her feet. Enemy fire from the ground tracked her. One of the Darkspawn fired a rocket launcher, and the warhead smashed against the side of the building in a roiling mass of orange and black flames.

Heat washed over Leah as the concussive wave drove her from her feet. She fell into a controlled roll and got to her feet again. When she glanced over her shoulder, she spotted the Blood Angel streaking for her again.

The Blood Angel had a feminine form and human

intelligence. Leathery wings stretched to ride the wind. Crimson runes gleamed on the demon's dark skin. This time the Blood Angel threw its hands forward and unleashed spectral bolts that missed Leah by inches and tore holes in the building's roof.

Leah leaped over one of the holes that suddenly opened up in front of her. She landed on the shuddering rooftop and barely managed to keep her balance. Fear spiced the adrenaline already racing through her system. Blood Angels were some of the fiercest demons that had poured through the Hellgate. Having no choice, she dropped the heavy sniper rifle and ran toward the building's edge. With the Blood Angel after her, no place atop the building was safe.

When she reached the building's edge, Leah propelled herself outward. She thought she screamed at that point, but she hoped she hadn't because that would have been embarrassing to be heard over the comm. In the next second, though, panic assailed her as she started the long fall toward the street.

FIVE

Achill breezed through Simon as he considered the Ravagers approaching from the east. Ravagers were at the low end of the mental spectrum of the demons, but they were definite threats. They lived to kill, and they always hunted in packs.

"If you've picked up a small group of them advancing on us," Simon said, "you can bet it's not the only one."

"I am," Danielle said. She'd been heavily blooded in the killing ground over the past four years. She'd trained all her life to be a Templar and had excelled in bladed weapons.

"Patch me in." Simon stood and surveyed his HUD view.

"Confirm upload of incoming information?" the armor AI asked.

"Yes."

"Streaming now."

As Simon watched, a window opened up in the upper left corner of his HUD. The view was a thermographic display of nine warm-blooded entities arranged along the ridgeline overlooking the hunting ground.

"Confirm preliminary identification of demon entities known as Ravagers," the suit AI said. "Size and general characteristics, including internal body temperature, match known values."

Simon booted the feed onto the other Templar harvesting the deer. They all grew silent and turned in the direction of the approaching demons.

"They're waiting," Nathan said.

"Yes." Simon clamped the knife back onto his armor. "Grab the deer that you can manage and let's get out of here."

"Run from a fight?" Campbell, one of the younger Templar, demanded. "From demon scum?"

"If we can," Simon said, "yes."

"We're here to kill the demons," Campbell protested.

"We're not here to get kacked by them, mate," Nathan replied evenly. "You've not been in any battles with demons."

"That's not my fault," Campbell replied. "I've been willing."

There were a lot of the Templar that hadn't been yet blooded against the demons. Simon tried to keep the young ones out of harm's way until absolutely necessary. Too many of the young, untried Templar found their way into early graves despite their training.

"There'll be plenty of time to fight," Danielle said before Nathan could reply. "And plenty of demons to fight. The main thing you need to realize right now is that Ravagers *never* hunt unless they outnumber their prey." She paused. "If we see this many now, there are more out there."

Simon draped the deer's body over his left shoulder. He gripped his main battle sword and freed it from the sheath across his back. The blade gleamed. Forged of palladium and steel, the sword was over three feet in length, double-edged, and straight as a ruler. The cross guard was solid and heavy, scarred from past battles. Runes along the blade held in the eldritch forces Simon and his father had beaten into the metal when they'd forged the sword.

"Over here," Trent said softly.

Simon accepted the additional feed patched into the HUD. Eleven Ravagers closed in from the north. Only a moment later, Linda Estep reported seven more to the south.

All three groups converged on the Templar.

"They're trying to box us, mate," Nathan said.

"Ravagers aren't this methodical." Simon jogged easily to the west, the only direction currently open to them. "Someone's guiding them."

"Too bad they didn't get to shut the door before we picked up on them," Nathan said.

Simon brought maps of the surrounding countryside up onto the HUD. The transparent overlays didn't block his vision. He'd trained since he was a child to separate the different video and audio input streaming to him at the same time. The Templar at the shelter he had put together four years ago stayed in the field nearly every day. Over the past few years, there wasn't much they didn't know about the lay of the land.

Problems lay to the west. The land turned steep and treacherous there. Hillocks became cliffs sixty and seventy feet high, above valleys of broken limestone.

The Ravagers acted as though they knew that.

"Bring the group together," Simon ordered. "We're going to try to break through to the south before they herd us to the cliffs."

The Templar gathered. Simon and Nathan took point. They stayed twenty feet apart and stretched their long strides into a distance-eating run. The onboard gyros kept Simon's gait smooth. He had the Ravagers on his HUD now. They were close enough that he no longer needed the piggybacked feeds from the other Templar to sense the Ravagers. Despite the speed possible in the armor, the demons closed the distance.

As he ran, Simon tried not to think of all the meat they'd left hanging from the trees to spoil. The deer had died for no reason, and the people at the shelter were going to go hungry soon if something weren't done. The whole turn of events offended him.

"Hostile forces one hundred twelve yards away," the suit AI informed him.

Simon used the light-multiplier programming built into the armor's optical array. The utility leached the color from the scene ahead of him and turned everything black and white with an undercurrent of green. The human eye was capable of detecting more differences in the color green than in any other color of the spectrum.

The seven Ravagers stood out against their surroundings. Their bodies were black as ink, heads too large for the narrow shoulders. They stood almost waist-high on Simon. As they traveled on all fours, the demons reminded Simon of crocodiles. Their tails, almost as long again as their lean, powerful bodies, switched back and forth in anticipation.

"Something's wrong," Simon said. "There are ten of us and seven of them. They should be giving ground, not staying there."

"Maybe they can't count, mate," Nathan offered.

It wasn't just counting, though. The Ravagers would have known when they didn't have the numbers they needed to bring down their prey.

A cold warning thrilled down Simon's spine as he watched the Ravagers holding their positions to the south. The demons from the north and east came on at a furious gallop.

Then the Templar closed on the Ravagers. Just before the two groups collided, the Ravagers issued their low, guttural barks. A warrior alone might have a chance to get clear of an encounter thanks to that habit of barking. But that wasn't going to happen tonight. The demons threw themselves forward with gaping jaws.

Simon dropped the deer carcass from his shoulder and hoped he'd have a chance to collect it before they had to flee. He freed the Spike Bolter at his hip and fisted it. The pistol was large, an L-shaped frame with six rotating barrels capable of delivering an amazing rate of fire. The ammunition was palladium spikes.

In the 360-degree HUD view, Simon saw Danielle free her second Molten Edge sword. The second one was slightly smaller than the one she held in her right hand. She'd been training long and hard these past few months to wield dual blades in battle. The Molten Edge blades held a high-intensity column of carefully controlled lava that followed the parameters defined by the sword.

Both weapons flared to life as she said the voice-activation prompts. Both blades resembled liquid fire and stood proudly against the darkness of the night. Danielle was hard to lose in a night battle.

The Ravagers shifted, but they didn't attack or retreat.

With liquid ease, the lead Ravager pivoted to face Simon. The horrible maw gaped open to reveal rows of serrated teeth that curved inward. Once a Ravager closed its jaws, the mouth was like a bear trap. A victim would almost have to hack off his own limb to get free.

Instead of waiting for the Ravager's attack, Simon sprang into action. He leaped high into the air and extended the Spike Bolter at the Ravager. When he squeezed the trigger, a steady stream of palladium spikes tore into the demon's scaly hide.

The Ravager roared in pain, but wasn't hurt badly enough to give up its single-minded obsession with seeking its prey. Next to the first, a second Ravager powered itself up to stand on its two rear legs as it lunged at Simon.

Nathan's Firefield Caster belched a pair of grenades that struck the second Ravager in the throat. The explosions knocked the creature back and covered it with a sheet of flame. Before it could recover, Nathan fired another pair of rounds that struck the Ravager's head. One of them exploded in the demon's mouth. It roared, breathing out fire, and whipsawed in a frenzy of pain.

"Anchor," Simon ordered the suit AI as he arced down. Anchoring spikes designed to hold a Templar fast against an assault fired from his boots. There were two twelve-inch spikes, one on each side of his ankles.

The first Ravager pulled back from the one that was on fire, but it moved only a few inches. Simon's left foot spikes smashed down through the Ravager's thick skull, but the spikes on his right foot only pierced the demon's neck. Simon's considerable weight drove the Ravager to the ground.

The Ravager yanked its head out from under Simon, who fell sideways, unable to keep his balance because his spikes were anchored into the demon. Its strength surprised him. He'd figured his move would have nailed it to the ground.

He landed hard on his back, but the armor and special anticoncussive liquid insulation that lay between him and the armor cushioned the blow. The Ravager came at him, but its head twisted awkwardly on its skinny neck. Still, it snapped at him and its fangs raked his armor.

Simon raised the Spike Bolter into position and fired at almost point-blank range. The spikes reduced the Ravager's left eye to bloody pulp and chewed through the socket and temple.

Bloodied, the Ravager refused to die. It snarled and dug its front feet into the ground, then surged forward again. Propelled by his opponent's weight and strength, Simon flopped like a rag doll.

"Anchor release," he commanded.

The spikes withdrew from the Ravager's head and neck. Instantly, it reared on its back legs and came down hard on Simon with its front legs. Unable to get out of the way, Simon felt the blow bounce him against the ground.

"Warning," the suit AI informed him. "Suit integrity at eighty-one percent."

Simon rolled to the side as the Ravager tried to repeat the attack. The ground shook as the massive front feet struck. After another roll, Simon got his feet under him. He surged up and fired the Spike Bolter again. The Ravager cocked its head sideways to see him with its good eye. Behind it, the Ravager that Nathan had shot rolled in agony as the clinging flames blistered the demon's flesh.

"Other demons closing in from the north and east," the suit AI said.

A brief glance at the HUD showed Simon the fresh waves of demons headed his way. He knew that trying to stand against all of them would be suicide. They had to make it through the Ravagers here.

SIX

Leah spread her arms and legs into a starfish pattern as she fell. Despite her panic over the long fall, she couldn't forget about the Blood Angel. The dive over the building's side had bought Leah a little time, but she knew it wasn't much.

Calm, she told herself. *You've done this before. Nothing to it.*

But she knew that was a lie. The equipment she was about to use had been used under optimum conditions. And she'd never used it at night.

She slammed her clenched fist into the activation pad just below her neck and waited to endure severe agony. The NanoDyne hang glider deployed from the low-profile backpack strapped to her. Thin black Kevlar mesh sailed along telescoping struts powered by Konstruk nanobots. In less than a second, the twenty-foot span of wings had spread and filled the frame.

The straps cut into Leah's flesh with a suddenness that took her breath away. She stifled a scream of pain. Every time she'd used the hang glider before, she'd deployed it from a standing start. As she checked the wings, she saw that they vibrated madly. For a moment she wondered if they were going to be wrecked by the headlong pace of her plunge. If they broke, it was over. The impact of the long fall would kill her.

At least the Blood Angel won't get you, she told herself grimly. She grabbed the controls depending from the wings, then straightened out her glide just in time to avoid one of the taller buildings. She adjusted her direction toward the O_2 and fired the microrockets filled with chemical propellant. They were capable of a sustained thirty-second burst that allowed the glider to gain altitude for longer flight.

The Blood Angel swooped down on Leah. The demon's claws tore through the hang glider's left wing as if it were made of paper rather than specially treated bullet-resistant fabric.

Abandoning the controls for a moment, Leah grabbed for the pistol in a shoulder holster under her left arm and the one at her left hip. The first weapon was an XM41 Thermal Bolter, a small rocket launcher that fired deadly warheads. The second was an SRAC machine pistol capable of a high rate of fire.

A twist in the harness allowed Leah to point the Thermal Bolter at the Blood Angel through the rent in the hang glider fabric. Hoping she didn't accidently hit the glider's wing, she squeezed the trigger and launched what looked like a small fireball as she closed her eyes. Protecting her eyes was second nature.

Bright light stormed across the back of Leah's eyelids as the rocket hammered the Blood Angel. A fresh wave of heat from the explosion clouded around her for a moment, then it was gone.

Flames wreathed the Blood Angel. It shrieked in pain and frustration as it tried to hang on. Aiming the weapon again, Leah fired one more time. The second rocket burst against the demon's skin as well.

The Blood Angel let go and shrilled as it fell away. Leah knew she hadn't mortally injured the demon yet, though. She reached up and tapped the gun butt against the small control panel that had slid into place above her. AUTOPILOT blinked into view across the small screen. Immediately, the wings adjusted themselves to a gentle glide approach path the shortest distance to the ground.

WARNING. APPROACH SPEED TOO GREAT, blinked the small readout. WARNING. NO CLEAR FLIGHT PATH AVAILABLE.

I know, I know. Leah followed the flaming Blood Angel with her eyes. Almost in the next breath, the flames around the demon extinguished. The Blood Angel flapped its wings and heeled over, streaking back to the attack.

Leah leveled the SRAC machine pistol at the demon and squeezed the trigger. The pistol bucked and kicked in her fist. Every third round was a purple tracer. Leah put the line of bullets on target with the demon. They smashed into the Blood Angel and tore holes in its body. Leah blasted the demon again with the rocket launcher.

Blinded by the flames, the Blood Angel hurtled straight at Leah. The demon fired more arcane energy and shrieked again.

Leah holstered the rocket launcher and grabbed the hang glider's controls. AUTOPILOT DISENGAGED. Her thumb slid over the rocket activation button. She pressed and held it, intending to hold on for a slow five-count.

Instead, the Blood Angel's energy blast overtook her. The hang glider spun as if seized in a miniature whirlwind. The support struts shivered and popped as they fought to maintain their shape.

WARNING! flashed the LED screen on the controls. WIND SHEAR IS—

Leah ignored the rest of the message. It didn't make any difference. All the guidance system could tell her was how bad everything was, and she already had a clue about that.

She pushed the controls forward and fired the rockets because up seemed to be the path of least resistance.

That direction also took her back into the path of the Blood Angel.

Fisting the SRAC machine pistol, Leah fired at the center of the demon's body. The explosive-tipped bullets smashed through the Blood Angel's scales, lodged in its flesh, and detonated. Small, fist-sized craters opened up in the demon's body and turned it into a moonscape of destruction.

Fighting the controls, Leah almost panicked when she saw the side of a building suddenly only a few feet away. She triggered the right rocket and tipped the hang glider sideways. The wingtip bounced intermittently from the side of the building. Orange sparks spewed in a torrent as the metal grated against stone. The scraping noise sounded as horrendous as the Blood Angel's cry.

Easy. Easy. Leah tried keeping a gentle but firm hand at the controls. The altimeter showed she was still seventy feet in the air. Plenty of fall remained to kill her.

The Blood Angel swooped in and smashed against the building. Rebounding from the wall, the demon spun down in a sudden tangle of broken limbs and shredded wings that still burned from the rocket attack.

A savage cry of exultation burst from Leah's lips before she knew it. In the next moment the hang glider's wingtip skidded against the building and heeled around. Panicked, suddenly focused on her own survival, Leah kicked her right foot against the wall and shoved. The hang glider's struts screamed and shuddered.

Knowing she had nothing to lose, Leah fired the rockets and hoped for the best. The propulsion kicked the hang glider out away from the building, but a crosswind caught it and slapped it back toward the wall again. Leah twisted violently, striving to keep the hang glider from crashing into the building. Then she blew past it and scooted once more into the open area above a street.

Maintaining control now, Leah angled for the street. She knew she was coming down far too fast, but there was nothing to be done for it. Darkspawn gunners were already tracking her. The air was suddenly alive with tracers and blurry energy bursts that heated the air, vibrated through her, or sparked electrical energy across her suit.

Fifteen feet above the street, Leah cut loose from the harness and dropped. She hit the ground on her feet and immediately tucked into a roll. The augmented strength of the suit would have allowed her to land standing, but that would have also made her an easy target for the demons.

"Here, Leah! Nip in!"

One of the orange dots identifying the agents suddenly radiated concentric circles to attract Leah's attention. She gathered herself and ran, pulling both her weapons.

Two men and one woman took cover behind an overturned double-decker bus beside the burned, rusting hulk of a tank that was a grim reminder that the British military had failed to stop the demon invasion in 2020. William Pittsfield, the man who'd called to Leah, was a veteran of both the military and a clandestine career that spanned decades. He was a survivor.

"A bit rough out tonight, eh?" Pittsfield asked.

"Perhaps a bit," Leah agreed.

Pittsfield leaned out around the bus and took aim with the Grizzly Rifle he carried. Energy pulsed and spewed during the two-second burst. A group of Darkspawn that had been closing in on their position went down like wheat before a scythe. Their smoldering bodies lay twisted and broken on the ground.

"One thing you have to say about this little tea party," Pittsfield said laconically, "there's no lack of targets." He recharged his weapon.

"What about the satchel teams?" Leah asked.

"We've lost one of them," Evelyn Herrington said. "There were more of these blighters here than we'd been told to expect."

Leah didn't say anything. It was hard to know the exact numbers of demons. So many of them looked alike, they could have been interchangeable parts. Added to that and making it even more difficult, the demons constantly moved.

"We need better intelligence about these sites," Leah said.

"Agreed." Robert Wickersham was the youngest among them. He had come to his majority while the war with the demons was under way. He ducked around the corner for a moment and fired the XM55 20-mm rifle he carried. A Darkspawn sniper located in one of the nearby buildings took a header out of a window and crashed to the ground below.

"Good shooting," Evelyn commented.

"Thank you."

A sudden explosion ripped across the street and jostled the bus. For a moment Leah thought it was going to overturn on them. Then it settled once more with a grinding clank.

Leah tracked the explosion.

"Satchel Team Three," Pittsfield stated grimly. "They didn't make it inside the dome."

"Are there any survivors?" Wickersham asked.

Pittsfield's masked head shook. "I don't know."

"If there are, we can't just leave them for the demons."

"I know." Pittsfield looked around at them. "Everybody saddled up then?"

"Yes," Leah said.

The other two echoed her.

"Righto," Pittsfield responded. "Then let's be about it, and be quick. We've riled these little beasties up." He glanced around the corner of the bus and took off.

Leah followed.

SEVEN

S imon swung his broadsword with all his amplified strength. The blade bit into the Ravager's reptilian face. Blood spurted over Simon's visor and obscured the forward 76 percent of his view—the suit ID verified that. He backed up automatically, holstered the Spike Bolter at his hip, and wiped the blood from his visor. His view remained streaked and smeared, but it was better than it had been.

In front of him, the Ravager's face had been split nearly in two by the sword blow. The weapon remained mired in the demon's flesh as it yanked back. From the jerky movements he observed, Simon judged that the creature was dazed. Simon used both hands to free his sword, weathered a mostly ineffectual blow that struck his chest, then rammed the broadsword into the demon's chest to pierce the heart.

Transfixed by the Templar blade, the Ravager shuddered and stood upright. Then its gory head fell to the side. The body followed it and the demon slumped to the ground.

"Carnagors!" someone shouted.

Slightly winded from his efforts, Simon wheeled around and looked past the blazing pyre that remained of the Ravager that Nathan had attacked. The other Templar had engaged the demons and fought for their lives. Thankfully all of the warriors still stood.

Beyond them, though, creatures burrowed up from the ground. At least a dozen of them broke the surface. Black soil scattered across the white snow.

The Carnagors resembled tanks. Massive as elephants, thick hide covered their bodies and provided natural armor. Tusks and rows of jagged teeth filled the cavernous mouths. Jagged spikes stood up from their spines. Hooked talons meant for digging and slashing jutted out from their toes. Carnagors could rip a Templar's armor open with those talons. Simon had seen it happen firsthand.

It was a trap. The cold realization of what had happened swept over Simon. This was beyond the capabilities of the Ravagers and the Carnagors.

"Sweep for demons," Simon ordered the AI. "Confirm known types."

"Sweeping. Confirm known demons: Ravager, Carnagor, and Minion."

"Isolate and display Minion." Simon lunged out of the way of a stampeding Carnagor. Even as fast as he was, he barely escaped the full brunt of the demon's attack. One of its shoulders caught his right foot and spun him into another Carnagor twenty feet away.

The second Carnagor whipped around and tried to bite its offender. Simon swept up a large rock and threw it into the Carnagor's throat. The rock gagged the monster for a moment. As it coughed and hacked, it pulled away and clawed at its mouth with its front feet. The razor-sharp talons scored its ugly face again and again. In its panic, the Carnagor didn't notice the cuts.

"Minion isolated," the suit AI said. "Displaying."

Simon got to his feet and reached around to his back for the Blockade Shield he carried. The shield had been hammered out on Templar forge, then overlaid with arcane energy and layered with NanoDyne tech. The nanobots gathered energy from the earth's electromagnetic field much as the spellwork served to do. When fully charged, the shield was a powerful weapon as well as a means of defense.

On the HUD, Simon spotted the Minion outlined in orange. Minions possessed intellect, were able to take commands as well as issue them. They weren't as powerful or clever as the Dark Wills or other demons, but they were dangerous foes.

The Minion sat astride a Fetid Hulk. Twelve feet tall and powerfully built with wide shoulders and a narrow waist, the Fetid Hulk was an engine of destruction. The green hide glowed with lambent energy.

Seated on the Fetid Hulk's shoulders, legs wrapped around the larger demon's neck, the Minion urged his savage mount forward. Covered in thick gray hide, the Minion looked as if it had been squashed into a squared-off form, condensed from something somehow larger, more solid and threatening. Minions' hands were removed at birth and the arms outfitted with organic links or technological implants that allowed the slotting of different weapons. They carried spare "hands" with them that gave them a range of attacks. The right hand worn by the Minion atop the Fetid Hulk sparked with electricity, and the left one glowed a dark violet.

The demons knew we hunted here, Simon thought desperately. *They were waiting on us.* He whipped his head around in time to watch Nathan go down before a charging Carnagor. The demon put its feet in the center of Nathan's chest and knocked him down.

Frantically, the Carnagor dug its feet in and tried to overcome its forward momentum as it struggled to turn around and go back after its fallen foe.

"Nathan!" Simon shouted as he ran toward his friend.

There was no response. Nathan lay half buried in the snow and loose dirt.

Simon placed his hand onto Nathan's helm. The suit-to-suit connection displayed Nathan's vital signs on Simon's HUD.

SINGH, NATHAN. CONCUSSED. READY STIM?

"Administer stim," Simon ordered.

Nathan's suit affixed a slap-patch to the Templar's body. Simon knew chemicals already raced through Nathan's body, but it would be a few seconds before he would be aware enough to save himself.

The Carnagor completed its turn and ran back in Nathan's direction. Knowing he couldn't grab Nathan, hoist the fallen man from the ground, and get them both out of the way of the rampaging Carnagor in time, Simon set himself before the demon and hunkered behind the Blockade Shield. It was almost three feet in diameter.

"Connect shield to armor power," Simon rasped.

"Shield connected," the suit AI replied. "Power levels at full."

"Anchor." Simon stared into the Carnagor's feverish red eyes as it closed the distance.

"Anchor not recommended at this time," the suit AI said. "Suggest evasive maneuvers. Personal safety is at risk."

"Anchor," Simon ordered. "Personal safety override." He felt the vibration as the spikes drove deeply into the ground. Just before the Carnagor reached him, Simon leaned forward to intercept the demon with the shield and hoped he hadn't foolishly gotten himself killed. *Death would be better than getting captured by the demons.*

At the moment of collision, the world seemed to go away. During his training as a Templar novice, during the years of extreme sports that included base jumping, as well as nanospring skateboarding with wipeouts at over sixty miles an hour and eighty feet in height, he'd never before been hit so hard.

The Blockade Shield was designed to offer anticoncussive resistance. Whatever force it defended against, the arcane energy and nanotech was designed to re-create, meet, and negate. That worked well in theory. The Templar that had designed it had suggested that it might stop a speeding automobile.

No one had ever tested that.

No one had ever used it in a head-on competition against a Carnagor, either.

Simon flew backward at the impact. Pain wracked his body, and he was certain that his legs had ripped free of his hips. The shield had slammed against his knees, shoulder, and chest so hard it knocked the breath from his lungs in spite of the anti-impact energies and natural resistance of the armor.

Then he landed on his butt and rolled through the snow and savaged earth. Somewhere along the way he lost the shield, but he kept hold of the sword. His vision swam as he tried to focus. He had managed to deflect the Carnagor from Nathan. Behind the demon, Nathan groggily got to his feet and reached for his sword.

"Are you trying to get yourself killed?" Danielle asked.

"I was really hoping not to," Simon replied as he stared at the charging Carnagor. He tried to move his feet, then discovered the spikes had yanked chunks of stone from the earth. He recalled the spikes and the stone dropped away. He pushed himself to his feet and turned profile as the Carnagor bore down on him. There was no time to get away.

Slightly before his left palm made contact with the Carnagor's head, Simon leaped and tucked himself into a forward roll across the demon's massive shoulders. Simon slammed his boot soles against the Carnagor's spine.

"Anchor," Simon ordered again.

Immediately, the spikes shot down from his boots and sank deeply into the Carnagor's body. At least one of them severed the demon's spine. The Carnagor's steps suddenly lacked power and went wobbly. But it lashed its huge head around and flashed its tusks.

Reversing his sword, Simon took a two-handed grip on it and rammed it through the Carnagor's neck at the base of the demon's skull. At that point the Carnagor became a pile of dead meat that was only just then realizing it.

Simon retracted the anchoring spikes and leaped from the demon's back. Landing, Simon plunged into a four-foot snowdrift and had to fight his way free. The suit AI located his shield and he made straightaway for it.

"Thanks for the save, mate," Nathan said as he joined him.

Simon nodded, then swept the grounds with his gaze. "Retreat," he broadcast over the comm. "To the west."

"The cliffs are that way, Simon," Danielle protested.

Simon saw her in the distance as she employed both the Molten Edge swords to disembowel a Ravager and then take the head from a second.

"The demons lie in all other directions," Simon said. "We don't have a choice. Do it now."

The Templar hunting party broke away from the demons and ran. Their amplified strength and speed gave them a slight edge on the demons, but—over the short distance they had to cover to the cliffs—that edge wasn't going to be enough.

Simon ran, but he kept the Minion on the Fetid Hulk's shoulders marked on his HUD.

EIGHT

The street was a war zone. Carnage erupted around Leah constantly. She kept her pistols up and fired continuously. As Pittsfield had said, there was no lack of targets.

After a few moments, they reached what was left of Satchel Team Three. Over a dozen blood zombies rooted among the remains of the six men and women. The foul creatures looked like blood-covered shambling mockeries of human beings.

Horrified, Leah realized that at least a handful of the abominations had been created from men and women who had died in this battle. Some demon somewhere was lifting them up from the gates of death and setting them on their comrades.

Pittsfield cursed and stepped out to fire the Grizzly Rifle. When the energy bursts struck the blood zombies, the creatures flew to pieces. Three of them disintigrated before the attention of the others riveted on Pittsfield. More blood zombies appeared from behind overturned vehicles and clumps of mortar and stone from nearby buildings.

"Run!" Leah added her own weapons fire to Pittsfield's. "There are too many of them!"

"One of the satchel charges didn't explode," Pittsfield said. He made no move to withdraw.

One of the blood zombies leaped to the top of a broken mass of building wall from a nearby structure. Its maw opened as it prepared to leap down onto Leah and her companions.

Reacting instinctively, Leah leveled the Thermal Bolter and put a rocket into the blood zombie's open mouth. The creature exploded into gobbets of charred flesh, and the smoky stink filled the air. Not even Leah's mask completely filtered out the smell.

Pittsfield barely held his own. The blood zombies massed on him and drove him back. The Grizzly Rifle was too long to employ effectively in such close quarters. Leah stepped behind and to one side of the man and opened fire with the SRAC. The blood zombies wilted under sustained fire, but they didn't stop coming.

"We've got to pull back," Leah said.

"No one has penetrated the dome," Pittsfield growled. "There's a satchel charge just lying there."

Leah saw the case that held the explosives. Two craters and blast markings showed where the others had exploded and only rearranged the wreckage along the street.

"If that bloody dome isn't blown," Pittsfield continued as he butt-stroked a blood zombie and shattered its head. He left the rest unsaid.

The blood zombie went down into a fetal position and started rocking. Leah knew from observation that the creatures sometimes regenerated. She kicked the blood zombie back and pumped a dozen explosive rounds into the corpse that scattered pieces in all directions.

If it comes back from that, she thought fiercely, *it's at least going to take a while longer.* She looked at the satchel charge. "I'll retrieve the explosives."

Pittsfield slung his Grizzly Rifle over his shoulder and drew a HARP pistol and an Eruptor. The HARP pistol was a Harmonic Resonance Projection weapon that used electronic and sonic generators to produce a beam capable of rapidly changing sonic waves. The technology had first been developed for mining because the field was controllable, and it disintegrated nonorganic matter such as rocks, metal, and glass.

The HARP technology also destroyed organic matter that no longer generated natural body rhythms. The hearts of the blood zombies were stilled, and blood no longer pumped through the veins and arteries. They registered as inorganic things to the HARP.

When Pittsfield fired the HARP pistol, the weapon emitted a wide cone of destruction. The blood zombies in the beam's path stopped moving, then shook and shivered to pieces. A second later, the parts of them—and sometimes whole blood zombies—broke apart into atoms and disappeared in the sudden blue-white arc of light that filled the immediate vicinity.

The blood zombies outside the destruction stumbled back. Evidently they felt some of the fallout of the HARP blast because they were too dead to know fear.

Leah also noted that two of the dead members of the satchel team had been hit as well. Only parts of their bodies remained where they'd fallen.

Pittsfield cursed.

Leah knew the man hadn't intended to do further injury to those that had fallen. *They didn't feel it,* she told herself. *And they can't be resurrected and turned against us now.*

"I've got the satchel," she said, and darted forward. She holstered the SRAC and kept the Thermal Bolter out so she could use it. Bending down, she caught up the satchel charge by its handle and kept moving forward. There was no time to think now.

A Darkspawn scout group appeared around the corner of a building and quickly knelt to take aim at her. She pointed the Thermal Bolter and fired a trio of rounds.

Only one of the rockets struck the group. The other two hammered the street and the building wall. Flames engulfed the entire area and clung to the Darkspawn that survived the initial explosion.

Leah ran, banishing all thoughts of survival or death. She concentrated on the effort it took to avoid her enemies and keep moving forward. The firefight had been so fierce that a smoky haze had mixed with the natural fog streaming in from the River Thames. The Isle of Dogs was barely visible out in the middle of the river.

"This is Blue Scout," Leah said as she leaped over the headless body of a Fetid Hulk. A dead man dressed in black lay twisted and broken in the demon's huge hands. Acid burns from the Fetid Hulk's throat sac had eaten away the protective suit and charred the flesh beneath.

"Reading you five by five, Blue Scout," Commander Hargrove replied.

"Blue Scout is now designated Satchel Team Three." Confronted by a horde of Darkspawn, Leah ducked into a nearby alley as energy bolts and rounds cut through the space where she'd been.

"Understood," Hargrove replied.

On the field generated by the datastream detailing the battle, Leah watched her designation change from BLUE SCOUT to SATCHEL TEAM THREE.

"Good hunting, Satchel Team Three," Hargrove told her.

"Yes sir. Thank you, sir."

The alley was a dead end. A twenty-foot wall blocked the way. On the map she had, the alley had been shown as unblocked. She cursed, knowing that the intel they'd had on the op was sloppy. She didn't completely blame the agents who'd done the recon. Keeping up with the demons and their machinations was almost impossible.

"Up, Leah."

She glanced over her shoulder and saw Wickersham there.

"I've got your six," he told her. Smoking ruin showed on his left shoulder where a Darkspawn shooter had winged him. Blood ran over the black material.

"You're injured," Leah said.

"We're going to be dead if you don't hurry."

Behind him, Darkspawn entered the alley.

Leah slung the satchel charge over one shoulder and holstered the Thermal Bolter. She pressed a button on her left control wristband. The suits they wore weren't as automated as those of the Templar. Many things remained manually operated.

Microscopic hooks shifted out of the pads of her gloves, elbows, and knees. More sprouted from the toes of her reinforced boots. When she reached the alley wall, she threw herself onto it and slammed her palms, elbows, knees, and boot toes against the stone and mortar. The hooks dug into the stone and provided her enough purchase to slither up the wall quick as a lizard. The climbing was a practiced maneuver, and she'd spent weeks perfecting it.

Wickersham followed her in the same fashion.

Near the top, Leah paused, gathered herself, and launched herself toward the wall's edge. She caught hold of it and hauled herself up. A heartbeat later, Wickersham landed beside her. Energy bolts crashed against the wall and sizzled through the air around them.

Leah ran along the wall toward the building in the direction of O_2. She threw herself against it and slithered up another two stories to reach the roof, then hauled herself over.

Wickersham came over as well, but he landed awkwardly and went facedown. He loosed a muffled yelp of pain, then a curse. He rolled into a sitting position and pushed himself to his feet.

"They're climbing," Wickersham said.

Leah reached into her pack and took out a HARP grenade. When she had it, she slammed the grenade against the rooftop to activate the timer. The grenade pulsed blue as it started its countdown.

Using the overhead recon available through the bot-supplied images, Leah shoved the grenade over the rooftop's edge and dropped it into the mass of Darkspawn Troopers forming a flesh-and-blood ladder to scale the building wall. It was two stories, but the demons had plenty of bodies.

The grenade landed in the writhing mass. A few of the Darkspawn recognized the threat and tried to bail from the top of the wall. It was wasted effort, though. The grenade went off, and the blue-white glare filled the alley.

Leah glanced over the side and saw that the largest knot of demons had disappeared. Arms, legs, heads, and torsos littered the ground to mark the radius of the blast. A large section of the wall had disintegrated as well.

And so had a huge piece of the building.

The rooftop shuddered and shifted with a groan.

Realizing the danger, Leah grabbed Wickersham's armor harness and yanked him into motion. "The support columns on this side of the building are gone," she shouted.

Both of them ran, barely managing to stay ahead of the building's collapse as the rooftop dropped. The destruction gathered force and intensity, sounding like a wave crashing in their wake.

When they reached the rooftop's edge, a forty-foot span opened over the street below. The four-story drop to the street level was manageable, but the demons held the area. If they dropped into the street, Leah knew they wouldn't last a moment.

"The other side," she gasped, and launched herself into the air with all the power of her augmented suit. "It's the only chance." She took flight like a human missile.

Wickersham was only a split second behind her. He flailed awkwardly through the air high above the street fighting. Some of the Darkspawn below saw them and recognized them for what they were. Bullets, beams, and arcane forces tracked Leah and Wickersham across the street.

Leah knew she couldn't hope to catch the building's rooftop. She angled her descent toward the windows because she didn't think her suit's armor would manage the collision with the building.

"The windows," she yelled to Wickersham. She didn't know if he heard her or tried to respond. In the next instant she smashed through the glass. Glittering shards arced through the air and caught the gleam of fires and weapons discharges.

Empty clothing racks covered the shop's floor. Everything worth taking had been taken years ago. Leah gasped as the impact drove the wind from her lungs. Then she lie on the floor, tucked into a fetal position, hands wrapped over her head and knees tucked in to protect her stomach.

When she was sure—and surprised—that she was still alive, Leah pushed herself to her feet and stared back out the shattered window. Darkspawn Troopers ran toward the store.

Behind them, the collapsing building fell into the street. Tons of stone, mortar, and glass slammed over the massed Darkspawn. What had only seconds ago been a mistake now became a savage blow struck against the demons.

Leah dived back down as stray bits of stone and mortar crashed through other windows in the shop. The suit's audio receptors struggled to keep up and finally failed out during the crescendo. She got her breath back as debris pelted her. After making sure she still had the satchel, she unlimbered the Thermal Bolter.

Three Darkspawn crawled through the broken window. Leah fired three rockets into them. The front of the store turned into an inferno, and the concussion of the explosions blew the Darkspawn back out onto the street.

Another demon tried to force its way through the door, but the entrance was obviously jammed. Wickersham shot the demon through the head with his M3 Perforator. Head and features obliterated, the Darkspawn staggered back and went down.

Through the window, Leah saw that the Darkspawn dead and other demons lay sprawled across the street, buried in the building's wreckage.

"Nice little bit of luck for us," Wickersham said grimly. "I guess you could say you brought down the house, Leah."

More Darkspawn arrived on the scene.

"Are you able to run?" Leah asked. Nearly all of Wickersham's upper body glistened with dark blood. A few jagged pieces of glass stuck out of his torso.

"Don't have a choice, love." Wickersham started to remove a shard of glass.

"Don't," Leah warned. She'd left the glass protruding from her body in place as well. "The glass might be the only thing keeping you from bleeding out."

"Oh." Wickersham took his hand back. "Well, I suppose we should be thankful for that then." Pain masked his derisive tone.

* * *

Leah led the way out of the shop's rear. The door let out into a small alley. She got her directions from the bot scans, then took off once more for the O_2.

They stayed with the shadows and discovered they were behind the demons' skirmish line. The scans also showed that the demons were winning the engagement, pushing the attacking team back farther and farther.

The dome stood less than eighty yards away. Wrecks littered the way. Carnagors or other demons not yet identified had torn up the ground.

"Once we're in," Leah said, "the river is our only hope."

Wickersham nodded. "Only one of us needs to go, love."

"Do you want to stay here?"

"No. I was suggesting that you might."

Leah shook her head. "I started this. I'll finish it."

"Then let's have at it before things become worse. For I'm certain they will." Wickersham held his Perforator and pulled the NanoDyne Firestarter he also carried.

Leah turned and ran, and Wickersham followed. They were flitting shadows among the fog, smoke, and twisting darkness in front of the dome. Instead of trying to force their way through the main entrance, Leah blasted a new one through one of the walls. The heated concussion blew through the barrier and hurled debris before them.

The O_2 wasn't anything like Leah remembered. She'd gone to athletic events and concerts there, and shopped with her mates. Now the building housed strange demonic devices. Green glowing power cells lit up the darkness. Strange conveyor belts and machines clumped and thumped and squealed and roared as weapons passed through the assembly line.

Darkspawn labored over the machines to keep everything running. Others ran toward the opening she'd blasted through the wall. Their weapons blazed.

"Satchel Team Three," Commander Hargrove broke in. "We show that you have penetrated the objective."

"Affirmative." Leah fired the Thermal Bolter at the arriving Darkspawn and knocked them backward. Wickersham added his own fire.

"Drop the satchel charge and go," Hargrove commanded. "We've started the countdown. You have ten seconds. Nine . . . "

Leah used the suit's augmented strength to hurl the satchel charge deep into the O_2. Combined HARP charges and highly concentrated plastic explosives made up the destructive package.

"Go," she ordered Wickersham.

The younger man turned and went back out the hole they'd blown through the wall without argument.

"Toward the river," Leah commanded as she followed. Something hit the right side of her face. Pain lanced through her skull and her vision suddenly collapsed and became smaller. Adrenaline fought off most of the pain as she forced herself to keep moving.

"Five," Hargrove said, continuing the countdown.

Wickersham stumbled as he ran toward the river. Leah caught the man by the arm and added her strength to his. They stumbled and managed to match stride.

"Two," Hargrove continued relentlessly.

Even with the augmented speed the suit produced, they weren't quite to the river's edge when Hargrove reached zero.

A massive flash of light blazed behind Leah and Wickersham.

"Jump," Leah said when they were thirty feet from the river. "Go as deep as you can."

Back when the River Thames had been full, rising actually, due to global warming, the river had lapped up onto the banks. Now that the Burn had taken away much of the water, the water level was five feet below the old banks. Leah only hoped it was deep enough from the trenching efforts in 2012 that had allowed more river traffic, to protect them.

The roars of the explosions caught up with them while they were in midair. But they hit the water before the air filled with fire and debris.

Leah went twenty feet down to the murky bottom and caught hold of a submerged boat that probably sunk sometime since the arrival of the demons.

Flames lashed out over the river and turned the water bilious yellow and orange. Wickersham clung to the boat's gunwales as murky blood threaded up from his wounds, and Leah did the same.

Her mask tightened over her face and changed shape a little as the safety features kicked in. Once the suit recognized the environmental change, it sealed around her face and the ten-minute air supply kicked on. Leah forced herself to breathe slowly even though her heart rate remained frantic.

Debris from the dome rained down into the river. A few charred demon bodies fell as well. Above the bank, it looked as though dawn had torched the sky.

"Good work, Satchel Team Three," Commander Hargrove said. "We confirm destruction of enemy target. Are you still with us?"

"Yes sir."

"There were two of you."

"Both of us, sir," Wickersham said weakly.

"Good. Make your way back to the rendezvous point and let's see how badly we've been bloodied."

"Yes, sir."

Wickersham stared at Leah. "Are you all right?" He reached out to touch her face.

Instinctively, Leah drew back. A fog of murky blood occupied the space where her head had been.

"Don't," she said. The blood convinced her that his touch would be painful although the whole side of her face felt numb.

"You're bleeding badly," Wickersham said.

"We both are. Let's go." Leah released the boat and swam underwater. With the burning dome so close by, she easily negotiated the river channel.

She hadn't counted on seeing the skeletons littered across the river bottom. The gleaming white bones, all of them human, lay mired in the mud. Leah didn't know if the river deposited them there when the demons destroyed some of the bridges or if the current swept the bodies there from shipwrecks and destroyed boats.

Or if the demons simply chucked them there like garbage.

The sight filled Leah with dread. From the beginning of the demon war, Control had stated that they would never be able to win the engagement. The best that the Agency hoped for was to keep the demons from winning as well. At the very least they wanted to at least force the demons to win more slowly and at a more costly price.

That's not enough, Leah told herself. She thought of the dead men and women she'd known before tonight that wouldn't return come morning. The Darkspawn were cannon fodder in the plans of the Dark Wills and Greater Demons.

The blow struck tonight had taken out a weapons factory, but that factory would be rebuilt within a few weeks or months. At best, even with all the death and sacrifice involved, this had been a delaying action.

Leah tried to forget about that as she kept swimming. But even that became too much for her as the throbbing pain in her head finally pushed her over into the blackest night she'd ever known.

NINE

The snowdrifts rose higher in the direction of the cliffs. By the time Simon reached them, the Templar plowed through drifts well over waist high. The disguised terrain made footing treacherous. Simon fell more than once and struggled to push himself back up.

As if sensing their prey had nowhere else to run, the Ravagers and Carnagors gathered. Overhead a few winged demons that Simon couldn't immediately identify flapped through the night air and became silhouetted against the starry brightness.

The Minion remained astride the Fetid Hulk. Reaching back over its shoulder, the demon drew a spear with an obsidian tip that somehow glowed black even in the night. The black light stood out against the pristine white snow.

"Templar," the Minion snarled in a guttural voice. "Do you want to give up?"

Simon strode forward. Three of the Templar had fallen in combat. Only seven of them stood on the windswept cliffs. No trees or boulders offered temporary cover.

"Who are you?" Simon demanded as he held his sword and shield.

The Minion took a deep breath and shook its blunt head. "For the moment, I am no one. I am not Named. I came to your pitiful world to fight and kill so that I might earn a Name. That's the way it has always been. Who are you?"

"Simon Cross, of the House of Rorke, and not one who's of a mind to surrender to demons."

The demon nodded. "Rorke. That House is known to us." It grinned, baring yellowed stumps of teeth. "We have killed your ancestors."

Simon didn't know if that was true. Human and demon interaction on this world had been slight. He stood there and tried to think of a way out, a way to still survive. Nothing came to mind. Burned by lack of sleep and the stimpacks he'd used to keep himself alert the last few days, he stood swaying.

"Tell me where the rest of you are," the demon said.

Taking heart in that, Simon stood his ground. If the demon didn't know where the Templar redoubt was, hope remained. When the hunting team didn't come back, the others would know that something had happened and would go on high-security alert. They would wait, as Simon had instructed, for a few days and then investigate. The possibility of getting the innocents out of harm's way still existed.

"There are no more of us," Simon said.

The Minion laughed mockingly. "Is that your answer, Templar, if I asked you to swear it upon your honor?"

"I have no honor for demons," Simon said. "Nor courtesy, nor mercy. My kind and yours, demon, only one of us will remain alive on this world."

"We will find the others," the demon promised. "Now that I have found you, I will take your head on my spear and let my masters know that other Templar hide out in the woods and hills here. Then we will find them and kill them all."

"You haven't killed us yet," Danielle retorted.

"That will take only a short time," the Minion said. He leveled his spear at Simon.

Simon barely had time to raise his shield in front of him before a black beam jetted from the spear. The shield dissipated most of the electrical charge from the arcane weapon, but the force involved blew Simon off his feet and knocked him backward.

"Warning," the suit AI informed calmly. "Defenses down to forty-three percent."

As one, the Carnagors and Ravagers attacked. Their taloned feet churned through the snow as they raced forward. In the end, though, their numbers worked against them. They got into one another's way as they strove to attack.

Simon stood and moved to the forefront. Smaller and quicker, the Ravagers struck first. Simon bashed the first one and snapped its neck, but even as its corpse slid down his shield, the next Ravager was already in line. It launched itself at Simon's head. He swung his sword and nearly cut the Ravager in half. His sword got stuck in the demon's spine. Stepping on his vanquished enemy, Simon ripped his blade free.

Before he could set himself, the Minion blasted him with the beam from the spear again. This time Simon spotted the green crystals that decorated the haft. They pulsed with energy.

The snow provided treacherous footing. Simon tried to anchor himself, but the spikes only pierced snow and found no purchase. Black flames clung to his armor and obscured his view.

"Defenses down to twenty-eight percent," the suit AI said.

"Analyze fire," Simon ordered.

"Analysis incomplete," the AI responded. "Not enough information in database."

Despite the armor, Simon felt the heat threatening to sear his skin. He shifted his shield to block the sustained burst, and barely got it into place before a Carnagor reared up in front of him. Simon thrust his sword forward and pierced the Carnagor's midsection, but the demon's massive feet slammed against the shield and knocked him backward.

He felt his right foot slide over the cliff's edge and tried to stop himself from falling. The gutted Carnagor struck him again, driving both feet forward again.

The demon's momentum propelled Simon over the edge, but the Carnagor failed to stop its own headlong momentum and ended up following after him. They both began the long fall to the broken ground below.

In mid-fall, Simon's reflexes and training took over. He'd learned a lot about falling and how to handle momentum in his Templar training, but his background in extreme sports had taken what was out of the ordinary and made it everyday for him.

Upside down in his fall, Simon slapped his empty hand against the cliff's sheer face. "Anchor right hand."

Immediately, the suit AI shot spikes out from the underside of his wrist that bored into the solid rock of the cliff. Simon's fall ended abruptly and uncomfortably as his hand stayed connected to the cliff face. He was suddenly right side up again, but his hand was trapped behind him. Pain flared through his wrist and arm. He slammed his boot soles against the wall and anchored them as well.

Shifting his shield to his back, Simon anchored his left hand and released his right. He swung out a little and stared at the Carnagor's broken body below.

Nathan cried out in panic.

Simon glanced up as a flood of snow poured over the cliff's edge nine feet above him. He barely registered the fact that Nathan fell before he reachinged for his friend. Nathan fell headfirst when Simon's hand closed around his ankle. For a moment Simon thought his shoulder might pop out of joint, but it held.

"Lord love a duck," Nathan breathed as he swung like a pendulum from Simon's hand. "I thought I was done for then, mate."

"Me, too," Simon said.

One of the flying demons dove from the sky. As it neared, Simon judged that it wasn't much bigger than an African condor, but that still made it bloody big. It had batwings and a forked tail over half again its length from nose to anterior.

The flying demon beat its wings fiercely and brought itself to a brief halt. Then it whipped its tail forward and attempted to drive the barbed end through Simon's visor. Minute fissures appeared in the high-impact polycarbonate.

"Warning," the suit AI said. "Repeated blows—"

The demon wheeled around, screamed in bloodlust, and attacked again. The fissures grew longer and wider.

"—may succeed in faceplate penetration," the suit AI finished. "Atmosphere integrity breached."

Simon swung Nathan toward the wall. "Lock on," he growled, then heard Nathan's suit anchors fire. Trusting the suit anchors to hold, Simon turned his attention to the attacking demon.

Staying with its usual method of attack, the demon swung around again and struck once more with its tail. This time, though, Simon seized the striking tail and stopped the wicked barb less than an inch from his faceplate.

The demon tried to escape by flapping its wings furiously. When it discovered that it couldn't escape, the demon curled over and attacked with a razor-sharp bill that scored Simon's armor.

Two other winged demons gathered in front of Simon. He whipped the demon to one side with its tail. Bones shattered when they met the cliff face. He released the dead demon and raised his free arm to defend against the two new ones.

Before they reached him, Nathan curled up with his Firefield Caster clenched in his fist. Flames belched from the pistol and charred both demons to ruin. Dead or dying, they dropped like stones.

"Thanks," Simon said.

"Don't mention it," Nathan replied. "If it weren't for you, mate, I wouldn't still be hanging about."

Turning back to the cliff face, Simon used the suit's anchors to climb. As he pulled himself up, he accessed the other Templar's video feeds through his HUD. Danielle and the other four battled desperately against terrible odds. Then Honeywell went down beneath a Carnagor's attack. The demon reared in savage, animalistic glee and pounded the fallen Templar.

Simon hauled himself over the edge and got to his feet. He freed his sword while on the run to aid Honeywell, hoping that he wasn't arriving too late. Nathan trailed behind him.

The Carnagor spotted Simon on the approach and tried to turn to face him. Before the beast set itself, Simon slit the Carnagor's throat with his sword. He rammed a shoulder into the demon to shove it from Honeywell.

Be alive, Simon commanded as he knelt and put a hand on Honeywell's chest. The suit-to-suit dataswap kicked in immediately and provided the fallen Templar's vitals.

Honeywell was alive. But only just. The list of broken bones and internal injuries spilled forth. She wouldn't return to the battle, and might not live to survive it.

"Initiate medical override," Simon said, contacting Honeywell's AI.

"Initiating medical override," the suit's AI responded.

"Full system shutdown."

"Affirmative. Kris Honeywell needs immediate medical attention."

"Noted," Simon replied. He stood and shifted his shield from his back. As soon as it locked into position, his suit powered it up again. By that time Nathan stood at his side, and the Ravagers had turned their attentions to them.

"What do you think, mate?" Nathan asked as he shot a Ravager with the Firefield Caster. Flames blazed up around the Ravager, and it howled in dismay.

Simon caught a leaping Ravager on his shield, bashed it to the ground, then stomped its throat to smash the trachea. He stomped again and put an anchor spike through its brain.

"If we can get Honeywell up, we can try to go down the cliffs."

"The Ravagers can climb."

"But the Carnagors can't."

"True."

Simon smashed his sword through a Ravager's skull and dropped another dead body at his feet. But they just kept coming. He called Danielle and the others to him. Bravely, the Templar fought their way through the tide of demons. Nathan and two of the other Templar formed a barrier with their shields, while Danielle and the other Blademaster fought with two swords each. Ravagers died before them and became a growing wall of dead.

The Carnagors held back. Simon suspected they did so due to the fact limited room to maneuver on the cliff's edge existed. The narrow expanse afforded them also shut down their chances of successfully tunneling under them. The Carnagors trumpeted in wild bloodlust.

"You're going to die, Templar," the Minion taunted from the shoulders of the Fetid Hulk. "Then I'm going to go back for reinforcements. We'll seek out those you've been protecting out here. We'll find them, and we'll kill them."

TEN

With Honeywell's unconscious body slung over his shoulder, Simon set himself to attempt the descent over the side of the cliff when he felt the ground vibrating. Searching the HUD, he found the source of the vibration: three ATVs with sleek black finishes plowed through the snow toward the demons.

Simon recognized them at once as three units from the redoubt. None of the Templar in London would have sent vehicles out this far from the city.

The undercarriages of the ATVs rode three feet above the ground normally, but now they had to break through the snowdrifts in places. The five-foot-tall spiked tires churned snow out behind them. Specially designed by the Templar, the ATVs were based on the British military Panther MLV, outfitted in reactive armor, and armed with antiaircraft weapons, missile launchers, heavy XM171 Thermo Cannon, and F-S Grinder Cannon. The Hound's Eyes, the onboard drones that painted targets for the ATV's weapons, shot forward and relayed information to the weps officer.

"Hold fast there, Simon," a familiar voice said.

"Wertham," Nathan quipped happily. "I didn't know you were still able to stay up this late."

Simon felt a little relieved himself. Wertham was one of the old guard, a man who'd helped train Thomas Cross when he'd been a young man. Few of the old Templar remained because most of them had followed Lord Sumer-isle to their deaths at St. Paul's.

"I made an exception when I found out you people hadn't returned tonight."

"You were also instructed to stay at the redoubt," Simon said.

"Was I?" Wertham sounded innocent. "You can't trust my memory at my age."

The ATVs fired without hesitation. With their targets lit up by the Hound's Eyes drones, there wasn't much chance of hitting the Templar stranded at the cliff's edge. Fireballs belched from the ATVs' cannon, and Palladium sabot rounds dropped smoking, ruined Carnagors in their tracks.

"Attack!" the Minion screamed at the Carnagors and Ravagers. "Attack!" At his command, the Fetid Hulk turned and loped across the snow-covered countryside in full retreat.

"Wertham," Simon called out.

"Yes."

"There's a Fetid Hulk headed east." Simon fed the co-ordinates to the ATV's weps officer through the suit's AI.

"We have him, Simon."

"He can't be allowed to run free."

The ATV's cannon swung round and fired. The Thermo Cannon's rounds fell short of their intended target. The Grinder's sabot rounds tore through the trees but didn't come close to the fleeing demons.

"Can't get a lock on him," the weps officer said. "The trees interfere with the Hound's Eyes."

Simon ran forward and used the suit's strength as he vaulted over the thinning line of attackers. He landed in deep snow, stumbled, and nearly fell. The nearest ATV's forward gunner blasted two Ravagers that attempted to follow Simon.

At the ATV, Simon laid Honeywell in front of the prow. "Get her inside," he commanded. "She needs medical attention now."

The ATV lumbered forward and shielded the fallen Templar with its body. Simon knew they would haul Honeywell aboard through the emergency access panel underneath the fighting vehicle.

Slogging through the snow, Simon reached the ATV that Wertham commanded. He leaped aboard the skirt and knelt. Studying the HUD, he watched as a Thermo Cannon burst blew a knot of Ravagers over the cliff's edge and sabot rounds exploded Carnagors.

Nathan and Danielle already led the Templar toward the ATVs and safety.

"Everything's in good hands here, Wertham," Simon said. "Take me to that Fetid Hulk and its rider."

"On our way."

Simon held on to the ATV. He banged harshly against the vehicle's armor as it got under way. The right-side tires stayed locked in position as the left side chewed through the snow and earth. Then they bounded across the rough terrain in pursuit of the fleeing demons.

"We lost a few, didn't we?" Wertham's voice didn't hold the bluster it had earlier. He was connected to Simon on a private frequency.

"We did," Simon admitted. "It was my fault."

"Weren't no fault of yours."

"I got too lax. I should have brought more people to station scouts."

"More people would have drawn more attention," Wertham told him. "You and I both know that. Small units travel fastest and less noticeably."

Simon silently agreed. Safety and stealth had always been the harsh balance he'd fought whenever he'd put hunting parties into the field. If they'd been able to sustain themselves within the redoubt, no one would have ever had to leave.

But then you wouldn't be able to save the stragglers that continue to find their way out of London, Simon chided himself.

"We can't become an island," Wertham said. "You and I and the other Templar discussed that at length when we first set up the redoubt. We all agreed that we couldn't turn our backs on those that we could save."

"I know."

"Not like the others."

"I know." The Templar in the Underground chose to wait out the demon invasion. The leaders of the Houses staged the massacre at St. Paul's to convince the demons that the Templar were all dead. They planned to train in secret and grow a new generation before attempting to fight back against the demons.

Simon hadn't agreed with that. The Burn scoured London. He felt that if they waited there would be nothing left to save before the Templar decided they had the army they needed.

In the beginning, only a few other Templar had felt the same way he did. When he'd first returned to London and subsequently fought with Terrence Booth, the High Seat of the House of Rorke, Simon had been banished from Templar rank. His privileges had been taken from him. But he hadn't walked out of the Underground alone. Over the past four years, especially since the other Templar had discovered that Booth had taken Simon captive under a flag of truce, more had come.

Am I just leading them to die? Simon asked himself bitterly. Things hadn't gone well at the redoubt. Booth and some of the other Templar that had chosen to remain in the Underground called him a pariah and claimed that he foolishly caused Templar to leave the safety of the Underground just to perish at the hands of demons.

He shook the dark thoughts from his mind, realizing that they came too easily these days, and focused on the fleeing demons.

The Minion had to die.

Simon clung grimly to the ATV as it tore across the uneven terrain. The pointed prow crested snowdrifts and exploded them into the air. Flakes landed on Simon's cracked faceplate and melted immediately as the suit fought to keep his vision clear. Water droplets formed inside the faceplate, oozing through the cracks left by the winged demon.

Twice the ATV went airborne and landed with jarring thumps. Simon knelt on one knee and felt hammered against the armor.

"Still with us?" Wertham asked.

"Yes," Simon replied.

"Can't go through the forest after the demon."

"I know." Simon peered through the tight cluster of trees. Thankfully the patchy forest allowed visual contact. The openings limited the demon in the areas he could attempt to hide. "Just get me close."

The ATV skirted the forest. Small saplings and brush went down under the fighting vehicle's massive tires. The constant crashing and snapping filled Simon's audio.

Moonlight occasionally exposed the fleeing demons through the trees. The Minion had obviously spotted the ATV and was making a concerted effort to stay as far away from it as possible.

"Stop here," Simon said, then flung himself from the ATV.

Even though the ATV sped at almost forty miles an hour across the uncertain landscape when Simon took his leave, the armor's gyros helped him stay upright. His trajectory still wasn't completely controllable, though. He caromed off a tree, shredding bark and taking off branches over two inches in diameter.

He hit the ground and rolled. The sword and shield across his back made it awkward, but he'd practiced such maneuvers for years. When he got to his feet, he gripped the sword in his hand.

He ran through the forest like a deer, leaping and bounding over fallen trees. The HUD showed him that Wertham had halted the ATV just outside the forest's edge. Three other Templar had deployed and ran in full pursuit.

As Simon closed on the demons, the Minion slid from the Fetid Hulk's back. Immediately, the large demon turned to face Simon. It lumbered through the forest awkwardly, ill matched to the terrain.

Sliding his shield around, Simon held it before him and used it to meet the Fetid Hulk's massive fists. The powerful impacts drove Simon back for a moment, then he stepped to the right, bashed the shield's edge against the outside of the demon's knee, and listened to it shatter.

The Fetid Hulk growled in pain as it collapsed to one knee. It flailed at Simon with a big fist but missed by inches.

"Take it," Simon ordered the pursuing Templar.

The three Templar mercilessly closed on the Fetid Hulk. The demon spat a huge splash of toxin from its throat sac, but one of the Templar held up his Domination Shield. Formed of spectral energy, the shield glowed and appeared translucent till struck. Then it grew more opaque, depending on how hard the blow struck. The shield took the brunt of the toxin as the other two Templar attacked.

Simon watched the battle in his HUD while he pursued the Minion. The demon leaped up, caught a thick tree branch in one cybernetic hand, and swung itself up. While taking cover behind the tree trunk, it slid a blaster hand onto its other wrist.

"You're stubborn, Templar," the demon taunted. "Coming all this way to die."

"I'm not going to be the one who dies," Simon said.

Lithe as a monkey, the Minion dropped to the branch below, caught it in its cybernetic hand, and fired the blaster as it swung. Caught off-guard, Simon fell backward as the energy smashed against his helmet. His faceplate shattered more.

"Warning," the suit AI said. "Primary defenses at eighteen percent. Other Templar presence detected. Shift to defensive mode only."

Hurting and near exhaustion, Simon forced himself to his feet. He tracked the demon as it moved through the trees. The three Templar still engaged the Fetid Hulk. He couldn't allow the Minion to get away.

The Minion tried to duplicate its attack, but Simon was prepared for the move this time. When it dropped and brought the hand weapon to bear, Simon raised his shield and blocked the energy blast.

Retreating quickly, obviously expecting Simon to retaliate, the Minion climbed through the branches. Simon slid the shield off, caught the edge in his hand, and turned to profile the tree. Back when he'd been involved with extreme sports, he'd thrown a lot of Frisbees to help develop hand/eye coordination. There had also been beaches and girls in bikinis involved. With the armor, the shield felt incredibly light.

As the Minion settled on a branch well out of reach, Simon whipped the shield forward. At nearly three feet across, the shield weighed close to forty pounds. The shield crashed through tree limbs and plowed into the Minion's head.

Almost decapitated from the blow, the demon dropped from the tree like a stone. By the time it hit the ground, Simon reached it with his sword in his hand.

Even with half of its head shorn away by the shield's edge, the demon still lived. It gazed at Simon with its malevolent black eyes. Convulsions wracked it as it tried to get up. Then it lay back.

"It seems I'm forced to accept my fate today, Templar," the Minion said.

"And you never earned a Name for yourself," Simon taunted. "Too bad."

"Maybe I'll make it back from the Well of Midnight," the demon said.

The Well of Midnight was the spawning place of the Shadow and the demons. Simon had heard the stories about it all his life. Even after years of trying to imagine it, he hadn't been able to think of a place that horrid.

"You have no soul, demon," Simon said. "When you die, you're destroyed. There's nothing left of you after this place."

The demon laughed defiantly. "Do you truly think so?"

"Yes."

"Then you're a fool. The Well of Midnight will succor me back into its embrace and make of me what it wishes. If I am strong enough, if I have followed the way of the Shadow truly enough, I will be back." The Minion wheezed as it labored to breathe. "If not, the Well of Midnight will still reclaim my essence and use me to make more demons."

The thought chilled Simon. *How can anyone face an inexhaustible army?*

"Your world will fall, Templar," the demon whispered. "All worlds before this one have fallen."

"Not this one," Simon said. "Our destiny is greater than yours."

The demon laughed. "Who told you that?"

"It has been written." Even the Goetia manuscript alluded to that. "It is the truth given by the Creator."

Something in what Simon said caused fear in the Minion. He saw the apprehension in the demon's widened eyes.

"The Truths," the demon whispered, "shall never again be—" Then it shivered and went still. The pupils of the eyes relaxed, then grew and became black pools.

Simon stared down at the creature and wondered what he'd said that had caused such a reaction. *Did the demon say "truth" or "truths"?* He wasn't sure.

"Is it dead, Lord Cross?"

At the mention of his hereditary title, Simon looked up at the three approaching Templar. Even though the Templar at the redoubt had been in the habit of calling him Lord Cross for the past few months, Simon still wasn't used to it. Lord Cross had been his father, and even Thomas Cross hadn't often gone by that.

"Yes," Simon said. "It's dead." He took his shield from the Templar who had gone to retrieve it, then knelt and washed away the demon's blood with a handful of snow.

"Sergeant Wertham would like to be away as soon as possible," another Templar said.

"Especially in light of the fact that you weren't supposed to be here tonight," Simon said, "I can understand how he'd want to feel that way."

"We're sorry about that, Lord Cross."

These faceplates totally suck when it comes to humor and sarcasm, Simon thought. He turned his faceplate translucent to show the Templar his smile.

Their faceplates cleared as well, and their youth astonished him. He'd trained all of them himself, and had even helped two of them forge their armor.

"It was a joke," Simon explained.

"Oh." But none of them relaxed enough to smile or grin with any real enthusiasm.

Simon led the way out of the forest. A quick check of the HUD showed that the other two ATVs had rolled in the direction of the deer they'd taken. Tonight wouldn't be a complete loss.

Except that there was no way to replace the three Templar that had gotten killed. Every one of those lives was precious.

With a heavy heart, Simon trudged through the snow, hoping for at least a few hours' respite before he was thrown once more into the fray. His thoughts strayed to Leah, and he wondered how she fared. They hadn't seen each other in weeks.

That was just as well, he decided. She had her secrets, such as who she actually was and what she represented, and he had his. Since he'd last seen her, Macomber had made considerable advances on translating the Goetia manuscript. He would hate lying to her about that, but he knew he would.

At least until he was certain their agendas matched more closely.

ELEVEN

T hey're not going to welcome us with open arms."
Studying the men hiding behind trees and brush before them, Warren knew that Naomi's words spoke the truth. People who lived outside London or managed to escape the metropolitan area weren't going to want to trust anyone coming down these roads.

The zombies made that trust even less likely.

"I didn't expect them to welcome us," Warren replied. In truth, he hadn't wanted to meet anyone while following Lilith's directions.

Only a short distance farther one, when no mistake could be made about the direction they took, a man stepped out of the shadows and stood near a copse of trees. He was gaunt and tense. Warren saw that in the man's aura. Of course, that tension was also easy to tell because the man pointed a shotgun at them.

"That's about far enough," the man shouted.

"We come in peace." Warren never broke stride, though Naomi fell back a couple of steps.

The man fired the shotgun over Warren's head. The explosive sound echoed over the marshlands.

"If you don't stop right there, you bloody fool, the people you're with will be carrying your body home."

Warren stopped.

"You don't have to follow this man's dictates." Lilith stood beside Warren with her arms folded imperiously. "You can order the zombies to attack."

"We could also try our luck at a more diplomatic approach." Warren resisted the impulse to blast his way through the men and women gathered there in the darkness. While he'd still be in Merihim's thrall, he didn't think he would have been allowed to back down.

"Showing weakness is a bad thing," Lilith said.

"Stopping to discuss this isn't weakness," Warren replied.

"I agree," Naomi told him. "But I don't think they're going to let us pass."

"Is there another way?" Warren asked Lilith. "Could we go around?"

"We could. But it would take longer, and you would lose more of the zombies. You don't want to be out in this country with no defenses."

Warren silently agreed with that assessment. "We'll lose some of the zombies to these people if we're forced to fight."

"Yes." The speculative smile on Lilith's face appeared genuine. "But the opportunity exists to make more zombies. You could raise a whole new army here."

The thought sickened Warren slightly. He hadn't thought as much about things like that when he'd been working with Merihim. He'd feared for his own life too much to acknowledge the lives of others.

Sometimes, when he was certain he was alone—which was seldom, between Naomi's and Lilith's attentions—he felt badly about how things had turned out with his roommate, Kelli. She'd never been a true friend, but upon occasion she'd been kind to him.

After his first encounter with Merihim, when he'd been burned and scarred by the demon, Warren had usurped

Kelli's will and made her his keeper. Even after she'd died, he'd resurrected her and kept her to watch over him. She had until the day he'd destroyed her when she'd tried to harm Naomi.

Warren didn't want to kill the people in front of them. Several were old, and many were not much more than children.

"You're soft," Lilith chided.

"I don't have to kill them," Warren responded.

"What?" Naomi stepped closer to him. "What did you say?"

The zombies grew restless.

Warren addressed the man with the shotgun. "We don't mean you any harm. We come in peace."

"Maybe so, but you'll go in pieces if you come any farther," the man grated. "We've got our own place out here, and we don't want anyone from outside coming around."

"We're just passing through."

"Not tonight, you aren't. You'd best just shove off and find another way to get where you're going."

"All right," Warren said. "Can you recommend a direction?"

The man hesitated. "Depends on where you're going."

Warren glanced at Lilith.

Her frown showed she was clearly unhappy with his choice of actions. "Deeper into the marshlands."

Warren relayed the information.

"You'd be better off waiting till morning," the man said. "Those marshlands can be tricky. Especially by moonlight. And we've heard stories about the things that live out there."

"What kinds of things?"

"You've got predators out there that fight for hunting territory. Wolves and the like. If not them, then lots of wild dogs that escaped from the city or from farms just outside London that were attacked by demons."

"Doesn't sound very hospitable," Warren said.

"It isn't."

"We just want passage. A chance to get to some place dry to sleep tonight."

"Anywhere but here."

Warren sensed danger and turned to look back along the road they'd traveled. He spotted an owl gliding silently by. Curling his silver fist, he concentrated on the owl, then closed his eyes and reached for the nocturnal predator.

When Warren opened his eyes again, he peered through the owl's eyes. Everything was in sharp relief, but it was in blacks, whites, and grays now instead of color leached by the silver moonlight. He also felt the owl's hunger. Hunting victories had been meager of late.

Usurping control, Warren forced the owl to turn around and fly back along the way they'd come. The bird flew just over the treetops, maintaining a low profile so it couldn't easily be seen. Its instincts for survival matched Warren's.

Only a short distance away, a motley crew of demons—most scavenging imps sent from the city to explore and map the surrounding terrain—moved steadily along the trail left by the lumbering zombies. The grooves carved through the snow were easy to follow.

One of the imps lifted its arm.

For a moment Warren thought the demon intended to fire a weapon at him. Heart pounding, forgetting for the moment that he was a separate entity from the night predator, he turned the owl around automatically and sent it winging away.

Instead of a weapon, though, or at least instead of the

pistol or rifle that Warren expected, a snake or eel un-
curled from the demon's arm and leaped into the air. It
spread its wings and took flight.

The owl's fear became Warren's. They both tried
to elude the impossible creature. Over the course of its
life, the owl had never seen anything like the eel-thing.
The demon was six or seven feet long, pallid, and had an
oversized, muscular head the size of Warren's fists put
together. When the jaws opened to expose serrated fangs
that glistened in the moonlight, the head looked even
bigger.

Despite the owl's graceful skill in the air, and its speed,
it proved no match for the flying demon. It swiftly overtook the owl, sailed above, then struck downward.

Warren felt the demon's fangs pierce the owl's neck as
if it were his own flesh. Burning poison coursed along his
body, reaching and then stopping his heart. Paralyzed, the
owl fell toward the snow-covered marshland as the demon
tore gobbets of flesh from it and devoured them.

Returning to his own body, Warren discovered his heart
pounded so fiercely he almost blacked out. He staggered
and would have fallen if Naomi hadn't stepped up to take
him by the arm. Her strength surprised him, but he knew
the demon transplants she'd done had changed her.

"Warren," she hissed.

"Stay awake," Lilith commanded. "If you don't move,
the demons will overtake us and kill you. Then we're all
lost."

"I'm all right." Although he wasn't sure if he could
stand on his own, Warren shrugged out of Naomi's grip.
She let him go.

"What is it?" Naomi asked.

"Demons," Warren gasped. "We're being followed."

Naomi gazed at him fearfully. "Why would they follow us?"

"I don't know." Warren looked at the people ahead of them.

"What's wrong with your friend?" the man with the shotgun asked.

Warren pointed back in the direction they'd come. "We're being followed by demons. They'll be upon us in minutes."

Frenzied curses broke out among the men. A few of them were of the opinion Warren should be shot on sight. Their way of thinking seemed to be gaining favor.

"I can help you," Warren insisted.

"You?" the man challenged. "With the dead things you've got following you?"

"I have powers," Warren replied.

"Demon's powers," someone said. "He's a demon-lover. One of them that wants to be just like the demons. Ain't no better than them, if you ask me."

"I don't want to be like them," Warren said. "They're my enemies, too. If I were with them, I would wait on them. I wouldn't have told you they were coming."

"It's a trick," someone else declared. "He just wants to bring his dead things among us to slit our throats when we let our guard down."

"Fools," Lilith snarled. "Leave them here to die."

Warren wavered uncertainly. He didn't want to face the imps.

Naomi looked at him and knew his thoughts. Her dark eyes held his.

"We can't just leave them," she said.

"Of course you can," Lilith argued.

"They don't want us here," Warren pointed out.

Naomi took his arm, his flesh and blood arm, and held it. "If we leave them here, they're going to die."

"They'll die anyway," Lilith said. "If not tonight, then another day. They're too weak to live in this world."

"They'll die anyway," Warren said.

"Do you think the demons will quit pursuing us after they slaughter these people?" Naomi asked.

Warren didn't answer.

"Because they won't," Naomi said. "The demons will kill these people, and then continue following us wherever it is you're taking us."

Anxiety spread through Warren.

"Those demons aren't out here for these people," Naomi said. "They came looking for something, and my guess is that they're looking for you."

"She doesn't know that," Lilith said.

"You don't know that," Warren stated.

"Merihim could have sent them."

Fear quivered through Warren. "I'm nothing to Merihim. Not since he reclaimed his hand."

"You shared the demon's mind," Naomi told him. "Maybe he fears what you might have learned."

Thinking about how powerful Merihim was, Warren couldn't believe that. He glanced back the way they'd traveled and tried to figure out what to do. His life had never been this hard before. Not even when he was being reared by his magic-obsessed mother and abusive stepfather. Choices in those days had seemed simpler.

But they were the same, weren't they? Warren asked himself. *Survive or not survive? The stakes haven't changed. The game has only gotten harder.*

TWELVE

W hen Merihim took his hand back from you," Naomi said, "he didn't expect you to live. It was a miracle that you survived. I saw you."

You left me, Warren couldn't help thinking.

"She abandoned you," Lilith said. "Only I saw to your needs. I gave you back a hand. Don't be swayed by her at this point. She thinks only of herself."

Warren looked at Lilith. *And who do you think of?* But he knew who she was most concerned with. He couldn't fault her for that, though. He thought mostly of himself as well.

"Merihim didn't expect you to live," Naomi said. "He didn't expect you to become powerful again. You may be a threat to him at this point."

Both of those things, Warren knew, were facts. In the distance, the group of imps stepped over a hill. They stood out darkly against the snowy background under the silver moonlight.

"She has a point," Lilith reluctantly admitted. "As powerful as I am, I couldn't have shielded you completely from Merihim. He may be looking for you as well."

"If Merihim wanted to find me," Warren said, "he'd find me easily enough. And he wouldn't send imps to do it for him."

"Wouldn't he?" Lilith asked. "You're not that important yet, Warren. Merihim doesn't yet know what I'm going to do for you. He doesn't know how powerful I'm going to make you."

Warren clung to the woman's words. If he was going to survive in the world as it now was, he needed to be powerful enough to do so. There was no other way around that. Even with all his innate ability, with the powers he'd already known, he wasn't strong enough to do that and he knew it.

"Merihim could have sent these imps," Naomi argued. "You can't take the chance that he didn't. If you're wrong, they're going to keep following us into the marsh and kill us."

"I know."

"We need to win these people over. Somehow convince them that we're stronger together than we are apart."

Warren fed off his fear, made it so big and so strong that he couldn't contain it. He'd done the same thing when he'd been a boy living in his mother's house. Once he was numb, he turned toward the group of armed men.

"I'm not the one you should be afraid of," he told them. "Our enemies are there." He flung an arm toward the advancing group of imps.

"He's one of them," someone said.

"He's just trying to fool us," another added.

Warren tapped into the power that constantly coursed through him. Now that he knew what it was, he'd realized that the power had always been within him. He'd had it even when he was a child. The power had allowed him to save himself the night his stepfather killed his mother and tried to kill him.

That night, with his mother lying dead only a few feet away and a bullet that had already ripped through his own body, Warren had seized control of his stepfather's mind. Despite the man's intentions to kill him, Warren had forced his stepfather to turn his pistol on himself.

"I wish you were dead," Warren had told him.

He still remembered the incredulous look in his step-father's eyes as he'd turned the pistol from Warren to his own temple. Martin DeYoung, his stepfather, had been a small-time drug dealer who hadn't been able to control his own habit or Warren's mother's need to believe in the arcane. That night, while under the influence of the drugs he sold, his will hadn't been particularly strong. He'd been angry, not afraid. Fear was much stronger than anger. Warren understood that because he couldn't remember a time when fear hadn't been part of his life.

His stepfather had screamed out in fear that night, but he hadn't been able to stop himself. *"No! Don't make me do this! No! Stop! Please!"*

But Martin DeYoung had held the pistol to his temple and pulled the trigger. The police investigation had ruled the shooting as a homicide/suicide. Warren had barely survived.

Warren gathered all his power, pulling it in through the silver hand that he wore, and pushed it over the group of armed men. All of their minds felt like padlocks. Some of them picked easier than others. He felt the tumblers falling into place as he pushed.

The effort of getting past the fear eased once he found the parts of the men that wanted to believe in something greater than themselves. Men, especially fearful men, always needed something stronger and larger and outside themselves to believe in.

"Those," Warren said with conviction, "are *our* enemies. *They* are who you should be afraid of. Not me."

"He's right," someone said.

"*I* can *help* you," Warren told them, and he *pushed* with all his strength. The imps came closer. Some of the eel-things among them took flight. "*I* will help you if you *let me.*"

"He has powers," someone said. "There aren't enough of us to stand against those demons."

"Let me help you," Warren said.

The man with the shotgun lowered his weapon. "Let them in."

"Bixby!" another man shouted in consternation. "What in bloody hell do you think you're doing?"

Bixby turned to face his men. "We don't stand a chance of stopping those demons by ourselves. And if we don't stop them, they'll slaughter our wives and children next. Do any of you want that?"

No one answered.

Turning back to Warren, Bixby said, "Come ahead."

Trying to appear fearless, Warren strode forward.

Naomi knew the men hated having to trust them. She felt their fear and anger all around her as she took her place among them. The men hated the zombies even more, though, and she held them blameless for that.

She hated the zombies, too. She suspected that her innate revulsion of them resulted, at least in part, in why she failed to raise them. Some Cabalists specialized in raising newly dead. They called forth bodies of comrades who'd fought at their sides only moments previously. Others only raised those who'd been interred in graveyards and sat patiently by while the resurrected zombies clawed from their caskets and from the ground.

Warren easily did both. She'd seen him do it.

She took cover behind a thick oak tree. The broad old trunk hid her and a young man in his late teens. She felt his gaze upon her and knew that he feared her as well as felt sexually aroused by her proximity and strangeness.

"Do you have a name?" the young man asked.

"I am Naomi."

"I'm Desmond."

Naomi looked at him briefly. Before the invasion, the world had seemed filled with such gaunt young men trying to find some way to assert themselves. At one time, she knew Warren Schimmer had been one himself.

The young man's coat and hat looked too big for him. He held a single-shot shotgun.

Since the invasion, Naomi had learned about weapons as well. Her knowledge base had grown in areas she'd never thought about.

"It's not just a shotgun," Desmond said defensively. He gripped the weapon as if embarrassed. "We modified the ammunition. Regular bullets don't do much to demons."

"No," Naomi agreed. "They don't."

"So we changed what we use." Desmond plucked at the bandolier of shotgun shells spread over his chest. "These are explosive rounds. Designed to penetrate demon hide and deliver a load of poison. It's a nerve toxin we got from some of the demon fish that's swum up from the River Thames." He swallowed. "They got all kinds of evil things living in that water these days."

"I know," Naomi said. "I've seen them." For a time, when she'd been with the Cabalist sept led by Hedgar Tulane, they'd studied the various demonic creatures that had crossed through the Hellgate. Not all of them had been warriors and savage animals. The Burn had brought a plethora of plant and animal life with it.

"The fish aren't any good to eat," Desmond explained, "but we found out the poison they carry is harmful to the demons."

"That's good," Naomi said. Man's ability to find destructive things in nature—any nature—seemed to be one of the constants in the universe. That affinity for self-destruction had been one of the things that had first drawn

Naomi to Cabalist beliefs. She'd wanted a peaceful way to live, one more along the lines she thought that nature and God had intended.

For a time, the Cabalist research had focused on improving personal health and well-being, using energy like the Reiki healing processes. Even then, though, some Cabalists had worked to master the more destructive arcane powers.

"Just hope it's enough." Desmond gripped his weapon and glanced fearfully at the approaching demons.

The imps spread out across the marshland. Although they came from a hothouse world, which was what the Burn was converting London into, they didn't show any real discomfort with the cold wind and snow flurries.

Without making a sound, the imps suddenly charged. They brought their weapons to bear and lit up the darkness with bright blazes and beams.

The ragtag group held their ground and returned fire. Naomi knew that bravery didn't make the villagers stand and fight. It was fear. They'd obviously learned over the years that if they broke ranks before the demons, they would only be hunted down separately and killed.

The explosive rounds used by the villagers did surprising damage. The demons obviously hadn't expected the attack. They dropped when they were hit by what would have normally been only a flesh wound. The poison in the rounds acted swiftly. Even in the blunted moonlight, Naomi saw the demons' skins become mottled, then turn a bilious yellow-green as festering sores erupted in seconds.

Urged by their commander, a wide-bodied imp carrying two pistols, the wounded demons tried to get up. Most of them failed and fell back onto the snow. The ones that did manage to get to their feet didn't stay there long before they succumbed to the poison's effects again. Those stricken quivered and foamed at the mouth for a short time, then went still.

Summoning her power, Naomi focused it and stepped forward. She spread her hands and unleashed a blast of energy. Immediately chain lightning erupted from her horns and blazed across the distance separating them from the demons.

The lightning tore through the demons, arcing from the first five it hit to seven behind them and three behind those. Flesh charred and fell from splintered bone. Dead demons collapsed in pieces.

"Set the zombies on them!" a man screamed. "Have the zombies attack!"

The zombies knelt in front of the trees and formed an undead barrier between the humans and the approaching demons. Naomi knew that Warren had learned a lot of military strategy from the games he'd played before the invasion. He'd learned more since.

Naomi felt sudden heat push across her as Warren stepped forward. He didn't set the zombies on the attack or respond to the demands of the men around him.

Holding his hands, one flesh and blood and the other gleaming metal, away from his body, Warren formed a triangle of his thumbs and his forefingers. Then he blew his breath over his hands.

Flames shot out of the triangle formed by Warren's hands. The swirling fireball plopped down in the middle of the imps and exploded.

THIRTEEN

Drenched in fiery masses, the advancing demon line crumbled just as the villagers poured another volley into them.

"Reload!" Bixby yelled. "Ready! Take aim!"

In the end, though, Naomi felt certain only a matter of time remained before the demons routed them. Too many demons stood before them. They swarmed again, driven by their dark master. Their weapons blazed once more. Caught by one of the blasts, Desmond stumbled back with half his head gone. He dropped to his knees and boiling blood hissed against the white snow.

Naomi summoned her power again and unleashed another lightning blast. This one drained her, and she knew she wouldn't have the reserves to do anything like that again for a short time. By then the demons would be upon them. She knelt and claimed Desmond's weapon and spare cartridges.

As the demons closed on them, the zombies lurched awkwardly to their feet. The undead battled the demons without any skill, using strength and near invulnerability because they stopped fighting only when they suffered damage to their heads or spines. The wave of demons washed up against the zombies like an incoming tide striking reefs.

For a moment, the zombies held the line. Bixby and the other villagers battled fiercely, only giving ground when their lives were certainly forfeit if they didn't. Explosions of gunfire—single shot as well as auto-fire—punctuated the night.

Demons blew apart as the poison-tipped bullets weakened their flesh. But they came through the line of zombies bearing grotesque trophies.

Holding a pistol in one hand, an imp swung a zombie's head at Naomi with the other. With the shotgun set firmly at her shoulder, Naomi pulled the trigger. The recoil drove her back a half step and bruised her shoulder, but the shotgun slug burst against the swinging zombie skull and splattered over the demon. Instantly, the imp's skin caught fire. But the demon kept coming.

Desperately, Naomi swung the empty shotgun like a club and battered the imp aside. One of Bixby's men fired a round through the imp's head and killed it.

The man grinned at Naomi for just a moment, obviously pleased with himself, and started to say, "You gotta look out once you've fired—"

Then his words died stillborn in his throat as one of the small, flying demons landed on his shoulder and chomped on his neck. Panicked, the man screamed shrilly and yanked the demon from his throat. A chunk of flesh came away as well. Blood fountained from the neck wound as the man tried to throw the creature away. It bit one of his fingers and held on.

Another man shot the demon with a shotgun, but he ended up blowing the man's hand off as well. The blood, demon guts, and human flesh blew over Naomi. Some of the poison splattered on her as well. Her skin tingled and burned, but she didn't have time to worry that the poison might kill her because another imp swung a knife at her eyes.

Naomi blocked with the shotgun and stepped back. Warren joined her, suddenly appearing at her side. He gestured at the imp, and it froze as though its joints suddenly locked. Wrenching violently, baying out in fear and pain, the demon exploded.

Naomi didn't bother trying to thank Warren. He wouldn't have heard her. And it wouldn't have mattered. He'd saved her because it suited him. The effort hadn't come through any kindness.

She fumbled with the shotgun and managed to get it open. Holding one of the fat cartridges tightly, she shoved it into the barrel and closed the breech. When she pulled the shotgun up to her bruised shoulder, she fired immediately. A new wave of pain tore through her arm, but she made herself break open the shotgun again.

"There are too many!" Warren called to Lilith. If anyone else on the battlefield heard him, they showed no signs of it.

The imps ranged deeply within the forest now, and they laid waste to the humans. They lost numbers as well, but they tried to kill everything before them.

Warren felt their bloodlust. It screamed and twisted through him as it found a resonance within him. He didn't know if his own feelings came naturally, or if Lilith somehow influenced him. Over the past few days, she'd gotten stronger.

But so had he.

"You can't run," Lilith said as she walked among the imps and remained untouched.

Warren believed some of the demons felt Lilith among them. They shied away from her at times. When she'd walked the earth all those millennia ago, when the human race struggled through infancy, demons like the imps had bowed down to her and recognized her as their cruel mistress. All the stories Warren had read of her agreed on that.

Some trace of her power must have clung to her astral self. Warren only wished that she could fight their enemies as well.

"If you try to run," Lilith went on, "the imps will track you down and kill you."

Aware of all the death and maiming around him, Warren believed her. He gathered his power and struck again and again. Handling the force blasts and fireballs was second nature to him. So were the shields that he raised and lowered in an eye blink as he needed them.

One of the small winged demons darted at him. He caught sight of it from the corner of his eye, gestured at it, and saw it explode into bloody bits of flesh and scale. He didn't try to separate the humans from the demons. If they were in a struggle together and anywhere near him, he blasted them all.

He told himself that he needed to survive no matter what, and that it wasn't his fault he was so much more powerful than Bixby and his friends were. He also told himself he wouldn't feel guilty, but he struggled to keep those feelings at bay.

Despite his best efforts at shielding himself, Warren became covered in gore—human as well as demon. Thankfully little of the blood was his.

As he fought and weaved among the combatants, he threaded the minds of some of the demons. They became his puppets and turned on their fellows when they failed to resist his control. Once they were in his thrall, the demons became like the zombies and fought independently of him.

Slowly, the tide of the battle turned. Sickness tightened in Warren's stomach as he lurched over the dead at his feet. Nearly all of the humans had been killed in the assault. Some of them had broken and run, causing some of the demons to chase after them.

If it weren't for the demons in my control, Warren realized, *we'd have already been overrun.*

Maintaining that control cost him, though. His head pounded from the effort, and his lungs worked like a bellows to keep flooding oxygen to his lungs. Although he focused as much as he could, double vision twisted everything before him.

An imp fired a weapon at Warren, but Warren lifted a shield into place. The ricochet speared through one of the few remaining human men. The victim dropped onto the blood-covered ground in halves. The man's death was so sudden he didn't have time to scream.

Warren changed the shield into a projectile in the space of a heartbeat and fired it at the demon. The energy bolt decapitated the demon. Before the creature's body fell, Warren summoned another shield. He used both hands separately and together, channeling all his reserves.

He fought as much against impending unconsciousness as he did against the demons. He didn't know which one of those was going to win out.

"Who are you, human?" a demon demanded as it battered at Warren's energy shield.

Warren didn't have the energy to answer. He felt the demon's blows against his shield as though they struck his body. He concentrated to keep his right leg under him because it felt weak and almost buckled several times.

"Where did you get that hand?" The demon slung its rifle and reached over its broad shoulders for a double-bitted axe. "It doesn't matter. I'll have it from you soon enough."

Warren's stomach lurched at the thought of losing the hand. It had already happened twice, and there was no way he could get inured to that. The panic overwhelmed him, and he lost control of his shield for a moment. The demon's axe slammed against the Kevlar vest Warren wore under his long coat. Although the blade didn't cut through, the force cracked one or more of his ribs. Breathing became painful as he jerked back from the imp's follow-up blow.

"Where are you going?" the demon taunted. "We've only now started to play."

Focus! Bloody hell! Focus, or you're a dead man! Warren tried to bring the multiple images of the imp swimming before him into one identifiable being. The task eluded him. Having no choice, he thrust his hand out and somehow managed to lock on to the axe blade with his metal hand at the last minute.

Metal grated as the keen edge slid along Warren's palm. He tightened his grip and halted the axe. The demon yanked on the weapon and almost got it free.

"You're stronger than you look." The demon brought up a taloned foot and aimed the claws at Warren's throat. "Not that it's going to do you any good."

Warren unleashed the power within him and channeled it through the axe into the demon. The imp locked up, talons grazing the skin of Warren's throat.

Fear and pain filled the demon's eyes as Warren kept feeding the raw power. The demon's flesh turned to liquid bags that ruptured and burst. The vile smelling mess oozed from the demon's bones in a handful of seconds, leaving only the creature's skeleton behind. Then the bones shattered into dust.

Gasping, unable to find enough air or the strength to stay on his feet, Warren sank to his knees. His metal hand hissed and melted through the snow. He worked to keep it from touching his leg in order not to burn himself.

A handful of zombies, most of them missing limbs and one of them dragging only its upper body because its legs were missing, formed a protective circle around him. Three imps joined the circle and killed other demons that tried to get through their defenses.

"You've got to get up," Lilith told him. Effortlessly, she stepped through the demons and zombies. She tugged on his metal hand and he was surprised that he actually felt it.

Warren willed himself to get up, but he didn't have the strength. The cacophony of death screams sounded all around him. His eyes closed and he couldn't open them again.

Terrified that Warren had at last been brought down, Naomi fought her way to him, relying heavily on one of the assault rifles she'd picked up from an unanimated corpse. Before the invasion, she hadn't known much about weapons. She'd learned, though. Everyone had.

As she got close to Warren, the zombies and controlled demons turned to her. She pulled up only inches away as they bit and slashed at her.

"No. Stop. I'm here to help." Naomi stared at Warren lying on the ground. Blood smeared his upper lip and he jerked in convulsions. "He needs help. Get out of my way."

The zombies and demons maintained their holding positions. Naomi turned the assault rifle on them and would have shot them if she'd been certain she wouldn't have accidentally hit Warren.

Frustrated, she stepped back. Only then did she realize that the sounds of the battle had lessened. Stunned, she gazed around at all the dead covering the ground and realized that they'd won the battle.

Not won it, she told herself as she caught sight of the few humans left alive. Most of them were wounded. *We survived it.*

Now all that remained to be seen was if this group of demons was the only one.

FOURTEEN

Despite the fatigue that filled his body and the yawning black hole created by dreamless sleep, Simon roused. He wanted to sleep more. His body craved it. Over the past four years, he hadn't gotten a good night's sleep unless he'd come in wounded and had been made to sleep by the Templar healers.

As a child, he hadn't slept much most nights. Usually he'd stayed in bed no more than five or six hours. That hadn't always been a good thing. His father had enjoyed his own sleep, and raising Simon by himself hadn't helped that.

The painful absence of his father filled Simon then as he lay still. The feeling haunted him often. When he was younger, he'd been restless to be away from his father, to get out and seeing the world for himself.

Thomas Cross had had too many rules. The Templar had had too many rules. Some days Simon had felt like he was growing up inside a straitjacket. That sensation had been unbearable. As a result, he'd often fought with his father. Even when Simon was railing against Templar rules, he'd fought against his father.

Thomas Cross had always been there.

Now he wasn't.

And Simon had never needed his father more than he needed him now.

Through training and experience, Simon pushed the

panic and fear away. There was no going back. He couldn't undo his father's death at the hands of the demons any more than he could undo the arrival of the Hellgate. He didn't accept that, though. He merely denied any other alternatives.

Templar training didn't include wishful thinking or berating the world for being unfair. That had been strictly the purview of the rebellious teenager and younger man he'd been. Neither of those two traits helped him now.

Wearily, knowing he wouldn't get back to sleep, Simon threw the covers off and sat up on the edge of the bed. His body ached from everything he'd suffered the previous night. Discolorations showed red and angry beneath his skin. In a few days, he knew from experience, he'd have riotously colored bruises.

He pushed himself up from the rack, grateful that it was his turn for the lower bed. The concrete floor felt cold underfoot. Although it was a blessing, the redoubt hadn't been set up with long-term living in mind. It had been designed as a waystop during emergencies.

Only a soft incandescence lit the room. Bright lights weren't allowed in the sleeping rooms unless there was an alert going on. Most of the other beds held sleeping Templar of both sexes. That told Simon that it was still "night."

Naked, because Templar didn't worry about nudity since the armor had to be worn that way, Simon took two steps away from the bed and began a series of tai chi exercises to oxygenate his blood and loosen up cramped and bruised muscles. After a few moments, the kinks unwound and he felt physically more prepared.

He stepped into the armored legs and felt the suit's AI automatically cinch him up. He pulled on the upper armor, and it sealed seamlessly. The helmet attached to his hip through covalent bonding, held at a subatomic level. Until the AI told the helmet it was a separate piece of equipment, it would remain immovable.

His weapons were already clean. He'd taken care of that before he'd gone to bed. His father had trained him to do that, and he kept up the practice not only for the good of the weapons, but to have a touchstone to his father as well. At the end of every day, before he went to bed, cleaning the weapons reminded him that he was grateful to be alive, and grateful to his father for training him to keep himself that way.

Ready for the day, Simon headed out of the sleeping quarters to find breakfast.

Seated at a breakfast table that had required new seating because it hadn't been designed with armored Templar in mind, Simon stared at his helmet on the table before him. The wireless connection between the helmet and the suit allowed them to interface. The faceshield also served as a computer monitor.

Simon didn't speak because he didn't have to. Small movements of his free hand brought up simple reports regarding the redoubt and the supplies they had. He ate with his other hand, absently spooning oatmeal into his mouth.

Oatmeal had grown old for breakfast. With supplies diminished and the hydroponics labs nowhere near ready to produce for so many people, breakfast had been limited. At least this morning's menu included deer steaks. After they'd defeated the demons, they'd gone back to claim their kills.

"You're not smiling."

Simon looked up as Nathan Singh sat down across from him.

Nathan pointed his spoon at Simon's helmet. "The reports must be bad." He spoke quietly so that the other Templar in the room couldn't hear.

A table in the corner held a group of small boys and girls that talked and whispered even under the stern gaze of their teachers. Demons loose in the world or not, Simon knew that kids acted like kids.

"The reports aren't good," Simon agreed. His oatmeal had grown cold while he'd been distracted, as had the meat, but he ate it anyway. It wasn't food at this point; it was fuel.

"I tell you," Nathan said sarcastically, "it's all these new people. They're eating us right out of house and home. They're like a bloody plague of locusts."

Although the situation was grim, Simon couldn't help grinning. Nathan, no matter what else was going on, had to laugh and joke. In his own way, he was as bad as the children in the corner.

"They have a table for blokes like you," Simon warned.

Nathan looked at the corner and shook his head. "You mean I'd have to sit at the little kid table? Not bloody likely. Cows would sooner jump over the moon, mate, and pigs would fly."

"You're up early." Simon pushed his empty bowl away and sipped his tea. It too had grown cool.

"Not exactly." Nathan folded a piece of deer steak and popped it into his mouth.

Simon cocked an eyebrow and looked at his friend.

"I haven't hit the rack yet," Nathan admitted.

"What kept you up?"

Nathan pulled a long, slow grin. "Natalie Cho."

"Oh?" Simon hadn't even seen that coming. Usually Nathan dated around and didn't stay around any one woman too long. He'd been that way before the invasion.

With the world hovering on the precipice, there was even less reason to get serious about someone now.

Nathan shrugged. "We . . . like each other a lot."

"I see."

Nathan waited. "Well?"

"Well, what?"

"Aren't you going to tell me?"

"Tell you what?"

"That this isn't exactly the best time to go and get romantically involved with someone."

"Are you getting romantically involved?"

Nathan blinked at Simon as if he were incredibly dense. "I thought that was what I was just telling you, mate."

"Oh."

Irritation knitted Nathan's brows. "Again with the 'oh.' I swear, your father named you appropriately enough. *Simple* Simon."

"Well . . ." Simon thought about responses he could or should make. "I suppose you like her."

"We *like* each other. And I told you that, too."

"You did. I'm just having trouble keeping up with you."

"What's to keep up with?"

"You. Natalie Cho. The redoubt. The lack of food, and the probable lack of water after summer comes. Or before then if the snow becomes toxic. And the funerals."

Mention of that took some of the wind from Nathan's sails. "The funerals." He took in a breath and let it out. Then he looked at Simon. "Maybe you should think about letting someone else handle those, mate."

"No," Simon said. "I took them out there. I got them killed—"

"The demons killed them. It wasn't you."

"If I'd—"

Nathan reached across the table and dropped a hand

onto Simon's shoulder. "Simon, if you could change any of this, you would. I'd help you. But if you start blaming yourself for everything that happens—casualties—"

"They weren't just casualties," Simon said bitterly. "They were friends."

"I know that. Truly I do. But I also know—and they knew—that no guarantees exist in what we're doing now. This—this is what we trained to do, mate. Give our lives fighting the demons and holding on to this world." Nathan nodded and held Simon's gaze. "They did their part. Respect them enough to acknowledge that they died trying to do what they promised their ancestors they'd do. And they died honorably. Let them rest honorably, and give them their full measure of respect. They weren't fools you led into battle. They were warriors."

"I know. I will."

Nathan lifted his hand from Simon's shoulder. "You will. In time." He paused. "You want to know what's really scary?"

Simon looked at his friend, aware that he should have known Nathan hadn't yet said everything that was on his mind. He waited.

"Natalie's pregnant," Nathan said. "We just confirmed that last night. The lab gave her a blood test. She's about six weeks along."

Simon tried to find some happiness for his friend and smiled a little, but he couldn't help thinking that in a few months—*too* few months—there would be another mouth to feed in the redoubt.

"Congratulations," Simon said.

"Yeah." Nathan was silent for a moment. "Natalie's upset. She cried when the nurses told her."

"Afraid it'll look like you?" Simon tried to keep the

humor going between them, but he felt the strain of the effort it took.

Still, Nathan grinned. "That was harsh, my friend." But the humor quickly died in his dark eyes.

"Maybe too harsh," Simon agreed.

"No." Nathan shook his head. "You did fine. I'd have said it if you hadn't. The thing is, Natalie had to stop and think about whether she wanted to have the baby."

That stilled Simon. Templar didn't have abortions. Life was sacred. God gave life as a gift. Even children who had handicaps remained in Templar families and were loved as gifts. Not many of those happened, with the way the Templar took care of themselves and maintained healthy lifestyles, but there were occasional birth defects. Children with missing or defective limbs were made whole inside the suits of armor.

Simon waited.

"She's still not sure what she wants to do," Nathan said. "Other than the fact that she's dead certain she doesn't want to have it now. She doesn't want to leave a child behind if she gets killed in the field. She's seen too much of that around here."

Simon knew that was true. One of those that had died last night had left children.

"Cryonics are a possibility," Simon pointed out. "You could freeze the embryo."

Nathan grinned mirthlessly. "Not here, mate. Back in the Templar Underground, sure. But not here. We're living out in the hinterlands." He twirled his spoon. "She's thinking of going back to the Templar Underground."

Simon didn't say anything. He kept his face as blank as he could. Under the circumstances, that was easy: he didn't know what to think.

"They can remove the embryo there," Nathan said. "Freeze it and save it for later. For when we kick the demons back to wherever it is they came from."

"What if that doesn't happen in this lifetime?" Simon asked.

"And here I thought you were going to come up with a plan soon."

Simon shook his head. "Not me. I'm in survival mode, not world conquering."

"I'm disappointed."

"Me, too."

Nathan rubbed his face. His whiskery cheeks crackled under his armored gloves. "Anyway, Natalie is trying to think about things. But if she should come to you and ask you about letting her return to the Templar Underground—"

"She can go," Simon replied. "Without question."

"I told her that's what you'd say, mate, but she's nervous. I'm not used to seeing her like this." Nathan hesitated. "There's something else you should know. If she goes back, I'm going with her."

Simon had known that was coming, but it was still hard hearing it.

"Just to take Natalie there and back again," Nathan said. "She won't want to stay. She just wants the baby— our child—taken care of."

"I understand."

"The problem is, given everything I've helped you do to Terrence Booth, he may not just let me walk back out of there."

"When you go," Simon said, "you'll go under my protection. If he tries to keep you there, I'll find a way to get you out."

"I have your word on that?"

"You do."

Nathan held out a hand.

Simon took it.

"Then make sure you don't get yourself killed anytime soon," Nathan said. "After you get us back, I'm going to need an uncle for my baby."

FIFTEEN

A t best, if we stay at the present rate of consumption, we can expect to remain viable for another five weeks. Is that what you're saying, Lord Cross?"

Simon glanced at the seven men and women gathered in the small room. They were the ones who had stepped forward on their own. Each of them had divided up the Templar warriors and children they chose to represent. With so many of them now at the redoubt, several of them fell along normal House lines.

All of them had come to him over the past four years. None of them had been with him the night they'd reoutfitted the train and hauled the first of the survivors out of London. Simon didn't hesitate telling them the truth because they'd joined forces with him after everyone saw how hard it was going to be.

To a man and a woman, each of the Templar in that room had known Thomas Cross and held to the Templar beliefs that they were supposed to help the downtrodden. They hadn't been able to turn their backs on the men and women and children trapped in demon-infested London, either.

"Five weeks of food," Simon said. "But that's only if we're able to take deer. I don't want to depopulate the forests of wild game—"

"Nor do we, Lord Cross," Genevieve Bowker stated. She was in her early sixties, but still quite formidable in her armor.

"—and I don't want to take the chance of having a hunting party ambushed by the demons again," Simon finished.

"We take chances every time we go into the city for supplies and clothing for the people we're sheltering here," Victor Carlyle said dismissively. He was in his early fifties, lean and fit. "You can't protect us or provide for us single-handedly, Lord Cross."

"I understand that," Simon replied.

"Then we'll just have to take our chances."

"The amount of food we're dispensing to the people is dangerously low," Marta Grimes said. She was in her late forties, fit and competent. "They're barely getting enough now. If anything, we need to give them *more* food. We can't starve the children. They need food to eat in order to grow strong and healthy. They are our future. Ignoring that is potentially lethal."

Simon knew and understood that as well. But he didn't say anything. None of the people in that room thought they were smarter than him. They just compared notes.

"Nor can we ignore the needs of the Templar," Micah Cuddy interjected. "The armor can compensate for physical weakness, but a malnourished warrior eventually makes a mistake that costs him his life or the lives of others." He was in his early thirties. "Keeping the Templar well fed is the first priority."

"Over the welfare of the children?" Marta Grimes looked ready to do battle.

"The Templar are our defense. A well-fed child is only going to make a better morsel for the bloody demons if they get past our warriors."

"You don't know that the demons are going to get past the Templar."

"We know that the demons are hunting us out here," Solomon Tremaine stated quietly. "Those men and women that gave their lives last night prove that."

"They haven't found us yet," Marta said.

"It's only a matter of time," Cuddy told her.

All of them, Simon knew, were older than he was. None among them had ever questioned their place in the world, or his ability to lead. If they had, he would have gladly stepped aside. *Maybe*, he admitted to himself. It would have been good to have the burden of responsibility lifted from his shoulders, but losing control of what was going on in the redoubt on a day-to-day basis would have been hard.

He owed the Templar something after abandoning them when he had six years ago. He'd also given promises to the people he'd taken in, and the warriors who arrived to stand at his banner.

Most of all, though, Simon knew he owed his father. After the way things had been between them, Simon couldn't simply step aside. His father deserved more than that.

"When it comes to time," Simon said in a clear, controlled voice, "we have five weeks. Food is the problem at the moment. Not water."

"What if we give the people a proper amount of food?" Marta asked.

"Then we're down to four weeks."

Marta locked eyes with him. "Is it worth it, Lord Cross? To plan for five weeks of slowly starving to death if the demons don't manage to find us? Or should we live and eat as people do when they're not saddled by fear for four weeks? If we have only a week before this place is discovered, how would you want these people to live that week? Hopeful? Or hungry?"

The headache Simon had nursed grew steadily between his ears. He was much better at tactics. And he'd rather face multiple armed demons than have to answer the questions of the men and women in that room. Fighting for survival was easy, and there was no holding back. But trying to stretch finite supplies through time was an exercise in frustration.

"It would be easier," Marta said quietly, "to make a decision on rationing if we knew a solution for the food shortage was at hand. I know what I'm asking you to consider is hard, Simon, but these are the times when you— when *we*"—she looked around the room—"need to trust in our faith. What we are doing is fair and just."

"Tell that to those Templar that died last night," Cuddy snarled. "Tell that to the men and women who'll have to take on extra shifts to pick up the slack. Or the young trainees who won't have the benefit of their full tutelage before they're asked to shed their blood."

"Enough," Simon said.

All of them quieted at once and looked at him. He didn't often take command of the meetings so directly. He felt uncomfortable pulling rank.

"We're recanting the rationing," Simon said. That hadn't been his idea to begin with. It had been theirs—all except Marta.

"I don't think—" Cuddy began.

Simon raised his voice and continued speaking. "We're going to send out more hunting parties. We'll work farther afield than where we've been hunting. We'll also double up on the number of hunters."

"That's going to leave us possibly shorthanded here," Carlyle said. He was ever the tactician himself. "Or the Templar worn to their bones."

"We'll supplement the hunting parties from the men and women here at the redoubt that know how to hunt or are willing to be trained." Simon shook his head. "It's something that I should have thought of before."

"You don't want unarmored civilians walking around out there," Genevieve said.

"They're better out hunting than here starving," Simon replied.

"We swore that we'd protect these people," Carlyle objected. "Telling them they have to risk their lives isn't defending them."

"We *are* protecting them," Simon responded in a loud voice. "*We* fight the demons, and *we* take the greatest chances. That hasn't changed. That's not going to change."

Silence echoed his words, and he knew they were shocked. *They don't have to supervise the funerals later,* he thought bitterly.

"We can't protect them by asking them to starve to death," Marta said quietly. She stood taller. "I, for one, quite understand Lord Cross's take on this matter. It isn't particularly elegant or esthetically pleasing, but it is the right thing to do."

"I won't allow anyone to be forced into hunting," Simon said. "We'll present the opportunity at general assembly. Those who are willing to help will be trained and outfitted with armor as best as we can manage." He paused. "The bottom line is that we need help saving these people. They can help us help them."

In the end, there were no more arguments. Whether they liked his handling of the situation or not, they knew he was right.

"I want to be a knight, Lord Cross."

Simon stared into the wide eyes of the six-year-old boy seated across from him. Talking to the young civilians was hardest for him. It wasn't that they were brave. They were fearless in the invulnerability of their youth, and that only made their offers more heartbreaking.

Even worse, the Templar needed the young ones most of all. Adults and teenagers learned too slowly. Older Templar candidates couldn't be trained to simply react without thinking. Demons could be incredibly fast, and the difference between surviving and being a casualty could be a nanosecond.

Simon knelt with one knee resting on the floor of the small office he'd claimed for his own. Danielle stood nearby and didn't say a word. From the conversations they'd had over the past few months since they'd started bringing the civilian children into the classes with the Templar children, she was as torn by the decision as he was.

"You're Chandler, aren't you?" Simon asked. He didn't even need a prompt from the suit's AI to get the boy's name. He made it a point to know all of those that had been at the redoubt for more than a few weeks.

Shock widened the boy's blue eyes. "You know who I am?"

Simon nodded. He had his helmet at his side and went bareheaded inside the redoubt so that any who saw him would know who he was. Being visible helped keep him in touch with those within the redoubt on a day-to-day basis.

"I do." Simon nodded at the boy's mother seated in one of the chairs before his metal desk. "Your mother's name is Nancy. Your father's name is Craig, and we're still looking for him."

A solemn look tightened the boy's face. Tears swam in his eyes. "I know. You'll find him one day. I know you will."

Simon didn't know what to say to that. With so much time gone, over eight months now, only a child would hold on to so much hope.

"Why do you want to be a knight?" Simon asked.

"To fight the demons," Chandler answered. He thought for a moment. "I'm going to have to fight the demons anyway, so I think it would be better if I knew more on how to fight them. Don't you agree?"

Simon heard the affected grown-up tone in the boy's words and knew that Chandler had given the matter a lot of thought before he'd requested a meeting. Surprisingly, most of the children who came forward had thought about the matter long and hard. In many cases, their thoughts surprised their parents.

Looking away from the boy for just a moment, Simon held Chandler's mother's eyes. Quietly, tears trickling down her cheeks, the woman nodded.

No mother should have to give her child over to something like this, Simon thought. Templar children and parents were different. They stayed immersed in the same world, male and females. But the civilian parents gave up time and a certain amount of control over their children. The Templar education, when taken by outsiders, was a rude awakening.

Looking back at the boy, Simon said, "I do agree. But you have to know that if you want this, it will be very hard. The training will be exhausting, and you won't have much free time."

"I know," Chandler told him. "I've seen the Templar kids. They're in school nearly all the time."

"They are. There's a lot to learn."

Chandler smiled. "It'll be okay. I'm a fast learner."

Simon almost winced at that. Those who didn't learn fast often died early. He thought about the funerals that would take place later. *Even the good ones die.*

"All right," Simon said, hoping that he didn't have to see the boy die in battle in a few years, "you can start training with the Templar children."

Chandler smiled broadly and looked a little nervous. "Brill." He hesitated. "Don't I have to say an oath to you or something?"

"Not yet."

Disappointment filled Chandler's face. "Oh."

Behind the boy's back, Danielle held up one crooked pinky finger. Simon almost grinned at that and had trouble keeping a straight face. He held up his crooked pinky finger.

"Pinky swear," Simon said.

Chandler grinned hugely and stuck out his own crooked pinky. "I pinky swear to be a loyal knight."

"And I pinky swear to be a loyal and fair leader," Simon said.

Chandler backed off hesitantly. "Will I see you in class?"

"Yes." Simon still taught the classes—martial arts, sword fighting, and basic knowledge of demons—whenever he could.

The boy's mother stood and came over to Simon as he got to his feet. Her mouth trembled as she looked at Simon.

"Mom," Chandler said. "Why are you crying?"

She looked down at her son. "Because I'm so very proud of you, that's why." She tousled his hair, then looked back at Simon. "Please . . . please take care of him. He's my boy. All that I have left."

There had been a daughter as well, older, Simon remembered, but she hadn't made it out of London.

"I will," Simon said.

The woman nodded, got control of herself, then took her son by the hand and led him from the room. Silently, Simon watched them go.

"You okay?" Danielle asked. She removed her helmet as well and looked at him.

"Yeah."

"The young ones are hard."

"I know."

"They trust too much."

"I know."

"Every time I tell one of them we're accepting them into Templar training," Danielle said, "I feel like I'm lying."

"About accepting them?"

"They think that if they become Templar, they'll be safe. That they can be heroes and everything will be fine."

Simon nodded.

"That's the lie," Danielle said.

"This evening," Simon said somberly, "should remind them that even being a Templar is dangerous."

Simon stood in front of the polycarbonate caskets that contained the mortal remains of the fallen Templar. Orchestral music piped into the great room that held for general assembly. From the size of the crowd, all squeezed in tight on the bleachers and folding chairs, Simon felt certain that everyone at the redoubt who wasn't too sick or too wounded to walk put in an appearance at the funeral.

After a time, they prayed. Simon led them. The words came easily to his lips. Too easily. He couldn't remember how many funerals he'd presided over in the past four years. He could remember their names, though, and if he stopped to count the names, he'd have a number. He remembered people, but he didn't like remembering the number of losses they'd had.

The caskets were simple affairs. The coat of arms for each House stood out in bas-relief. Tri-dee images of the individuals played over the tops of the caskets.

The Templar formed color guards of the different Houses, and some of them gave eulogies. Simon followed them and felt hollow inside while feeling brittle outside. Standing there with everyone watching was one of the hardest things he'd ever done. It always was.

He paused for a time when he came to an end of the memories he had of the fallen and why they should be remembered. Then he strengthened his voice.

"We're burying brothers and sisters here today," he said. "Husbands and wives and lovers. Fathers and mothers and sons and daughters. Most of all . . . we're burying friends."

Tears ran down even the gruffest of faces. There wasn't a dry eye in the room.

"If these Templar were here today," Simon said fiercely, "they would tell you that they died for one thing and one thing only." He raised his sword. "They died so that the others might live on. For the living!"

The other Templar took up the chant as they lifted their weapons—swords and axes—toward the ceiling. "For the living! *For the living!*"

Even the civilians took up the chant. It was the Templar battle cry, the fierce promise they made to the demons and the Darkness.

In the back, Chandler—now outfitted in Templar novice robes—lifted his fist and joined in. Hope swelled in Simon's heart when he saw the fierce determination in the boy's eyes. They still had that hope. The demons had not yet managed to wrest that away.

SIXTEEN

Warren slept for hours among the dead.

Naomi wanted to move him, but every attempt she made was blocked by the zombies that stood protectively around him. The imps had finally started to slip from Warren's control, though she wasn't sure if that was because they'd gotten stronger or Warren had grown weaker. As a result, the zombies turned on the demons and slew them before they could defend themselves. More demon corpses added to the wall of dead flesh surrounding Warren.

At first, Naomi worried that he might die. She couldn't tell how wounded he was. Blood covered him, but she knew from the quantity that not all of it could possibly be his. No one human could bleed so much.

No one human. The words echoed in Naomi's thoughts. Warren wasn't human anymore. Merihim's machinations had twisted him to begin with. The strange book he was so careful about seemed to have been the catalyst that changed him now.

When she'd first met Warren, he'd been badly scarred from a fire. Now his skin was smooth and unblemished. He didn't possess any demonic transplants or tattoos that helped anchor a Cabalist in the arcane forces that had quickened to life with the opening of the Hellgate. By everything that Naomi understood, Warren should have had little to no power.

The pockets of dead demons and the zombies that ringed him offered mute testimony that such thinking was wrong. He possessed more power than anyone Naomi knew.

She gazed at his silver hand and watched the slow rise and fall of his chest. If he died, she wondered if she could remove that hand and use it herself.

"Miss?"

Startled, not happy with the fact that someone slipped up on her from behind and feeling especially vulnerable because of it, Naomi looked up at the thin old man behind her. He carried a steaming metal bowl in his hands.

"I've brought soup, I 'ave," the old man said in a Cockney accent. "Me missus insisted. Allowed as 'ow it was the Christian thing to do. It's not so much, p'rhaps, but me missus always puts 'er 'eart into it, she does. It'll warm ye some'at."

Naomi reached for the bowl. Despite the distance back to the village—or the nearness, when she thought about how close the imps had come to finding it, the bowl and its contents were still warm. She used a small spell to check for poisons or hallucinogens but didn't detect any. More at ease, she dipped her nose near the bowl and inhaled the soup's aroma.

"Chicken soup, miss." The old man stood uncertainly. "The old bird what gave 'is life to make that was gamy an' toff, an' there weren't much to 'im, but 'e makes a fair soup when the missus was through with 'im."

"Thank your wife for me."

"I will, I will."

Most of the survivors had left to take the wounded and bad news home. But they'd left guards with weapons to watch over Warren and the zombies. During the past few hours, they'd rotated out. None of them spoke to her. Not a one of them trusted her. She was fairly certain they were convinced that she somehow kept the zombies in one place.

"'E's still alive, innit 'e?" the old man asked.

"Yes." Naomi sipped the soup, relishing the fluids as much as the mushy vegetables and noodles, and the stringy chicken bits. She'd found clean snow to slake her thirst, but she hadn't gotten hungry enough yet to eat the rations they'd brought with them.

"Is 'e gonna be wakin' up anytime soon?"

"I don't know." Naomi scanned the blanket of white snow that hugged the terrain. Except for the trail they'd followed, and the tracks left by the imps that had pursued them, the snowcapped landscape appeared pristine. London remained a dark smudge in the distance, but the sun hung in a blue sky and the snow glittered.

"'As 'e done this before?"

"No."

The old man wrapped his arms around himself and hugged fiercely. "Don't seem normal, does it?"

Looking at the dead demons and the zombies that stood guard, Naomi couldn't help thinking that "normal" somehow didn't apply to the world anymore. But she agreed with the old man's assessment.

"No."

The old man stood there awkwardly.

"What is it?" Naomi asked.

Hesitating, the old man wouldn't look at her. "It's just that some of the people back to the village, well, they were wonderin' when the two of you might be movin' on." He hurried on. "Not that anybody's in a rush or anythin'."

Naomi quelled her immediate anger. Getting angry wouldn't help them, and might even tilt the delicate balance the villagers had about merely watching them instead of trying to kill them.

"I don't know," she said. "Not until he's on his feet, at the least."

The old man scratched his head. Gray wisps of hair stood out under the edges of his cap. His nose and cheeks burned red with the cold.

"I guess, then, that they'll be 'opin' 'e's on his feet before evenin' then."

Naomi didn't say anything. She supposed they were lucky the villagers didn't try to kill them. Concentrating on the soup, she savored the flavor and the warmth and drank it more quickly when she got down to the dregs because they cooled so much more quickly. When she was finished, she handed the bowl back to the old man.

"Thank you," she said. She'd been taught to always be polite. Even when around imperfect company.

The old man took the bowl, nodded, wished her well, and departed. His footsteps crunched through the icy crust over the snow. Somewhere in the distance, a branch cracked as it finally surrendered to the burden of snow and split from the trunk.

Naomi watched Warren's chest rise and fall. *Wake up,* she thought angrily. *Wake up.* But she wondered if Warren was going to recover. She'd never seen anyone harness that much raw power.

Imp bodies lay in pieces for a hundred yards. Many others were twisted into improbable shapes, or burned almost beyond recognition—other than being demonic.

What did it take for a man to do what Warren had done? And what had it cost him?

Naomi glared out at the bleak countryside. More than that, what were they doing out here? He'd been keeping to himself lately, not telling her anything she wanted to know about his new hand.

Frustrated, she laid her head back against the tree she sat next to, pulled the thick wool blanket one of the villagers had given her more tightly around her, and slept.

Without warning, Warren woke. Bright light lanced into his eyes before he opened them. *Day,* he told himself, then immediately wondered if that were any better than it still being night.

He felt unaccustomed weight over his body. He shifted, terrified for a moment that he'd been buried alive, then quickly reminded himself that he couldn't very well be buried if he could see the sun.

Senses alert but so weak he didn't know if he could defend himself if he had to, Warren opened his eyes. Quietly, he took in the destruction all around him. The zombies stood tirelessly over him. They didn't look at him, but he knew they felt his presence.

"Warren?"

He tracked Naomi's voice. She stood just beyond the reach of the zombies nearest her. She looked worried. And mad. He almost smiled at that. Like she could do anything to him that the demons hadn't already tried to do.

Beyond her, a handful of the villagers shifted and pulled their guns into ready positions. *The trust department is bankrupt,* he thought. Looking at all the human bodies scattered around him, he couldn't blame them.

"Warren? Can you hear me?"

"Yes." Warren lurched to his knees. His back and leg muscles screamed in protest. When he smelled himself, the gore that covered him, sickness twisted in his stomach. He swallowed with difficulty. "Is there any water?"

Naomi tried to pass him a canteen, but a zombie flailed at her. Cursing the undead thing, she stepped back.

Warren forced himself to his feet and stood swaying for a moment. His senses swirled. Then he stepped through the zombies and took the canteen. He removed the cap and drank.

"Don't go so fast," Naomi said. "You're going to get sick."

He couldn't stop, though. It felt as if someone had gripped him in a hard fist and squeezed him dry. He barely had time to take the canteen away from his mouth before he threw up.

Real impressive for the locals, he thought bitterly as he wiped his mouth with the back of his coat sleeve.

The second time he tried to drink, he went more slowly. As he sipped, he gazed around the field of carnage and tried to spot Lilith.

"What's wrong?" Naomi asked.

"I was looking for someone."

Naomi looked around and spoke quietly. "Most of the men that were with us last night died. They took the bodies back to the village to get them ready for burial. They couldn't reach some of them because of the demons and zombies."

Warren felt the wave of resentment and fear that boiled off the men in the brush. If they thought they could kill him with impunity, he knew they would.

"We're not going to win any popularity contests," he said. "But that's all right. I wasn't looking for a country home anyway."

"It would be better if we could go."

"I know." Warren passed her canteen back and walked toward the nearest villager.

Gray streaked his hair and beard. He held a large-bore pistol naked in his fist and kept it between them. Despite the zombies at Warren's back, the man didn't back away.

"We need supplies," Warren said.

"We've barely enough to feed ourselves as it is," the man grumbled.

"Only enough for two people." Warren refused to beg. He and Naomi needed food and water, and he was powerful enough to take it without asking. They all knew that. "For no more than a week."

The man looked as though he thought about lifting the pistol and shooting Warren in the face. Warren knew the man *wanted* to do that because he felt that emotion within the man. But fear won out.

"C'mon with me, then. We'll see what we can do."

Warren followed and Naomi joined him. The zombies fell into step around him.

"They're only giving us the supplies because they want us gone," Naomi said.

"I want us gone, too," Warren replied. Without Lilith, though, he didn't know exactly where to go. He didn't like feeling lost and not having a plan. His whole life after he'd entered foster care had been planned out. He had never been able to afford the luxury of mistakes.

"They also know that we could take the supplies if we wanted to," Naomi told him.

Warren remained silent. He counted the zombies shuffling around him. Their numbers had dwindled during last night's attack. Besides the food, he needed reinforcements. He knew the villagers weren't going to be happy about that.

While the supplies were arranged, Warren ate homemade bread baked in a small woodstove. The heat circulated through the exhaust pipe, and another pipe allowed the heat to bleed off to bake the bread. To him, the whole system appeared quite ingenious. He also ate a bowl of stew that held a lot of vegetables and a little rabbit meat.

He sat at a table by himself. Naomi supervised the gathering of the supplies, and no one among the villagers ate with him. The zombies hunkered and stood outside the door of the small house. Until the undead arrived, the small town had resembled a rather pastoral setting.

He stared into the glass of tea he sipped from. It was strong and black, and he knew not to drink too much or it would make him sick. He needed to keep the food down to get his strength back. As he stared into the dark depths, he saw Lilith's eyes, then her face became more clear.

"You must not tarry there long," she told him.

"I'm not. Where are you?"

"I've gone on ahead." Lilith appeared distracted. "There were things I needed to check on."

"Did you see any more demons?"

She hesitated.

Warren knew that she would lie to him if she thought she had to. He hadn't met anyone who wouldn't lie when they felt it was necessary to get what they needed or wanted.

"I didn't," she replied. "But that doesn't mean that there aren't more out here."

"That lot that found us," Warren said. "Did they come looking for me? Or did they come looking for you?"

"I don't know." She maintained eye contact with him from the dark depths of the tea.

Warren knew at once that she lied. He felt good about that. Getting to know how to tell someone was lying was almost as good as keeping them honest.

"I think they came after you," he said.

"Perhaps. But it doesn't matter. You and I, we're after the same thing."

"I want to be safe. I don't think that's anything you have to worry about."

"No one is safe now that the Hellgate has opened. We've all been put at risk. The only thing we can do is grab enough power for ourselves that we can put the demons at risk." She paused. "I can help you do that."

Warren let that go without comment. It might have been true. And even if it wasn't, it wasn't worth fighting over.

"When are you going to leave?" she asked.

"I'd rather stay the night."

"Doing that would be a mistake. The villagers will only grow more bold with you among them. Familiarity breeds contempt."

Personally, Warren felt certain the zombies bred contempt even faster.

"Finish what you need to do there," Lilith said, "then I'll join you outside the village." Her image disappeared from the tea.

Warren finished his drink, then sat and waited.

Less than an hour later, with only a few hours left before nightfall, Warren changed into the fresh clothes Naomi asked for and received. He shouldered one of the packs Naomi gave him. She kept the other for herself.

No brass band waited to see him off. The armed villagers stood and watched without saying a word. Warren didn't speak, either. They blamed him for bringing the demons to them, and maybe they were right.

But what he was about to do next would cause them to hate him forever. And fear him.

The dead had been laid out in the street. Some of the

men worked across the street to dig a mass grave for those that had fallen in battle against the zombies. The imps had rated only a petrol-soaked pyre at the end of town, and only then to keep away the predators.

Warren stopped before the dead. He counted twenty-three whole bodies. It was twice as many zombies as he currently had.

"What are you doing?" Naomi asked.

Warren didn't answer. She knew what he planned to do.

"You can't do this." Naomi came and stood at his side. "This is wrong."

Gazing into her eyes, Warren asked, "Do you want to wander around out there without protection?"

Naomi cursed, but she didn't tell him to stop. However, she did step away from him.

Summoning his power, surprised at how quickly his strength had come back, Warren held his metal hand out toward the corpses.

"Rise," he commanded them.

Immediately, the corpses twitched and jerked. A wave of horrified cries and curses sounded behind Warren. He ignored them because working the spell took all of his concentration, and he hoped that no one decided to shoot him in the back of the head.

"Kill him!" someone shouted.

"Don't let him do this!" a woman cried out. "Merciful God, don't let him turn my son into a soulless monster!"

From the corner of his eye, Warren saw a man taking aim at him with a rifle.

"Don't," Naomi said, holding a hand out to the man.

He ignored her and set himself. Before he pulled the trigger, Naomi waved her arm at him. An invisible wall of force struck the man and knocked him backward nearly thirty feet. When he came to a rest, he was unconscious or dead.

None of the other villagers tried anything.

Warren watched the zombies stand and turn toward him. He didn't know how many zombies he'd raised in the past four years, but the number had to be staggering. Yet, no matter how many times he'd done it, he'd never lost his fascination with what he was able to do.

He looked at the zombies. Covered in garish wounds and their eyes glazed over, they were walking nightmares. Most of the zombies Warren had left London with were in stages of advanced rot and decay. Many of them carried the dead husks of maggots that had hatched inside them in the warmer area of London and frozen in the winter cold.

"Come," he told them, and he led them out of town without a backward look. The pained cries of the villagers followed him into the snowy outlands.

SEVENTEEN

"A re you in pain?"

Leah gritted her teeth against the violent agony that twisted through her thoughts. She tried to open her eyes and couldn't.

"No," she answered. She tried to raise her arms and couldn't. After a moment, she felt the straps around her wrist, elbow, and across her chest that kept her secured to the bed.

She was in a hospital. She knew that from the medicinal smells and the chronic beeping of the machines around her. The last thing she remembered was passing out in the river.

"You're in pain," a man's voice said.

"I can handle it. Why can't I move my arm? What's wrong with my arm?"

"You need to calm down," the man said. "It will only make the pain worse."

"The pain is nothing," Leah lied. "Help me out of this bed." She tried to open her eyes and couldn't. "Is something wrong with my eyes?"

The machines beeped into the ensuing silence.

"Did you hear me?" Leah demanded.

"She has a high pain threshold," the calm man's voice stated. "But as you can see from this readout, she's in indescribable pain."

"I see that, Doctor," a woman's voice replied. "Thank you."

Leah thought she recognized the voice, but with the noisy machines and the agony she was in, she couldn't be certain.

"Can you increase the Demerol?"

Demerol? No wonder Leah's nose itched. She always had that reaction to that particular anesthetic.

"If we increase the drugs in her system, she's going to be unconscious or so out of it that she may not understand you."

"That won't do," the woman said. "Can't you give her something that will keep her awake?"

"And pain-free? No."

The woman sighed. "Then put her back out."

"No." Leah struggled against her bonds. She deserved some control. She wasn't a child. Panic filled her. She desperately wanted to see what kind of shape she was in. One of her greatest fears was that she might not come back whole from one of her missions. "Talk to me. Let me decide—"

Warmth flooded her arm and she knew they'd injected more anesthetic. She fought against it, cursing and willing herself not to surrender to the effects.

Blackness closed over her.

When Leah came awake again, the dark room waited for her. Her head was clearer and most of the pain was gone, but a fierce throbbing continued to reside in her skull. She tried to lift her arm and couldn't.

She turned her head to look at her arm and it felt as if her brain smashed against that side of her skull. Her vision rolled, then finally cleared. Straps held both her arms down.

Both her arms.

She was ecstatic. She also had both her legs. And everything else in between seemed to be mostly together. That was always a good sign.

If it weren't for all the bandages around her head and over her right eye, she would have thought nothing out of the ordinary was wrong with her. *It's nothing they can't fix,* she told herself.

Then she slept again.

"Awake, are we?"

Dully, Leah turned her head to look at the speaker. In her middle thirties, the blonde had shoulder-length hair and green eyes. She was trim and athletic, and if she hadn't been, the form-fitting black armored suit she wore would have revealed that. A webbing of scar tissue showed at her right temple and cheek.

Her name was Lyra Darius. She'd been the one at the agency who had ferreted out the truth about Lord Patrick Sumerisle. In addition to being a heavy player in the Home Office ministry's Internal Affairs division, Lord Sumerisle was also the leader of the Templar.

"I'm awake," Leah agreed.

"Good. I thought you might be. You roused earlier. Excited the hospital staff enough that they called me."

"Sorry. Don't mean to be a bother." Leah intended her response to be subtly sarcastic. Lyra Darius held a lot of power in the organization. After all, she'd been the one who had proved the Templar existed while MI-6 and other intelligence agencies had searched for them.

"You're no bother," Lyra said. "I'm just glad that you made it back. A lot of those men and women didn't."

For a moment, memory of all the death and destruction claimed Leah's thoughts. The sights and sounds promised to haunt her for the rest of her life.

Lyra got up from the chair and put away the book she held. She stood at the side of the bed and gazed down with what looked like genuine compassion. It was hard to tell. Compassion was one of the first emotions they'd all been trained to fake.

"I had water brought in," Lyra said. "And I got permission that, if you felt you were up to it, you could drink it."

"I'm thirsty," Leah said.

Lyra poured a glass of water from a carafe and added a bendy straw. She held the cup low for Leah to sip from the straw if she wanted.

"If you would unfasten the straps from my arms," Leah said, "I could tend to myself. I don't much care for being treated like a mewling brat."

After a brief hesitation, Lyra nodded. "All right, but you're going to have to go slow. The doctors aren't yet sure how much you'll be affected."

"Affected by what?"

Lyra released the restraints. "You lost your right eye, Leah. You also suffered some slight brain damage that may affect motor control."

Adrenaline dumped an overload into her system. "My eye?"

Lyra looked at her sympathetically. "Yes."

If the world were a normal place and not stuck in a demon-infested nightmare, Leah would have sworn that she would have been seriously freaking at about that time. She also thought that part of her calm was because she had control over her body now.

Unfettered, she sat in the middle of the bed and sipped water through the straw. Her head still maintained a dulled pulse beneath the bandages. Having the wires and sensors connected to her body made her feel weak and fragile.

"It's a lot to take in, I know," Lyra said.

"It's better than being dead." But not much. Losing an eye meant losing more than 50 percent of her vision. It was actually closer to 60 percent. And her depth perception would be gone as well. *Better than being dead* was going to be her mantra for a time.

"It is better," Lyra said.

Leah put the cup on the small table by the bed. "Is there anything else wrong?" She asked herself if losing an eye and potential brain damage weren't enough of a laundry list of problems.

"Other than a rather astonishing collection of cuts, scrapes, and bruises, you're in fine shape."

"We did destroy the weapons plant, didn't we?"

Lyra nodded. "That set the demons back, but they're already building another plant somewhere else in the city."

"Do we know where?"

"No. But if we've learned anything at all about our adversaries over the past four years, it's that they're committed."

"You'll have to forgive me," Leah said. "I'm not up on how good our medical technology is these days. I've been out in the field."

"They can't replace your eye." Lyra's voice remained soft, but no sympathy sounded in her words, nothing that Leah could attack. It was just a statement of fact. "Our technology hasn't come that far yet."

Barely quelling the nausea that twisted her stomach, Leah forced herself to nod. She wanted to tear the bandages from her head and prove that she *could* see. All she had to do was open her eye.

One of the machines beeped more quickly.

Lyra glanced at it, then said, "I can summon a nurse back to give you something to calm you down."

"No." Leah glared at the machine as she worked on taking deep, rhythmic breaths. The beeping slowed and kept slowing. *I'm in control. Not my fear or anger. I can just . . . be.*

Lyra smiled a little. "Very good."

Controlling the body's reactions was one of the things Leah had learned early in her career. She'd gotten educated in that at about the same time she was shown how to kill an opponent in hundreds of different ways.

"They replaced your arm," Leah said.

Lyra wore a black glove over her right hand to mask the metallic surface. She hadn't opted for a cosmetically more appealing hand. She'd chosen something that was as much a weapon as a pistol or a knife.

"An eye is more . . . complicated," Lyra replied. "There is a prosthesis that can be wired into your brain. A helmet, if you will, that will cover that side of your face and provide visual feedback in programming uploads that your brain will understand."

"Doesn't sound especially chic."

"It's not. It's cumbersome and ugly. But it's better than being half blind."

"Nice to hear brutal honesty."

"If I tried to sugarcoat it, you wouldn't listen to me."

"No," Leah agreed.

"The headpiece also lacks the ability to see in color, which is going to take some getting used to."

"Different images for the brain to process."

"Yes. I'm told that the user will, eventually, layer the two images into one. It gets smoother with use."

Leah didn't say anything.

"I know this is a lot to take in, Leah," Lyra said.

"Yeah."

"But you don't have a choice."

"What will I be allowed to do?"

Lyra regarded her seriously. "When you're released from the hospital—and I said *released*, not *escaped from* or arbitrarily decide to forgo medical treatment—you'll be evaluated."

"I'm going to be stuck in a bloody desk job, aren't I?"

"Support positions are as necessary as any other."

"I wasn't trained to be a support person," Leah said vehemently. "I was trained to be a covert operative. A force to be reckoned with."

Lyra was silent for a moment. "How long do you think you're going to need to protest the injustice of the universe and feel sorry for yourself?" Her words were blunt and hard.

Leah looked at the woman with new respect. Although she'd met Lyra Darius only once before, it had been during a time of trouble as well.

"You don't mess about, do you?" Leah asked.

"We don't have time to."

"Good to know."

"You're still a valuable operative, Leah. You've got qualities and connections that I value highly."

With her one good eye, Leah glared at the woman. "You don't know me. We've met only the one time."

"Once was enough."

Leah studied the woman with more speculation. "Someone like you, someone as high up in the organization as you are, wouldn't have come down here to offer me a pep talk."

"Not unless I thought you needed one."

"I don't."

Lyra smiled and the effort pulled a little at the scar tissue on the right side of her face. "Then I'd best get on to the exploitative part of my visit here."

"What part would that be?"

"You have friends among the Templar."

Leah didn't argue. The last time they talked she'd been in trouble for exactly that reason. As much as she dealt with Simon Cross, the organization had believed she'd been compromised.

"I want to *exploit* the friendship you have with them," Lyra went on.

"How?"

"Control is wondering how amenable Simon Cross would feel to being sponsored in a bid to put him in charge of all the Templar."

EIGHTEEN

Warren woke just before the dawn. He'd spent the night with his back to a tree and huddled in a thick quilt he'd gotten from the villagers. An icy glaze from new-fallen snow lay spread over the quilt, but it continued to be warm inside the folds. The heat inside his body was generated by the arcane power he commanded. The quilt helped trap it.

Only a few feet away, wrapped in another quilt and dug into a hillside, Naomi slept with her head covered. Although she'd tried to generate warmth the same way Warren had, she hadn't been able to maintain it. During the night Warren had lent his strength to hers. He sensed from that connection that she was well.

"You worry about her too much."

When Warren glanced back up, Lilith stood in front of him. She faced the gray dawn and looked incredibly pale.

"I don't think I do," Warren responded.

"Yet you weaken yourself to care for her."

"She's an ally."

Lilith turned and frowned at him. "She's a dependent. Taking, but not giving."

"When I passed out after the fight with the demons, who took care of me?"

"The zombies. The demons you held in thrall."

"They didn't talk to the villagers and persuade them not to kill me while I was defenseless."

"Even unconscious, you aren't defenseless," Lilith told him. "The hand I gave you takes much better care of you than the one Merihim gave you."

Talking about his hand like that made Warren uncomfortable. Nightmares about the night four years ago when the Templar Simon Cross cut his original hand from his arm still haunted Warren. And he didn't like Lilith pointing out that she'd given him the hand. It made the fact that she could take it back even more real.

"Naomi is human," Warren said. "She can take care of me in ways you can't."

Lilith strode toward him and her gown rippled in the cold winter breeze even though snowflakes drifted through her. She clearly wasn't happy, but Warren didn't think she would attack him.

"What? Are you talking about the physical relationship she has with you?" Lilith asked.

Warren's cheeks flamed with embarrassment. Even after all that he'd been through these past four years, after having survived a childhood that was anything but safe or loving, he remained modest about some things.

"No," he said. "That's not what I'm talking about. Naomi exists on a physical level that you don't. And she can interface with humans."

Lilith approached Naomi and hunkered down beside her. Warren's heart tightened in his chest. He pushed himself to his feet and shrugged out of the quilt as Lilith ran a hand along Naomi's sleeping form. Lilith couldn't touch her, though. Her trailing hand didn't even disturb the wrinkles in the quilt.

"Your concern for her is going to get you into trouble one day," Lilith said.

"Why?"

"Because she's here only to use you for her own gain."

Warren couldn't dispute that. When Merihim had taken his hand back, Naomi had left him. Of course, he hadn't been fit to be with at the time, either.

"We use each other." Warren pinned Lilith with his gaze. "*All* of us."

Lilith laughed at him. "It amuses me to think what you would do if I, too, had a physical form." She looked back at Naomi. "Then one of us would be expendable."

Not thinking happy thoughts, Warren told himself.

Lilith returned her gaze to him. "Since I lack a physical form and you follow me anyway, I don't think I would be the one who felt threatened."

Warren struggled to think of something to say to that but failed.

"Get her up," Lilith commanded. "We've still got a long way to go."

"How much farther?"

"We'll be there by this afternoon. If you don't tarry."

Warren knelt down beside Naomi, took her by the shoulder, and gently shook her awake.

"Is there someone else?" Naomi asked.

Confused, Warren glanced at her. "Someone else?"

"With us."

Warren glanced at the zombies that flanked them, then searched the nearby brush and marshlands with his arcane senses. Nothing hit his radar.

"No," he answered. "We're alone."

For a moment, Naomi remained silent. Then she said, "I get the impression that someone else is out here with us. I've had that feeling since we left London."

Warren knew Lilith walked beside him, but he ignored her while under Naomi's scrutiny.

"Perhaps," Lilith said, "she's not as stupid as I'd thought."

Anger stirred inside Warren, and he wondered if Lilith chose to make Naomi feel her presence now. Even in the past few hours, Lilith had started looking more substantial.

"Is that it?" Naomi asked. "Is someone else here?"

"If someone else were here," Warren said irritably, "don't you think you'd know it?"

"I think I do. That's why I asked." Naomi fixed her gaze on the patchy dirt road they followed. The leaden gray sky beat down on them through the whirling haze of snowflakes. "I couldn't see Merihim, either."

"That's because he didn't want you to see him."

"I was thinking this was the same thing."

Warren remained quiet.

"You told me about Merihim, though," Naomi said. "I just wanted to know why you weren't telling me now." She paused. "I also feel this is connected to that book. The one that you can read but I can't."

"How much longer are you going to allow her curiosity to threaten you?" Lilith asked.

Warren concentrated on walking. He still hurt from the battle the night before.

"I trust you," Naomi said.

"Lie," Lilith hissed.

Warren knew Naomi lied. He felt the lie on her. But he didn't blame her. She trusted him some, but that wore thin.

"I trust you," Warren said.

Naomi took his hand, his flesh and blood hand, and held it. "Then tell me what's going on."

Feeling the warmth of her, remembering the four years they'd been together and apart, Warren took a deep breath and told her about Lilith. He didn't tell Naomi everything, but he told her enough.

Lilith hissed like a scalded cat and walked away. Fear quivered inside Warren as he watched her go. He didn't want her to desert him, but he honestly felt that she wouldn't. If Lilith had had anyplace else to go, she'd have already gone.

You need me, Warren thought at her.

For a moment, Lilith glanced back at him. "Don't get too arrogant for your own good, human." And in that one word, she reminded him of the vast divide between them.

"Do you believe she's *that* Lilith?" Naomi asked. "The one who was supposed to be Adam's first wife?"

"I don't know."

Curiosity chafed Naomi as she considered the question. They sat beneath a scrub tree on a log. Warren had dragged another log over and set it ablaze with his powers. She took a loaf of bread from their supplies along with a ham. Using her knife, she sliced the bread and meat and made sandwiches for them both.

"Do you know much about Lilith?" Naomi asked.

"She isn't very talkative."

"Not her." Naomi glanced around and tried to find the woman Warren said accompanied them. Her inability to do so aggravated her. Warren described her as beautiful and young looking despite her thousands of years of existence. "The one in the legends."

"I've researched her," Warren replied. He stood and walked closer to the fire to warm himself.

Naomi held a hand out. The energy she'd used to keep from freezing in the winter cold had been enough to do that, but only just. The warmth from the fire seeped into her and felt so much better than what she'd been able to do.

"She's supposed to be the mother of demons," Naomi said. "Legend has it that when God first created her, she was attached to Adam. Then he separated her from him and evidently opened up a path to a world of demons. Some sources called it the Great Abyss, but that could have been the Well of Midnight."

"I suppose."

Warren's obvious lack of interest in the matter irritated Naomi. "Aren't you the least bit curious?"

"Of course."

"You could ask her, you know."

"I have. She won't tell me. Also, I've learned that asking too many questions can sometimes get you killed." Warren looked at her meaningfully.

"Me? You're talking about *me*? That she might kill me?"

"Yes."

"Why?"

"Because she doesn't like you very much."

For a moment, Naomi thought that she heard a mocking peal of laughter. She hoped it was only the wind, but she feared it wasn't.

"Has she at least told you what we're out here looking for?"

Warren quietly wished that Naomi would just be quiet. Telling her about Lilith was a mistake. For the past hour, since they'd resumed their trek, Naomi continued to pummel him with a barrage of questions.

"No," he said.

"Then why did you come?"

"Why did you come?" he replied.

"Because you asked me to."

"Lilith asked me to come."

Naomi frowned in displeasure at that. For a while, she was quiet, but Warren knew it wouldn't last. As soon as she thought of a new way to ask the questions she wanted answers to, she'd ask once more.

Warren studied the countryside. Snow covered the sides of the hills and hung in the branches of evergreens lining the valley. If it weren't for the zombies lurching around them as the undead things tirelessly kept up, the scene would have looked idyllic.

They were far from the beaten path now. He hadn't seen houses or signs of habitation in over two hours.

Lilith suddenly stopped and walked toward a tree to her left. Unconsciously, Warren followed.

"Where are we going?" Naomi asked.

"I don't know." Warren pushed through tall dead weeds and brush as he trailed after Lilith.

A moment later, Lilith stopped and pointed at a tangle of snow-covered vines. "Here," she said.

"What?" Warren asked. Then he saw that the vines and bushes wrapped around an artificial form. Excited and fearful, he grabbed a fistful of vines and tugged. Snow drifted to the ground, and the vines came apart with brittle snaps in his fist.

Naomi joined in. She took her knife from her belt and slashed at the vines and brush.

In a few moments, they cleared part of a low stone wall held together by cracked and weathered mortar. Several gaps showed. Warren studied the stones, hoping for some kind of markings.

"What is this?" Naomi asked.

"I don't know." Warren glanced up to where Lilith stood watching them.

"It looks like an old Roman wall."

Warren agreed. England was covered in structures and walls left by the Romans, as was most of Europe. That empire had covered continents and spanned centuries. For a time, Hadrian's Wall had separated northern England from the south, holding back the Picts.

"A Roman wall in this part of the country isn't anything special," Naomi said.

"Looks like no one knew this one was here," Warren replied. Dread laced his excitement at the discovery. Whatever Lilith searched for couldn't be good. He hoped it wouldn't kill him.

You don't believe it will, he told himself. *Otherwise you wouldn't be here.*

"You'll need to clear more of the wall," Lilith said.

"What are we looking for?"

"A mark."

"What mark?"

"I'll know it when I see it." Uncertainty touched Lilith's features, but she shook it off. "This has to be the place. But so much has changed."

Warren stepped back from the wall and called to the zombies. "Here. Rip this away."

With zombies, it was hard to tell what they understood and what they didn't until it was sometimes too late. Simple commands that a living, breathing person understood immediately became difficult to issue. But in this case, the zombies understood immediately. They fell upon the wall like locusts and tore the brush away.

"Stop them," Lilith ordered.

At Warren's command, the zombies stepped back from the wall. They'd worked hard for ten or fifteen minutes. Many of them now had broken fingers, and the freshest zombies from the village had lacerated palms. The undead stood nearby, twitching and jerking.

Lilith peered more closely at the wall and traced stones with a manicured forefinger. Accumulated dirt peeled away under her nail. Warren couldn't imagine any other woman he knew risking her nails in that fashion. But every now and again, Lilith's nail looked like a curved talon.

"She's touching the stone?" Naomi asked.

For the first time, Warren realized that Lilith interacted with the physical world. Something had changed, and change—at least in his experience—wasn't a guaranteed good thing. Wariness rose up within him.

"Yes," he whispered.

Seconds later, a shape carved into one of the stones stood revealed. Warren thought it was maybe a bird, or maybe an insect.

Lilith stood and looked around. She smiled and turned to him. "This is the place. I feel the power here." She reached down for a loose stone atop the wall. She tried to pick the stone up, but in the end she succeeded only in causing it to shift and topple from the wall.

"What place?" Warren asked.

"*My* place." Lilith strode from the wall in carefully measured paces. At thirty-two, she stopped and turned back to Warren. "You must dig here."

"Why?"

"Because what we seek is underground."

Warren looked at the virgin snow and knew the hard-packed earth below it would be frozen. "I didn't bring any shovels or trenching tools. I didn't know there was going to be digging involved."

"Find a way," Lilith ordered. "You didn't come all this way to fail."

NINETEEN

When she was released from the hospital a few days later, Leah wore an eyepatch over her right eye. The patch and the strap holding it itched and constantly bothered her. Beneath the patch, the socket remained empty. The surgeons chose to remove the eye rather than risk infection so close to the brain.

A prosthetic replacement—nonfunctional except for the possibility of an image recorder or poison dart air gun, both of which were readily available—wouldn't be feasible till the flesh healed. Even then the prospect of putting an artificial eye into her head didn't sound pleasing.

Leah returned to the rooms she'd been given inside the secret complex maintained below London. The city, it seemed, held enough spaces belowground to hide many secrets. There were several such complexes, but her organization didn't have access to all of them.

Even after four years, the rooms didn't feel personal. Instead, she felt like a hotel guest. She tried to watch recorded movies and programs, and she tried the few books she'd managed to get her hands on. She even cooked her own meals instead of simply going down to the commissary to eat.

Nothing worked. Each day—and there were five of them in a row, five times as much as she'd ever spent there in a row—got harder to manage. She needed something to do, and she felt that need incessantly.

The only times she got out of the rooms were to get supplies and to exercise. Despite the physical recovery ahead of her, she pushed her body to get back into shape. Physical conditioning mattered out on the street, even inside one of the bio-enhancing suits.

Mostly she slept and she waited for the time when Lyra Darius cleared her for an assignment. Leah petitioned daily in the mornings and afternoons by e-mail. But she didn't know if she was ready to undertake the assignment she felt certain she would be given. She wondered what Simon Cross would say about Lyra's offer to make him the supreme leader of the Templar.

Will it tempt Simon? she wondered. *Especially in light of what Booth tried to pull only a few months ago?* She knew if it simply meant getting High Seat Terrence Booth out of his position then Simon would be more tempted. She'd been with the other Templar when they'd broken Simon out of Booth's trap.

Simon respected many of the other Templar. Usurping power over them wouldn't be easy.

And that was only if Lyra Darius could make good on that offer. If she couldn't and Simon tried to do that, he could end up in a worse position with the Templar than he currently was.

In the meantime, all Leah could do was watch and wait to see what happened. She had no way of getting in touch with Simon Cross to discover if he was alive or dead. Lyra's offer might not even be viable.

On the morning of the sixth day, Lyra Darius sent a message through the Internet channels set up inside each of the rooms. Eating dry cereal from a box and watching news footage of the invasion, Leah hoped once more that she saw something about the Hellgate that she—and no one else—had ever before noticed.

Letters printed across the television screen. LEAH CREASEY.

Leah picked up the room interface pad from beside her on the couch. She brought up the small computer application and wrote: I'M HERE. The device translated it into typed letters on the screen. She pressed SEND.

The television monitor blanked the news footage it showed from around St. Paul's and brought up a fresh screen. Lyra sat at a desk in an office somewhere in the underground complex. The office location was known only to a handful of people. Leah wasn't one of those people.

"How are you feeling?" Lyra asked.

"Better." Leah hated the fact that she struggled unsucessfully to focus on the image the way she used to. Things just *looked* different these days. She kept telling herself that her vision would improve, but she really didn't think it would. Or that she would get used to it over time. She didn't think that would happen, either. Constantly noticing what she'd lost terrified her and made her feel claustrophobic.

"Good."

"I'm ready to get back to work," Leah said before the woman said anything else. "I . . . I *need* to get back to work." She wanted to say more. She wanted to tell Lyra that the business they were in didn't really include a friendship basis.

Over the years, she'd gotten to know a few of the other operatives, but only on ops, never to go out and get a drink with. Their training precluded them from seeing one another after they went out into the world. Even a demon-infested one.

Safety lay in staying apart and getting together to secure

intel or destroy something. Hit and git remained the only way they worked effectively. Staying in a dwelling made a target of agents.

"We're going to see if we can accommodate you. I'll meet you in the intelligence block in twenty minutes. Can do?"

"Can do." Leah felt embarrassed about the excitement in her voice. As soon as the monitor blanked, she launched herself into motion.

Leah felt naked in street clothes and not in the black armored suit. For the moment, the doctor handling her case hadn't cleared her for that, either. She wore jeans, boots, and a sweater against the chill in the room.

Lyra and three agents sat around a conference table. Leah knew the two men and other woman, but only tangentially. Computer hardware filled the walls, and the whole room hummed.

The tri-dee projector in the center of the table kept cycling through images of Simon Cross. Leah felt almost guilty watching Simon. It reminded her of how she'd taken advantage of his protective nature to get inside the Templar Underground and steal away with as much information as she could.

"As you all know," Lyra said, "Control has come up with a working strategy regarding the Templar."

"Not exactly a big fan of those armored goons," one of the women said. "They tend to be in this thing for themselves, not out of any real desire to bring down the enemy."

"Simon isn't like that," Leah said automatically. She'd spoken before she'd even known she was going to. She was immediately embarrassed. *In for a penny, in for a pound,* she told herself as all heads turned in her direction. "He's worked to get civilians clear of the city, and to provide for them. If he could kill every demon in England single-handedly, he would."

"Well," Clarice Thompson said as she steepled her fingers against one another, "it appears as though someone is carrying quite the torch for the Templar." She was in her early fifties, a thin woman with a pinched face and gray-white hair.

Leah forced herself not to respond to the comment. She liked Clarice, and she knew that if she were sitting in any seat but her own, she'd have felt the same way that the other woman did.

"Simon Cross," Lyra said, "is different than many of the others. Just as Lord Sumerisle was."

Clarice lifted her chin and dropped it. "I'll defer that to you."

Lyra returned the woman's gaze full measure. "Good. This will go much more quickly if you do."

A nerve twitched along the underside of Clarice's jaw. All of the different teams within the organization remained separated. They didn't work well together. They weren't designed to. In theory, they all worked without knowledge of one another. Being together proved hard for them.

"Control wants to find a way to unite the Templar," Lyra said.

"I thought they were united," Bernard Carpenter said. He was in his early sixties, sleek and silver.

"No. Simon Cross's arrival from South Africa split the Templar to a degree. We know that most of the Templar died at St. Paul's."

"And the rest of them are hiding out," Craig Gordon snarled. In his late forties, he held a reputation as a master espionage player.

"We have a plan to change that," Lyra said.

The statement, uttered so matter-of-factly, blew Leah away. She tried to wrap her throbbing mind around it. The pain in her head made her regret not taking her meds, but she'd wanted a clear mind for the meeting.

"We know there are at least two groups of Templar," Lyra went on. "One within London and one—Simon Cross's group—somewhere outside London."

"Somewhere?" Carpenter echoed. "We don't even know where this Cross fellow is?"

"We don't."

Clarice eyed Leah speculatively. "But you say that Agent Creasey can get in touch with Cross."

"She can."

"Then she knows where this hiding place is." The woman's tone ended just short of an accusatory slap in the face.

"She does," Lyra agreed. "And I've agreed to honor her request not to divulge that information."

"Since when do we make deals with lower echelons within this organization?" Gordon asked.

"How do we know Agent Creasey hasn't been compromised?" Clarise asked.

"*I* made this deal," Lyra said, "and I'm on equal standing with all of you. As for Agent Creasey being compromised, she put her life on the line for our efforts to destroy a demon weapons plant only a week ago. She bears her wounds from that encounter now. That's enough credibility for me."

No one else in the room said anything, but Leah felt the waves of animosity directed at her. *They're scared,* she realized. That surprised her. All of her career she'd figured the people at the top tier of the organization would be cold, collected individuals with ice water in their veins. It shocked, and potentially a little scared her, to realize they weren't that much different from her.

"Besides that, Cross's operation is almost bankrupting itself just to take care of the people they brought into their ranks," Lyra said.

"If the man is overwhelmed by his own undertaking," one of the men asked, "why would he be of any value to us?"

Lyra looked at Leah. "Perhaps you could answer that, Agent Creasey."

Caught off-guard, Leah struggled to recover quickly. She hadn't expected to have to answer any questions. "Simon Cross's family has always been important in the history of the Templar. Also, many of the Templar hiding in the Underground have become sympathetic to his efforts. A few have deserted the Underground, knowing they'd never again be allowed in that place, and joined Simon."

"He's in a position to sway the rest of the Templar?" one of the men asked.

"We believe so," Lyra answered. "From what we've seen, the Templar holed up in the Underground have no intention of taking a truly active part in the battle against the demons."

"They're waiting to build up more warriors," Leah said. "All of that was in my report."

"You should all know that. I disseminated those reports."

No one disagreed.

"We can't afford for the Templar to wait," Lyra continued. "We need them in the streets fighting back against the demons."

Because we're running out of operatives, Leah thought.

"Yes," Lyra said, gazing at her hard enough to let Leah know she'd guessed her thoughts. "For the moment, Simon Cross hasn't concentrated on winning the battle against the demons or trying to shut down the Hellgate."

"Simon's trying to save people," Leah said, feeling defensive. She didn't want anyone to mistake Simon's motives. "His people operate mostly as scavengers and search-and-rescue."

"But he's also training civilians to fight," Lyra said. "And he's giving them armor. Templar armor." She pointed at the tri-dee in the center of the conference table. A tri-dee image ballooned up from the center of the table. Eight others followed the first.

Leah didn't recognize any of the faces, but she knew the look of death they all wore. She shook her head and instantly regretted it when pain exploded inside her skull.

"None of these people were ever Templar," Lyra said. "When we found their bodies, we traced them back to credit histories and medical information from before the Hellgate opened. Prior to their deaths, prior to the invasion, they were normal British citizens."

Gordon leaned forward and looked at the dead faces. "Cross is drawing from the population."

"Yes."

"For an organization that has been ultrasecret for hundreds of years, that's pretty radical."

"I agree."

"Is the other Templar group doing the same thing?"

"No," Lyra answered.

"They wouldn't," Leah added. "They've got a bunker mentality. I've been there in their Underground." She knew that was going to cause further suspicion, but that couldn't be helped. "The other Templar are all sticklers for their code of conduct, and that speaks strictly against involving outsiders."

"Yet it was you who saved young Jessica Sumerisle," Clarice told Lyra.

"It was," Lyra admitted.

"Then why don't you pursue an alliance through her?"

"She's a child."

Carpenter shook his head. "Cross isn't much more than that himself. What is he? Twenty-six? Twenty-seven?"

"Twenty-nine," Lyra answered.

"Hardly an elder statesman," he noted derisively.

Leah's voice was hard and flat when she spoke. "Simon Cross isn't a statesman, elder or otherwise. The man is a champion. He's one of the best the Templar have ever turned out. A warrior and a leader, and he stands for all the compassion and rules that are in the Templar code."

"Quite the fan, aren't you?" Clarice asked sweetly.

TWENTY

Angered almost enough to lose control, Leah turned on the woman. "When was the last time you were out there laying your life on the line?"

Clarice's face mottled with anger. "That's not what I'm supposed to do. I'm supposed to gather intelligence and direct—"

"Simon's out there every day," Leah said. "He never asks anyone to do something he wouldn't do himself. Or *risk* himself. That's why he has the unconditional support and respect of his warriors. He doesn't hide behind chain of command. He sets the standard."

Her face a mask of rage, Clarice looked away.

"That's precisely why we want him in our camp," Lyra said into the silence that followed. "Agent Creasey, I'm authorizing you to take a team to Simon Cross and inform him—within parameters that you'll be given—that this organization stands ready to support his bid to establish himself as leader of the Templar."

"No team," Leah said.

Lyra folded her arms and looked unhappy. "I can hardly ask you to go out there alone."

"With all due respect, I can't take anyone there," Leah said. "I gave my word to Simon that I wouldn't reveal the location of the redoubt he's established."

"Ridiculous," Carpenter objected. "Given the current nature of how volatile the situation throughout London has gotten, a lone woman can't hope to get through those streets."

"I'll get out of the city," Leah said to Lyra because that was the one she knew she'd have to convince. "I've done it before."

"In the condition you're in?" Gordon's tone made it sound as if everyone should know how impossible that was. "I don't mean to be overly blunt, but you're less than what you were the last time you were out there."

That stung. Leah bit her lip in order to keep from responding.

"I'm confident in her abilities," Lyra stated.

"If Agent Creasey is the only asset with which we can pursue this endeavor," Carpenter said, "she needs to be protected. Not risked."

"We're all risking," Lyra said. "Every day that we live in this city under demon occupation, we're risking all that we are. And all that we will be." She looked at Leah. "Your med clearance came through. Draw what you need from weps and the motor pool. Let me know if there's anything else you need."

"I will. But how do you plan to give Simon control of the Templar? Booth and the others aren't going to just willingly cede control."

"We've tracked some of the Templar from those underground bunkers," Lyra said. "We've found enough of them to make a point to the Templar that we can work with them or against them. I'm also willing to make it costly for them to decide not to play along." She paused. "But I'm betting on one other thing, too, Agent Creasey. The Templar organization—every man, woman, and child that grew up in those Houses—was trained to love heroes."

Remembering what Simon had revealed to her when she'd gone down into the Templar Underground with him, Leah knew that was true.

"I want to remind them that not all the heroes in the world died that night at St. Paul's," Lyra went on. "And that not all of them wear Templar armor."

Clarice shook her head. "You know as well as I do that one of the first things we do in this organization is disabuse new recruits of the notion that they're going to be heroes. Heroes die far too quickly in the field."

Lyra looked at them. "The world has changed. Before, we served best by staying within the shadows, and I'm not saying we should step out of them now. But I believe the time *has* come for heroes. At least, heroic enough to pull more assets to our side of the game board for a time." She paused. "Is there anything else?"

No one spoke, but clearly no one was happy.

"Agent Creasey," Lyra said, "I want to wish you good luck." She crossed over to Leah and extended her hand.

Leah shook hands. "Thank you. And if it's all the same, I'm going to be leaving straightaway. I've sat around my apartment for the past five days. I feel as though I'm about to go mad."

"Of course."

Leah left the room, but none of the others made an effort to move. She wondered what else the group would talk about in her absence. Then she cleared her thoughts and concentrated on the trip to see Simon Cross. She couldn't believe how much she looked forward to that. The excitement felt almost sinful.

By three that afternoon, Leah sat astride a matte-black finish Enduro motorcycle and sped through the metro area with a Blood Angel screaming in pursuit. Clad in the blacksuit, her mask securely in place, and feeling the unfamiliar heavy weight of the eyepiece she was forced to wear that augmented her vision, Leah checked the Blood Angel's pursuit in the vibrating mirrors.

The demon swooped down again and opened its mouth.

Leah stomped on the rear brakes, locking the tire up and sending the motorcycle into a controlled skid across the street. At least, she mostly controlled the skid. The cracked street surface offered constant challenges to her driving skills.

The Blood Angel flashed by overhead. Not as much resistance existed in the air as on the street. Leah braked quicker and sped faster in the straightaways than the demon.

She had a problem with distance, though. Adjusting to the vision augmentation was going to take time. She skidded uncomfortably close to a wrecked Mini Cooper that housed two shattered skeletons. For a moment, the compact car's rear bumper held her leg trapped against the motorcycle.

Leah grabbed the handlebars and shoved backward. Without the blacksuit's strength augmentation, she probably couldn't have moved the motorcycle, and definitely never in time.

The Blood Angel heeled over in the sky. Two buildings down, a gargoyle that wasn't actually a gargoyle suddenly took flight. Leah didn't recognize the type of demon it was. New ones seemed to come through the Hellgate every day.

You're not going to hang about and find out what it is, she told herself. *Move.*

She twisted the throttle and roared through the streets again. Turning her inside leg out during turns, she leaned the Enduro over so far that her knee at times kissed the rough street surface. Beams and bullets from demon snipers tore through the air, missing her by inches and punching through the corpses of vehicles as she deliberately sped by close to them for cover.

In the mirrors, the Blood Angel flew after her.

Leah hit the brake again, dropped the shifter into a lower gear, and made a tight turn into the first narrow alley. The alley was hardly wide enough for a lorrie to get through, let alone a Blood Angel with wings fully extended.

With a scream of rage, the Blood Angel pulled up out of pursuit and pushed off one of the buildings to keep from colliding with it. It unleashed a burst of arcane fury that set the alley on fire right behind Leah. The motorcycle's big engine filled the small space with rolling thunder.

Two Stalker demons, looking like overgrown lizards mixed with wolves and equipped with alligator's jaws, occupied the alley in front of Leah. Corpses and rotting garbage provided an obstacle course out of Hell. The stench of death and decay fouled the air and made it thick.

The Stalkers turned toward Leah and opened their jaws to reveal rows of serrated teeth. They launched themselves at her. Leah wasn't sure if the demons were smart enough to think or merely operated on instinct, but if they did think, she felt certain they were convinced she was going to see them and stop or try to turn back to escape.

Leah gunned the engine and headed straight toward them. At the last minute she aimed the motorcycle at a demon corpse to one side, clutched and revved the engine, then popped the clutch and pulled back on the handlebars. The front wheel hit the demon's dead body and shot into the air.

She sailed a good twenty feet before touching down again, well over the snapping jaws of the Stalkers. The handlebar dragged against the side of the wall for just a moment, and Leah fought to keep control.

Then she raced forward again, mentally mapping her route through the city. Getting out would be the most dangerous part.

The Burn had spread past London's geographical boundaries and sent uneven tendrils into the countryside surrounding the suburbs. The gray buildings of the inner city gave to homes with yards and space in between.

Although the line between the Burn and the snow-covered landscape beyond couldn't be laid with a straight-edge, enough of a change existed to make the difference immediately visual. The land closer to the city was dry and cracked. Inside London only acid rain had fallen in the past few weeks, and that had only been liquid death and not really any moisture.

The land beyond reminded Leah of Christmases with her family, long trips to her grandmother's house, and a world where seasons still took place all over. Those, at least for the moment, were things of the past.

She glanced at the mirrors as she sped into the countryside. So far, it appeared that she'd left all the monsters behind. Demons filled London, but they weren't everywhere.

Not yet.

She relaxed only a little as she gave herself to the road. She told herself that the safety she felt was only an illusion, not something to be trusted. The illusion shattered when she passed a roadside stand filled with rotted fruits and vegetables. Bloated corpses hung over the stand like grisly piñatas.

Leah knew the corpses weren't the people who had owned the stand. Those people would have left years ago, when the Hellgate had first opened.

Something hunts regularly in this area, she told herself. *It uses the stand to display its kills like trophies. It's something that takes pride in its work.*

She forced herself to look away from the dead and not remember that at one time they had been individuals with hopes and desires. At the same time, she hoped that she didn't get so inured to switching off her feelings that one day they didn't come back.

Kept warm by the blacksuit, which had now turned white as part of its camouflage technology, Leah trudged through the snow. The motorcycle was seven miles back, parked in the barn behind an old farmhouse. Stealth mode through the hill country didn't involve a motorcycle that would easily get mired in the deep snow. She gazed at the hills and valleys, and at the snow-laden evergreens butted up next to the stark skeletons of oaks and ash.

The prodigious amount of snow impressed her. She couldn't recall it ever snowing so much, and it just kept coming. She wondered if the proximity to the Burn caused the amount of snowfall's increase. Maybe nature herself was trying to strike back at the demons.

A quarter mile farther on, she spotted the Templar scout high up on a ridge. When he didn't move, Leah thought possibly the man hadn't seen her. She wondered if she should turn off the camouflage utility on her suit or try to flag the man down.

Then two Templar, one male and one female, stepped from the brush ahead of her. They aimed machine pistols at her.

"Stop," the female commanded.

Leah stopped and held her hands out at her sides.

"Who are you?" the woman demanded.

"I can remove my mask," Leah offered.

"Do so slowly."

Gingerly, Leah touched her finger to her mask and opened the electromagnetic seals. Once the mask disconnected from the blacksuit, it became as limp as fabric except for the extra Kevlar plates over the back of her skull, her forehead, around her eyes, her chin, and across her cheekbones. The constant electric current conducted through the suit "hardened" the fabric to near steel.

"My name is Leah Creasey," she said. "I'm a friend of Simon's. I mean, Lord Cross's."

The Templar stood still for a moment, then the man waved her forward. "We've identified you. You have clearance. Come along then."

"May I put my mask back on?" she asked. Her breath made small gray puffs. "It's cold out."

"You may."

Gratefully, Leah pulled the hood back on, fastened the electromagnetic seals, and felt the mask "harden" as the electricity was generated by her suit. In seconds, it was once more a form-fitting, bullet-resistant shield.

"Is Lord Cross at the redoubt?" Leah asked.

"Yes," one of the men answered. "Would you like us to get a message to him?"

"No, thank you. I'd rather surprise him."

"This really isn't a good time for surprises, miss."

"Give it a rest," the female suggested. "Lord Cross will

be glad to see her. And something like this? Well, it makes a good surprise."

Leah hoped so, but she didn't think the offer she'd come there to make would get a good reception. Simon Cross was one of the most fascinating men she'd ever met, but when it came to affairs of honor, he tended to keep everything controllable, neat, and honest.

She felt certain she knew what his answer to Lyra's offer would be. She just hoped that he wasn't so angry that he tossed her out flat on her arse.

TWENTY-ONE

How big do you think it is?"

Warren stared at the buried structure and shook his head. "I don't know."

"Is it Roman?" Naomi asked. She stood beside him at the edge of the ditch dug by the zombies over the past five days.

The irregular ditch sometimes measured four feet wide and at other times closer to ten and even twelve feet wide. The zombies had dug up anything that looked as if it might be part of the structure, but since they didn't think too well independently, they required constant monitoring.

Warren needed to sleep occasionally, though the way he felt made it seem as if he hadn't. It had been more like passing out for short periods. And at times he got consumed by what the excavation revealed. The structure was roughly rectangular, sixty feet wide by another hundred feet long. It was, so far, at least nine feet high, but the digging hadn't reached the bottom yet.

"I don't know that either," Warren answered.

"Hasn't she told you?" Naomi asked, referring to Lilith.

"She hasn't been around much." Warren hated admitting that because it made him feel vulnerable so far outside of London. He'd never enjoyed big, wide open spaces. He didn't have agoraphobia exactly, but he knew where he belonged.

"Why hasn't she been around?"

"I don't know."

Naomi frowned suspiciously. "It seems like there's a lot you suddenly don't know."

Ruefully, Warren admitted to himself that there was a lot he suddenly didn't know. "Well, that's one thing I know."

The zombies continued digging. They still didn't have any shovels or picks, but they made do with broken branches, rocks, and even their own bones. It was possible that they would have been farther along if they'd actually had tools, but the zombies worked tirelessly. They never got fatigued and continued chopping and hacking into the ground through the night. Every now and again, when Warren was asleep or distracted, one of them wandered off, never to return.

"Have you tried to get in touch with her?" Naomi asked.

"Yes." Warren tried to mask his irritation, but he didn't think—according to Naomi's icy stare—that he succeeded.

"Did you do anything to make her angry?"

"No." Warren took that back. "Not that I'm aware of."

"What did you do?"

"Pretty much the same thing you've been doing. Asking a lot of questions about this."

Naomi didn't say anything, and Warren wondered if she made the correlation. The *chuff, chuff, chuff* of the zombie's makeshift tools kept cutting into the ground.

"Who would construct a building," Naomi asked, "and not build a door?"

"Maybe it's on the end we haven't uncovered yet," Warren suggested.

"Do you know why anyone would build something that big with only one entrance?"

"One entrance would make it easier to control."

"And why put it so far out here? Alone?"

"For all we know," Warren replied, "there's a whole city buried out here."

"We don't know a lot, though," Naomi replied coldly, and she walked away from him.

Warren didn't mind her inattention to him because it allowed him to focus on his own questions. He believed that Lilith wouldn't have brought him all the way out in the middle of nowhere just to have him dig up a building with no entrance.

In earlier frustration, he'd had the zombies try to break through the stone walls, but they hadn't been able to do it. He'd even tried using the arcane forces at his disposal but hadn't had any luck. So far, the building remained impenetrable.

Warren slogged through the ditch. The melted snow had accumulated under the zombies and turned to treacherous mud.

Writing on one of the walls caught his attention immediately. He couldn't help wondering how long the wall section had sat there uncovered and no one had drawn his attention to it.

The writing was some kind of pictograph. Beautiful people and garments adorned the wall. Warren held his torch closer and willed himself to read the images on the wall. Simply gazing at them hadn't made any sense.

Nearly all of the images were of the woman, and several scenes bordered on pornography. Whoever the woman was, she'd had great appetites for nearly every wanton thing ever done.

"Once you learn to read the language, the inscriptions become simple."

Feeling the heat of someone's breath on his cheek, Warren turned and found Lilith standing beside him. She looked the same as she always did, but she seemed to have more color. Then Warren realized he'd felt her breath on his cheek.

He reached for her automatically, simply trying to put a hand on her shoulder. When his hand met the space her body seemed to occupy, his hand sank through her, but he felt the heat of her and a small resistance.

"Do you know the language?" Warren asked.

"Yes." Lilith smiled. "I was the one that invented it." She leaned closer to the pictographs. "The writings are beautiful, aren't they?"

"They are," Warren agreed. "They seem to focus on one woman."

"Me."

Warren hesitated and checked again, but he didn't see the resemblance. The woman in the pictographs could have been anyone. "You're sure about that?"

"Yes. All men see me as they wish to see me." Lilith looked at him. "Your own desire created the image you see before you."

"Does that mean you're not real?"

She smiled at him. "There's still so much you don't understand. I'm real, Warren. As real as that hand I gave to you. But you aid in my realness. You help give me form. Without you, I would be just a dream."

Warren didn't ask any more questions about that particular topic because it was too confusing. He concentrated on the building.

"Who built this?" he asked.

"I ordered this building built."

That surprised Warren only slightly. His imagination had already gotten days ahead of him.

"Why?"

"I needed some place to wait."

"To wait?" Warren directed his torch at her. "To wait for what?"

"Isn't that apparent? For the Hellgate to open." Lilith walked farther along the ditch and continued her study of the pictographs.

"I don't understand."

"Once the Hellgate opened, I didn't have to wait anymore."

"Why did you wait?"

"Because humans couldn't tap into the arcane energies in the world enough. And because there wasn't enough arcane energy here to begin with. It had all been diffused as humans stepped away from it and embraced science." Lilith frowned and said *science* as if it were something disgusting.

"Humans have always been able to tap into arcane energy?"

Lilith smiled at him. "Of course. You had a lot of natural ability before the Hellgate opened. After all, you killed your stepfather when you were just a child."

"He was going to kill me." Even after all these years, and knowing that his stepfather would have killed him, Warren had residual guilt over the act. He'd tried to bury it, but that had been easier when he didn't think magic existed or that he'd had the ability to do such a thing.

"I know."

Warren followed her, wondering what she looked for.

"The Templar have always had access to some of the arcane energy because of their beliefs and their nature," Lilith said. "Other humans had it as well. But they never managed to have a lot of powerful people in one place so I wouldn't have to wait."

"You need the arcane energy to manifest."

She cocked her head and looked at him. "That's one way of explaining it. It's too simple, of course, but you're not prepared to completely understand what I'm talking about. Perhaps you never will be."

Warren wasn't sure if he'd been insulted, but he ignored his own immediate anger and focused on the questions he had.

"Demons come from the Well of Midnight," Lilith said, as if sensing his frustration. "We never lose our connection to it, and the higher you go in the demon hierarchy, the more connected to the Well of Midnight you are. I became isolated here."

"Because humans stopped using the arcane energies."

"As you've noticed, not all humans can summon those energies, much less control them. Not all demons possess magical natures. Many are simply vicious. However, humans have always been a jealous species."

And demons aren't? But Warren didn't give voice to that question.

"Demons are the most jealous of all," Lilith said. "Here in this world, humans resented the arcane energy users enough that they persecuted them. They named them witches and wizards and, even though wrongly, demon-possessed. And they killed them."

Warren thought immediately of the witch trials that had gone on in England, elsewhere in Europe, and in America.

"Using arcane energies became a thing of the past more than seven thousand years ago," Lilith continued. "The last place that saw any really confluence of it was Lemuria. Atlantis had long since sunk, and the fools in Lemuria ended up triggering the same kind of underground cataclysm and sank their world to the bottom of the ocean as well. By that time, I decided I had to wait."

"Why here? Why in England?"

"Because I get glimpses of the future. I knew that when the demons came, and that they would, they would first come here. So I had this place built and I had the Book you have made."

Remembering the female Cabalist that Merihim had given his hand to, Warren asked, "Why didn't Merihim have his new pawn take the Book from me when he took away his hand?"

"Because he's forgotten all about it." Lilith smiled. "I made him forget. Just as I first whispered into his ear that the Book existed and that he should send you to seek it out."

"You wanted me to receive the Book?"

Lilith regarded him. "You have a lot of potential. Merihim is too egotistical to believe in anything outside himself. Were it not for you that night the Cabalists pulled him through the portal, Merihim would not be in this place. Were he not here, had he not laid his mark upon you, I wouldn't have been able to communicate with you. All of these things are part of a pattern that we're still exploring."

"What pattern?" Warren didn't know whether to feel threatened or elated. He finally decided that he should probably feel both.

"We're still exploring that." Lilith paused and reached out to the wall in front of her.

"Where have you been?"

"There are things I must see to elsewhere."

"You haven't ever left me like this before."

"I wasn't strong enough earlier. Now I am. And there is much I must do if we're to be successful."

"Successful at what?" Warren asked.

"I'm owed a place in this world. That was arranged

when I was first sent here. I wasn't supposed to be here for so long by myself. I was betrayed. When I'm done, I'm going to have my vengeance for that." Lilith's beautiful face hardened into an unforgiving mask.

Warren found that threatening. Not because she would direct any of her ire at him, but because he knew she would expect him to stand on the front line of any attempts at revenge she made. He wanted no part of that.

"Our goals, at least part of the way," she said, "coincide. If you listen to me, if you are loyal to me, you are going to be more powerful than you've ever before dreamed of."

Power wasn't what Warren wanted. It was what he needed. In order to be safe, he also had to be powerful. These past four years, and even the ones before that, had taught him that lesson.

"It will be all right," Lilith said in a sincere voice. "I'm not Merihim."

You're not, Warren thought before he could stop himself, *but you're still a demon.*

"Press here." Lilith pointed to a section of the wall.

Warren moved his torch and threw more light over the area she'd indicated. There was no difference in any part of the surface that he discerned. He put the silver hand over the spot and felt an immediate connection with *something.* Startled, he pulled his hand back and retreated.

"It's all right," Lilith told him. "That hand and this place are connected."

Cautiously, Warren put the silver hand back on the spot and pressed. After a moment, something *clicked* within the wall. Stone grated as a section of the wall moved. The noise repeated within the vault of the room, offering testimony that the area beyond was mostly empty.

Curiosity pulled at Warren. He'd had a hard time not investigating things that caught his attention when he was younger. He wasn't any less curious now, but he'd learned through bad luck to be patient. But he didn't step into the darkness that yawned beyond.

"Go carefully here," Lilith whispered.

"Why?"

"There are death traps all along the way."

Lovely, Warren thought bitterly. *Like I needed another distraction while we're doing this.* But he slowly pushed his hand with the torch into the room.

TWENTY-TWO

I can let Lord Cross know you're here," offered the brawny woman at the doorway to the blacksmith. She perspired heavily under the leather smock she wore. Protective goggles hung around her sweat-stained neck. A leather strap tied her dark hair back, but loose hair hung in soaked ringlets.

Leah declined the offer. "Please. Leave him to his work. I can wait until he's finished."

The woman smiled at Leah. "Well, I have to admit the view *is* rather good." She stared pointedly in Simon Cross's direction across the room.

Embarrassment stung Leah's cheeks. "I just didn't want to interrupt him."

Simon stood in one corner of the large room in front of a fiery forge that glowed yellow and orange from the heat. Like the women and most of the other people in the room, he wore a leather smock. He didn't wear a shirt, however. Back and arm muscles rolled under glistening skin slightly reddened by the heat. A small boy, similarly dressed but with a shirt on under his smock, stood beside Simon.

The smell of metal and coal tainted the thick air inside the room. Hammers rang against a dozen anvils in a cadence that almost sounded planned. Leah knew it had to be a subconscious thing, though.

"If you're not in a hurry, you could wait elsewhere," the woman said.

"That's all right."

That brought on another smile from the woman. "You might be a while. Lord Cross is a lot like the other men when it comes to smithwork. Tends to lose himself in it."

"I didn't know you had a smithy here."

"Somebody's got to make the armor and weapons. It doesn't grow on trees, luv."

"I thought with all the technology you had that you'd be using nanoforges."

"My name is Angela, by the way." She offered a hand.

Leah took it, felt the power of the grip, and said, "Leah. It's nice to meet you."

"And you as well. I've heard lots of things about you."

"Oh."

"We might be Templar," Angela confessed, "but we're not above a bit of gossip now and again."

"I'll keep that in mind."

Angela crossed her muscled arms and blew a stray lock of hair from her face. She gazed out at the smithy with pride.

"For some of the armor and weapons, sure, we could use nanoforges. But the weapons that are made here don't do as well when machines make them. These weapons need the hands of the person that's going to be using them upon them. They need to feel the souls of the people giving them shape and meaning."

"Why?"

"The men and women here fold arcane energy into the metal. You can't do that with machines. Power like that is put into the metal through blood, sweat, and tears. Through desire and need. There's no replacing that."

Across the room, Simon used a pair of tongs to lift a length of metal. He pulled his goggles back on, then handed the tongs and metal to the boy beside him.

Over the years of their friendship, Leah had seen Simon

around kids on several occasions. In the redoubt, it was almost impossible to go anywhere without having children underfoot. Leah didn't mind because their presence made the cavernous underground vault feel more homey, which she'd believed more than once was the strangest thing she could have thought. She'd been in hotspots around the world and wasn't looking for a home.

Simon had a natural knack with kids. Leah had seen him with them in the saddest of times, such as when he'd had to tell them that a parent had fallen in battle, and when playing conditioning games in the Templar exercise rooms. Under the right circumstances, Simon acted just as big a child as any of them.

With Simon watching, the boy held the length of metal in the forge. Then he pulled it back out and carried it back to the anvil. Simon demonstrated how to strike the metal with a hammer, and the boy followed suit. It wasn't long before the boy's cadence echoed that of the other smiths.

"Is he training the boy to make swords?" Leah asked.

"Yes, but not like you think," the woman replied. "Simon's training young Chandler how to make his own swords. He'll have to make his own armor before he's done, of course. But for now they're going to make a sword for him to practice with."

"Oh."

"If you want, I've got a chair over at the forge I'm working at," Angela offered. "You can come and have a sit. And watch your man."

"He's not my man," Leah said.

"Sorry. That's not what I'd heard."

Leah started to ask the woman what she'd heard.

Angela cocked an anticipatory eyebrow and looked entirely too predatory for Leah's tastes.

"Never mind," Leah replied.

Angela looked a little disappointed. "Come along then. I've also got water. You're going to need that if you're going to stay here."

As Angela had predicted, Simon stayed wrapped up in the sword smithing for almost two hours. Leah had felt certain the young boy with him would have lost interest in the work, but he hadn't. In fact, he seemed somewhat saddened when Simon gathered the sword blade up and rolled it into protective cloth.

Holding his bundle in both arms, the boy went out the door smiling. Leah studied Simon as he watched the boy go through the entrance. Simon appeared strained and not happy. He hadn't even noticed Leah was there.

"One of the new recruits," Angela whispered into Leah's ears.

"What do you mean?" Leah asked.

"I mean that's not a Templar child, luv. By his age, Templar children already know how to make swords, bows, and other weapons."

Simon is recruiting from the civilians. Leah remembered Lyra Darius telling her that and felt slightly sickened. Sending civilians up against the demons was tantamount to murder.

Then Simon's eyes fell onto Leah's face and she saw the haunted look in his gaze. For a moment, Leah stood frozen, unable to speak. Taking long strides, Simon joined her. He reached out to take her hand, but ending up feeling her sadness and anxiety at the contact.

"What happened?" he asked, touching the side of her face with his fingers.

"It's a long story," she said.

"I've got time. Let me get back into my armor, and we'll find a place to talk."

* * *

The whole time that she related the tale of the destruction of the demon weapons plant, in far greater detail than she'd intended, Simon sat quietly and let her talk. They sat at the desk in his office in the quiet dark with only a single light on.

"The people you're with," Simon asked, "they can't replace your eye?"

"They gave me a prosthesis." Leah hated even talking about the subject. Discussing it seemed to magnify the helplessness she felt at her situation. She took the half-helmet from her backpack and handed it to him.

Simon studied the device. "I don't know much about this."

"It allows me limited vision when I wear it." Leah tried to keep her tone light. "It not something I can wear to a cocktail party." She tried a smile, but it didn't fit right. "I think the eyepatch makes me more mysterious and provocative."

Simon handed the prosthesis back to her and she put it away. He remained quiet for a moment, then he said, "If you would like, there are physicians here that can replace your eye."

Trying not to show her surprise, Leah took a deep breath. Finally, she said, "No one can do that. The technology—" Her voice grew tight and she stopped speaking.

"The technology we have goes beyond what anyone else has," Simon said. "When the Templar first began getting ready for the coming war with the demons, they knew it wasn't enough to study weapons and weapons systems. Or armor. If they were going to stand a chance against anything that would come here to prey on mankind, they would have to find a way to prevent casualties and repair damage done to soldiers in the field."

Leah tried to adjust to what Simon had said. She felt sick with anxiety. *Don't let this be a fantasy.*

"Every time there's been a war," Simon went on, "like when the United States had their War Between the States in the 1860s, and the Iraq wars of the past century and this one that took place, munitions have taken large leaps in knowledge. The medical field has kept up. It's had to."

Voice so tight that she had to force it, Leah asked, "Are you sure you can do this?"

"The physicians can," Simon replied.

"Have you seen it done?"

"Do I know anyone who's had an eye replaced, you mean?"

"Yes."

"I do."

Less than twenty minutes later, a young Templar joined Simon and Leah in the office. He had dark red hair, freckles, and an honest smile. He carried his helm in his off hand and looked all of seventeen. He introduced himself as Eoin Murdoch.

"You sent for me, Lord Cross?" the young man asked.

"I did." Simon gestured to Leah. "Miss Creasey was recently wounded in battle. She was told it was impossible to replace what she'd lost."

The young Templar grinned. "No, ma'am. That's not entirely true."

"May I?" Leah asked.

"Yes, ma'am."

Leah got up from her chair and walked over to Murdoch. Only faint traces of scarring remained on his face. She studied his brown eyes from several angles, then shook her head.

"I can't tell," she said.

"Tell what, ma'am?" Murdoch asked.

"Which eye you had replaced."

Murdoch smiled a little. "Begging your pardon, ma'am. It wasn't one eye. It was both. Eight months ago, I was totally blinded during an encounter with the demons. They had to do some patchwork on my face as well. It was a very uncomfortable time."

Leah couldn't believe it. There was nothing to see that would tell her the young man's eyes weren't the ones he'd been born with.

"Was there anything you wished to know, ma'am?"

"How well do you see?"

"I see just fine, ma'am. Better than I did with my old eyes. There's only so much human DNA can do."

"Thank you," Leah said.

Murdoch looked at Simon.

"That's all, Mr. Murdoch," Simon said.

The young Templar spun and walked back out of the room.

Weakly, Leah sat back in her chair. She stared at Simon.

He didn't say anything.

"Yes," she replied in a hoarse whisper. "Bloody *yes* I want my eye back."

TWENTY-THREE

The hidden doorway was only four feet tall. Warren had to scramble through in a duckwalk. On the other side, he held his torch over his head. Dust motes danced in the pale amber glare.

Air is going to be a problem, Warren told himself.

"Why didn't you call me?"

Warren turned as Naomi clambered through the opening. She switched on her own torch and played her beam over the walls as well.

"There's no rush," Warren said, then looked away as her torch beam caught him squarely in the eyes.

"How far were you going to explore before you decided to let me know about this?"

"We can't go any farther," Warren said. "Not at this moment."

Naomi shone her torch against the opposite wall. The beam stopped somewhere short of touching any other surface than the floor, ceiling, and side walls. The same kind of writing as on the outside of the structure covered them all.

"You need to get this one under better control," Lilith said.

"What?" Naomi spun around and shone her torch on Lilith. The light touched the demoness but only enough to make her resemble a hologram.

She's becoming more solid, Warren realized.

Surprised annoyance flashed across Lilith's beautiful face.

"Who's this?" Naomi demanded.

"I am Lilith." She drew herself up to her full height. "And you would do well for yourself to have care around me."

Naomi looked at Warren, and he nodded.

"Why can I see her now?" Naomi asked.

"She's getting stronger," Warren replied.

Cautiously, Naomi closed the distance to Lilith, then held out a hand to touch her. Lilith held her ground. Naomi's fingertips at first sank through the demon as Warren's had. Then a sudden blaze of electricity filled the room, and Naomi sailed backward over ten feet. She convulsed and jerked on the ground, then lay still.

"What did you do?" Warren raced over to Naomi's side.

She wasn't breathing. The whites of her eyes showed through her parted lids. Frantic, Warren laid his flesh and blood hand against the side of her neck and felt for a pulse. There wasn't one.

"She annoys me," Lilith replied.

"That doesn't mean you can just kill her."

Lilith looked at Naomi curiously. "It appears that I can."

"If she dies," Warren said before he stopped to think about what he was saying, "I'm going to walk out of here. I'll be done. Do you hear me?"

Lilith walked over to him. For a moment Warren thought he was a dead man. He struggled to think of something he could say—*anything* he could say—that might appease her. Nothing came to mind.

"You would defy me?" she asked. "Knowing all that I could do to you?"

Warren thought desperately. Even if he took back what he'd said, it was too late. He'd already said it. Neither of them would forget.

"Yes," he breathed hoarsely. "You will not kill my friends."

"She isn't your friend. She seeks only to use you."

"You're not my friend, either."

"I gave you a hand when you had none."

"You put me in Merihim's path and let him hurt me."

Lilith didn't deny that.

Painfully aware of the time passing, reminding himself that the human brain lasted only for around four minutes once the heart stopped beating, Warren returned the demon's stare. He couldn't show weakness or he was as dead as Naomi was.

"You have placed me in harm's way," Warren said, "and you intend to put me there again."

"I do," the demon said softly.

"It can't go all your way. I learned that from Merihim. You need me only until you find someone to replace me. But you're not going to find that out here. You're not going to find many as naturally powerful as I am. You know that."

Lilith smiled at that. "Now you begin to see your own worth. You're not going to be such a timid little mouse anymore, are you?"

Timid little mice die, Warren told himself. He'd been lucky against his stepfather. His luck wouldn't work against the demon.

"I want her alive," Warren grated.

"So that she may betray you?"

"So that she may live. I owe her that at least."

"You don't owe her as much as you think you do. You've already given her more than she would have managed on her own."

How much time has passed? Warren wondered. "Do it, Lilith. Save her."

"Remember this spirit that possessed you," Lilith said. "Remember that it will get you killed ... and that it will help you achieve what you desire. You have to be hard in this life, Warren. You can't give in to others all the time."

"Save her," Warren whispered. "Now."

Lilith leaned down and placed her hand over Naomi's chest. Sparks suddenly crackled into the air. A surge of electricity spurted from Lilith's hand and bathed Naomi's chest. Naomi jerked inches off the ground, then crashed back down.

Afraid that the demon had short-circuited Naomi's body and fried her brain, Warren placed his hand on the woman's neck. Her pulse felt strong and steady. As he moved his hand back, she took a breath.

Relaxed and exhausted, Warren slumped back on his heels. He looked up at Lilith, who had retreated a few feet away and still managed to look irritated.

"Thank you," Warren whispered.

"Let this be a warning to you," Lilith said. "Never let this woman come between you and your service to me. If she does, I will end her life. And yours as well."

Warren looked at her but wasn't as afraid as he had been. Lilith had returned Naomi to life, or at least restarted her heart. Maybe Lilith didn't like being held account-able for her actions or admitting that she wasn't strong enough to do what she wished when she wished to do it, but Warren knew he possessed that power. A balance existed between them—somewhere. He needed to find it to better use it.

He didn't respond to her threat, and he figured that was rebellion enough for the moment. He turned his attention back to Naomi, who remained unconscious.

"You need to come," Lilith said.

"As I started to say," Warren said calmly, "we have to wait."

"Why?"

"The air is bad. Let some of the air from outside wash through the building for a little while. You don't need me somewhere in the middle of this place collapsing and dying, do you?"

Lilith just faded from sight.

Warren panicked a little when the demon suddenly disappeared, but he felt certain she was only piqued and would be back as soon as he was ready to venture more deeply into the building. He retreated outside to his pack long enough to get a blanket for Naomi.

The snowfall had picked up. A layer of new-fallen white powder covered the building as well as the terrain. The zombies continued working in the awful cold and looked blue in the moonlight.

Warren wrapped Naomi, made sure she was breathing all right, then warmed both of them using his power. He leaned back against the wall to rest and somehow found sleep.

"Warren."

Since the voice didn't offer any immediate threat, Warren ignored it and stayed wrapped in his coat. He was warm there against the winter cold seeping into the room around him.

"Warren."

It was Naomi. Warren kept his eyes shut. Then he sensed something hurtling at his head. He jerked his head up and instinctively put up a shield. Senses spinning so fast everything looked as if it were taking place in slow motion, he glanced up and saw the rock headed toward his face.

He gestured and the rock froze less than a foot from his

face. He plucked the rock from the air and held on to it as he looked over to find Naomi standing on one side of the room.

"What?" she asked, exasperated. "It's time to get up."

"I'm tired," Warren said, "and cold and hungry." He rolled the rock between his fingers, and they both knew that he could turn it into a much worse weapon than she'd used it as.

"I let you sleep," Naomi countered. "I've been awake for over two hours. It's daylight outside."

Warren looked through the door and saw a blurred grayness reflecting on the snow and indicating that the sun had risen. He closed his fist—the silver one—and crushed the rock to powder, then let it leak between his fingers.

"Where's Lilith?" he asked.

"I haven't seen her."

Warren struggled to his feet. He hated letting go of the warmth he'd built inside his coat. The winter chill nipped at him at once. His body ached from sleeping in a seated position, and from all the walking and manual labor he'd been doing over the past few days.

"I'm out here," Lilith called.

Wary, Warren stepped back through the opening. Lilith stood atop the ditch that the zombies had dug out to reach the buried structure. The zombies continued the excavation, but Warren wondered if any of them had wandered off in the middle of the night. Their numbers were once again thinning.

Warren climbed the uneven steps he'd cut into the wall. Although the zombies could dig, he hadn't been able to get the concept of steps across to them.

"Stop," Lilith said.

Calmly, Warren froze where he was and watched her.

She'd changed. She looked more real than she had before. Her color was back. More than that, she actually left footprints in the snow.

As he watched her, she stretched out a hand and crooned in a strange melody that beckoned to Warren at the same time it frightened him. Movement darted in the brush ahead of her. After a couple of moments, a fat rabbit hopped across the snow-covered ground and came to a stop at Lilith's feet as she coaxed it to her.

Still singing, the demon leaned down and tentatively stroked the rabbit. In the next instant, she grabbed the rabbit by its scruff with one hand and took its head in her other. She twisted violently.

The sharp crack of the rabbit's neckbones pierced the cold air. For a moment, the rabbit kicked furiously, then it was still.

Before Warren figured out how he was supposed to react, Lilith tore the rabbit's throat open and drank its blood. He heard Naomi cursing behind him, then throwing up.

When she'd drunk her fill, Lilith cupped a handful of snow and washed the blood from her mouth. She looked at Warren with too-bright eyes.

"I haven't eaten in thousands of years," she said in a slurred tone. "I'd forgotten what the taste of blood was like."

Warren didn't know what to say.

"Come on," Lilith coaxed, shaking the dead rabbit at him. "I've got breakfast waiting. She can eat, too. There's enough, and I'm feeling generous."

For the first time, Warren noticed the smell of cooked meat hanging in the air. His stomach growled in spite of what he'd just witnessed.

She led him to a windbreak she'd arranged in the brush. A cheery campfire burned there. The overhanging branches defused the smoke and disappeared against the leaden sky that promised only more snow.

Three rabbits hung on spits near the fire. The flesh was cooked and browned. Warren salivated when he saw them and smelled them. It had been weeks since he'd had fresh meat, and he'd had to barter with one of the survivors still hanging about London.

"Sit," Lilith encouraged. "Eat. If this isn't enough, there are more rabbits."

Warren had never eaten rabbit before, and he'd drawn the line at rats caught inside the Metro area. He wouldn't have eaten rats anyway, but he knew that many of those in Central feasted on dead humans that had recently been killed or succumbed to injury, sickness, or starvation.

Rabbits don't eat meat, he told himself. *They haven't eaten anything foul.* He brushed the snow from a fallen tree, folded his coattails under him, and sat. He took up one of the spitted rabbits and pinched flesh from it. The meat fell off the bone, and it tasted divine.

Although she'd looked appalled, Naomi sat beside him and picked up one of the rabbits as well. She ate tentatively at first, then more hungrily. Grease dripped down her chin.

"Have you rested?" Lilith asked.

"Yes," Warren answered.

Naomi said, "Yes."

Lilith didn't look at Naomi. "Do you think the interior of the tomb is safe for you to go into now?"

"Is that what it is?" Warren asked. "Your tomb?"

"I haven't died," Lilith pointed out. "I only fell into near-death. My death, as long as I stayed protected, was still a long way off."

"Are you flesh again?"

"Not yet," she said. "But soon." She tore the rabbit's

TWENTY-FOUR

Simon stood beside Leah's bed in the surgery. From the tightness round her good eye and her elevated respiration, he knew she was nervous. He didn't need his armor to tell him that. Round them, the OR team prepped her for surgery.

"I never much cared for hospitals," Leah admitted.

"Neither have I, but I'm glad we've got a good one." Simon felt awkward standing there as the other people worked round him.

"The surgeon's done this before?"

"He's the one that put Eoin's eyes in."

"Can they match my eye color? My eyes aren't exactly off-the-rack, you know."

Simon did know. Those violet eyes sometime haunted his thoughts.

"They'll match," he told her. "The nanobots pick up color from the DNA and push it right into the new eye they build for you."

"I'm going to hold you to that," she said. "I've always been a little vain about my eyes."

"You've got lovely eyes," Simon told her.

Some of the tension in her face went away as she smiled at him. "You've never told me that before."

"No." Simon suddenly felt awkward.

"Are you trying to hit on me?" Her tone was playful.

"I was going to wait until they anesthetized you."

"Maybe you should. It would be less painful that way."

Despite the tension of the moment and all the bad things that loomed before them with the dwindling food supplies, Simon laughed. Leah joined him. Everyone working on the prep stared at them.

"Well now," a matronly Templar woman that Simon had known since he was a boy said, "look at the two of you. Like you're out on a lark."

"Not quite," Leah said.

"Scandalous is what it is. My name's Jenny." The woman inspected the machines hooked up to Leah and made a notation on the digital notepad she carried. "Everything here looks shipshape. Can I look at your eye, luv?"

Since she'd been in the bed, Leah had made the OR personnel keep her voided socket covered with a towel. Simon knew she hadn't wanted him to see her.

"After Lord Cross leaves, you may," Leah said.

"Well then, Lord Cross," the nurse said, turning to Simon, "I believe it's time to say your good-byes."

"All right." Simon focused on Leah. Her hand sought his and held it for a moment. "Quite the death grip you've got there."

She frowned at him. "I'm nervous. The thought of miniature robots crawling through my brain creeps me out."

"Oh," Jenny said without turning around, "if those robots crawl *through* your brain, the surgeon's doing it all wrong."

"Lovely thought." Leah grimaced.

"I wasn't the one that had it. Let's get a move on, you two."

Simon looked into Leah's good eye. "You're going to be fine."

"When my new eye is built, what happens to the nanobots?"

"They deactivate and get flushed out with white blood cells. After your eye's repaired, using your body's building blocks and some of the wiring the nanobots will string, there's nothing left for them to do."

"You've seen them do this before?"

"I've had them work on me. Two years ago, while fighting with demons, a Blade Minion skewered me." Simon tapped his chest. "The blade ruined my heart. I was barely alive when Nathan and Danielle brought me back here. The suit kept me stabilized, kept my heart and lungs going, but I would have died if I'd gone to an OR like the ones you're used to. The nanobots saved my life and repaired my heart."

"If they're so good, why didn't the Templar turn them over to the rest of the world?"

"Because it's easier to provide the rest of the world with new armor or new weapons than it is to give them new medical technology," Jenny said sourly. "That's the way it's always been. New technology, new procedures, and new medicines all mean corporations, insurance agencies, and politicians get involved."

"A trifecta of terror," a young male nurse stated.

"Exactly," Jenny said. "Corporations fight against anything new if they don't have a version of it, too. Insurance agencies have to rewrite policies, and they don't like doing that. And politicians use emerging technology and the threat of science to win or intimidate voters."

Simon shook his head. "The Templar made the breakthrough in this field while I was in South Africa. It's new."

"Given time," Jenny said, "the Templar would have given the technology to the world. We just never got the chance to do that." She frowned and looked at Simon. "And you've really got to be on your way."

"All right." Simon squeezed Leah's hand a final time. Then he bent down and kissed her. "Sweet dreams. When you wake, you'll be back to normal."

"Aren't knights in shining armor supposed to kiss sleeping damsels awake?"

"Don't go confusing them with princes," Jenny said. "They aren't that. And enough of them have overinflated opinions of themselves as it is. They don't need any encouragement."

Simon grinned, mirroring the one Leah had.

"Wake me," Leah said, "after I'm out of surgery."

"I'll be there."

"Promise?"

"I promise." Simon stepped back and left the room. He told himself again that Leah was going to be fine. The surgery handled much harder cases on a regular basis. Replacing arms and legs with cybernetic units had become something of an everyday occurrence.

The only thing tricky about this procedure was whether or not Leah would regain her vision. He stood at the doorway and watched as the OR team trundled the bed down the short hallway.

"Have you known Lord Cross long?" Leah asked the older nurse. She tried to concentrate on the questions running through her mind so she wouldn't give in to the panic that threatened to tear her apart. She was more scared now than she'd been while waiting to hear from the physician after the attack on the demon weapons plant.

"I've known Simon since he was a boy. I knew his mother, too, before she died."

"It's nice to meet you, Jenny."

"Why yes," the nurse said brightly, "yes, it is." She checked off something on her digital notepad as they rolled down the hallway. "The two of you seem to be close."

"We're friends. We've fought together off and on over the past four years."

"You're sure it's not anything more than that?"

"I'm sure."

"Because he didn't kiss you like a *friend*."

"Friends kiss."

"Friends also become something more than friends."

Leah felt uncomfortable. "Maybe this isn't a good time to have this conversation."

Jenny smiled. "Oh really? You don't think talking about possibilities like this won't give you something to look forward to? Something to get you on the other side of this operation?"

"No. What you're suggesting could possibly be more trouble than Lord Cross or I can handle." Still, her mind traveled down pleasant avenues that, she had to admit, it had traveled down before. It was hard not to remember that Simon Cross was a good-looking man.

"I think you and Lord Cross can handle a lot."

"Besides that, I'm quite sure Lord Cross has other *friends* among the Templar that are much more suitable."

"If he does," Jenny said, "I don't know about it. And trust me when I say that I would know."

"He's good at keeping secrets."

"Oh, I'll grant you that he's good at keeping things to himself. Better than most men. But I also know that any *friend* he was *friendly* with wouldn't keep her mouth shut. Plenty of women have noticed that Lord Cross is a handsome man. There were plenty of them that noticed that before he left us all those years ago. None of them were shy about it then, and Lord Cross didn't mind spending time with them."

A wave of jealousy shot through Leah, but she quickly got control of it. She hadn't gone without a few *friends* herself before the invasion.

"Well aren't you the busybody," one of the male nurses asked.

"I'm just saying, is all," Jenny said. "It would be good for Lord Cross to have something for himself. All he does is near kill himself every day trying to take care of this place and these people."

"Maybe you should tell him that," the male nurse said.

"Maybe I will."

Leah stared up at the high-powered medical lights above the operating table. She folded her arms across her chest as they transferred her from the bed.

Waves of fear radiated through her. She thought she was going to be sick, but there was nothing in her stomach. She concentrated on being numb inside, using all of the training she'd received.

In just a couple of moments, they attached her to all the computerized equipment necessary for the procedure. It had all been explained to her the day before, but she didn't know if that was a good thing. She honestly felt as if she knew too much now.

Thinking about the nanobots being injected into her eye almost drove her out of her mind. Images of runaway robots tearing through her mind kept her on the thin edge of terror. They weren't clunky or awkward-looking the way they were in the movies. Several of them could fit on the head of a pin.

Like angels, Simon had said.

"All right, Miss Creasey," the surgeon said as he leaned down to address her. He was probably in his early thirties and calm. "We're going to give you something to help you to relax. Then we're going to see about giving you two good eyes. All right?"

Leah nodded. She liked the surgeon's gung-ho attitude, but she'd been around enough bad things in her life that she knew things didn't always turn out that way. She was already lying on this hospital bed minus one eye.

Jenny fitted an oxygen mask over Leah's lower face. A burning sensation flowed along her left arm. Then she breathed in.

"Count backwards from one hundred," the surgeon said.

Leah tried, but it didn't work for her. She spotted Simon above her in the observation deck. It was funny. She hadn't even noticed the deck earlier.

On her second breath, she reached ninety-two. Then her head spun, and she was gone.

TWENTY-FIVE

S
omething clicked beneath Warren's left foot. He knew that couldn't have been good. Since nothing had immediately happened, he left his foot where it was and scoured the darkness with his torch. The dying batteries gave off weak light.

"Stay back," he told Naomi.

"What is it?"

"I appear to have stepped on something."

Naomi backed away slowly.

They'd already found three booby traps in the vault and disarmed them. All of them had been nasty things with spikes and sharp blades. Whoever had finished off the vault for Lilith had possessed a sadistic mind and a thirst for blood.

Warren figured the man—or woman, for that matter—had been disappointed by using such elaborate cunning but then not being able to know if anyone got caught up in them. At the moment, Warren hoped the nasty mastermind had gotten caught in one of his own twisted traps at a later date and had a horribly agonizing death.

"Lilith," Warren called.

She didn't answer. Since they'd returned to the building, she'd gone off exploring. Evidently her present form interacted with the physical world, but that was by choice. She still walked through walls, and she didn't set off any of the traps.

"Can I do anything?" Naomi asked.

"Besides come up here so that we can both be killed?" Warren asked sarcastically.

"I wasn't offering to do that."

Warren didn't blame her. He wouldn't have, either. Gingerly, he knelt and took a closer look at the stone beneath his foot. In their exploration of the first two levels, there were five in all, none of the stonework had been loose.

Unless it had been part of a trap.

The torch burned just bright enough to show that the stone beneath his foot had slid down a fraction of an inch. It had to be a pressure plate. But what was it connected to?

"Well?" Naomi asked.

"It's a switch."

She cursed.

Focusing on the positive—that he wasn't already dead—Warren tried to figure out what he was supposed to do. *You can't stay here,* he told himself.

"Perhaps you can jam it," Naomi suggested.

"How?"

"I don't know. Can you slip a knife blade down between the stones?"

Warren looked, but the torch's dying light wasn't good enough to show him if he could. Even if he had a knife blade thin enough, he wasn't able to see well enough to do the job.

"No," he said. "I can't."

"Then you're going to have to move."

Warren knew that was all he could do. He was lucky he'd heard and felt the click. The first time they'd had no warning. He'd nearly ended up skewered on a trio of spears that had suddenly jutted from the wall. If his reflexes weren't as fast as they were, if he'd been only marginally slower, he'd have been a dead man.

Now . . . was he fast enough again?

The decision to be made was which direction he should take. What would the trap maker have thought? Warren blew out a breath. He would have thought no one would have been fortunate enough to notice the pressure switch.

"All right," Warren said as calmly as he could. "I'm going to jump for it. Watch yourself."

"I will."

"On three," Warren stated. "One. Two. Three." He leaped forward as far as he could. A rustling noise sounded above. From the corner of his eye, he caught sight of a great shape swinging down at him.

The next room was twice as tall as the one above. That explained a lot about how the first floor had been constructed and hadn't stepped off the way he'd thought it should have.

Warren didn't have any time to think about that, though. The large object turned out to be a spike-laden hammer that swung toward Warren without a sound. In the darkness with the torch failing, he saw that the hammer was brutal and ugly.

Turning at the last second, he managed to let the spiked hammer whip by him. His chest stung. He hit the floor on his hands and knees and scuttled forward. Knowing the hammer would come back toward him, he hugged the floor.

Ratcheting sounded overhead. When Warren looked up, he saw that the hammer mechanism had allowed it to come down farther, jerking into place. Being low wasn't going to work. He rolled to the side and barely stayed ahead of the hammer.

His torch lay against the wall twenty feet away. Darkness surrounded him. Almost effortlessly, he switched over to the night vision the arcane energy allowed him to have. Maintaining it for long gave him a headache that prevented searching the building with it. But it helped now.

The hammer ratcheted again and jerked lower. This time it slammed into the ground only a few feet from where he'd been. If he'd been faster, if he hadn't noticed the hammer was descending, it might have gotten him then.

Drawing a deep breath, Warren stood up on shaking legs. He glanced down at his burning chest and saw that his shirt and coat had been shredded. Long scratches marred his chest, and blood stained the material of his shirt.

"Are you all right?" Naomi shone her torch over him, coming to a rest almost immediately on his wounded chest.

"Not really." Warren mopped at the blood with his shirttail.

"You're going to need stitches," Naomi announced after her preliminary inspection. Her torchlight played over his chest. She'd pulled open his tattered shirt to reveal the wounds.

"Later." Warren rummaged in the kit he'd brought. He brought out bandages and handed them to Naomi. "For the moment, bind them. We've got to keep moving. Whatever is down here that Lilith wants, we have to get."

Naomi cursed as she accepted the bandages. She helped Warren take his coat off, then she ripped away the ruined shirt. After she had the gauze bandages in place, she taped them to him and tore the shirt into strips. She used those to further bind his chest.

"The bleeding's slowed," she told him when she stepped back, "but it hasn't stopped."

Carefully, Warren bent and retrieved his torch. He shone it around to make certain it still functioned properly. "There we go," he said. "There's a bit of luck."

With the torch raised, they saw that the room held rotted crates and sealed jars. Ill-made wooden bowls held crude gold coins and gems. Bolts of what had at one time been fabric sat in the corner.

"What is this place?" Naomi asked.

"Treasure room." Warren shoved his hand into a bowl of gems and drew a fistful out. He let them trickle back through his fingers. They flashed emerald, sapphire, ruby, and purple in the torchlight as they fell.

"How much do you suppose is there?" Naomi asked.

"A queen's ransom. At the very least. By standards before the Hellgate opened, at least a considerable fortune." Warren shrugged and found the movement almost excruciating. "Now they're just pretty stones. Same with the gold. You can't trade them to anyone. A man who has food or a safe place to live from the demons has all the treasure he needs."

"It wasn't so long ago," Naomi said, "that men killed each other over things like this."

"Amazing how the prospect of sudden death changes priorities, isn't it?" Chest on fire, Warren played the torch around and examined the rest of the room.

Drawings and the strange language adorned the walls and drew his eyes. He walked close to them and brushed away the layers of dust. The cloud came back into him and he turned his face away.

The drawing beneath stood revealed in his torchlight. In it, a figure that was obviously a woman sat on a massive throne and warriors knelt before her.

"Lilith?" Naomi asked.

"Couldn't imagine it being anyone else."

"It would be good if we could read the inscriptions."

Warren moved down the wall and started brushing again. He felt the same way. There was a story written into the wall, perhaps several of them, and he wanted to know them.

"Who do you think the people were that she ruled?" Naomi asked.

"I'm not that familiar with British history," Warren admitted. "I know the Picts were here. The Angles and the Saxons. The Romans."

"Maybe these were Roman warriors."

Warren studied the images. "I don't think so."

"Why?"

"The armor seems wrong."

"You'd know about armor?"

Warren smiled a little at that. "I'm a war-gamer from way back. I know armor. The Romans used short swords, spears, and occasionally axes. If these drawings are representative, the swords are too long."

Naomi moved away and started working on the wall on the other side of the room.

"Careful," Warren advised. "That hammer might not have been the only trap."

"I know, but I don't think anyone who constructed this would want to hurt this room."

"A treasure room? If I were building this as a dungeon for my mates to rumble through, I know I would."

"This isn't a game."

Feeling the pain of the wounds across his chest, Warren silently agreed.

"There were demons here," Naomi said.

Warren crossed the room and joined her. He added his torch beam to hers. The ghastly image on the wall tightened his stomach and dried his mouth. Looming over the warriors around him, a gigantic demon wielded a massive club and took out horses and riders, oxen and carts, and dozens of men. The image was stark and savage, violent death frozen on the wall.

"Giants," Warren said. "A lot of mythologies always include stories of giants. Always fierce and, more often than not, cannibalistic."

"Cannibals?"

"Jack and the Beanstalk." Warren moved his torch farther down the wall and revealed another image of the large giant picking up men in his fists and eating them. "He warned Jack that he was going to grind his bones to make his bread."

"I'd just thought it was something scary to say when I was a girl," Naomi said. "I never really thought about the giant eating Jack."

"That's because you never saw the giant doing it. This gives a little more credence to that threat."

Naomi moved to the next section. A woman stood in the middle of a forest. She carried a spear in one hand. A mysterious door opened in thin air behind her.

"Lilith?" Naomi asked.

Warren peered more closely, then brushed at the accumulated dust to better reveal the lines. "Maybe. Looks like a door behind her."

"A miniature Hellgate?"

"Hard to say. But something." Warren moved his torch and wiped the next scene clear. On it, the woman figure battled with human warriors, obviously beating them with ease.

"She fought them," Naomi said. "The question is, did they come to see her as a friend or as a conqueror?"

"This is a room full of treasure," Warren pointed out.

"So they revered her."

"Or they were deathly afraid of her."

The next image also showed the woman battling demons. She'd killed two of them and fought with the third. Her spear set poised to pierce the demon's heart.

"If she's one of the demons," Naomi asked, "why would she fight them?"

"Demons fight each other," Warren said. "Merihim had me kill demons in his name. To gain power and prestige among the demon hierarchy. Everywhere you go, it's always about power. The Cabalists aren't any different."

The next image showed Lilith standing in front of a group of cheering warriors. She carried the black spear in one hand and held up a demon's severed head by one horn.

"She became their hero," Naomi said.

"Woman as savior. That's another recurring theme in mythology. You have to wonder how much of this story got out and how much of it influenced so many of the cultures around the world."

"They didn't have telephones or the Internet back then."

"No, but in those days traders traveled everywhere. There's evidence that Vikings discovered the Americas long before Columbus claimed them. Some of the Eastern steppe tribes are related to the Celts. They could have carried the story back and forth."

"Or other demons popped up in other places," Naomi suggested. "Stories about them are far too prevalent to be one event."

"I agree."

The next image made Naomi gasp. The hair on the back of Warren's neck stood up. Captured on the wall, Lilith—or the woman figure they assumed to be Lilith—ate the heart of a man she impaled with her spear.

"She's a cannibal," Naomi said.

"Not a cannibal," Warren whispered hoarsely. "A cannibal only eats the flesh of the same species. Don't forget that she's a demon."

He stared at the picture and wondered again what they were supposed to do in the building. A noise scuffed the floor behind him. He turned and shone his torch ahead of him.

Lilith stood there. She no longer looked virile and self-assured. Weariness draped her and bowed her shoulders. "Come," she said. "I have need of you." Her eyes flicked to the wall where Naomi stood with her torch on the incriminating images. "Ah, I see that they added a history."

"This is you?" Naomi asked.

"Who else would it be?" Lilith snapped.

"You slew the demons?" Warren said, hoping to distract her from the image with the man's heart in her hand.

"Yes. They were sent here before I was. They weren't pleased that I was sent to do what they could not."

"What was that?"

"Subjugate your species if I could. Prepare the world for eventual invasion." Lilith stared at the images. "It was far harder than the Dark Wills believed it would be. And our presence here seemed to awaken the latent ability to use the arcane energy of this world."

"That must have been disappointing," Naomi said.

Lilith's dark eyes flashed. "In the end, it's not going to matter. You'll all be dead or in servitude."

TWENTY-SIX

Tensely, Simon watched the operation taking place in the operating room below. A nearby monitor showed a close-up of the actual work taking place. On the operating table, Leah looked small and vulnerable. He had second thoughts about his decision to stay and observe.

She asked you to be here, he told himself. *You're going to be here.*

The doctors moved with economic efficiency. First they evacuated the eye socket again, opened up the tissue at the back, and inserted a string of nanobots that wired into the brain's appropriate visual centers. Simon wasn't sure what those were called. The surgeon had explained the procedure to him earlier, as had Eoin Murdoch. The particulars hadn't stuck.

While the nanobots connected the neural pathways that restored Leah's sight, the doctors prepped the implant that the next set of nanobots would build around. The implant was a highly sophisticated camera that the nanobots would weave into the eye as they rebuilt it from flesh and blood and the camera. The finished eye wouldn't be completely human, but the construct needed something to work with. The outer layer of tissue would remove all chances of rejection.

The head surgeon looked up. "Lord Cross."

Simon tapped the speaker control beside the observation window. "Yes, Doctor."

"At this point we do have the option of installing a tracking module in her eye as well," the doctor said.

Someone's been talking, Simon thought irritably. Not everyone at the redoubt shared his trust in Leah. Many were suspicious of the fact that she knew more about them than they did about her. The lack of knowledge was an area of concern to Simon as well.

"No," Simon said.

"She wouldn't know unless someone told her," the doctor persisted. "Whoever this woman ultimately works for, they don't have equipment sophisticated enough to find what I could install."

"I said no, Doctor. I appreciate you telling me this." Simon knew the man could simply have installed the module and told him after the fact. Most bothersome about the whole affair was the fact that Simon's command of the redoubt fell into question. With the problems of food supply facing them, though, he knew he shouldn't have been surprised. Fear of not having basic needs met divided people quickly.

The doctor turned his attention back to the eye replacement.

Simon watched the operation on the screen. The doctor used a syringe to deposit the nanobots into Leah's eye socket. For a moment it only looked as if the space were half filled with silver.

"It will be a few minutes before you start to see results, Lord Cross," the surgeon said.

Automatically, Simon cued the suit's AI to let him know when five minutes had passed. He wasn't wearing his helmet, but it still projected audibles.

The observation room door opened and Nathan entered. "Hello, mate." He held up a cup. "Heard you were here. Thought maybe you could do with a spot of tea. Maybe a bit of company."

"Thanks," Simon said.

Nathan joined him at the window. They stood in companionable silence for a few minutes. "You just going to stand here the whole time?"

"The chairs weren't built to handle the weight of the armor. Standing's the only option."

"Right. You and I know that, but do you think that doctor is going to feel at least a little bit intimidated?"

Simon knew his friend was right. He took a deep breath and relaxed. "I promised Leah I would be here."

"You are. Even if you weren't here, you'd be here. There's nothing you can do here. She's in good hands, mate. You knew that or you wouldn't have brought her here."

"I know."

The suit's AI chimed. "Five minutes have elapsed."

Simon studied the monitor. He made out the new blood vessels and nerves that the nanobots created and grafted to the inside of Leah's eye socket. The surgery team had set the program up to identify the various parts of the eye the nanobots were working on.

"That," Nathan said, "is gross, mate."

"You're queasy? After all the fighting we've been doing for the past four years?"

"It's eyes, mate. I've always had a thing about eyes." Nathan shivered and looked away.

A twinge of queasiness settled like a rock in Simon's stomach as well. But he couldn't look away. The chances were good, 93 percent, that Leah would get her sight back better than before. There was no anxiety about that. But Nathan was right: there was something about eyes that invoked the gross-out factor.

"Don't you have anything else to do?" Simon asked Nathan as he continued to stand beside him. Nathan pointedly didn't look at the screen, though.

"Nope. I'm all yours, mate. Thought maybe I could help you through this."

"I appreciate it." Simon had to admit that it felt good having someone there.

Three hours later, the eye began to look like an eye. It stared, vacant and without reaction, up into the OR's bright lights. The sight of a nonreactive eye disturbed Simon because it looked repellant and artificial, but it took on the same violet hue that he remembered Leah's eyes had.

"How long does this take?" Nathan asked.

"I was told the eye construction would take between twelve and thirteen hours. Creating a new kidney or liver is done in less than half the time. The eye mechanisms and nerves are more complicated."

"I heard Murdoch's had an eye replaced."

"Both eyes, actually."

Nathan shook his head. "Personally, I don't like the idea of those robots crawling around inside me. I'd be wondering all the time when they were going to try to take over."

"It doesn't work like that. Once the nanobots have completed whatever they've been tasked, they deactivate and flush out of the system."

"Lovely. I don't even want to know how."

The observation door opened and Wertham stepped through. He was broad and stocky, with gray hair and a short gray beard.

"Lord Cross," he greeted.

Simon knew nothing was wrong. Otherwise he'd have

been notified over the suit's AI. He said hello to the other man and waited.

"How's everything going?" Wertham glanced down into the OR.

"Good so far," Simon answered. "But you didn't just come by to inquire about Leah's health."

"It is a concern, of course, Lord Cross. I happen to like the young lady quite a lot. But inquiring after her health is not the reason I looked you up. Professor Macomber and Brewer would like to have a word with you. They appear to have made some breakthroughs."

"In the Goetia manuscript?"

"Yes, my lord. And in the construction of the Node fields."

Simon hesitated.

"The doctor will call you if there's anything that goes on that you need to now about," Nathan said. "Macomber and Brewer have been pushing themselves for months to get a handle on their projects. They haven't been talking to anybody. I, for one, am curious that they'd want to see you now."

"Let's go see what they've discovered, then."

Wertham opened the door, and Simon led the way out.

"What we've discovered is that the Goetia manuscript was written in eight different languages," Professor Archibald Xavier Macomber told Simon.

"Possibly ten," Gerald Brewer put in. Despite the quiet of the lab where they worked, his voice boomed.

Macomber waved that away. "As you can see, we're not quite in agreement over that."

Simon wasn't surprised. The two men didn't often agree on anything until they felt they had a true answer to some of the questions they had about the manuscript. Unfortunately, there were a lot of questions.

In his sixties, Macomber was a frail man with slow, thoughtful movements and a soft voice. Scars showed on his face and hands from the hardships he'd suffered while an unwilling resident of a Parisian sanitarium. There were more over the rest of his body. Simon knew the mental scars would never show, but he also knew they were there. Macomber was bald with a fringe of silver hair and a short beard.

"Luckily," Macomber went on, "between us we've had the skills to decipher most of those languages."

"That decryption has been even harder," Brewer said, "because all of the languages are artificial. What's more, they haven't shared a connective base. So for every endeavor we've made to decipher one, we've had to start from scratch."

"A very laborious process," Macomber said.

Brewer nodded. Evidently they agreed about that. Brewer was in his fifties, with dark hair and an intense gaze. Before the invasion, he'd been a professor of history and computer science at Harvard. He'd used both those skills to create computer games that had been quite popular. There were, in Simon's opinion, few men who were more intelligent.

"We just deciphered one of the newest languages," Brewer said, taking up the thread again. "It's been quite interesting." He touched the wireless computer he carried.

Instantly, a page from the Goetia manuscript appeared on one of the large wall screens that surrounded the room. The page showed smoke stains and charring around the edges.

"As you can see," Brewer said, "this is one of the pages in the manuscript that suffered the most damage during your recovery efforts."

"It wasn't exactly something we could avoid doing at the time, mate," Nathan said defensively. "What with the demons filling that bloody sanitarium and all. Retrieving that manuscript and saving our lives got to be sticky."

"I quite understand." Brewer smiled reassuringly. "I meant no disrespect. I know you suffered trying circumstances. What I simply wanted to impart was why it has taken us so long to decipher this page."

Simon couldn't help but grin. "You mean, in addition to the fact that it was—until now—an artificial language that no one but the author of that manuscript knew."

Brewer's smile broadened. He looked even more tired because of it. "Exactly. You do grasp what we were up against."

"I do." Simon noticed cots in the corner of the room. He also noticed that both men appeared to have slept in their clothing. "Have you been getting enough rest?"

Brewer and Macomber swapped looks.

"We've been getting what we could," Macomber said. "We're all desperate for whatever knowledge might be contained in this manuscript."

"Get more rest," Simon suggested.

"The work we're doing here," Brewer protested, "is very—"

"—important," Simon interrupted. "I get that. I also know that you two are the only ones capable of breaking that language—*those* languages—down. But if you become ill or exhausted, we lose time."

"We've been getting what rest we could."

"Get more," Simon said, "or I'll station a guard in here to put you to bed at night."

"All right," Brewer said. Macomber nodded as well.

Simon glanced at the screen. "I suppose you know what we're looking at."

"We do." Brewer indicated sections of the strange look-ing text. "We've spent weeks decrypting this language. Whoever wrote this original manuscript was incredibly intelligent. I would have loved to have met him. This sec-tion of the manuscript deals with the Truths."

"What truths?" Simon asked. "The truths about the de-mons?"

"That concept at first stymied us, Lord Cross. We thought it was a generic term as well. The manuscript basically states that it's going to unveil the nature of the Truths. We believe it referred to the fact that demons had been hidden away for so long that no one believed in them anymore."

"The Templar never forgot the demons existed," Na-than said quietly.

"No," Brewer agreed quietly. "But not all of us believed quite so fervently as others." He looked at Simon.

Guilt surged through Simon.

"You weren't the only one that didn't believe, Lord Cross." Sadness darkened Brewer's eyes. "I'd become quite complacent in my university calling, and in design-ing video games. I didn't spend much time thinking about demons outside of the ones I created for the video games. No one could have been more shocked than me when the Hellgate opened."

"But these Truths represent something else," Ma-comber said. "We don't know if they're ideals or if they're physical things."

"Physical things?" Simon asked.

"Yes. They way they're referred to in the manuscript leads us to believe they're physical things." Brewer turned back to the image on the wall and read. "'In order that the demons may be turned back, that the evil tide will be stilled before it is a plague upon the world that cannot be removed, the Truths must be found.'"

As Brewer read, the words formed in English over the manuscript page.

"'This world is protected against the demons,'" Brewer continued. "'When this world first was made open to the demon hordes, so also were the Truths placed here. For the first time, the Light sowed the seeds of destruction among a world that the Well of Midnight would one day threaten.'"

"'The first time,'?" Nathan echoed. "How many worlds have these demons invaded?"

"We don't know," Macomber admitted. "This manuscript says there are hundreds of worlds out there. Not all of them are populated, but many of them are."

"And they've all gone down under the demons," Brewer said.

"What made this world special that these 'Truths' would be placed here?" Simon asked.

"The manuscript mentions there are warriors of Light in this world."

"We believed at first that it referred to the Templar," Macomber said. "But the time period was too far back. The original manuscript was written before the Templar Order was created."

"In that," Brewer said, "we disagree. Although the Templar Order got officially established at a later date, the ideals of what the Templar stood for were around for a long time before that. I believe these Truths were given to those men."

"Then how did they lose something so important?" Nathan asked.

Brewer shook his head.

Macomber did as well. "We don't know. The manuscript has a way of raising more questions as it gives answers."

Simon studied the page. "So we don't know what the Truths are or where they might be found?"

"It's a conundrum," Macomber said. "The manuscript simply says, 'The Truths will be found within, then without. The unlocking of the inside door shall unlock the outside door.'"

"I don't suppose whoever wrote this could have been a little plainer," Nathan said.

"It would have helped," Brewer said. "But at least we know there is some hope out there."

TWENTY-SEVEN

Warren shone his torch around the latest room they had reached. It was directly under the treasure room. They'd gained access to a hidden stairway Lilith had guided them to.

Naomi remained by the oval door at the bottom of the curling stairway they'd followed down into the hollow earth. Judging from the number of steps he'd followed, Warren felt certain they stood at least a hundred feet below the surface. Whoever constructed the room had been serious about keeping it hidden.

"There may be more traps down here," Naomi said.

"I know." Warren glanced at Lilith. She walked at his side.

"When I was buried here," Lilith said, "this room held no traps. The architects who built this place didn't expect anyone to get this far."

"That doesn't mean they didn't put traps in," Naomi said. "You didn't mention that hammer one upstairs."

"I didn't know about that one."

"And what do you mean, when you were buried here?"

Cautiously, Warren moved across the floor. He took time to examine the space with his senses. This time he used his arcane powers as well.

Nothing triggered his alarms. But the wall on the opposite side of the room drew him. The weakening glow of his torch revealed a number of beautiful and deadly images carved into the wall. But in these images, Lilith fought only monsters.

She lifted her hand, and an incandescent blue light glowed brightly enough to fill the room. The return of her powers bothered Warren. For months he'd grown used to her being powerless. She'd *needed* him. Now, potentially, she didn't. The thought that she might try to relieve him of the silver hand he wore lurked in the back of his mind.

"I was a hero to them," Lilith said. "They worshipped me."

"Because you killed the demons that offended you," Naomi said.

"Yes. Until they found out I was one of the demons." Lilith smiled more brightly. "Then they feared me. Of the two, I have to be honest: fear was far stronger. It always is." She turned to Warren and stroked his face with the fingers of her free hand.

Warren felt as if a spider glided across his skin. He struggled to keep from stepping back away from her.

"I miss the fear I was able to inspire in others," Lilith said quietly. Her eyes locked with Warren's. "Do you fear me, Warren?"

He wanted to lie to her and tell her that no, she didn't frighten him. But that wasn't true, and he was certain she'd know if he lied.

"Yes."

Lilith laughed aloud and drew her hand back. "Good," she said. "You should be afraid of me. Very afraid."

"I am," Warren said.

"Good. Fear will keep you alive much longer," Lilith told him. "As long as you and I are in agreement, you will be safe with me."

That wasn't true, and Warren knew it. He was safe only as long as she needed him. The instant that changed, the minute she found someone else to do the things she asked him to do, she'd turn on him.

But not until then, Warren told himself. *Until then, learn and grow strong.*

"Why are we here?" Naomi asked.

Lilith frowned at the woman. "I need you to reclaim my mortal shell. The flesh that I once wore."

"You're not a ghost," Naomi said.

"No." Lilith ran a hand along her lean body. "I am power incarnate, that which lives on after the body has died. If I were dead, I'd be drawn back to the Well of Midnight to be recast and born again. Nothing is ever created or destroyed." She paused and turned to survey the wall. "But I would not lose myself in that place. I am Named. And I will be greater than I am now."

Warren held his torch up and inspected the pictographs on the walls. All of them were of Lilith. Some of them showed her in a large forest area with a man. They stood in water up to their hips, both of them naked. Fish in the water clustered around them. Birds in the air hovered by their heads. Large animals lay along the bank of the river or lake they were in. Small animals occupied the spaces between or hung in the trees.

"Is this—" Warren couldn't bring himself to say it.

"The Garden?" Lilith smiled. "Yes. Before that troublesome woman showed up. Things then were not so bad. It's only after I taught evil to the children that your species became so chaotic and hard to control. I suppose I'm partly to blame for that."

There were other images. Warren thought he remembered some of them from the Bible stories he'd learned while in foster care, but he wasn't sure what the artist intended.

"Your body is in this room?" Naomi asked.

"Yes." Lilith approached one of the walls, studied it a moment, then put a palm against the stone. "This one."

Warren joined her and inspected the wall. "If I'm going to take that down, I'm going to need a sledge."

"There is a sequence . . . here." Lilith pointed, one at a time, to four different stones. None of the stones in the wall appeared to be the same size. They'd been stacked so that they worked together, then mortared between.

Following Lilith's prompted cues, Warren pressed the sequence of stones. Something *clicked* deep within the wall. He stepped back and held the torch high, trying to guess which direction an unpleasant surprise might come from.

Instead, a section of the stone wall jutted out a couple of inches.

"Behind this wall," Lilith said. "You'll have to move it the rest of the way."

"Bring that torch over here," Warren directed Naomi.

Reluctantly, she brought her torch over and shone it against the wall.

Warren pocketed his own torch and slipped the fingers of both hands through the crack in the wall. He expected to pull back bloody stumps. At least, on one hand. He thought the metal one might hold up. He hooked his fingers behind the wall and pulled. The hidden door had to weigh hundreds of pounds and was hard to move. Then, inexorably, it moved by inches at a time and grated across the floor.

When he had the door open enough to shove his head and shoulders through to see if he could enter the space beyond, Warren entered the hidden area. He took out his torch. Everywhere his beam touched, metallic surfaces gleamed back at him. More riches awaited inside.

"Is that what I think it is?" Naomi asked.

"If you're thinking that that's another room filled with treasure, then yes," Warren whispered in awe. He squeezed through.

"Before the invasion," Naomi said, "this would have been a fortune."

A stone sarcophagus occupied the center of the small room. Curiosity pulled Warren to it.

"A sarcophagus isn't something you'd expect to find in the middle of England," Warren said. "Unless you'd brought it in from Egypt."

"It's not a sarcophagus," Lilith said. "It is a preservation chamber."

Warren felt the arcane energy given off by the coffin-shaped box as he walked over to it. The outer casing was carved in the likeness of a beautiful woman.

"Before the Flood drank down the wicked empires that had turned from the Light, in order to end the madness and evil loosed in this world by the demons, men heard stories from those who prepared my burial chambers," Lilith said. "I tried to keep my secrets from them, but stories get told all the same. Some of those who served me fled these lands and became the Egyptians. They remembered this preservation chamber and tried to construct some of their own."

"Because they thought the sarcophagus would return them to life as well," Warren said.

"Yes." Lilith smiled. "Theirs didn't, of course, but they kept believing that one day it would happen."

"You were in the Book Merihim sent me after." Warren looked at her.

"I was."

"How?"

"The Book is an arcane object as well. It allowed me to travel the world without harm."

"It was a safe place."

Lilith nodded. "It was. I needed my body protected, but I had to be out in the world in order to know when the Hellgate opened and to arrange my own return here. Merihim wanted the Book because he'd heard of it, as he'd heard of other objects that ended up in this world through one means or another from all the worlds out there. This place, this world, has a tendency to draw things of power to it. That's why the demons had to conquer it. The Book allowed me to fall into the hands of people I could . . . persuade to my cause."

Warren knew she meant her *use*. He looked at the preservation chamber.

"What do you want me to do?" he asked.

"I must be reunited with my body."

Kneeling, Warren searched the container for hidden releases. He trailed his fingers along the sides. Lilith took him by the hand and guided him.

"Here," she said, and indicated two intricately carved tiles.

"Press?" Warren tried, but nothing happened.

"Not with your hand," Lilith said. "With your mind. These are sealed with arcane energy."

Warren concentrated and ignored the pain in his chest. He felt the arcane energy within him and pushed it through his fingertips.

A hum vibrated through the preservation chamber. A crack suddenly split it and formed a lid. Pale emerald light glowed from within, and jade smoke roiled out of the chamber.

Fearful of what was about to happen, Warren stepped back. He used the arcane energy to build a shield in front of him. Naomi stepped behind him, but she didn't get too close.

The lid rose on its own and flipped open. In the next instant, the body within floated outside. Horror filled Warren when he saw what condition the body was in. Naomi cursed in disgust.

The body was withered, the flesh wrapped tight to the bone. If Lilith had been pretty at one time, none of that showed now. Her face was disfigured, and her black hair was patchy and falling out in clumps. Her sticklike arms lay crossed over her bony chest. Ribs showed beneath the gold sheath dress that looked several sizes too big for her.

"In my time," Lilith said, stepping close to the crypt and peering in with a smile, "I was lovely."

"That time," Naomi whispered, "is *so* over."

The young Lilith started turning translucent. She reached for her desiccated self, but her hand passed through. Grimacing, she turned to Warren.

"I require your help."

"What do you want me to do?" he asked.

"I need to be rejoined with my body so that I can come back to my full strength. You have to be the conduit. Come." Lilith waved to him. "Take my hand."

Reluctantly, Warren told Naomi to hold her torch up, then he shut his off and placed it within his pocket. He crossed the room to Lilith. She reached for him and took him by the hand.

"Hold on to my body," she instructed. "You must be the conduit that connects us."

Stifling the gag reaction that turned his stomach to

acid, Warren took the corpse's hand. He found it surprisingly limber and *warm* to the touch. That made the nausea swirling inside him even stronger.

Lilith cried out in pain. Warren almost let go of the corpse.

"Hold on," Lilith told him. Pain wracked her beautiful face. "This will only last a moment more."

It lasted longer than that. Warren thought later that at least a half hour passed while Lilith screamed as she became one again. But when it was done, the two halves of Lilith existed obviously in one body. Her translucent features surfaced occasionally in the dried-up crust that leathered her skull.

When Lilith was completely gone from sight, Warren concentrated on the body he still had hold of. He felt the power within it. It was so strong that there was no escaping it.

Jade fog poured into the room and obscured the surroundings. As Warren watched, the corpse took a breath, inhaling the fog. In the next moment, the dead woman's eyes fluttered open, and Lilith stared at him from within the desiccated corpse.

"Very good," she whispered dryly. She stopped floating and stood on the ground in her bare feet. "I . . . am still . . . very weak . . . in this . . . form. I cannot . . . allow that." She looked down at her cadaverous body. "You will . . . continue . . . to protect . . . me. I shall . . . reward you."

Warren thought fleetingly of turning and running. Lilith was too frail to pursue him. But as he gazed into her eyes, he felt certain she knew what he was thinking. He also knew that she was far more educated in the use of the arcane forces that he'd only lately started tapping into.

Without help, he wouldn't learn everything he needed to in order to survive quickly enough.

"All right," he said. He felt Naomi's eyes boring into the back of his skull and knew that she was opposed to his decision.

The corpse tried to smile, but her lips resembled dehydrated worms. She appeared more horrid than ever. "Good."

She turned and walked to the wall behind her. Her body was so dry and tight that Warren heard ligaments crack. She touched the wall slowly, arthritically, and a section slid open with a grating crunch.

"Take . . . these," she said, waving toward the contents of the hidden space.

Warren took his torch back out and pointed it into the space. A spear made of black obsidian, a leather robe, and a pendant with the horned head of a demon Warren didn't recognize lay inside. He took all three items out.

"The coat . . . provides protection," Lilith said, "from arcane forces . . . and weapons. The pendant . . . is a foci . . . that will enable . . . you to use . . . the powers that you . . . command . . . with greater efficiency. And the . . . spear . . . can pierce . . . demon hide . . . like it was . . . tissue . . . despite physical . . . or arcane defenses. Worse than that, it will pull them into the spear and make it even stronger."

Warren took off his other coat and pulled the robe on. He immediately felt more protection from the bitter cold that filled the underground structure. But he didn't care for the robe's appearance at all. He wished it looked more stylish, like a long overcoat.

Almost immediately, the coat altered its look, becoming a dark trench coat.

"It responds . . . to your wishes," Lilith said. "So . . . does . . . the fit."

Now that he thought about it, Warren was certain he wasn't looking for a good fit. He was looking for something that would protect him. But the fit had been so good, he hadn't even marveled as its changing to suit him there as well.

"The time . . . has come . . . for us . . . to return . . . to the city," Lilith went on. "There is . . . much . . . we have left . . . to do."

Warren wasn't looking forward to the long walk.

"We aren't . . . walking," Lilith said. "I would . . . rather get there . . . sooner."

"I'm all for that," Warren said.

Guttural noises cascaded through Lilith's throat. Her voice sounded like rusty nails being pulled from a two-by-four. When she finished, she gestured, and a glowing, six-foot scarlet oval irised open in midair. It looked like a glowering lizard's eye, but Warren felt the power it contained.

"What's that?" Naomi asked.

"A portal," Lilith wheezed in her rusty voice. "It will . . . transport us . . . back to London. But we . . . must . . . be careful. Power this . . . strong . . . can be . . . sensed . . . by demons. They will . . . rush to it."

"If we walked back," Warren reasoned, "we could get back inside the city with no one the wiser."

"Walking back means trying to pass by that village again," Naomi said. "The one where you raised all their dead into your own private army? I don't think they'll just let you pass."

Warren suspected that was true.

"Not only that," she continued, "but Miss Creaky Bones here isn't up for running for our lives if it comes to that."

Lilith glowered at Naomi. "You presume . . . too much, woman."

Warren stepped protectively in front of Naomi but didn't say anything.

With a snarl, Lilith whipped her glower to Warren. "You should . . . pick your friends . . . more wisely . . . in the future."

"I don't think any of us had a real choice," Warren replied. "Until something better comes along, we're going to make do."

Lilith held his gaze for a moment, then she nodded. "Until . . . such time." Then she turned and slowly strode into the portal.

Warren waited to see if there were going to be any ill effects, but Lilith simply vanished. He took a deep breath and started forward.

Naomi pulled him back.

"What?" he asked.

"How do you know she's not going to put us in the demon world?"

"Because I don't think that's where she wants to be." Warren pointed at the wavering oval. "And if we don't hurry, that may close. Like you said, it's a long walk back to London."

"Maybe it's worth it. To be rid of her, I mean." Her eyes held Warren's. "She doesn't mean you any good, no matter what you think."

"I never once thought that." Warren gripped the obsidian spear more tightly. He felt the vibrant arcane energy in it, and it only made him want more. "I can learn from her for now. I learned some things from Merihim."

"You're not safe with them."

"I'm not any safer with the Cabalists. None of them trust me."

"I do."

Warren looked at her and felt sadness at the untruth in her words. But he didn't say anything. He wished Naomi did, but he didn't blame her for being unable.

"I could," Naomi amended. "Given time."

"You'll trust me more," he replied in a flat voice, "when I know more. That's how this has always worked with you. Now, make up your mind. I'm going." He held the spear in one hand and stepped into the oval.

Intense heat blazed through Warren. He tried to scream in agony, but he didn't know if he'd managed that. Electricity vibrated and jerked through his body and he felt his limbs twitching spastically.

However, the spear remained cool in his hand. He focused on it and used it as his anchor. Red light dawned around him, only slightly paler than the oval. In the light, he saw demonic faces stretched and squashed and turned inside out. He smelled their foul breath and heard the threats they made and their cruel laughter.

He searched for Lilith and Naomi, but he found neither of them. For a time, he felt lost. Then the portal suddenly ended, and he was vomited out into free fall.

Off balance, Warren tried to remain on his feet and failed. He viewed a spinning panorama of a city street covered over with wrecked, burned-out hulks that had once been vehicles. Then the rough asphalt bit into the palms of his hands. The impact against the ground, then against the alley wall, knocked the breath from him and caused the wounds on his chest to hurt again.

Only a few feet away, Lilith got to her feet in a painful and disjointed way that held no grace or strength. Warren used the obsidian spear as a brace to force himself to his feet. A moment later, Naomi materialized in midair and tumbled to the ground.

A handful of armed ragged men and women hunkered fearfully in the alley. All of them pointed their weapons at Warren.

"Demon lover!" one man accused in a harsh voice. He squeezed the trigger of his pistol, and the sharp report filled the alley.

Warren barely had time to get his shield up. The bullet froze in midair less than a foot in front of his face, then dropped to the ground. Scared and angry, Warren gathered the arcane energy inside him and *pushed* at the man. Invisible force slapped into the man and knocked him backward through a pile of debris. When he stopped moving, no life remained within him.

"Run!" one of the women yelled. They ran, and Warren gratefully let them. He didn't relish killing when he didn't have to.

"You should have killed them all," Lilith said.

"There was no need."

"It would have served them right."

"We scared them."

Lilith shook her head. "They scared themselves. We just became targets of convenience for them."

"Let's get home," he suggested. "I want to sleep in a warm, dry bed for a change."

"There is much to do," Lilith said. "Now that I have returned, some of the Dark Wills will hunt me."

"I've got good defenses at my house. You know that. You helped me construct them."

TWENTY-EIGHT

Leah struggled between nightmares and wakefulness. Drug-induced fatigue wrapped her brain in layers of thick cotton that kept the world away. She thought she heard the bleating of hospital machinery, but she wasn't sure. Some distant part of her knew that she should hear such things.

"Breathe," Simon said.

Some of the anxiety that the nightmares had left with her disappeared. Simon was there, just as he'd promised. If he'd asked, she would have told him that she never doubted him for an instant. But she had.

"Deep breaths," he told her. "Blow out. You've got to get the rest of the anesthetic out of your lungs."

"Am I going to be in pain?" she mumbled. "Because if I'm going to be in pain, that whole waking up thing doesn't sound so brill."

Simon chuckled. "No pain. I promise. The physician who talked to me said you might experience headaches for a few days till your body adjusts, but nothing truly horrible."

Leah hoped not. It was one thing for her to fraternize with a confirmed risk, but it would be another for her to admit she'd had surgery done by them. But to be able to see again . . .

"How did it go?" she asked. "Was the operation successful?"

"Everything went swimmingly, I'm told."

"Do I still look human?"

"Yes."

Leah hesitated. "Can I see? Am I not still blind?"

"Open your eyes."

She wanted to, but she was afraid. It bothered her that she was afraid. Fear was one of the first things she'd learned to control, and to use. She knotted her hands into fists.

Simon wrapped her right fist in his big hand. "Just open your eyes," he told her.

Swallowing hard, Leah told herself it wouldn't matter if she was still blind. Or if her vision wasn't as good as she'd been promised it would be. She'd had nothing to lose and everything to gain.

She opened her eyes. Instantly, she noticed how bright the recovery room was. She raised a hand to block the light from her eyes.

"It's bright in here," she said.

"To both eyes?"

Leah closed one eye, then the other. She saw through them both. Smiling but still brain-fogged from the anesthetic, she turned to Simon. "I can see," she whispered. "I can really see."

"Good," he said, smiling back. "The next step is going to be getting you back onto your feet."

Simon stared at the glowing energy field on the lab tabletop. It was roughly oval, about eighteen inches across at its widest point.

"Tell me what I'm looking at," he said.

"That's an energy field capable of keeping demons away," Macomber replied. "The Goetia manuscript referred to it as a . . . Node. It was the most apt name we could agree on."

"This thing keeps demons away?" Nathan leaned on the table and studied the energy field.

"In theory at least," Brewer said. "Reality's yet to be tried."

"If we can get this energy field under control," Macomber said, "we can set up areas that the demons won't be able to invade."

"They'd have to be awfully short people," Nathan said dryly.

"This is just a prototype," Brewer retorted. "Once we understand the forces we're dealing with, we can build it bigger."

"How does it work?"

Macomber shook his head. "We believe that it sets up a harmonic dissonance."

"Sound waves?" Simon asked.

"Yes," Brewer replied. "A combination of lasers, masers, and arcane energy create the sound waves." He shook his head. "I have to be honest, Lord Cross, even as technically advanced as the Templar are, we were barely able to create this thing. We're not certain it even functions properly."

"You say it creates a harmonic," Nathan said.

"That's correct."

"I can't hear or feel anything."

Simon couldn't, either. He tapped into his suit's audio field and heard a high-pitched whine that threatened to give him a splitting headache almost immediately. He broke the connection.

"You're not supposed to hear anything," Brewer said. "You're human."

"Only demons can hear this?"

Brewer nodded. "Without aid, yes. We've been able to detect the sound range on other equipment."

"So it's like a dog whistle? Hurts the demons' ears?"

"According to the manuscript," Macomber said, "this field does much more than that." He tapped the computer keyboard and brought up a new image on the wall.

Simon studied the image and saw a monstrous demon take shape. The giant creature in the picture confronted a glowing shield. Half of its arm had been melted away. "I don't remember seeing this in those pages." He'd studied the manuscript as well.

"The picture was encrypted in the manuscript," Brewer said. "Professor Macomber found it."

"I wouldn't have found it if you hadn't caught on to the code."

Brewer shrugged modestly, but he stood up a little straighter. "It was a joint effort. And a lot of work. The code was set up to emulate the points on a graph, which—when connected—gave us this image. Quite ingenious, actually."

"What's happening to the demon?" Simon asked.

"As near as we can figure it," Macomber said, "this harmonic can be adjusted not only to defend an area and establish a defensive perimeter but also can be used as a weapon. Contact with the Node causes the demons to discorporate on a cellular level."

"Or transports them elsewhere," Brewer said. "Until we see it actually function, we're not going to know." He shrugged. "It's possible we won't know then."

"Is it portable?"

"No," Macomber said. "You were thinking of using it as a tactical weapon?"

Simon nodded.

"A demon death ray would be a very brill thing," Nathan said.

"When a Node is built," Brewer said, "like this one, it locks into the earth's electromagnetic fields. The harmonic projection depends on the stability of that field. If you move this Node"—he reached through the lights and moved the Node slightly, and the bright energy field disappeared—"even slightly, you will lose it."

"So when you get to the point that you could build a field big enough to protect people or a structure," Nathan said, "you're going to have to make sure the Node is settled in permanently."

"Yes," Macomber said. "And it can't just be one Node. In order to protect something as large as a building, it will necessitate several Nodes working together to create a field large enough to handle the demons."

"How long before you can create a Node that I can take out and field test?" Simon asked.

Brewer and Macomber looked at each other. "A few days. Surely no more than that."

"All right. Let me know when it's ready. We need to know where we stand with this before we spend any more time on it."

Three days later, the doctor released Leah from the hospital. She was glad of that because lying abed as a patient had never been easy for her. Simon visited her when possible, but his visits were infrequent and short. And he always seemed distracted. She didn't fault him for that, though. She knew he had his hands full trying to take care of his Templar and those they'd sworn to protect.

Being ambulatory again meant she could spend more of the day with him. But not all of it. There were still a lot of things that he did without her. That was frustrating, but she understood it. If he'd been the only one at risk, she felt that he would have trusted her. The other Templar wouldn't have been quite so generous, though.

In the mornings, they had breakfast together and Simon made the rounds of the complex. Then they had lunch, which was generally interrupted by someone who needed information or permission. After that, they separated. Leah worked with the rehab teams to get her eye/hand coordination and depth perception back in sync.

One of the interesting conundrums of having the replacement eye was that it became her dominant eye. Shifting her reactions to that eye took hard work and diligence, but it came quickly.

In the evenings, Leah met up with Simon as he drilled and worked with the young Templar. She didn't take part in the sword classes because she had no urge to take up the sword. The Agency believed in guns, the bigger the better, and she was trained on all of those. While Simon put his young students through their paces, Leah worked out, regaining strength she'd lost after her initial injury and the follow-up surgery.

Afterward, she and Simon worked on martial arts forms and ran through self-defense sparring matches. Being physical with him felt good and right. He didn't hold back. He used his size and strength against her, and she knew that he went at her with everything he had because the demons were even bigger than he was. If she couldn't defend herself against him, she wouldn't be able to hold her own against a demon.

She got her shots in because she was quick and creative. But time after time, Simon's prowess in close was too much for her to handle.

"I'm much better at a distance," she said during one of their rest sessions. "Give me a rifle and you wouldn't stand a chance."

Simon grinned at her and wiped the back of his neck with a towel. "That depends on whether or not you saw me coming."

"I'd see you," Leah told him. "A big, heavy-footed oaf like you would be easy to spot."

"'An oaf,' is it?"

"You heard me."

"When we get back on the mat," Simon promised, "we'll see who's the oaf."

Leah toweled off for a moment. It felt good to concentrate on just the physical exertion for a while. When she sparred with Simon, she had no room in her mind for any thoughts other than survival and getting as many shots in on him as she could.

Now, however, she couldn't help but think about the assignment she'd been tasked to do. She hated that it was going to interrupt and potentially spoil the friendship that they'd shared.

"Have you been in contact with the other Templar?" she asked.

Simon looked at her. Pain and wariness showed in his eyes. He hung his towel around his neck and kept hold of it with both fists.

"No," he answered. "Not since you and the others rescued me."

Leah tried to go carefully. "As you know, I'm with an organization myself."

"I do. Military or spook in origin, I should assume."

Leah didn't answer, not knowing what to say. Trying to deny it wouldn't endear her to Simon, who was usually painfully point-blank honest, and unable to admit it because all of her training had been geared toward her *not* telling anything about the service. She decided to go with honesty even though she was uncomfortable with that.

"Yes," she said.

TWENTY-NINE

I didn't expect you'd admit that," Simon said.

"If I didn't, one of us would have been the fool. I can't tell you any more about it." Leah regretted that, but she had her own promises to keep.

"I'm fine with that," Simon said. "You and your mysterious benefactors have been helpful to us in the past. As long as what you know about us doesn't harm us, we're willing to exchange information."

"The people I work for," Leah said softly and slowly, "would like to be more helpful."

Simon crossed his arms and drew himself up to his full, imposing height. "How helpful?"

"Your situation here isn't good, Simon," Leah stated blatantly. "The demons are hunting you out this far, and you're facing a supply shortage."

"Yes."

"The Templar Underground, from what we know of them and their stockpiles—"

"And you're the one that brought your people most of that information," Simon said.

"I did." Leah refused to feel guilty about the subterfuge she'd used to get into the Templar Underground. "As I was saying, from what we know of them, they have enough food and medicine to take care of your people here."

"They're not willing to take on extra mouths. I tried that already."

"Maybe you can't change them," Leah said. "But maybe you can change who's leading them."

His eyes flashed and he looked at her more squarely. "I'm not going to challenge anyone for the leadership of the Templar, Leah," he stated softly. "So whoever's putting those ideas into your head is wasting his or her time. And yours."

"Not challenge anyone there," Leah said. "Simply . . . let the Templar know that you want back in."

"I don't."

"They would let you come back."

Simon hesitated. "How would you know that?"

"Because this is what we do."

He shook his head. "If you ask me, that's a nasty business to get into."

That stung a little. Leah chose not to be defensive. Her job contained bad elements. "Perhaps. But what we do has its uses. Secrets save lives."

"They also claim them," Simon said.

"We have people around the Templar," Leah said. "No one within the Underground, mind you, but a few on the periphery of their operations."

"They don't have any operations outside the Underground."

"No, but they do—upon occasion—venture forth to save someone or just to explore how badly things have gone." Leah smiled at him crookedly. "And we have a few friends among the Templar Underground. Some of the Templar used to be in my line of work."

"I can see that. But they would still have definite lines of allegiance."

"Really?" Leah stared into his eyes, knowing her next statement was risky. "Like the allegiance you had toward the Templar, Simon?"

Simon folded his arms. For a moment she thought he was going to walk away.

"I'm different," he said brusquely. "I broke with Templar ways a long time ago."

"Really? Is that why you're here, then, risking your life to save others?"

Simon hesitated. "My father would have wanted—"

"You're not here because of your father, Simon. You don't risk the things you do because of him. You're here because Lord Thomas Cross raised a fine son and guided him in the ways of being a Templar."

"I'm not that good."

"The other Templar here aren't following you because they want to help you with your guilt over your father, Simon."

Angry spots of color blossomed on his face.

Leah knew she'd come perilously close to hurting him or offending him. "They believe in what you're doing. That's why they came out of the Underground to risk their lives with you. You're doing everything they believe they should be doing." She paused. "They believe in you."

"That's a lot of responsibility."

"Then give it away."

"I've offered."

"And no one's accepted."

Simon was quiet for a moment. "No."

Leah remained silent for a time to let his answer sink into his mind. "Not only do you bring fugitives here, Simon, but more Templar join you as well. This operation you've set into play grows larger than you expected, and you're not able to hand off the survivors like you believed you would."

"I know."

Leah took a deep breath. "One of the people I work with has the ear of Jessica Sumerisle."

"She's just a child."

"And the heir to the leadership of the Templar. Not only that, but this is no time for children. I saw you training children to fight and kill earlier this evening."

Simon's voice took on an edge. "I taught them to survive."

"Yes, and part of that involves fighting and killing. Otherwise they're going to die without hope, afraid, and alone."

Simon didn't argue.

"Just as those children are no longer children because this world can't allow them their childhood, Jessica Sumerisle has grown up as well. She doesn't have the power she will one day have because her uncle runs things at the moment, but she does have some power. She has enough to bring you back into the Templar."

"There's a reason I left them. I don't want to have to fight their mind-set again. I can't wage a war with two fronts."

"I know. But more and more of them are drawn to your view of things. They know people still survive in London. Fewer and fewer each day, but there are survivors."

"What about the people you work with?" Simon asked. "Do they believe in saving those survivors as well?"

"We're not set up as the Templar are," Leah said. "We don't have the resources, manpower, or space to handle search-and-rescue operations. But we believe in what you're trying to do."

"Sounds like another way of shifting responsibility, if you ask me."

Leah couldn't keep all her anger from her voice then. "No. It's recognition of fact. You don't realize how far my organization has come just to make the offer to use what influence it has to help you and these people here. We weren't organized to save lives, Simon. We were organized to take the lives of our enemies. We've been doing that. Now, they know they're not going to be able to get rid of the demons on their own. That's been a very humbling experience, trust me."

"It has been for all of us." Simon looked away for a moment as if thinking something over. Then he met her gaze again. "There's something else I'm working on, though. Something that may offer more respite than trying to crowd all of these people into the Templar Underground."

Interest surged in Leah, and she knew what he had to be referring to. "You found something in the Goetia manuscript, didn't you?"

"Yes."

"What?"

Simon shook his head. "I can't discuss it too much at this point."

Angry frustration sloshed inside Leah. He didn't trust her. That much was evident. She pulled in a deep breath and let it out.

You can't blame him, she thought. *You wouldn't trust you, either.*

"I wish you luck with it," Leah said.

"If it works," he said, "we'll all benefit in the end."

If any other person told Leah that, she would have felt certain she was being patronized. But this was Simon Cross, and she knew him well enough to know that he wouldn't lie to her or tell her something just because he thought that's what she wanted to hear.

"And if I decide I want to talk to the Templar again," he said, "I'll let you know."

She forced a smile she didn't feel, because she wasn't

as truthful by nature as he was, and said, "Care for a re-
match?"

Simon tossed the towel aside. "Sure."

Leah wasn't restricted to the redoubt in any way. Simon
gave her the full run of the complex, except for secure
areas. She exercised and did the rehab treatment to get
her eye/hand coordination back, exceeding the surgeon's
expectations.

She still stared in the mirror in the mornings and tried
to tell the difference between the eyes and couldn't. In a
way, that was frustrating because she felt she ought to be
able to tell an artificial construct from her own flesh and
blood. Even more interesting, she couldn't remember the
ragged hole she'd seen in her face a few days after her first
surgery.

Old habits wouldn't die, though, and her curiosity
about whatever Simon had learned from the Goetia manuscript chafed her. She knew his habits inside the redoubt.
When he broke them and left, he even politely told her
that he'd be gone for a few days and welcomed her to stay
as long as she liked.

After he'd gone, she pulled her armor on, then some
winter clothes on over that, broke her rifle down so she
could lash it to her back under the winter coat, and filched
a few supplies from the cafeteria. When Simon had a half-
hour start, she set out in pursuit.

"Wait."

When she heard the woman's voice directed at her,
Leah thought her intended subterfuge had been seen
through. She calmed herself and turned around.

The woman was one of the Templar. Fiery-haired and
full-figured, looking like an Olympic athlete in her armor,

the woman stood half a head taller than Leah. Part of that height difference was the boots, but not much.

"We haven't gotten to speak," the woman said.

"I've seen you," Leah said. "In the dojo."

"My name is Kyra."

"Pleased to meet you, Kyra." Leah shoved her hand out. "I'm—"

"I know who you are."

At the unfriendly tone, Leah drew her hand back. She waited.

"No one here blames you for coming to Simon to have your eye repaired," Kyra said.

"Actually," Leah said, "I hadn't been aware that was something that could be done."

"They worry because you seem to know more about the Templar than you should."

Leah folded her arms. "What's that supposed to mean?"

"No one here trusts you."

"Simon does." Even as she said that, though, Leah felt guilty, since she planned to go spy on him. That wasn't very trustworthy behavior on her part.

"Simon is an innocent to a large degree," Kyra snapped. "Someone like you—"

"Like me?"

"A woman."

"Ah." Leah nodded. She understood a little more then. Jealousy was attached to the woman's words. It was a tribal response. Leah represented an outsider female threatening to cut one of the males from the group.

"For all that Simon is," Kyra said, "he can be played a fool by someone like you."

"I suppose I should feel flattered," Leah replied coldly. "But somehow I don't. You could be suggesting that I'm overly attractive, or that Simon is dense. Frankly, I don't think he'd be flattered, either."

"This isn't flattery. I'm suggesting that maybe when you leave this time—*soon*—that you shouldn't come back here."

While Leah tried to figure out how to respond to that, Kyra turned and walked away. Beyond her, three other Templar—all women—lounged in the hallway and made it apparent they supported Kyra. Feeling angry and disrespected, Leah almost headed into the middle of them just for spite. Even three on one, and them in Templar armor, Leah thought she might make a good stand.

It's not worth it, she told herself. *You don't need the drama.* But she didn't like being told what to do. She never had. Without a word, she turned and headed for the door.

THIRTY

B it of baiting the bull, don't you think?"

Simon glanced over at Nathan and barely saw him against the stone wall of the underground tube. They were near Charing Cross, away from the Templar Underground. In addition to that, one of the Templar redoubt scavenging crews had reported a group of survivors had settled into the area. If they could recover those people and guide them to safety, they were going to do that.

"If there was another way to do it, we would," Simon replied. He slammed his armored palm down on the steel stake he held in his other hand. Metal struck metal with the sound of an explosion. Sparks spat out from the contact. The stake drove down into the ground several inches.

Nathan leaned down and attached the laser projector Macomber and Brewer had built in the lab. It was slightly smaller than Simon's armored fist, built with lenses and wiring that Simon didn't quite understand even after repeated explanations. The composite blue polymer was teardrop-shaped and high-impact resistant. Nathan cupped the device for a moment.

"I'm ready to bring Number Three online, mate," Nathan said.

"Go ahead," Quincy Hartsell replied. "We're ready." The Templar knelt nearby at a control box that had come with the projectors. The control box was about the size of a slim briefcase but was crowded with electronics.

Nathan fired an electric current through his armor that activated the field projector. Two amber lights winked to life, one after the other, then turned green.

"We're go here," Nathan said.

"And go here," Quincy said.

"Four is set," Danielle called from across the tunnel.

"Bringing Four online." Quincy tapped on the keyboard. "Reading Four. Now I'm going to initiate the recognition sequence."

While he stood there, Simon cycled through the button cams they'd strung along the tube. The armor AI was set to warn him of the approach of anyone not scanned into the Templar security, but maintaining constant visual watch over the area was old habit.

Debris filled the dark tube. The last passenger trains had traveled the tracks over four years ago when the Hellgate opened. Wrecked train cars piled like child's toys less than a mile from their present position. Judging from all the skeletons in the cars, few must have survived the wrecks back then.

A low-pitched hum filled the tunnel. Gradually, it grew louder and more piercing. Simon's suit dampened the audio, then the noise went away. The green lights on the projectors grew brighter.

"Phasing harmonics," Quincy announced.

A few seconds later, purple-tinted haze spread across the distance between the poles they'd set up. Then it cleared and gradually disappeared altogether.

"Is it working?" Nathan asked.

"Step into it, mate," Quincy suggested. "If it zaps you, I'll know I've got it calibrated wrong."

"I don't think so."

From the other side of the tunnel, Danielle walked into the cube of light. Her armor sparkled just for a moment, but nothing happened after that.

"Well, we know that it won't harm humans," she said. The nervousness in her voice was barely detectable.

"Doesn't mean it's unfriendly to demons," Nathan said.

"There's only one way to discover that." Simon pounded the stake again and knocked it into the ground so far that none of it projected. The stake was built thick at the piercing end, then thin at the rear of the shaft so the projector was protected by the profile. He reached into the nearby duffel bag and brought out a canister of foam-crete.

When he sprayed the contents into the hole and they interacted with the air, a dirty gray silicon plug formed and filled the hole. After a moment, when the camouflage particles sparked into life to change the gray-white color, it was almost indistinguishable from the original floor. He tossed the can to Danielle, and she did the same thing to the stake she'd knocked into the ground.

Once all four stakes were properly buried, Simon said, "Recalibrate the field again. Make sure we didn't tear anything up."

Quincy went through the process again. The purple cube came to life once more, then faded. Again Danielle stepped through the field and into the cube without a problem.

"I have to admit, mate," Nathan said quietly, "it doesn't give me much confidence watching her walk through it so easily. Could be the demons will walk through it just like it was a warm spring rain."

"There's only one way to find out." Simon reached over

his shoulder and took out his sword and shield. He turned and started down the long tube tunnel.

After Simon and the others had gone, Leah eased out of the shadows of the tube station's waiting area. Finding the Templar hadn't been hard. Almost no humans headed into London these days, and the tracks left by the armored suits had been simple to follow. The hardest part was to follow without being seen.

On the tube platform, she gazed at the area where the Templar had worked. She'd gathered from their conversation that the stakes and electronics they'd driven into the ground were some kind of demon deterrent, but she had no idea what it was.

Kneeling, she opened the command console that one of the Templar had used. She captured images with the ocular over her right eye and stored them on the gel-drive hidden in the subcutaneous tissue of her left thigh. As she worked, she told herself that the guilt she felt was misplaced. She had a duty to her organization. Those men and women had given their life's blood to keep London safe for a long time before the Templar admitted they even existed, in the show of force at St. Paul's.

Her comm-link chirped for attention.

Leah straightened as she answered.

"Black Orchid, this is Nightingale. Do you copy?"

"Black Orchid copies." Nightingale was Lyra Darius. Leah had contacted the woman as soon as she'd left the Templar redoubt.

"Do you know what this device is that we're looking at?"

"No." Frustration chafed at Leah. "If I'd known, I would have told you earlier." She took a deep breath. "Did you get anything from the audibles I captured?" She'd aimed a shotgun microphone concealed in a fingertip at the Templar in hopes of picking up conversation.

"We didn't. Their helmets and suits didn't broadcast any of their conversations. If you can, stay on-site there and see if you can get any more information."

"I will. But that's increasing the risk here."

"I doubt that the young lord would do much to you even if he did find you out. I get the impression that he's quite taken with you."

Under the armored faceplate, Leah's face reddened. "I think you're reading more into it than what is there."

"We'll see. Have a care down there, Black Orchid. We want you to come back to us."

"I will." Leah closed the case and stood. She switched her view in her ocular through the visible light spectrum. For a few seconds, she thought she could make out the cube of light being projected.

Heart at the back of her throat, Leah stepped forward. Her suit's sensors picked up vague traces of the laser light, but not enough to set off any alarms. According to the seismograph built into her armor, there were sonics involved as well.

She studied the configuration of the cube, but it offered no clue as to what she dealt with. A moment later, her sensors picked up the sound of demons growling down the tube in the direction the Templar had gone.

She freed her rifle and almost ran down the tunnel. Then she realized the demonic baying and wild screams came closer. They raced back up the tunnel.

Outrunning the Stalkers wasn't always possible. The demons were incredibly fast. Not only that, they could also run along the sides of the tunnel as well as the ceiling, evading the tumbled-down wreckage. The Templar had to negotiate the overturned train cars and debris that had choked the tunnel.

"I hate running from these things," Nathan growled, then cursed as he stumbled over loose rock and went down. He caught himself on his off-hand and pushed himself back up. By that time, though, one of the Stalkers had launched itself from the ceiling. The Stalker sailed toward Nathan like an arrow.

After a quick twist to set himself, Simon said, "Boot anchors." He felt them chug into the stone floor as he shoved his shield out to protect Nathan's back. The Stalker smashed into the shield, rolled away, and yelped in displeasure.

Another Stalker sprang from the wall on the left and slammed into Simon with enough force to rip his left boot anchor free of the concrete. Unable to bring his sword into play with the demon in his face, Simon smashed his doubled fist into the Stalker's open and slavering maw. Teeth shattered under the impact. Nearly unconscious, the demon staggered away.

The Stalkers hurled themselves at Simon then, giving him no quarter as they swarmed him. Buried by sheer numbers, he went down. The suit's AI warned him about the diminished defenses.

Nathan, Quincy, and Danielle stepped in and hammered the Stalkers back with their swords. They used their shields to hold back other Stalkers. When there was a break in the attack, the Templar turned as one and fled back up the tunnel.

"You better hope that Node works," Danielle said. "If it doesn't we're going to have a long fight on our hands."

"I know." Simon ran, eyes forward as he used the suit's 360-degree view to spot an attacking Stalker leaping from overhead. Pivoting slightly, he slammed the sword hilt against the demon's brow. Bone gave way with a loud *crack!* The Stalker dropped to the ground and lay twitching.

The tunnel turned gently to the right. A quick check of the map inside his helmet showed that they were only seventeen yards from the Node. Even with the amplified night vision possible due to the helmet, he barely made out the environment.

As he ran through the first side of the cube, Simon experienced a brief thrill of fear. He caught himself holding his breath, expecting the worst. Then he was through. The Stalkers were on his heels, only inches back.

The demons reached the protective Node less than a second after he crossed the threshold. With the 360-degree view, Simon watched as the first eight or nine Stalkers passed through the invisible wall.

Bright purple sparks suddenly flared to life and ignited into deep lavender conflagrations that consumed the demons. Stalkers that had thrown themselves hard enough to penetrate the wall completely also turned to ash completely. Other Stalkers that didn't quite make the distance found themselves only partially incinerated, but since the part that was harmed was generally the head, they died on the spot. A few Stalkers got knocked into the protected area by the demons behind them.

"Bloody brill!" Nathan exclaimed. He stood nearby with his sword and shield raised, obviously not trusting the barrier to stop all the Stalkers. "I didn't expect it to work as well as all that!"

Simon silently agreed.

The surviving Stalkers drew back and growled in confusion and fear. A couple pawed at the barrier and succeeded only in amputating part or all of a paw.

"What about the power source?" Simon asked. With

the rate that the field had disposed of demons, it had to have expended a lot of energy.

"The power levels dipped for a moment," Quincy said. "But they came back up. Macomber and Brewer said the field should feed on the inherent arcane energy of the demons it destroys. It's a self-contained system."

"Power supply isn't as big a problem as you thought we'd have, is it?" Danielle asked.

"No," Simon answered.

"You can't get much better than self-perpetuating."

"I know." The redoubt didn't need any more stress on their meager resources. As necessary as the protective field was, powering a huge drain might have come close to breaking the fragile balance they kept. No only that, but supplying that protective field also meant it would be vulnerable to attack.

On the other side of the barrier, the Stalkers paced restlessly. They barked and yelped, and Simon trusted the barrier.

"If Macomber and Brewer can figure out how to enlarge the field, we'll be able to protect the redoubt," Nathan said.

"They'll get it," Simon said. "It's just a matter of time." For the first time since the invasion began, he felt real hope about the outcome of things.

THIRTY-ONE

Leah waited until Simon and the Templar were gone, then she crossed the tube platform and dropped into the tunnel. The patches that had sealed the devices into the ground hadn't quite assumed the same temperature of the floor around them. They were visible in her thermographic vision.

She slipped the combat fighting knife from her right shin and knelt down. Hesitation held her up for a moment.

"Black Orchid," Lyra Darius said. "Are you experiencing difficulties?"

Yes, Leah wanted to answer. *Simon trusted me.*

Except in this, she told herself. *And this is something that could change the face of this war.*

"Black Orchid, do you copy?"

"Black Orchid copies," Leah responded. "I'm worried I'm going to damage the device."

"If you're not certain of your abilities, I can get an extraction team there."

The only drawback to that was the fact that the Templar could return for the devices at any time, or that the devices might be uncovered by demons. Some of the demons were quite ingenious.

"No," Leah said. "If these are to be gotten, now is the time." She drove the knife blade into the patch and worked carefully. As she unearthed the device, she set her ocular to capture images automatically and send them to the base.

After she finished the first one, she moved to the second. However, she noticed a still, silent form standing in the shadows near the tube platform doorway. Recognizing the blue and silver armor, she knew exactly who it was. Ashamed and angry at the same time, she turned to look at Simon Cross.

"Do you need help?" he asked in a quiet voice.

Leah stood, but she didn't know what to say. "I thought you'd gone."

He stood with his arms crossed. "I knew you were here. Somewhere. I figured if it looked like we left that you'd show up."

"How did you know?"

"I was told you'd escaped the redoubt."

"'Escaped' implies that I was a prisoner. You told me that I was free to come and go."

"You were. That's why no one there tried to stop you from leaving. You chose to 'escape' when you slipped away instead of merely informing anyone you were leaving."

Leah felt foolish. "I was seen?"

"Yes."

"Black Orchid, do you need help?" Lyra asked.

A movement of Leah's chin muted the outside broadcast so she was heard only inside her armored mask. "No. By the time anyone could get here, this will have played out." She didn't want a confrontation between the Agency and the Templar. Things were bad enough. "Let me handle this."

"We're closer than you might think."

That angered Leah. Not only had she been following Simon, but evidently Lyra Darius had assigned others to follow the Templar—or her—as well.

"Hold them back," Leah directed. "Give me some time to work on this."

"Are we going to have company?" Simon didn't appear worried about the prospect. Of course, that was only through reading his body language. Leah couldn't see a bloody thing through the helmet's faceshield.

"No," Leah answered. "But they aren't far away."

"So the offer to help me gain influence among the other Templar was . . . what? A subterfuge?"

"No. It's real."

"I see." His cold, impersonal response hurt her.

Leah hated talking to him this way. The masks they wore disguised everything about them. They shielded every human emotion as well as their appearance, and the device-modulated voices they projected were as cold as ice.

"There's just not a lot of trust on your part," he continued.

It's not me, Leah wanted to tell him. *It's the Agency. It's just the way I work.*

"That trust seems to have broken down both ways, Lord Cross." Leah held the device out in her hand.

"Don't," Lyra admonished. "He could destroy that."

Leah didn't worry about that. If Simon hadn't wanted her to have the device, he would have destroyed it before now. Or at least tried to. She wasn't going to discount her own ability to get away.

"What are you talking about?" Simon asked.

"You didn't tell me about this."

"Until today, there wasn't anything to tell."

"You have a means of destroying the demons with relative ease."

"We have a means of defending against them. This Node—this field—isn't portable. Once it's set into place, it has to remain there."

"It's an advantage that you kept from us."

For a moment Simon didn't speak. His faceplate remained blank and unyielding. "It didn't become an advantage till it worked a few minutes ago. Until that time, it was just a hope."

"This changes things. A lot."

"In areas, perhaps. But this defense is only a last resort. If we use it—if we're *forced* to use it—that means the demons have found us. We can wall ourselves away from them, but they can still lay siege to wherever we've holed up. You've seen for yourself how desperate we've already become. And that's with our being able to hunt on a regular basis. Can you imagine what it would be like if we couldn't take deer? Or scavenge for food in the city?"

Leah could. While she'd been in the redoubt, she had imagined that. Simon had taken on a Herculean task in providing for his community of survivors.

"And I didn't keep this from you," Simon went on. "I'm quite certain that the copy of the Goetia manuscript you gave me wasn't the only copy that was made. Especially not after seeing you in action."

The loathing in his voice came through in his words despite the mechanical quality of the suit's speakers. His accusation—especially in light of the truth of it—cut deeply. The Agency wasn't a trusting lot.

"You had access to as much information as I had," Simon said.

"No," Leah said coldly. "You have all the Templar knowledge that's been gathered for hundreds of years."

"We paid for that knowledge. The Order was attacked, turned on by its friends, saw its fortunes stripped from those to whom it belonged, and it was forced underground."

"You could have come forward."

"And told the world that demons really existed? *I* didn't believe they existed, remember? I left the Order. I left my father. I left everything I knew here because I didn't believe." Simon paused. "No one wanted to hear about demons. Not until they were among us."

"You have Macomber. He's been helping you translate the Goetia manuscript."

"Yes. But only because I've got someone else who supplements what Macomber doesn't know. If your . . . *organization* had kept Macomber, which they decided *not* to do, they wouldn't have been able to do what we've done."

"I know that. The people I work with know that. But you can't expect us not to try to fight back. Whatever advantage you've gained—"

"Is yours," Simon interrupted. He flicked a hand and a small rectangular computer disk case sailed across the distance.

Leah easily plucked the case from the air and looked at it. The case contained a nanospring microdot computer drive. It was red as a drop of blood and no larger or thicker than her fingernail.

"That contains everything we've discovered from the Goetia manuscript," Simon said. "It also includes the instructions on how to make the Node fields. At least, what we've managed to figure out about them so far."

"Do you believe him?" Lyra asked.

"Don't you?" Leah asked her.

After only a brief hesitation, Lyra answered, "Yes, I do."

Pride surged inside Leah. Simon Cross was exactly what he presented himself to be: a knight willing to sacrifice his life so that others could live. Leah's training ran counterpoint to that. She was supposed to sacrifice others, let them die for their countries or beliefs.

"What you've seen in the tunnel there?" Simon asked.

"That's as large as we've been able to make the fields up to now. Macomber and the others are still working on the problem of enlarging it, but they've not reached a solution yet. When—and if—they find one, I'll let you know."

Leah remembered the harsh words the woman at the redoubt had given her. "Your generosity is surprising, Simon, but I know not all Templar feel the way you do."

"They don't like trusting people."

"They would have kept the secret of the Nodes to themselves."

"Yes. But that decision isn't completely theirs. It's mine. And I persuaded them to see that knowledge of the Nodes benefits all of us. The more others fight back against the demons, the longer we'll last. In the end, they saw that."

Leah closed her hands around the disk and wished she didn't feel so miserable. But part of that was Simon's fault. A large part of it. She held him accountable.

"You could have brought me with you today," she told him. She knew her voice was cold with accusation.

"Another choice I made."

"You tried to keep this from me."

"I wanted to keep you out of harm's way," Simon said. "I knew this was going to be a bloody bit of business."

That's something you would do, she thought angrily.

"If the field failed, it wouldn't have mattered," Simon said. "I saw no reason to get your hopes up. That's why we haven't told anyone else at the redoubt. And we won't until we find a way to increase the Node's parameters. Having a protective field over a couple dozen people isn't going to help enough."

She chose not to argue that.

"You're welcome to the research," Simon said. "I'd ask that if your people find a way to enlarge the parameters that they tell us."

Leah wanted to answer but knew she couldn't.

"Tell him yes," Lyra said.

"Am I lying to him?" Leah asked. *Are you lying to me?*

"No. It's the truth. I swear it."

Leah knew the promise didn't mean anything. Lying was one of the primary skills among agents. But she wanted to tell Simon.

"If we find anything," Leah said, "you'll be informed."

Simon nodded. "Thank you for that." He let the uncomfortable silence drag between them for a moment longer. "Given the circumstances, especially in light of the fact that most people in the redoubt know you 'escaped,' it might be better if you stayed away for a while."

His words hung dry and lifeless in the distance between them. Leah felt hurt and confused. Resorting to her training, she walled those feelings away.

"All right," she said. "If that's how you'd like it."

"It's not a matter of how I'd like it," Simon said. "I've found I've got little control over the things I'd like. This is just how it has to be."

Leah tried to think of something to say but couldn't.

"Will you be able to see your way to safety from here?" Simon asked.

"Yes," Lyra told Leah. "I've got an exfiltration team standing nearby."

"I will," Leah answered.

"Then take care out there, Leah. I wish you well." Simon turned on his heel and disappeared through the door to the tube platform waiting area.

Unable to move or to speak, Leah watched him go.

"You did what you had to do," Lyra said.

"That doesn't make it right," Leah said.

"It will. You had no way of knowing what Lord Cross planned to do."

"I could have waited for another time. Or asked him about these devices."

"If he'd wanted to tell you, he'd have told you before now."

"He was going to tell me."

"That's what he says now."

Leah headed for the platform and hauled herself up. "Didn't you come to me and want to push him further up in the hierarchy of the Templar?"

"Yes."

"Then you must believe in him."

"That doesn't mean—"

"Do me a favor," Leah interrupted. "Stay out of my head for a while." She cut comm and kept walking through the darkness.

THIRTY-TWO

G et up, Warren!"

The frantic voice dragged Warren from his sleep. He pushed the pillow from his face and glanced around groggily. It was light outside, but dawn had started when he'd gone to bed. He'd been up all night working on mastering new ways to use the arcane energy he tapped into. Since they'd returned to the building he'd claimed for himself in the Soho District, he'd worked with Lilith. Naomi had grudgingly remained around, but even she had set her enmity with the demon aside to learn more.

Naomi stood by the bed and pulled her clothes on. Her eyes locked on the security monitors on the wall by the bed.

"What's going on?" Warren asked. He stared at the blank monitors. They shouldn't have been blank. He'd set up a generator in the basement of the building, and shielded it so the noise wouldn't be heard or otherwise sensed by the roving demon patrols. A large petrol tank guaranteed that it would run for weeks at a time. He'd filled it again upon their return.

"The security system is down," Naomi replied as she stomped into her boots.

"I see that."

"I heard a noise and woke up. When I checked the security monitors, they were dead."

"How long have they been dead?"

"I don't know."

Warren stepped into his pants and pulled a rugby jersey on. The combat boots took a moment longer. He roomed on the fourth floor. It would take a moment for anyone arriving at the building to climb the stairs.

Not winged demons, he amended. He glanced through the steel security bars that blocked the windows. Many of the buildings in the neighborhood had had those in place to keep out looters before the invasion. They didn't draw any special attention.

He touched the coat Lilith had given him and it flowed over his body as if it had a mind of its own. Perhaps it did. He still wasn't sure about that, but it had offered better protection than any of the body armor he'd worn. Just thinking of the obsidian spear brought it into his hand. It flew across the room and settled into place.

Warren reached into the messenger satchel he habitually carried, which contained various artifacts he'd created. He knew where everything was located simply by touch. An individual pocket held Blood Angel eyes he'd harvested and tied to his own senses. He sorted out four of them that still felt wet and slimy. Two of them had dried out.

He filled the eyes with arcane energy, mapped the way each individual eye was supposed to go, and threw them into the air. They paused in the air for just a moment as if sorting out the command, then flew into action. Two of them sailed through the window, and two shot away through the door to the room.

"Where's Lilith?" Naomi asked.

"I don't know."

Naomi frowned. "Awfully convenient of her not being around while this is going on."

"She doesn't want anything to happen to me." Warren

opened his mind to the Blood Angel eyes, tapping into what they saw. "She still needs me."

"Don't be too sure about that."

Warren was, though. Until Lilith got her body back to full strength, she'd need him to care for her and help her.

One of the eyes that had flown outside broke away and flew over the top of the five-story building. The other aimed for street level.

Dozens of Gremlins poured in through the building's front door. Massive and vaguely human-shaped, they stood on wide, two-taloned feet. Misshapen and powerful, they were fierce foes in battle. Their flat faces held several beady black eyes. Three horns jutted from the tops of their large, bulbous heads and two others stabbed down from their square jaws.

The eye viewing the other side of the building showed more Gremlins coming in through the door on the Old Compton Street side. The demons breached the security doors without problem.

The two eyes inside the building sped down the two stairwells at either end of the main hallways. Since Blood Angels saw in the dark, they easily spotted the Gremlins surging up the stairwells. They arrived at the second landing.

As Warren watched, his mind desperately racing, one of the Gremlins spotted the eye hovering on the third-floor landing. The demon pulled his rifle to his shoulder and fired.

Bright light sizzled through Warren's vision. Pain split his temples. He cried out.

"Warren?" Naomi took his arm.

Impatiently, and more than a little afraid, Warren brushed her off. "There are Gremlins in the building."

"How did they find us?"

"I don't know. They're at the second floor now. We've got to get out of here."

Movement caught the attention of one of the Blood Angel eyes outside the building. It spun and focused on a flying demon just before the creature caught the eye in its razored beak.

Another wave of pain shot through Warren's head. He kept from crying out, but nausea swirled in his stomach. When the front door of the suite blew open, he raised the spear to defend himself.

Lilith floated before him. Her feet dangled inches from the ground. She couldn't walk fast enough to escape. Her body had begun to gradually resume some of its shape and flesh, but that left her grotesque and weak.

"We've been found out," she said.

Naomi cursed. "How did they find us?"

"Now isn't the time for questions," Lilith stated. "Warren, get the Book. If we're going to live, we need it."

Warren sprinted to the ornate desk he'd found and had zombies bring up to the room for him. He laid his hand on the drawer that held the Book and pulsed arcane energy into the lock as he spoke the code phrase.

The lock released with a series of audible clicks.

Out in the hallway, the demons had reached the third-floor landing. Then that vision blinked out as one of them shot the Blood Angel eye hovering in front of them.

Warren sagged against the desk for a moment, then got control of himself again. He reached inside the desk drawer and withdrew the Book.

Eighteen inches by fourteen inches and six inches thick, the Book was covered in virulent purple leather that had lines—by design or by accident—that looked like blood veins. As always, the Book purred liked a cat. An eye the amber-green of a cat's opened in the center of the Book. Below it, a fanged mouth took shape.

"I am in danger," the Book said.

"I know," Warren said. "I'm going to get you out of here." For a time, he'd believed that the voice he'd heard from the Book had been Lilith. But after she'd separated from the Book, it had still continued to talk to him. Lilith hadn't given any explanation.

"Good," the Book said. "I do not wish to be destroyed."

"You won't be. Trust me."

"I do trust you, Warren Schimmer. Otherwise I would kill you."

It was funny, Warren reflected, how many demons and people—and *things*—claimed to be his friend, yet offered to kill him if he ever betrayed them. But not funny in a good way. That tendency of the demons and demonic things reminded him a lot of how his life had been before the invasion.

He pressed the Book against his duster. Immediately, a pocket formed there and swallowed the Book. The eye watched him until the pocket sealed. For a moment, the bulge in the duster was obvious, then it disappeared. The garment could make any number of pockets, and Warren could store innumerable things in it. The amazing thing was that none of them had any physical weight or shape after the pockets sealed. He could even open a pocket over the top of a pocket.

The clamor of the approaching demons sounded out in the hallway.

Naomi stood at one of the windows and held the security bars.

"You can't go out," Warren said. "More of them are out there."

Exasperated and scared, Naomi turned on him. "Then what are we going to do?"

"The first rule of having any sanctuary," Warren said, "is to have a way out." He crossed the room, took her by the hand, and pulled her into motion.

An explosion ripped through the window where Naomi had stood. The concussion knocked Warren and Naomi from their feet. Masonry and steel bars shot across the room. Two of the steel bars embedded in the wall on the opposite side. Lilith flattened against a wall but didn't seem any worse for wear.

"Lilith!" a monstrous voice boomed.

"Korhdajj," Lilith snarled.

Warren stood and pulled Naomi behind him. The duster he wore offered more protection than her armor.

Korhdajj clung to the side of the building. He had to have been at least twelve or fourteen feet tall, and was immense. Huge batwings helped him balance on the wall, barely visible through the hole he'd created. Iridescent red scales covered him and gave him the appearance of being on fire.

However, silvery metal that seemed constantly in motion sealed over parts of the demon. It wasn't armor, Warren saw. It was fixed to his body like skin grafts. The metal covered half of the demon's face, including one eye.

Lilith pulled herself from the wall. Warren felt the arcane energy building around her.

Do not fear him, Warren, Lilith spoke into his mind. *He's big—*

And powerful, Warren thought.

—but he can be destroyed. Strike quickly with the spear when I tell you.

We should run. I have a way out.

If you run, he'll destroy you.

Warren gripped the spear. Naomi grabbed him from behind, pulled on him, and whispered, "Let's go. Let them kill each other."

Not speaking, Warren shrugged free. "Wait."

"We're going to get killed."

"Wait."

Lilith floated above the floor and looked incredibly frail and used up, facing the giant clinging to the wall like some demonic King Kong. Winds filled the room and blew furniture and papers everywhere. Sheets and bedding billowed off the bed and swirled madly.

"I thought you were dead, Lilith." Korhdajj knocked more of the wall away with a huge fist. Chunks of stone rained down into the street as vibrations shook the room.

"I was abandoned," Lilith said. "Sydonai betrayed me."

Korhdajj laughed.

"Do you understand them?" Naomi whispered into Warren's ear.

Warren did. Until that moment he'd thought they were speaking English. "Yes."

"What are they saying?"

"Be quiet. You're going to get us killed." Warren took a fresh grip on the spear.

THIRTY-THREE

Korhdajj pulled himself into the room. He ducked his head to fit inside. He peered down at Lilith, and she looked almost childlike next to him. She certainly looked defenseless.

"Where have you been all these years?" Korhdajj asked.

"Waiting for Sydonai to make good on his promise. He sent me here to defeat these people and make way for the Hellgate."

Warren watched her face and wondered if the flesh wasn't dead and gripped her skull so tightly that she couldn't show fear.

"You failed," Korhdajj taunted.

"The humans are more skilled and powerful than we'd thought."

"But they die so easily. Even the Templar wither and perish before us."

"Is Sydonai here?" Lilith asked.

Gremlins suddenly filled the doorway behind Warren. He faltered for a moment as he felt their baleful stares burning into his back.

Do not think of them, Lilith commanded. *They will be dealt with.*

"Sydonai is where he wishes to be," Korhdajj replied. "He is the Eldest. His will is law. You had best learn your place with him. Otherwise you'll find yourself crawling out of the Well of Midnight as far less than you ever were."

"I see you still bear your scars."

Self-consciously, Korhdajj ran a three-fingered hand over the metal side of his face. Then he caught himself and grinned. "This was your doing."

"You should remember your place with me," Lilith said.

"Once, perhaps." Korhdajj shook his head. "But no longer. You're not the Eldest's protected anymore."

"I will be again."

"If I were inclined to let you live, I might be interested in seeing the outcome of that. But since I sensed you in this place, working your power, I knew that I wouldn't suffer you to live again."

"Have a care, blunderer. I'm more powerful than I appear."

Korhdajj grinned, and the effort bared huge fangs in a double row of teeth. "I don't believe you. All I see before me is a shriveled *dakmuwah*, hardly worth the trouble to skin and eat. I'd wager your skinny flesh sticks in my teeth. But I'll pick you out with your own bones."

Ready, Lilith told Warren.

Yes.

When the time is right, you must strike for his neck. Pierce it and we will live.

Warren swallowed hard. His hand felt sweaty. Heat from the demon washed over him. For the moment, the Gremlins held back at the door.

"I gave you those wounds that you cover," Lilith said. "I was merciful and let you live. For thousands of years, they've remained with you and never healed."

"For thousands of years they've served to remind

me why I hate you so much." With a quick movement, Korhdajj wrapped an impossibly huge hand around Lilith. In just that slight movement, his hand grew so large that it covered the withered demon from shoulders to knees. "Today, though, I'll have my revenge." He lifted Lilith and opened his mouth.

An explosion of light suddenly blazed in the room, slammed against Warren, and rocked him on his heels. He barely kept his balance. The Gremlins cowered back from the door.

Korhdajj's hand flew open, and he screamed in agony as flames covered his palm and fingers.

Now, Warren! Lilith commanded. *Strike now!*

Fear pounded Warren's temples as he set himself and threw the spear as hard as he could. The obsidian shaft flew true and sank into Korhdajj's neck just below his jaw.

The demon's eyes widened in sudden fear. He turned to face Warren. "No!" Korhdajj bellowed in disbelief. "What have you done?" He reached for the spear, but his neck abruptly turned to soup and ran down his shoulder. Only his bones remained intact.

Lilith flew forward as Korhdajj started to fall. Her arms moved arthritically, but she caught his massive head in her hands. Unbelievably, she held the demon up as he fought for his life. Then a bold blue light dawned in Lilith's hands.

Warren felt the exchange of arcane energy passing from Korhdajj to Lilith. Some of it spilled over onto him, and he pulled it into himself. The energy was too strong, though, and the pain of containing it lanced through him. He needed to release it before it tore him apart.

Hold on to it, Lilith said. *You're going to need it. Wait for my signal.*

Warren's eyes brimmed with tears as he fought the pain.

Korhdajj shrank, dwindling into himself like a rotting jack-o'-lantern. But Lilith grew younger, till she looked like a woman in her twenties. Her hair grew in full and luxuriant. Her eyes held Warren's as she turned to face him.

Now. Call the spear to you and use it to channel the energy within you against the Gremlins.

The connection to the spear throbbed in Warren's mind. He threw out his hand and called it to him. With a quiver, it broke free of the demonic corpse and streaked across the room to slap into his palm. He spun as the Gremlins, spurred on by their commanders, streaked into the room.

As if he'd handled the spear all his life, Warren set himself and swung the weapon around. The spearhead ripped the first wave of Gremlins open. Some of them died immediately as the blade pierced their hearts. Others received lingering deaths from sliced throats, punctured lungs, and disembowelment. The floor ran thick with gore that flooded the area like a tidal wave.

The Gremlins backed off in awe. Warren couldn't believe the damage he'd wreaked and stood frozen himself for a moment.

"Stand there and you'll die," Lilith yelled at him. She threw out a hand and a massive charge of electricity surged through the massed Gremlins. Many of them blew up, their limbs twisted free by the discharge that ripped through their bodies.

Several of the Gremlins at the door raised their weapons and took aim at Warren and Lilith. With a gesture, Warren raised a shield. Projectiles came to a sudden stop in midair, held by the shield. Beam weapons, acid, and swarms of insects fired by even stranger weapons smeared harmlessly across the shield.

"There are too many," Naomi shouted in Warren's ear. "We'll have to go out the windows."

"No," Warren replied.

"We can slow our fall with our powers."

"No. There are too many of them waiting out there."

"We're not going to get out of here."

"Yes we will. Stay with me." Warren held the spear in both hands before him. He channeled the supercharged arcane force now at his disposal and created a massive wall of fire that blazed back over the Gremlins. Only Warren's shield kept the flames from consuming them as well.

The demons had no chance for escape. Almost to a creature, they caught fire and burned like kindling, dropping to the floor in twisted, blackened lumps. Some of them shattered into ash.

For a moment, the room was empty.

The heat washed over Warren in spite of his shield. He focused again, once more channeling the energy through the spear, and directed a shockwave at the wall beside the door where Gremlin corpses blocked the way.

With a thunderous crash, the wall shattered, then blew outward to leave a gaping hole. The Gremlins standing behind the wall were flattened or blown away. Beyond them, the elevator doors caved in with a metallic shrill.

"Come on!" Warren grabbed Naomi's hand with his human one and got her into motion. He ran through the hole. Lilith followed.

Never breaking stride, Warren ran across the downed Gremlins and straight for the elevator shaft. He threw the spear out and directed another blast of force toward the doors hanging askew. The doors ripped away and fell down into the dark shaft.

"Jump!" Warren shouted. Naomi fought against him, but Gremlins had already recovered enough to fire at them. He tightened his grip on her hand and yanked her after him as he went over the edge and fell into darkness.

Naomi screamed.

Warren didn't blame her. Hurtling down the dark elevator shaft proved terrifying. He switched over to his night eyes and saw the elevator cage rushing up at them. Of course, it wasn't actually moving because he hadn't wired it through the emergency generator, but it gave the appearance of doing so.

Tapping into his power, he halted his downward plummet and held on to Naomi. Her weight hit the end of his arm and dragged him off balance. They fell again, but the shorter fall lessened the impact greatly. Still, Warren felt ribs on his right side crack as he struck the top of the elevator cage.

Lilith floated to a graceful stop above him. "You've trapped us," she snarled.

Unable to draw a breath against the pain of his cracked ribs, Warren managed to stand. He swayed and felt sick, and he regretted what he had to do next. Concentrating, he blasted another force wave through the elevator cage. It crumpled beneath them and they fell again.

His ribs burned as he pushed himself to his knees. He placed his free hand against the elevator doors and blasted them. They ripped from their moorings as the Gremlins leaned over the opening on the fourth floor. Bullets and beams rattled the shaft.

Warren lurched through the opening. Lilith floated by him before he got through. He pulled Naomi from the wreckage and hauled her into the building's basement.

The Soho District was old. The building was one of the oldest and didn't have a parking garage beneath it. Abandoned machinery, crates, and boxes halfway filled the storage area.

Finally the deathgrip of pain in Warren's side released its hold, and he sucked in a breath just as black comets whirled in his vision. He cried out, but even that hurt.

"Where are we?" Naomi asked.

"You're taking us from one trap to another," Lilith complained.

"Always," Warren wheezed, "always . . . have a way . . . out." He crossed the room and gestured at a stack of crates. Swept by an invisible wind, the crates tumbled out of the way to reveal a blank section of wall.

"There's no door," Naomi said.

Warren drew another breath. "No door," he agreed. "Escape routes . . . should be . . . marked." He pressed against the wall. "There's an . . . an old tunnel . . . next to . . . this basement. Probably . . . used it . . . for smuggling. Or supplies. Found it . . . on blueprints. I chiseled . . . through the wall . . . reset the blocks . . . with weak mortar."

He blasted through the blocks. They cascaded before him, shattering and spilling across the rough-hewn floor of the tunnel just beyond.

The passageway reeked of age and mold. Lampblack stained the ceiling, visible to Warren's night vision. Scuff marks scarred the stone floor.

"Which way?" Lilith asked as she floated out into the passageway.

"Left." Warren stepped through after her. He breathed easier now, but pain still gripped him.

"Where does it go?"

"Away from here." Warren paused to flick the arming trigger of a remote detonator he'd placed on the wall when he'd broken into the tunnel.

"What's that?" Naomi demanded.

"Plastic explosive." That was easy enough to find these days with armories left undefended. There were even manuals that told him how to use it.

"You're insane."

"We can't . . . outrun them."

"Can we outrun the blast?"

"Have to . . . find out." Warren leaned into his stride, and found he couldn't quite manage to get up to a run. Naomi grabbed his free arm and yanked him to greater speed.

A few of the faster Gremlins reached the opening before the plastic explosive went off. The explosion filled the tunnel with light and noise. The concussive wave knocked Warren flat. He hovered on the edge of consciousness, barely aware that a large section of the tunnel—more than he would have guessed—had collapsed.

Then he spiraled into darkness.

THIRTY-FOUR

"What are you still doing here, Creasey? Everybody figured you'd be out there hiding with your Templar buddies instead of risking your life with the rest of us."

Be cool, Leah told herself. *Ignore them.*

It was hard, though. Since she'd returned to the Agency complex, the obvious lack of acceptance by her peers was sandpaper to an unprotected nerve. There had already been some of that before she'd gone to take Lyra Darius's message to Simon. The hostility had escalated.

She lifted a boot to the bench in the coed locker room and started on the buckles. Her boot, like the rest of her armor, was covered in blood. Most of the blood had belonged to demons, but some of it had belonged to human wounded and to two men who had died in her arms tonight.

"Are you listening to me, Creasey?" Dockery roared.

Let it go, Leah thought. She almost had the boot off. Blood turned her gloves slippery and made the task more difficult.

A heavy hand dropped onto her shoulder and yanked her around. Dockery stood a head taller than she was, a massive man with a barrel chest. He was in his early thirties. He had his helmet mask off. Close-shaven black hair covered his head and five o'clock shadow stubbled his jaw. His features looked broad and mulish.

Leah swung her forearm up and batted his hand away. She kept both of her fists on either side of her face in the ready position.

"I heard you, Dockery," Leah said. "Back off. I don't want to talk to you."

"Maybe I want to talk to you, love," Dockery snarled.

"I'll bring charges against you."

Dockery laughed. "I go out there every day and wage war against demons, love. Do you really think having charges brought against me worries me?"

Leah felt foolish. Before the invasion, charges within the Agency were serious matters.

"I was in the Royal Marines before all this went down," Dockery said. "I knew about hard times even then while you were still learning spy tricks. We fought people face-to-face in those days. None of this hiding-in-the-shadows crap you people are taught."

A crowd had gathered in the locker room. No one seemed interested in stepping in to break up the potential fight.

"You've had a hard night," Leah said evenly. "We all have."

"Not all of us have had a mate die in his arms tonight," Dockery said. "Wendell Tate was a good man. A Royal Marine. Easily worth four or five times as much as the likes of you."

That drew some remonstrations from the crowd. Even though the spy organizations and military departments had come together under the same covert umbrella as a result of the Hellgate invasion, that joining of forces wasn't seamless.

"A lot of people died tonight," Leah said. "A lot of good people."

"I know. And you insist on running off to hook up with those cowardly Templar."

He's just baiting you. Leah took a deep breath and let it out slowly.

"I want you to leave me alone," Leah stated.

"Too bad. I think it's time you figured out where your loyalties lie." Dockery shoved a big hand forward and slammed her shoulder.

Leah caught his wrist with her left hand, grabbed his elbow with her right, and tried to force him into an arm-bar hold. Dockery kicked a foot out and tripped her as he rotated his upper body. Off balance, Leah had no choice but to release her hold and step back quickly. She lifted her hands again and barely got them up before Dockery came at her.

"You shouldn't have done that, love," he rasped. A malicious grin pulled at his mouth. "Now see, you're going to regret that."

Leah avoided a jab and let it sail by her ear. Intentionally, she backed toward a stand of lockers. The observers gave ground reluctantly behind her, not wanting to lose their front-row positions, then jockeyed for those same positions as the circle broke into a semicircle. Savage voices filled the locker room.

Dockery feinted, but Leah realized by his stance that he wasn't putting any commitment into the effort. She closed her hands and let his next blow hit her. Flush with success, Dockery swung again, stepping forward and powering the punch this time.

Bending her knees, Leah dropped below the vicious punch. Dockery's big fist smashed into the locker and punched through the flimsy door. He struggled to get his hand free of the torn metal. Before he got loose, Leah slid out beside him, then whirled in a downward axe kick behind her opponent's knee.

Dockery's leg crumpled and he went down. The angle further trapped his fist, which was an unexpected bonus. Leah grabbed a fistful of his hair and yanked his face around to look at her.

"Don't you come at me again," Leah told him calmly. "Not ever again."

The big man cursed and tried to get up. Leah slapped her palm against the back of Dockery's neck and unleashed the fifty thousand volts stored in her suit's capacitors. Dockery jerked wildly for a moment, every muscle in his body taut with stress, then he slumped into unconsciousness.

"You're going to pay for that," one of Dockery's fellow Royal Marines threatened.

Leah dropped back into a defensive posture. The room remained divided, but Dockery and the military contingent formed a tight little group. She doubted anyone would step forward to her defense.

"That'll be just about enough of the roughhousing," a crisp voice announced. "The next one of you to throw a punch will be joining Sergeant Dockery in lockup."

The crowd parted as Lyra Darius walked among them. Four heavily armed security staff trailed in her wake. She stopped at Leah's side and stared at the gathered crowd.

"Riordan and Jacobs," Lyra said. "You claim to be friends of the sergeant. Get him to medical and have him checked over. Once the physician declares him fit, escort him to lockup. I'll be along to make sure that happens. If it doesn't, you'll be joining him. Are we clear here?"

"Crystal, ma'am," one of the two men replied grudgingly.

Lyra glanced at Leah. "You're coming with me."

Leah quelled the immediate impulse to fight against being treated as if she were guilty of anything. "Yes, ma'am."

When they entered Lyra Darius's private office, Leah stood at attention in front of the desk. Her gaze roved around the room. Nothing personal existed in there, nothing to hint at who Lyra Darius had ever been before or after joining the intelligence agency.

"Don't be silly. You're not in any kind of trouble. It's just better if Dockery and his lackeys think I'm reading you the riot act. Have a seat."

Feeling a little relieved, Leah sat in one of the two non-descript chairs in front of the metal desk. Lyra sat across from her.

"Things must be difficult for you," Lyra said.

"I'm doing fine, ma'am." Leah kept her face neutral.

"Yes, I can see that. Brawling in one of the common rooms with your teammates is a perfect indication of how *fine* you're doing."

"That fight was not my fault."

"Of course it was." Lyra leaned back in her chair.

Leah barely managed to remain seated. "Begging your pardon, ma'am, but I didn't start that."

"You did. The minute you stepped outside Agency lines and got involved with Simon Cross four years ago."

Not with the *Templar*. With *Simon Cross*. Leah took note of the distinction.

"Are you upset with me, ma'am?" Leah asked.

"Not with you. With the situation." Lyra shook her head. "And more upset *for* you than with you."

"I don't understand."

"You've placed yourself in an untenable position."

"I don't see how."

"Because you're getting special dispensation from the Templar. The rest of the people here are not."

"They don't want it."

"Of course they don't. This lot is too prideful and mired in their elitist thinking. They believe they're better than the Templar, so they are."

"Not hardly."

"They see themselves as taking the war to the demons. That's what they've always trained to do. Make the other side lose as heavily as we do. Unfortunately, none of the people these soldiers and agents have been up against in the past have ever been so willing to expend troops. Nor were they ever as well equipped. Not even the Middle Eastern terrorists in the early years of this century."

Leah remained silent.

"One way or another, this will sort itself out," Lyra said. "It would have been better if so many people here didn't focus on you as being part of the problem." She looked at Leah with concern. "I am loath to send you back out into the field."

"Why? Because you don't trust me?"

"I trust you. I just don't trust all of those people out there to stand with you if it comes to that."

"I can take care of myself."

Lyra smiled sadly. "The days of us taking care of ourselves are over."

"I still have a few friends," Leah said.

"Yes. I know that you do. And when they are shunned by men like Dockery? What do you do then? How far will this division go before our center no longer holds?"

Leah thought about that. "Are you suggesting that I leave?"

Lyra regarded her calmly. "Not yet. At the moment, I don't think it's come to that. But it might. When it does, I'll let you know."

Leah gave a tight nod.

"And if it does, do you think you could take safe harbor with the Templar?"

With practiced ease, Leah lied. "Yes, ma'am."

Lyra frowned. "A pretty deceit if I've ever seen one. Even as good-natured as Simon Cross is purported to be, I daresay he may have had enough after this last meeting with you."

"Possibly."

"Before I turn you out of here, I'll find another place for you. You have my word on that."

"Yes, ma'am. Thank you. Will there be anything else?"

"Yes." Lyra leaned onto the desk and spoke kindly. "Step easily while you're out there, Leah. Animosity like this isn't always given the time it needs to work through. The friend you think you have at your back . . . may not be."

"Yes, ma'am. I've already been aware of that." Leah stood and saluted.

Lyra stood and saluted back. "There is one more thing I'd ask of you. In case anyone asks, tell them that I was rude and offensive to you."

"Yes, ma'am." Leah left the room and stepped out into the hallway. Before she'd entered Lyra's office, the complex hadn't felt like a safe haven, but she was surprised at how much less so it felt now.

THIRTY-FIVE

Warren woke in the middle of a forest instead of the underground passage. Confused, he stared around at the sunlight streaming through the emerald trees and bushes surrounding him. He clenched his right hand and found that it was still there, still made of metal, and it was still tight around the spear. Some things hadn't changed.

Birds sang in the trees and fluttered from branch to branch. Somewhere off to the left a brook gurgled as it passed. The scent of pines and grass filled his nose, and he thought he smelled apples as well. His stomach rumbled at the apples. It had been over three long years since he'd had fresh fruit. The only apples that existed these days were in cans or dehydrated packages.

He realized the fiery pain in his side was gone. He decided to take hope in that. There was no way he'd gone numb to that, and no way the damage had healed on its own.

"Get up, Warren," a familiar voice urged. "In this place, no one will try to harm you. This is a safe place."

The ground vibrated slightly as someone walked toward him. Screwing down the fear that throbbed within him, Warren rolled over and got to his feet. He brought the spear up in both hands. The duster felt solid and impenetrable around him, hardly shifting except to conform to his movements.

A strange creature stood in front of Warren. It took a quick step back from the spear.

"I would appreciate it if you wouldn't wave that in my direction," the being said. "That's a powerful weapon. If I'd had my choice, I would have left it behind. But it, like the coat that you wear, seems to have bonded with you."

"Who are you?" Warren demanded.

The creature stood barely four feet tall. Slender and elfin, it didn't look like a threat. That didn't mean anything. Warren had seen demons no bigger than his little finger burrow into a man's flesh to seek out his heart or his brain and kill him.

The being's features looked mismatched, as if they'd been forced together instead of growing naturally. Its nose was a large oblong that dangled almost to its upper lip. The eyes were too small and pushed too far together. The mouth was a slash. Dark, curly hair framed the elliptical face with a chin so crooked it looked like a comma. More hair covered its bony legs. A yellow breechcloth fluttered in the gentle breeze.

"I am Thakelrot," the being announced, and smiled hesitantly.

"That's a name," Warren said. "It doesn't tell me who you are, what this place is, or how I got here."

"You haven't died and gone to some afterlife, if that's what you're thinking."

"No."

"You humans have interesting ideas about that."

Warren stepped forward and thrust the spear to within inches of Thakelrot's throat.

The little being held up his hands. "This is what I get for the kindness I've shown you? After I pulled you from that passageway to this place and healed your wounds?"

"If you've done all that, then you can tell me what I want to know."

Thakelrot looked into Warren's eyes. "You know me, Warren. You know my voice and you know this place."

It took Warren a moment more, but he did know the being. "You're the Book."

A smile curved the slash of a mouth. "Yes."

Warren lowered the spear but didn't let down his guard. He looked around.

"You've been inside the book before," Thakelrot said.

Warren had. "It didn't look like this then."

"The Book has many pages. You've not seen them all. No one has."

"And you weren't there."

"I was. You just didn't see me."

Warren considered that. "You pulled me into the Book?"

"To save your life, yes."

"What about Naomi and Lilith?"

"Naomi carries the Book. She saw me pull you into it. She couldn't very well carry you. And now that I've finally managed to separate myself from Lilith, I don't want to endure that again."

"I can get back out?"

"Of course. I am not a jailer."

Warren studied the homely face. All of his life, Warren had been lied to. His mother had lied to him first, followed by his stepfather, and continuing on through the foster homes and "friends" he'd made who leaned on him because he could be counted on to come up with his portion of the rent and utilities.

He couldn't tell if the being in front of him was lying.

"I wanted to you to be safe," Thakelrot said. "When you were knocked unconscious, they would have had no choice but to leave you behind."

They could have stayed, Warren thought.

"They're afraid. The passageway didn't completely close as you'd hoped it would. The Gremlins dug through."

"Will my companions get away?"

"Yes. There is time. You planned well."

"I need to get back there."

"Take a moment. The last time you were inside the Book you only saw one of the wars the demons have waged in the past. You can learn from this experience."

Warren gazed around at the forest. "Where are we?"

"Inside the Book."

"I meant, this place."

"This is one of the worlds that the demons devoured. Better yet, this is a memory of that place. It no longer exists, but within the pages of this Book, this place can live on forever. At least, as long as the Book remains whole."

Thakelrot walked down to the slow-moving brook. "Follow me."

For a time, Warren walked in silence beside the small being. The beauty of the forest overwhelmed him. Before the invasion, he'd taken parks for granted. Then, once the Burn had started consuming London and it had become unsafe to be in wide, open spaces, he'd regretted not having gone to the parks more often.

Thakelrot paused at an apple tree. The red fruit hung heavily on the limbs. After eyeing the fruit judiciously, he plucked one and tossed it to Warren.

Warren caught the apple and examined it. The fruit looked perfect. Good enough to—

"Eat it," Thakelrot encouraged.

"Is it safe?"

"Yes."

"I've heard too many stories of evil witches and jealous queens to easily accept apples as gifts."

"I don't want to hurt you. If I did, all I had to do was leave you in that passageway. The Gremlins would have killed you."

"Maybe."

"If you'd been conscious, you'd have seen the truth of what I'm saying." Thakelrot plucked another apple and tore it apart in his bare hands. The being dropped pieces of it into the brook. Almost immediately, fish surfaced and nibbled the bits. None of them died.

Hungry, wanting to remember what an apple tasted like that wasn't pureed and poured into a can, Warren shined the fruit on his coat and took a bite. The apple was sweet and just tart enough to make his jaws ache. Juice ran down his chin. Despite his strange circumstances, he had to smile.

"Good, right?" Thakelrot asked.

"Yes."

The creature turned and walked along the brook again. Warren followed, still munching on the apple.

"I wanted to take this opportunity, now that we're finally alone, to talk to you. There is much I have to share."

"Why didn't you tell me before?"

"Because Lilith was here. Hiding among us. There are things she must not know. Or at least things that she must not know that you know. Otherwise she will kill you. And never trust for a moment that she won't as soon as she's through with you anyway."

"I don't."

Thakelrot grinned over his shoulder. "No more than you trust me, eh?"

"No more." Warren flipped the apple core into the brook. A dozen fish set upon it at once.

"You have to trust someone."

"I trust myself."

"You don't know enough."

Warren didn't argue that point. "What are you?"

"For now, perhaps for always, I am this Book. But once, I was like you. A creature of my own place and world. I had a family. A spouse. Children." Pain showed in the little being's eyes. "The demons killed them all."

Warren didn't know what to say, especially since he didn't know whether he believed the story or not.

THIRTY-SIX

I n my village, I was an historian," Thakelrot said. "I kept the old tales. The ones that no one really wished to hear anymore. But it was my place and I did it. No one believed those stories anymore."

"Why?"

"Because they were about demons. No one believed in demons in those days. All believed that the Darkness had passed us by. Or—as many began to say—never existed at all."

"The demons had been to your world before?"

"Yes. Just as they had yours. They monitor young worlds. Send Heralds and Seekers into them to judge when they'll be ready for the harvest."

"What time is that?"

"When the population has flourished," Thakelrot said. "In the beginnings of all worlds, there are only a few. But given time, intelligent creatures continue to breed and multiply, till they threaten to overpopulate a world. No other creature on any world does that with the same dogged success as the intelligent species. Once a world is burgeoning, when the demons judge they can no longer continue without imploding under their own weight, they strike. Just as when a fruit is ripest so that they can suck all the juices out."

"How do they know?" Warren asked.

"Demons never truly leave a world. They always have some who stay and observe. Like Lilith."

"She said the demons planned to return before now." The hill beside the brook rose steeply. Warren's thighs burned with the effort of the ascent.

"Perhaps they were," Thakelrot said. "Your people have had many setbacks as a species. I've seen them. Wars. Famines. Plagues. All those things set you back and threatened eradication."

"Why were you made into a book?"

"It was a joke on me. Because of what I'd been."

"Lilith did this?"

"No. She was there, but my fate wasn't through any decision of hers. Another of the Dark Wills took my body and the life barely beating within me and broke my bones and twisted me until I became this book."

"What was the point?"

Thakelrot sighed. "When I was alive, I knew how to hurt the demons. How to hurt them and kill them. What I knew helped forestall the inevitable, but it was too little, too late. Our destiny was ashes, and we were slow to get there. More than that, we didn't have the Truths in our world. Not like they are in this one."

"The Truths?"

Thakelrot stopped and looked at him. "Yes."

"I don't know what those are."

"Neither do I. Not entirely. I only know that they are the greatest weapons you can ever have against the demons. By your nature, you are a Cabalist. As such, you are tied most closely to the Truth of the Mother."

"What mother?"

"I don't know. I only know that when the time is right, the Cabalists must recognize that Truth and free it. Only then can the demons and the Hellgate be defeated."

"Where did these Truths come from?"

"Where all good things do. From the Fountain of Light."

"How many Truths are there?"

"Seven. They must all be found and united."

Warren's head reeled. "Where are the Truths?"

"Somewhere in your city," Thakelrot said. "You must find the Sigil, then you must find the Truths."

"How do you know this?"

"Because the story of the Seven Truths was one of the tales I knew in my world. I thought the Truths were there as well, but we searched for them and couldn't find them."

"They're physical things?"

"Of course they are. They'd have to be. They're going to be weapons that can be used against the demons."

Warren marshaled his thoughts. "You said the Truth about the Mother is tied to the Cabalists?"

"Yes."

"What other truths are there?"

"One will be tied to the Templar. They are too important to be discounted. And another Truth will be tied to the secret warriors."

"Isn't that the same as the Templar?"

"No. There are warriors within your world. I've seen them. They will be tied to the Truth about the Soldier because they only believe in fighting. The Templar will be tied to the Truth about the Brothers, because they are a house divided against itself. They stand for unity, but they became divided when the Hellgate first opened. Some of them died, while others were commanded to stay behind. Shame has tainted the living."

"Who will find those Truths?"

"Whoever seeks them." Thakelrot smiled hopefully. "I only wish that you're one of those. That's why I'm telling you about them. You have a chance to make a difference, Warren. But not unless you let go of the fear and anger that you cling so desperately to."

Warren wanted to argue that he wasn't fearful or angry, but he knew he couldn't. "Where would I start looking for them?"

"I don't know. But you must be prepared to act on anything you see. I've wanted to tell you that for months, but Lilith cannot find out that I know these things and am willing to tell you. If she learns of my knowledge, she will destroy me."

Warren just looked at the little being in front of him. If what he said was true, Thakelrot had had a horrible life for thousands of years.

"I won't tell her," Warren said.

"Be careful too how much you think around her. She can pull thoughts from your head easily."

"I know."

"As long as you have me with you, I can help keep some of your thoughts shielded."

"Then I'll make sure you stay with me."

"Come with me up to the top. There's something I want to show you."

At the top of the ridgeline, Warren thought he was going to be sick. Beyond the foothills, the terrible blackness of the Burn stretched forth in all directions. Pulsing ulcers that streamed sulfurous gas filled the wretched and diseased land. The sky above resembled a deep, dark bruise.

"This," Thakelrot whispered in a strained voice, "is what's become of my world. And if steps are not taken, if the Truths are not found, this is what will become of your world as well. Do you understand?"

Warren did.

"Even if you live, which is doubtful on your own because the demons will not suffer you long without making you pay for your own life, this will be all that you have to inherit," Thakelrot told him. "Living like this is no victory."

"But you live?"

"Do I?" Thakelrot seemed genuinely puzzled. "Most days I believe I am only a memory of myself. You are the first person I've talked to on my own in thousands of years. What kind of life is that?"

Staring out at the charred expanse, Warren felt afraid. "Are you sure?" he asked in a quiet voice. "Are you quite sure the demons can be defeated?"

"From this place? Yes. The Truths must be found and the secrets must be unlocked. The forces of Light put them here so that champions could rise up and strike back against the Darkness."

"Why here?"

"Because your people have great capacities for passion, for violence and for love. Because they can know the Truths and still yet be strong enough to wield them." Thakelrot paused. "Because, in the end, they have to be found here or your world has no hope for survival."

"How will I know them?"

"I don't know the answer to that riddle. I only know that when the time is right, the Truths will reveal themselves to you. You must make sure you and others are prepared."

"Why others?"

"Because the Truths must come from all three groups that have formed to fight the demons. None of you can stand against the demons alone. You must use each other's strengths in knowledge."

"No one trusts anyone out there."

"Some do. That trust must be made stronger. You must find a way."

"I'm not the guy for this."

"Then tell others," Thakelrot stated slowly. "Don't let what I tell you go to waste. This is a chance to strike back."

Warren silently thought that Thakelrot should have found someone else to have a bonding moment with.

"There is no one else," the little being said. "The Light gave me you."

"I'm not a champion," Warren protested. "I'm not even a good person. The things I've done, the people I've hurt . . . if you only knew."

"What you did before doesn't matter," Thakelrot said. "It's what you do now that counts. Every hero has a failing."

"I'm not a hero."

"Then be a messenger." Thakelrot grimaced and shook his head. "Our time is over. *She* searches for you."

"Lilith?"

"Yes." He scrunched his eyes up in pain. "You had best go. Before she becomes suspicious. If she asks, simply tell her that you were unconscious the whole time in here."

"All right."

"I'll be in touch with you when I can."

One moment, Warren stood on the hill overlooking the black desolation of the Burn—

—and the next he stood in the underground passageway. The suddenness of the transition left him light-headed. He staggered, then caught himself with the spear.

Lilith eyed him with vague suspicion. "Where have you been?"

Warren looked around the passageway. "On a battlefield. Somewhere else." He paused. "How did I get here?"

"You were in the Book," Naomi answered. She held it close to her.

"Did you enter the Book?" Lilith demanded.

"No. The last I remember was the blast in the tunnel."

"Were you injured?"

Warren looked down at himself, as if only then thinking to check. "I don't seem to be." Then he did what he always did when others made him feel uncomfortable with their questions: he asked questions of his own. "Who was the demon back there?"

"An old adversary. He's dead now. You no longer have to concern yourself with him."

"How did he find us?"

"That doesn't matter."

Warren made his voice more harsh. "It does matter. If that demon can find us, then others can as well. We need to be—*I* need to be—prepared for that eventuality."

Lilith glared at him. "Do you really think it matters if you're prepared?"

"Does it matter to you if I'm still alive?"

Her nose flared then, proving that she was once more breathing in her withered body. Warren wondered if that made her more vulnerable.

"It does matter," she answered.

"Then it matters if I'm prepared. I've just lost my hiding place. We're going to be vulnerable."

"There are other boltholes in the city. As for how Korhdajj found me, I have taken care of that. I've masked myself. I hadn't thought myself powerful enough to have warranted attention."

"You obviously have a list of enemies I don't know about."

"Demons have always been a jealous breed. You don't think humans invented that emotion, do you?"

"How many other demons will want to kill us?"

"Many. For a time, I was favored by Sydonai. There are many who never knew his beneficence." Lilith turned and floated away. "Come. We have much to do. I need to further regain my strength, and you have to raise a host of disciples to follow me into battle."

"How am I supposed to do that?"

"You're creative, Warren Schimmer. That's why I chose you. You'll think of a way."

Warren followed her, but part of him wished he were still inside the Book.

THIRTY-SEVEN

W e've got an inexperienced crew here, Leah."
"I know that, Marrick, but it's what we
have to do the job with." Leah knelt in the
shadows draped atop a building that offered a view of the
Apple retail store on Regent Street in the West End.

"For something like this," Marrick grumbled, "it seems
like upstairs would have found more to send than wet-
nosed pups." He was in his fifties, a slim, dapper man
who'd spent most of his years in the killing fields of for-
eign countries.

"We don't know if this is anything yet." Leah scanned
the front of the building. Back when it had opened in
2004, the computer store had been all the rage. Her father had taken her there to pick out her first tri-dee player
when she'd been just a girl.

The once-fashionable building was now a wreck. The
large, ornate glass windows were shattered. Computer
parts littered the sidewalks, either dropped by the early
looters or cannibalized by survivors trying to find a way to
make contact with the outside world.

"Upstairs reported organized demon activity here?"
Marrick asked.

"Yes."

"What's that supposed to mean, exactly?"

"It means that we're here watching for organized
demon activity."

"And we'd recognize it?"

"Upstairs seems to think so."

"Jolly good for them."

Undeterred, Leah kept surveying the building. They'd been there for over an hour since sunset. So far there'd been no demon activity.

"The demons are building new things," Leah said.

"Like the weapons plant."

"Yes."

"You have to wonder why they waited so long."

"I don't think they believed it would take quite so long to terrorize and take over this world," Leah said.

"Meaning we're fighting back harder than they expected us to?"

"Perhaps."

"It's not like they gave us any bloody choice."

"Nor any place to go," Leah agreed. Activity down on the street drew her attention. She refocused the binoculars.

Regent Street was a curving boulevard designed to take advantage of the Crown Estate lands, and to set off the disreputable Soho District from the shopping elegance of Mayfair. As a barrier between the haves and have-nots, it hadn't succeeded too well. Pickpockets simply lived across the street from their work environment.

Through the binoculars, Leah watched as a group of Darkspawn led four humans in chains toward the Apple building. Two of them were women. One was a man. And the fourth was a teen that might have been either.

"They're bringing them in alive," Marrick said.

Leah said nothing.

"It would be better if we killed them now than let the demons torture them. They're as good as dead already."

"If we do that, we give away the fact that we know this place."

"You've seen what the demons do with their prey, Leah. Putting a bullet through the heads of those four people would be merciful."

"I know, but they're going to be inside that building before we could get ourselves into position to fall back to safety. We'd just lose our team."

Marrick sighed. "I know."

Below, the Darkspawn herded their prisoners into the building. They disappeared into the darkness.

Leah opened the comm-link. "Red Raven Six, this is Red Raven Leader."

"Red Raven Six reads you, Leader," came the prompt response. The young woman's voice was confident and ready.

"You've got Spy Eyes, don't you?"

"Yes."

"Why don't you navigate that building? Let's see what's around it."

"All right."

Even though she looked for it and knew where Red Raven Six was, Leah barely spotted the drones speeding across Regent Street. She tracked her binoculars constantly, but didn't see anything amiss.

"Negative, Leader," the young woman reported.

"No guards?"

"None."

"Set up eyes overlooking the area. Let's give it a few minutes." Leah muted the broadcast and glanced at Marrick. "Why wouldn't they have sentries?"

"Because they're not afraid of anything," the older agent replied.

"I know." That answer irritated Leah more than she was prepared to deal with.

* * *

Forty minutes later, with no demons in evidence and no return of the hostages—after all that time spent trying not to be consumed by thoughts of what had happened to those people—Leah decided to lead a small team into the building.

"My advice," Marrick said, "is not to do it."

"Upstairs sent us out here for answers. We're not going to get them sitting on the rooftop."

"We're not going to get them *quickly*," Marrick replied. "Doesn't mean we're not going to get them. Going inside that place is risky."

"So is coming back to this rooftop—"

"Doesn't have to be this rooftop."

"—or one like it, seems at the very least *as* risky."

Marrick scratched his jaw through his tight-fitting mask. "Then my next bit of advice is to let one of the young pups lead the insertion."

"They don't know enough."

"Then send your seasoned pro."

"You?"

Marrick shrugged. Due to the faceless appearance of his mask, the effort looked strange. "That's what we underlings are for."

"Sending other people to do my scut work isn't my way."

"You'll never get into an upstairs position."

"I see that you didn't, either."

"No, ma'am."

"I'm depending on you to get me out of there if this thing goes badly."

"I will." Marrick offered his hand. "Godspeed."

"You, too." Leah shook his hand, then laid a palm on the side of the building and swung over. Nanowire hooks slid out of her armor from her palms, boot soles, forearms, and knees. They bit into the mortar and held her like a human fly as she crept down the building's side.

Three of her team met her at the bottom of the alley. Together, they ran away from Regent Street a block deeper into Soho District, then six blocks down. Crossing Regent there, they crept back up to the Apple store.

Carrying the Cluster Rifle she'd chosen as her lead weapon for the insertion, Leah crept through the shadows leading to the target building. The way the structures had been built along Regent Street, all butting into one another and standing shoulder to shoulder, hadn't allowed for alleys. But with the carnage that had occurred during the invasion and the continued depredations by the demons, most of the buildings in the area stood Swisscheesed with holes and gaps.

She crawled over rubble, then made her way across debris-strewn floors. She'd deliberately chosen to enter on the second floor of the building adjacent to the Apple store. Once there, they crossed through shattered walls. They maintained radio silence.

Over the main showroom floor, feeling a vibration pulsing below, Leah pressed her left little finger against the floor, straightened her wrist, and fired a monofilament link through the concrete and acoustic on the ceiling below. The vid-link came online just in time to reveal the small puff of dust that floated down from the ceiling. That was the only disturbance that the penetration created. The small cloud of dust vanished before it floated three feet.

A quick survey showed that macabre machinery honeycombed the area. Leah had never seen anything like it. A rectangular mass of wiring and components, all of it looking jury-rigged instead of finished, occupied the

center of the room. Darkspawn demons labored slavishly
over it.

Bilious green and yellow lights flashed within the machine's interior and made it look like the gaping maw of
some great creature. Power umbilical cords snaked across
the floor and threaded through the machinelike veins and
arteries. For the first time, Leah realized the vibration she
felt came from the machine below.

Looking up at her team, Leah held out her hand. Taggart took it, then the suit-to-suit stealth link booted so
that they saw what she saw through the vid-link. All of
them kept watch for demons.

A demon yanked one of the four hostages to her feet
and shoved toward the machine. She didn't go willingly. The Darkspawn slapped her with his gun butt and
knocked her down. When they stood her up again, she
swayed drunkenly.

Another Darkspawn fitted a collar around the woman's
neck. A moment later, a demon attached an umbilical as
well. The woman fell backward into the arms of one of
the waiting Darkspawn. They carried her to the machine.
Another demon opened a recessed cubicle that slid out of
the machine. Without care, they dumped the woman into
the cubicle and closed the hatch.

Looking at the hatches on that side of the machine,
Leah realized room for forty or more people existed
within. Nausea twisted sharply through her stomach.

A shadow moved in front of her. It took her just a moment to realize it was in the room with her, not something
in the horror below she was watching.

She retracted the monofilament snooper wire and
reached for the Cluster Rifle as dozens of Stalker demons
slithered out of the shadows around them.

"Run!" Leah ordered. "Back the way we came!"

Bright lights from energy blasts and muzzle flashes filled the room. The building vibrated with the assault. Leah pointed the Cluster Rifle at one of the largest groups of Stalkers in the room and squeezed the trigger. A salvo of missiles tore into the demons and blew her backward. She remained on her feet, but only just.

Pieces of shredded and flaming demons stuck to the walls. A cavernous hole opened in the center of the ceiling and started spreading. She took brief satisfaction in the destruction, but her survival instinct quickly eclipsed that success.

She ran after her team. Weapons fire from the demons below broke through the ceiling and shattered the surface. Sections of it buckled and dropped, leaving holes.

Then they reached the gap leading to the next building. Taggart stepped aside, pulled the pin on a grenade, and slipped the spoon. "Fire in the hole!" He counted down and tossed the grenade.

The incendiary blew up and filled the immediate vicinity with flames. Some of the fire clung to Leah's suit, but she ignored it. The material was fire-suppressive. Once the flames burned through their fuel source, they'd go out.

Before they reached the wall breach that led to the alley outside, a Fetid Hulk rose up from the debris. Muzzle flashes and the flames briefly lit up the creature's dark green scales. The demon lashed out with its clublike fists, dropping them like hammers.

Leah lifted her weapon, aimed at the center of the Fetid Hulk's chest, and fired. Missiles streaked on target and blew the creature back several steps. Before she reached her downed teammates, another Fetid Hulk reared up beside her.

She tried to turn, to bring up her weapon and back away at the same time. Her back foot slipped on loose

THIRTY-EIGHT

Hatton Cross tube station stood silent and empty, but Simon knew that didn't mean the place had been left unprotected. Especially not with the secrets it held.

The familiar red, white, and blue sign advertising the London Underground hung askew. The windows held shards. Several sections of the train tracks under the cut-and-cover housing of the tube trench had been ripped up. Simon didn't know if the destruction had been done by demons or by scavengers looking for steel.

A pulling engine and several cars lay overturned and broken inside the tube trench. The cargo had been jettisoned by looters—or survivors, depending on when the action had taken place—and covered the ground. There wasn't much use for electronic equipment after the invasion. Food and medicine had become everything.

Just as it was in the redoubt, he reminded himself grimly.

"We're not going to stand out here all night, are we, mate?" Nathan asked.

Simon waited a beat more, scanning the area one more time. "No."

"So which do you least want to run into?" Nathan asked. "Templar from the Underground? Or demons? I mean, if we get busted by the Templar, there's all that embarrassment to factor in."

"I want to get in and out quietly," Simon replied. "No muss, no fuss. I just hope the supplies are still there and in good shape." He waited just a moment more, then gave the order to close in. Once they were moving, some of the indecision and worry went away.

Long, quiet minutes passed as they sifted through the wreckage inside the tube station and cleared the underground section. They used their armored hands like miniature steam shovels to dig through the wreckage. Once they had the way cleared, they crept deeper into the tunnel. Simon shoved buttoncams into the walls and ceiling at regular intervals. He linked them to the HUDs of the team and used them to mark the distance.

Five hundred seventeen yards into the tunnel, Simon turned to the wall and scanned the surface. Neon-bright graffiti stood out on the concrete. A broken skeleton lay at the bottom. Another was scattered across the tracks.

"Let's put up a Node there," Simon said, indicating a tube section fifty yards away. "That should give us breathing room enough. And I want buttoncams, heat sensor, and motion detectors a hundred yards farther on from that."

The team moved into position and started working. The security alarms were in place before the Node generators were. They'd gotten faster at implementing them.

When everything was in place, Simon turned his attention back to the wall.

"Doesn't look like anyone's been this way in some time, mate," Nathan said.

"No." Simon struck the slab surface with an armored fist. Concrete plugs concealing bolts shattered and fell out of the holes. "This supply dump was set up as an auxiliary.

A way station for anyone that got locked outside the main areas. Or if the main areas were lost."

"So what kind of swag are we hoping to find?"

Simon had the suit form and ID Spike and rammed it into the six bolts. Trying to get at the hidden door without properly releasing them would trigger an explosion that would destroy everything within.

"Dry goods. Cereals. Powered milk. Powdered eggs."

"Any chance of those little sausage tins?" Nathan asked. "I've missed those."

"Beggars can't be choosers," Danielle told him. "You may just have to forgo that pleasure a little longer."

Once the ID Spike recognized Simon as a member of a Templar House, the bolts released. He grabbed hold of the wall section and pulled it away. A gleaming security door lay beneath. The steel oblong looked like a submarine hatch.

"How did you know about this storage facility?" Nathan asked.

"My father made me memorize the locations of all of them," Simon said. "At least, he tried. He knew them, all of the lords did, but I could never remember them all."

"Good thing you remembered this one. We've got meat and water to last for a time, but the dry goods will help."

Simon agreed. They'd still been taking deer, but he feared they'd already overhunted the area and that the herd might not recover. That didn't agree with the conservation the Templar taught.

"But I'd kill for some cheese, mate. And a bottle of wine."

The door unlocked with a series of rapid-fire clicks. An automated voice sounded inside Simon's HUD.

"Welcome, Lord Templar."

Simon pulled and the heavy door opened on a sheen of

frictionless metal liquid. Lights dawned inside the hallway. He stepped inside.

Danielle grabbed his shoulder and halted him. "This isn't the only way in and out, is it?"

"It's a Templar storage facility," Simon said. "There are *two* ways out once we're inside."

"Oh. Okay. I was just checking. How big is this place?"

"Two stories."

"There should be quite a lot of supplies in here."

"If no one's gotten to them—"

"Which I doubt," Nathan said. "Going by the shape of the concrete wall."

"—there should be enough to help us for months," Simon finished. He strode down the hallway.

"Then why haven't we come here before?" Danielle asked.

"I didn't want to take anything from the Templar."

"*We're* the bloody Templar, mate." Nathan slapped the wall. The metal-on-metal contact reverberated through the hallway. "Not those people still in hiding."

"Not all of them want to hide," Danielle said.

"So far," Simon said, "we've been able to work things out for ourselves. We haven't asked for anything."

"We're not asking now," Nathan said.

"And we haven't taken anything that we haven't earned, either," Simon went on.

"Sometimes, mate, you play it too straight and narrow. If my father had been a lord of a House so that I knew about a place like this, we'd already have been here."

"Simon's right," Danielle said. "If we'd taken this straightaway, Booth and some of the others would have had cows over it. They'd have reduced what we're doing to thievery, not survival."

"It's not thievery or survival," Simon said. "It's taking care of the innocents that rely on us. We're not going to break that faith."

He stopped at another door, fed it his ID, and opened it. Beyond a two-story vault sat filled with packaged cereals, powered milk, powdered eggs, pastas, and canned goods.

"Bloody brill," Nathan whispered, and the relief in his voice sounded strong. "We need bigger lorries, mate."

Simon hated stringing the Templar out on a supply line, but trying to move everything together would have taken far too long. They were already exposed and vulnerable. At least the suits' extra strength and speed helped cut off some time.

They'd located two lorries nearby that had been in decent shape. Both of them remained capable of carrying big loads. The dry goods wouldn't necessarily be heavy, but they took up a lot of space. After making sure the engines worked and there was enough petrol to get them at least to the edge of London, they'd pushed both of the lorries less than a mile to the tube station. A band of survivors watched from hiding, but there was no sign of demons.

In short order, they loaded the first lorry and worked on the second. The buttoncams picked up movement aboveground.

"Alert," the suit's AI said. On the HUD, a square melted down and showed a nearby street corner.

"Nathan," Simon called.

"Got it, mate."

"Carry what you have, and let's get it loaded. Everybody out of the tunnel."

Once everyone was out of the storeroom, Simon sealed

the hatch, replaced the wall, and screwed it back into place. Sword in one hand, case of nutrient bars in the other, he headed back up the stairs.

Dawn remained hours away, so full dark lay over the city. The eternal pall of black smoke blocked out whatever moon there might have been.

"Load the lorrie," Simon said. "If we can get out of here in one piece, that's what we'll do."

Before the Templar had the loading finished, an amplified voice announced, "Stop what you're doing and step away from the lorries."

Simon's team bristled with weapons. He sheathed his sword and held his hands up. "Everybody just relax."

"It's going to be hard relaxing," Nathan said, "knowing we're looking down gun barrels now."

"This is Simon Cross," Simon said. "I—"

"We know who you are," a harsh voice replied. "Step away from the lorries."

"I've got people who need this food."

"That belongs to the Templar. To us."

"Since when did the Templar own anything that they weren't prepared to give to the first person they saw who needed it?" Simon asked. "My father, Lord Thomas Cross, taught me that we're knights first and foremost. Our duty in this life is to make the burden of others easier to bear when we're on the road together." He pointed at the lorries. "That food is going to women and children who will otherwise starve without it."

"That's not our problem."

"It should be," Danielle said. "You should be embarrassed to call yourselves Templar."

Not exactly what I would have said at this point, Simon thought ruefully. But he let it stand and waited to see how it would go over.

"High Seat Booth gave orders that you're not to be allow—"

"Enough," a deeper voice growled. "You're givin' me a headache, you are." One of the Templar stood and walked out of the shadows. His armor was gray matte and olive, sleek and rounded. He carried a two-handed battle axe.

"Get back here, Sergeant Harstead."

"No sir, I won't," Harstead replied. "Not when there's hungry people waiting on those supplies. You won't catch me taking food out of the mouths of babes and women. On *nobody's* orders. Including the High Seat's." He laid his massive axe over his shoulder and looked back at the other Templar taking shelter there. "Is that how the rest of you want to handle your duties here?"

A chorus of nos rang out.

Simon's gut unclenched a little.

Harstead turned back to Simon. "Is there anything else you're gonna be needin', Lord Cross?"

"No," Simon said. "We've taken almost as much as we can carry, and we've overstayed. We've locked up inside. Thank you."

"Have you got safe passage out of the city?"

"We're going to find out. I've got armored vehicles waiting for me at the city's edge."

"Perhaps we could ride along," Harstead volunteered. "We've got four armored units. If you get into a sticky wicket on your way out of the city, maybe we could lend a hand."

"That would be appreciated. If you're sure you're not going to get into any trouble."

"I'm a Templar, Lord Cross. Maybe some of these other men and women have forgotten what that is, but I haven't. I knew your father. I would have died with him if I could have."

"I'm sure he would have wanted you to live," Simon said.

Harstead yanked a thumb over his shoulder at the first speaker. "That's the High Seat's cousin. We've noticed that a lot of positions have gone to Booth's family within the House of late. This one has brains and is good with a sword, but he's still in the process of learning to think for himself. Still busy kissing his cousin's boots."

"Keep a respectful tone, Harstead," the younger man replied.

"I will, Lieutenant, just as soon as you give me something I can stomach, let alone respect."

"You can't just take over this patrol."

"Do you really want to put it to a vote, Lieutenant?"

The officer was quiet for a moment. "No."

"Good. Then I'll let you come with us instead of tying you up and shoving you into the back of one of the vehicles."

Behind his blank faceplate, Simon grinned. With the extra security, travel across the city would be safer, but it was still a long way to get through the city.

THIRTY-NINE

A painful slap woke Leah. Agony ripped through her face. She blinked through a haze of tears up at the monstrous demon above her. Automatically, Leah tried to grab her weapons and blast it, but she couldn't move her arms. In fact, none of her moved. She'd been strapped naked to one of the modules in the machine.

The demon above her had an elongated head and a curved proboscis that looked as if it could strike through palladium alloy. The thin frame looked too weak to support the bulbous head.

"Are you awake now?" the demon demanded. It spoke English haltingly.

Leah didn't reply.

A grin curved the demon's lipless mouth. "You're close enough." It reached back and took out a collar. His thick fingers manipulated it for a moment, then it sprang open.

Leah fought as the demon encircled her neck with the collar. Vibrations and heat raced across her flesh as the device started working. She growled in helpless rage.

"Struggle," the demon encouraged. "It only makes the inevitable more pleasant to watch."

Pain screamed through Leah's body. For a time, she heard her own screams, then she either went deaf or lost her voice. After a while, she passed out.

* * *

Leah stared at the featureless metal walls of the small room around her and struggled to remember how she'd arrived there. There were obvious gaps in her memory because the last thing she recalled was having the collar around her neck.

She raised a hand to her neck and felt nothing. More than that, instead of being naked, she wore her blacksuit again. She opened a comm-channel.

"This is Raven Leader. Does anyone read me?"

There was no reply.

"This is Raven Leader. Is anyone out there?" Anxiety ratcheted up inside Leah. For a moment, she thought a shadow drifted along the ceiling. She ducked, raised her left arm, and drew the Thermal Bolter and SRAC machine pistol from her holsters.

Her distorted reflection formed a large, fuzzy patch on the metal ceiling. Even when she recognized it, Leah didn't lower her weapons. The sense of dread remained strong within her.

No door existed in the ceiling. She scanned the floor. No door existed there, either. How could she have entered a sealed room?

She stomped the floor, but it sounded solid. Unable to accept the fact that no opening existed in the room, she sheathed the Thermal Bolter and rapped the SRAC's folding butt against the wall. She took a sounding every six inches.

When she'd made her way around the room along all four walls without finding anything, she took a break, calmed herself, and started from top to bottom. On the second wall she detected a hollow *bong* that let her know the area beyond wasn't solid.

Trying not to get overly hopeful, Leah concentrated

on the section of wall. She ran through the various light bands open to her goggles and finally discerned a hairline crack in the surface.

An image floated to her mind and she remembered the strange machine she'd discovered with the demons in the Apple store. Where had that gone? How had she gotten away from that?

Heat filled the room till it felt like an oven. She placed her palm against the section and sprung the nanohooks that allowed her to cling to walls. Released, the hooks bit into the metal. She pushed a foot against the wall to gain leverage, then pulled.

The wall section creaked open reluctantly. Darkness filled the narrow opening behind it.

"Raven Leader," a weak voice called over the comm-link.

Thank God. "This is Raven Leader," Leah answered. "Who is this?"

"Geoffrey," the voice responded. "Geoffrey Timms. I need help. I've been wounded."

Geoffrey Timms was one of the younger men who had been assigned to the team.

"Stay calm," Leah said. "Tell me where you're at."

"I don't know."

"Look around."

"Some kind of room. Metal walls."

"Do you remember how you got there?" Leah asked.

"No. I just woke up here." Geoffrey broke into a fit of coughing. When he started speaking again, he sounded weaker. "I'm bleeding bad."

"I'll find you," Leah said, even though she didn't know how to manage that. She closed her eyes and thought. "Bang on the wall. Let me hear you." She prayed that he was close by.

A moment later, thuds sounded behind the wall to her left, not the wall with the opening.

"Can you hear me?" Geoffrey asked.

In answer, Leah banged on the left wall. "I can. Do you hear me?"

"I do." Geoffrey laughed in relief, but that quickly ended as another coughing fit started.

"Hang on," Leah said. "I'll find a way to find you." She sheathed the SRAC and hauled herself into the narrow hole in the wall.

The darkness inside the short tunnel was complete. She couldn't see anything. Now that she thought about it, though, she didn't know where the light in the small room behind her had come from. Just as she thought that, the light went out.

Leah couldn't tell how far she crawled. It didn't make sense that it was far, but it seemed like forever. Her ragged breath sounded like a bellows in the confined space. It was worse because she couldn't see. Her imagination filled the darkness with all kinds of demons. None of her suit's light emitters worked.

"Geoffrey," she called out because she didn't want to be alone anymore, "are you still with me?"

"Yes. Barely."

"Just hold on. I'll be there soon."

"What's taking so long?"

"The way is confusing. Just keep talking to me." The comm-link suddenly spat painful static into her ears. She almost ripped her mask off before it stopped. "Geoffrey?"

There was no answer.

"Geoffrey?" Leah crawled a little faster. She wondered if the demons had found him.

Then she reached the end of the tunnel. Her fingers

brushed against it, then she put a palm against the smooth metal surface and found that it completely covered the end of the passageway.

Panic vibrated through her. She tried getting leverage against the end but couldn't push hard enough. It didn't make any sense that the passageway went nowhere.

Machinery hummed behind her and a light came on. When she glanced back the way she'd come, she saw that the other end of the passageway was now closed as well. Even worse, a series of spinning blades fired into motion and came inexorably toward her feet.

Desperate, she glanced around and spotted another wall section to her right. She slammed her palm against it, fired the nanohooks, and yanked the cover from the opening behind it. Hoping to jam the spinning blades coming for her feet, she spun the metal at them. Without pause, the blades turned the metal cover into confetti in a harsh buzz that deafened Leah.

"Leah!" Geoffrey called.

His communicatio came as a surprise. Leah had barely enough room to twist her body and pull herself inside. She imagined the blades were only fractions of an inch from her feet when she got clear.

"Leah!"

The blades stopped moving an inch or so from the wall. For a moment Leah had feared they were going to turn and pursue her. Instead, they blocked her return.

"Geoffrey," Leah said. "It's okay. I'm here."

"That noise sounds horrible."

"I know. It's nothing." *Now.* Leah crawled forward more and reached a ninety-degree turn to a tunnel that went straight up. She barely managed to negotiate the turn, then had to use the nanohooks to climb into the waiting darkness.

The opening slammed shut behind her.

"Geoffrey," she called. There was no answer.

Leah found four more openings and two more death-traps. She kept the turns in mind, mentally mapping the way, and believed she was at least headed in the direction of the thudding she'd heard earlier. It was impossible to know, however.

"Leah." Geoffrey's voice sounded weaker than ever when she heard it again.

"I'm here," she said.

"Thought I'd dreamed you."

"No."

"I've been having a lot of weird dreams."

"It's probably fever." Leah reached another dead end and wanted to scream in frustration.

"I'm cold."

"Just hang on." Carefully, Leah felt around the wall blocking her way, then the sides of the passageway. "Can you bang on the wall for me again?"

"Yeah. I think so."

Leah listened intently. A moment later, she heard slow, weak thumping from below. She silently cursed the fact that she couldn't see in the darkness even with the new eye and all the tech included in her suit.

"I hear you," she said. "You sound closer." She thumped the walls.

"So do you."

"I'll be there in just a few more minutes. Just hang on." Leah slapped a palm against the bottom of the passage-way and tried to shift a loose cover. Then her knee banged against the passageway and she heard the hollow boom. Excited, she pushed herself back down and slammed a palm against the surface there. A plate pulled away. Light dawned at the end of the tunnel some ten feet below.

"Leah?"

This time Leah heard Geoffrey's voice over the comm-link as well as with her own ears. He was below.

"I hear you, Geoffrey. I'm almost there."

She resisted the impulse to drop down feet first because she wouldn't have been able to see what—and who—was inside the room until she was already there herself. She shoved her head and shoulders into the opening and crawled through. Blood, drawn by gravity, rushed to her head.

At the bottom, she looked around. The low-level light barely revealed the metal walls of the small room and the man lying on the floor. Blood gleamed dark and wet on the metal.

Geoffrey looked pale as he lay there. His eyes were burning hollows that struggled to focus on her. He kept both hands tight to his middle.

"Hey," he said.

"Take it easy," Leah said. "I'm going to help you." She placed a hand on one side of the opening, then the other hand on the other side. When she had herself anchored, she slithered out and flipped to land on her feet.

"Can't believe you found me," Geoffrey croaked.

"I did." She walked toward him.

"Do you have any water?"

Leah started to say no, then she felt the familiar weight of a water canteen at the back of her equipment belt. She handed the flask to the man.

"Go easy with that," she admonished. "You look like you're burning up with fever." In the end, she had to help him. The odd thing was that even though she poured and

Geoffrey drank, no explanation existed for why water pooled on the floor.

Then, as she watched, Geoffrey's skin faded away and left only a skeleton behind. She'd poured the water through the open, ivory grin of a dead man.

Chilled, Leah recoiled and sealed the water flask. Depending on how long she was going to be trapped inside the maze, she needed to conserve water.

Mentally fatigued and emotionally wrought, Leah stared at the skeleton and wondered how it had gotten there. When she closed her eyes just a moment to rest them, she was unprepared for what faced her.

The skeleton had disappeared. She was once more back in the featureless room.

FORTY

They're not going to like you being there," Naomi said.

"Not at first," Warren agreed. "But when they hear what I have to offer—"

"They'll hate you even more. They'll want to believe you, but some of them will still be afraid."

"—they'll hear me out." At least, Warren hoped that was true. Two days had passed since he'd lost his refuge. He and Naomi had slept in squats while seeking out a Cabalist sept that he could influence. This morning they'd found one.

They were down in Piccadilly, sorting through the wreckage of flats and shops. Naomi had heard about some of the Cabalist groups gathering in the area. The one they'd found was on the sixth floor of a tenement building.

Guards posted at the perimeter challenged them. All three men were large, obviously chosen because of their size. Tattoos covered their faces and exposed arms, necks, and chests. Their armor had been fashioned from demon beasts, pieces of hide stitched together with sinew because artificially made thread or fishing line would have robbed what little arcane energy they possessed.

"What do you want?" The speaker was a gaunt-faced young man with a Mohawk. His face was discolored by the red tattoos he bore. He held a machete in one hand and had another slung over his shoulder.

"I'm Warren Schimmer. I need to speak to the Voice of your sept."

The three guards swapped knowing looks.

"Our Voice won't want anything to do with you," another man said. Blood leaked from wounds in his head where he'd recently grafted three small demons' horns. They were from a flying demon no larger than a spider monkey, but which had the ability to throw off waves of electricity.

"I think he will," Warren said confidently. "When he finds out what I have to offer."

"Don't be too proud of yourself, demon thing."

"I'm not." Warren gestured at the man.

A wave of shimmering force slammed into the man. His knees buckled and he went down to the cracked pavement. He cried out in pain.

The young man with the machete brought his weapon toward Warren's head with startling suddenness. Almost effortlessly, Warren blocked the strike with the spear, turned the heavy blade to one side, and banged the spear's butt against the ground. A wall of force erupted from the ground and blew the man backward.

The third man, this one shaved bald to show the tattooing across his skull, drew a blocky-looking pistol. A strange liquid reservoir attached to the top *glugged* as he fired.

With one hand, Warren raised a shield. Four small demons no bigger than the end of his little finger embedded in the shield. They wriggled horned tails angrily, striking the shield again and again.

Naomi choked back a curse and retreated. The demons had weapons that fired living ammunition, insect swarms and things like this, but Warren had never seen them in the hands of Cabalists.

"Interesting," Warren commented. "Did you make the weapon yourself? Or did you learn how to use it?"

The Cabalist leveled his weapon again.

Warren gestured and the wriggling ammunition flew back from the shield and stopped only inches away from the Cabalist's head. The man got the message and lowered his weapon.

The Cabalist with the three small horns stood. A look of amazement showed on his face as he ran a hand over his horns. "My head feels strange," he said.

The pistol-wielding Cabalist looked at him. "Your head has been healed, mate. The horns look like they've grown there forever."

"Healed?" The Cabalist ran his fingertips around the horns. Surprise filled his features, too. He looked at Warren. "You did this? You healed me?"

"Yes," Warren answered.

"How?"

"This is one of the things I have to offer."

The Cabalist kept pulling at his horns as though he couldn't believe it.

"I want to see the Voice," Warren repeated.

"All right," the man said. "Let me send someone to let her know." He gestured to the Cabalist with the Mohawk.

Growling curses, the younger Cabalist got to his feet and went inside the building. As an afterthought, Warren imploded the live ammunition and let their lifeless bodies drop to the ground.

The building's interior was a wreck, but a few areas had been cleaned out to make living space. Warren counted as many as thirty people, but there might have been more. None of them appeared happy to see him. Watchful eyes stared at him as he walked up the stairs to the third floor.

A large section of the second floor held garden containers. Herbs and vegetables flourished. Judging from the size of the vegetable boxes, everything was designed to be immediately mobile.

He recognized some of the herbs and spices as things that were used in natural medicines, but there were several plants that looked warped and twisted. Some of them only grew in areas the Burn had claimed.

A young woman stood waiting on the third floor. She looked nineteen or twenty, slender and Asian. Her shoulder-length hair was electric blue, and she had almond-shaped green eyes. Tattoos covered her face, arms, and legs. She wore a tunic top, cargo shorts, and hiking boots. Although she didn't look like someone who would be a Voice of a Cabalist sept, Warren felt the power rolling off her.

"I'm Daiyu," she said. Four Cabalists stood around her.

Warren almost smiled at that. Although the woman was petite, probably not even five feet tall, the power he sensed about her offered more protection than the men.

"I'm Warren Schimmer," he said.

"I've heard of you. They say that you belong to no sept."

"I don't."

Daiyu studied him with open interest. "I also heard that you command power without wearing tattoos or sigils."

"I don't need them."

"They say that's because you wear the demon's hand and his mark." Daiyu's eyes rested on Warren's silver hand.

Warren flexed the hand to show that he owned it and that it worked. "It allows me to focus my power, but the power I have is my own."

"I see." Daiyu focused on his eyes again. "What do you want here?"

"To make you a deal you can't refuse," Warren said.

"There's nothing you can give me that I can't take for myself."

Warren gestured to the man whose horns he'd healed. Reluctantly, the man approached them.

"Your people try to emulate the demons by wearing their trophies," Warren said. "All they do is make themselves weaker by opening wounds into their bodies. I can heal them, and I can teach you to guarantee that the transplants you're attempting take hold and become permanent."

"Look at my horns," the Cabalist entreated. "He healed them only moments ago."

Daiyu waved the man down to his knees, then examined the horns. Cautiously, she touched one of them with a forefinger. An electrical spark stung her flesh, and she jerked back.

"Once the transplants are in place," Warren said, "they become foci and allow a greater control of the arcane forces your people can control."

The young woman eyed him suspiciously. "Will the body later reject them?"

"No. Not unless the person wearing them decides they no longer want them."

Conversations around them grew louder. More Cabalists came from the other floor to listen in.

"We're supposed to accept your word on this?" Daiyu asked.

"If you have another offer," Warren said, "then you should take it." He made himself sound brave, but he'd never interacted with people well. He wasn't forceful by nature, and he wouldn't have been now if he hadn't been so desperate. He had nowhere to run, no hiding place, and Lilith seemed bent on dragging him to his destruction if he couldn't take care of himself.

"You said you came to make a deal," Daiyu told him.

"Yes."

"But it's not a deal until you get something out of it."

Warren was impressed. She was smarter than he'd expected.

"I want the same thing you want," he told her. "I want more power. I can't get any more without help."

"You want my help?"

"No."

"Then what?"

"I want you to follow me."

"I follow the First Seer."

"That's fine," Warren said. "Follow the First Seer if you want to. But follow me in this. I can make you more powerful. The First Seer can't. I can give you power that no other Cabalist has."

Daiyu studied him for a moment, then nodded. "I'll have to discuss it with my Savants. I'll get back to you."

"Soon," Warren warned. "I have other people I can talk to."

Naomi took a package of flavored noodles from the bag she'd filled only moments ago from a grocery store a few blocks away. Although there were survivors in the city and it had been four years since the invasion, enough food remained in places to keep many people fed. All the perishable items were long gone.

She opened the package and poured it into a small pot she'd found a few days ago. She missed having proper kitchen equipment like what she'd had at Warren's building. Within a few minutes, a small fire blazed inside the basement apartment where they'd holed up after speaking with the Cabalists under Daiyu. She poured water over the noodles and added the flavor packet.

Warren stood at the window and stared out through the dirty, cracked glass. He appeared calm, but she knew him well enough to know that the appearance deceived.

"What's on your mind?" Naomi asked as the smell of the food filled the small apartment.

"The Cabalists." His distracted tone told her that was only half the truth.

"Are you worried about the decision they'll reach?"

"No. They'll reach the right decision. They don't have a choice. I can do things for them and teach them things they can't do on their own."

"I have to admit, I thought they'd be more afraid of you."

"They are afraid of me," Warren said, "but they're more afraid of not ever being able to do what I can do."

A little jealously, Naomi knew that she had the same fear. "Are you going to teach them those things?"

"Yes."

"Why haven't you taught me?"

He looked at her. "Do you really want to learn?"

Naomi thought about that. She was torn. Having more power, especially with all the danger around her, was a good thing. The only part that worried her was how close she'd have to get to the demons in order to have that power.

"Perhaps," she answered.

Warren smiled a little sadly. "That's why I haven't taught you. Something like this, you have to want it."

"Did you?"

"Not at first, but I knew I was going to have to learn everything I can if I'm going to survive. There's no guarantees even then."

Naomi stirred the pasta. "Have you seen Lilith lately?" The demon hadn't been around in two days, so far as Naomi knew.

"No."

"Where do you think she's gone?"

"I don't know."

"Will she be back?" Naomi silently hoped not.

"Yes."

"If the Cabalists come back to you and accept your offer, what are you going to do?"

"I'm going to teach them to fight the demons."

"I thought you were convinced anyone who did that was only going to get killed."

"Not," Warren said, "if you win."

"Do you think we can really win?"

"Hiding is no longer an option. Since the beginning of this thing, I've been drawn into the demons' battles." Warren paused. "I've fought for everyone but me."

For a moment, Naomi saw the fear in him. Many times she'd mistaken it as selfishness, but she'd learned that it was fear. There was something broken inside Warren that had never been fixed.

"What about you?" Warren asked. "Are you going to stay or go?"

Naomi had been asking herself the same question. As soon as the building where they'd been hiding had been destroyed, most of what Warren had had to offer her had been lost. Without the sanctuary, he was a lightning rod for demons.

"Does it matter?" she asked.

He hesitated. "Yes."

"What do you want me to do?"

"I'd like you to stay, but it's going to be dangerous. I don't want you to get hurt."

"I don't want to be hurt, either. But I'm going to stay."

Warren nodded, tried to speak, and couldn't. He just nodded again.

"The pasta's ready," she said. "You need to eat."

Together, using chopsticks they'd found in the debris of a Chinese restaurant, they ate from the bowl and listened to the screams of demons and victims out on the streets.

FORTY-ONE

L eah strained at the wall. The nanohooks on her palm locked deeply into the metal. Just when she thought the panel wasn't going to move, metal screeched and it slid free. Instead of a passageway as she normally found, a breeze loaded with the scent of pine and fresh grass wafted in.

In disbelief, Leah stared out at the forest beyond the opening. She didn't know how the machine she'd been buried in had ended up in a forest, and she wasn't going to waste time questioning it. She shoved her head and shoulders through the opening and fell out onto the soft earth.

Heart hammering, she pushed herself to her feet and ran. Fog partially obscured the landscape and blocked the sunlight when she glanced up and tried to get oriented. She didn't know in what direction she fled, but anywhere away from the demon machine had to be good.

The marshy land held water in puddles and pools. She ran through them, getting soaked and chilled almost at once. Her clothing, cold and heavy with mud, clung to her as she ran. Her breath gusted out in gray puffs.

At the top of the grade, winded and unable to run any farther, she stood in the shadow of a gnarled spruce tree and gazed back. The demon machine looked as big as a three-story building. She knew it couldn't be because it had fit inside the Apple store.

That's where it fit the last time you were outside of it,

Leah told herself. *The demons could have added to it. But how did they move it? How long have I been trapped in there?*

While getting her breath back, she scanned the countryside. At the very least she expected roving patrols. There was nothing. Not even a bird broke cover.

How many other people are in that thing? She didn't know. She was certain she'd been inside it for days, but she couldn't be sure she'd ever seen or heard anyone else. Everything she'd encountered inside the machine had been an illusion.

It had to be. She'd witnessed horrible things.

Breath regained, she turned and ran down the other side of the hill. She didn't know where she was. The ground was springy and damp. Verdant growth clutched all the way up her legs to her knees.

She ran until she couldn't run anymore, and she thought she'd gone for miles. The countryside never changed. The fogbound landscape was impenetrable. Finally, exhausted, she lay down. Just to rest. Somewhere out there birds chirped. Although she didn't want to, she slept.

When Leah woke, she was dreaming that she was back in the attack on the munitions plant. She was hunkered down behind an overturned freight van. The SRAC machine pistol and Thermal Bolter felt heavy in her hands.

"Leah!"

She stared at the dead man at her feet. His name was Jamey Capps, but she'd never met him in her life.

"*Leah!*"

When she glanced up, Leah saw Robert Wickersham standing in front of her. He looked just as young and vulnerable as that night she'd lost her eye.

This is impossible, Leah thought. *I can't be here.*

"Leah, are you with me?" Wickersham reloaded his assault rifle.

"Yes."

Concern fired his eyes as he looked at her. "You looked like you were somewhere else."

"Where are we?"

Wickersham studied her. "You sure you're all right, love?"

No. "Where are we?"

"Trying to shut down the weapons plant. Where did you think you were?"

Leah shook her head. *Not true! Not true! Something's wrong!* Her senses spun. "Never mind."

"Not like we have any bloody choice. The satchel charge is at your feet. You want to ferry that thing? Or me?"

When she looked down, the satchel charge lay there on the street. Blood dotted the scuffed surface.

"We're Satchel Team Three now," Wickersham said. "Are you ready for this?"

Leah nodded, but she felt anything but ready. She holstered the Thermal Bolter and scooped up the satchel charge.

"Let's go." Wickersham led the way out. He spun round the corner and froze.

"What's wrong?" Leah asked. Then she noted the bloody claw sticking out of Wickersham's back.

He stumbled backward and leaned heavily against her. When she shifted, he flipped round to face her. Blood dripped from his parted mouth. He tried to speak but didn't have any luck. His eyes glazed as she watched, and he slid toward the ground.

No! Leah thought in horror. *That's not what happened! Jamey Capps didn't die, either! These deaths aren't real!*

Even as she denied it, though, a Blade Minion stepped

up in front of her and grinned. Leah tried to bring the SRAC up, but the demon batted it away easily. In the next moment, it thrust its blade hand through her armor and her stomach. With a sideways jerk, it spilled her intestines to the ground.

Unable to remain standing, Leah dropped into the steaming pile of her own body. The pain hammered her mercilessly for a moment, then went away. When it did, she went away with it.

"Can you get the door open?"

Panic welled inside Leah when she realized she wasn't dead. She ran her free hand down her body and found that her stomach was whole and intact. There was no blood. Her other hand held a Scorcher, a pistol designed to spew Greek Fire. It was a Templar design, scavenged from a fallen warrior.

"They're coming. Can you get the door open?"

Dazed, not comprehending, Leah looked over at the speaker. Her night vision barely pulled in enough light to see the four other people in the room. All of them wore black armor.

The big man beside her let out a vicious oath and shoved her out of the way. "What's wrong with you? If we stay here, we're going to die. Those zombies have us outnumbered."

Leah stepped to one side and tried to fathom where she was. It was a tunnel, maybe an auxiliary passage off the tube.

At the back of the passage, the big man worked frantically at a door that was rusted shut. He yanked on the release lever, but it only snapped off in his hands with a banshee screech.

"Here they come!" someone shouted.

"Get set! Hold them back till Pete gets the door open!"

Leah knew the door wasn't going to open. They were at a dead end. Literally.

Zombies lurched into the passageway ahead of them. Blood glistened on their mottled skin, offering silent proof that they'd already succeeded in their hunt for victims.

"Pete! Are you gonna get that door open, mate?"

Looking back at the big man, Leah saw that fear had claimed him. He stood frozen and mute. Then weapons fire filled the tunnel. She fired the Scorcher, feeling it buck and twist in her hand as flames sprayed out over the zombies. Although the first line of them caught fire and jerked in response, the dozens behind them kept pushing them forward. The zombies that succumbed to the flames got trampled on by the undead behind them.

"Pete! *Pete!*"

Explosive weapons blew pieces of zombies in all directions. Limbs, heads, and chunks of dead meat stuck to the ceiling and dropped over the battlers.

The line broke as the first of the zombies reached them. Leah couldn't blame them. The dead eyes, sunken and flat black, were horrible to contemplate.

This is wrong, Leah told herself, trying to calm the mindless terror that reached for her. *I've never been in this situation. I've always escaped.*

Unable to hold against the onslaught of the undead, the line buckled. The frightened cries of men and women choked the small space.

Leah tried to fight clear of the confusion of limbs. Many of them were no longer attached to the original bodies. Blood filmed her lenses and the world took on a red tint. Panic filled her, and she fought against everything and everyone that touched her.

She fired the Scorcher directly into the ravaged face of

the zombie in front of her. Head on fire, the undead thing wrapped its one good arm around her and bore her to the ground.

The living and the dead stepped on her. Pain rattled through her mind as her arms and legs broke beneath the weight. Then her ribs shattered and pierced her lungs. She drowned in her own blood.

"Do you see how it is, human?" a raucous voice asked. "Do you see how you are being used?"

Weakly, Leah pried her eyes open. The demon's features slowly came out of the darkness enveloping her. The solid, flat surface behind her told her that she was once more inside the chamber.

"You never left," the demon barked. "Not physically. Only your thoughts. Only your fear. And you have spread it to all those people you know."

The creature was unlike anything Leah had ever seen before. A segmented, dark green carapace covered the demon, and it gleamed wetly, as if it had just been polished with oil. The face was a narrow blade with bulging, bulbous eyes that gleamed orange. A cluster of antennae, at least a dozen stalks nearly two feet in length, sprouted from the top of its head and brushed its narrow shoulders.

The thing radiated fear. A massive cloud of the emotion slammed into Leah. Her gut reaction forced her to squirm back from it. The wall kept her from going anywhere. Unable to sit still, she kicked at the demon's face.

It moved with incredible swiftness, shifting even as she started the kick. She kicked again and again, but only met defeat.

"You can't touch me," the demon taunted in that hoarse voice. "But I can touch you." A six-fingered hand flicked out. Light flashed on the gleaming black talons.

Before Leah could move, one or more of the talons scored her face right above the eye the Templar surgeons had replaced. Blood wept into her eye and blinded her. Panic screamed through her when she thought it had taken her eye. She pressed back against the wall, dug her heels in as hard as she could, and created as much distance between the demon and herself as she could.

"We know you," the demon said. "We know what you're afraid of. We use your fear to awaken the fear inside your fellow humans. When you sleep, you work for us. So sleep. Sleep and dream the most horrible things so that you can take them into the minds of those who are with you."

Despite her fear and the proximity of the demon, Leah's eyes closed. She slept. And then she dreamed.

Timothy Robinson slept, and Leah slid into the twisted nightmares that had haunted the young man for the past three weeks. That night, he'd nearly died at the talons of a demon patrol. His team had been scouting, marking enemy targets, lurking in the shadows and trying to decide which of those targets were more important, more vulnerable.

They'd been found out by a Templar under the spell of a cursed weapon. Their intel had found out about such things, and even people among their organization sometimes fell prey to them.

Timothy was in his early twenties. When the invasion had come, he'd still been wet behind the ears, just recruited out of Sandhurst Academy. None of his training had prepared him to fight monsters, or the undead.

The Stalkers had erupted out of the darkness and dropped on him and his team. In seconds, the low rooftop where they'd set up their surveillance had turned into a bloody battlefield.

"Run!" Parker, the team leader, had cried.

Timothy had pulled up and run immediately. He laid down covering fire out of habit. In three seconds, five of his scout team were down. In real life, he'd been the only one to escape that rooftop that night, and that hadn't been without cost.

In his nightmare, he didn't get away.

As Leah watched, helpless to do anything, Timothy was brought down by the pack of Stalkers. One of the demons caught him by the ankle. He tripped and fell, managing to catch himself on one hand. He twisted and brought up the machine pistol. When the event had really happened, he'd filled the demon's face with exploding bullets. Tonight, though, the pistol misfired.

Before he cleared the action, another Stalker leaped forward and seized his throat. Fangs passed through the protective armor with effort. It was even money whether the pressure would collapse his throat or the fangs would rip it out.

Timothy gagged and tried to draw a breath. Leah felt his fear and pain. She ran to his side and reached for the Stalker before she thought about what she was doing. Her hands passed through the demon.

"No!" Leah said, certain she was going to be forced to watch the young man die.

"Help!" Timothy croaked. He beat the demon with his fists. "It didn't happen this way! I got away! I didn't die! I didn't *die*!" He jerked and fought.

In the next instant, Timothy woke in twisted sheets. He realized that he was in the barracks in the underground complex. He was safe. But his heartbeat felt as if his heart was going to explode at any second.

Leah stood at his bedside. Somehow the young man was still locked into the dream. She was still with him.

He drew the SRAC machine pistol hanging from his bed and leveled it at her. "Who are you?" he demanded. "What are you doing here?"

"I don't know," Leah answered. Even to her ears, her voice sounded like it came from a million miles away.

"Get out of my head," Timothy ordered. "Take those bloody nightmares with you."

Leah backed away. All around her, other men and women writhed in their beds. She felt the nightmares forming inside their minds.

Face pale and splotchy, Timothy climbed from the bed and kept his weapon trained on Leah. She knew it wouldn't hurt her; she wasn't really there. This was just another nightmare.

"You," Timothy said. "You're the one causing all of this."

"No," Leah said. "It's not me."

"I saw you in my dream."

More people in the barracks came awake. They were lethargic, haunted by sleepless nights and past horrors. They looked at Timothy.

"You weren't there," Timothy said. "You weren't there the night all of them died."

"It's not me," Leah said. "They're using me."

"Who's using you?"

"The demons," Leah said.

"Timothy," a burly man roared. "Who are you talking to?"

"It's a woman." Timothy never took his feverish gaze from Leah. "She's dressed like one of us."

"Timothy," the burly man said in a calm voice. "There's nobody there. Just put the pistol down. Before somebody gets hurt."

A man and a woman crept up on Timothy from behind.

"They can't see you," Timothy growled. "Why can't they see you?"

"I don't know," Leah said. "I don't know how you can see me."

"I want you to get away from me," Timothy said. "I want you out of my head."

"I'm not going to hurt you. I promise."

"You brought the nightmares."

"No."

"Timothy, put the weapon down."

"No, Sergeant. It's this woman." Timothy pointed at Leah. "She's messing with all of our heads. She's bringing the nightmares."

The sergeant slowly kept coming. "Just take it easy, mate." His voice sounded soft and soothing. "Nobody here is going to hurt you."

"Can't you see her?" Timothy demanded. "She's standing right here."

Desperate, knowing that the connection she had with the young man had to have been unexpected by the demons, Leah said, "Keep calm, Timothy."

"*Don't* tell me to keep calm!" Timothy exploded. "I've been watching people around me die for years! I'm tired of it! I'm tired of going out there every night wondering if I'm going to be the next one that gets his ticket punched! You can't live like—"

The two people behind Timothy launched themselves at him. They wrapped him up in arms and legs and took him down to the floor. The big sergeant stepped in quickly and snatched the SRAC pistol away. Timothy fought to get free, but the people lying on top of him had him in cunning grips that he couldn't escape.

He yelled and cursed, and struggled as much as he was able. "She's here! She's the one causing the nightmares!"

"Somebody get a tranquilizer in him," the sergeant said.

Helpless, Leah watched as one of the captors injected the young man. He squirmed and cursed her, then his eyes grew tired and started to droop. Everything around Leah grew fuzzy.

"You've got to listen to me," she told him. "I'm not doing this. I need help. You've got to—"

"—help me." Leah blinked and she was back inside the sterile steel cage. Her heart thudded and pain throbbed at her temples.

The demon was gone, but its mocking laughter lingered.

Get control, she told herself. *Calm down and think.* But all she could think about was that somehow the demons had found a way to use her to get into the sleep of everyone at the complex.

FORTY-TWO

S imon helped log in the latest haul the Templar teams
had brought in from the storage area. It felt good to
have that much food all in one place. Crates, boxes,
and barrels of the dry goods lined one of the caverns
they'd claimed when they'd moved into the underground
bunker.

"I have to admit, this makes things a little easier," Sarah
Kerosky said. She was in her early fifties and served as one
of the nutritionists. "In addition to having a more rounded
and balanced diet, it's good that people are talking about
how much we have instead of how we're doing without."

"I know." During the past five days, since they'd
returned with the first shipment, words of hope and encouragement to the Templar scavenger teams filled the
redoubt.

"We've got meat and grains," Sarah said. "The only
thing I could wish for at this point is fresh vegetables and
fruit."

"Maybe in the spring," Simon said. "I know big farms
exist outside London proper."

"Do you think those will be tended?"

"I don't know. If they aren't, it's possible that some of
the plants could have volunteered. Just come up with new
plants from seeds that dropped in previous years. Plus, we
have seeds now. We could plant those fields."

"You're talking about farming them?"

"No. That would be too dangerous."

Sarah looked wistful for a moment. "They'd do better if they had someone looking after them."

"There's no way to make that happen," Simon replied. "Not yet. But it's something we can think about."

"Someone's looking for us, mate," Nathan stated quietly.

With dawn just bleaching the sky behind him, Simon stood below the rim of a snow-covered hill overlooking the valley where the deer had retreated. Anger and help-lessness surged inside him as he surveyed the dead deer scattered across the hillside.

At least three dozen animals sprawled in the snow. Their limbs were twisted and broken. Some of them had been decapitated. Others had bite marks on their bodies. The small herd had been massacred down to the last deer.

Mixed in with the deer tracks, demon footprints and hook marks shone in the gleaming snow crust. Blood stained the snow and melted it in places.

"They know we're hunting the deer," Nathan said. "So they're going to try to starve us out by killing the herds."

Simon had nothing to say. They'd become more vul-nerable, and he'd known it would happen.

"What are we going to do?" Danielle asked.

Simon stood. "The first thing we're going to do is har-vest the meat here that we can. Send for extra crews to help take the meat. We can at least make sure that the meat's not wasted."

"That's today, mate," Nathan said softly. "This demon, whoever's doing this, is going to come back tonight and find more of the herds."

"We don't have any choice about what we're going to do," Simon said. "The demons are escalating the stakes, so we're going to have to do the same."

"What do you mean?"

"When night comes on, we're going hunting for the demons," Simon said. "We're going to be the predators for a while, not the prey."

Harvesting the meat was bitter, bloody work. Simon rotated the teams between butchering the kills and keeping guard. Getting the meat back to the redoubt proved problematic. They had to make certain they didn't leave a blood trail back to the sanctuary.

Inside the redoubt, the story of what the demons were doing had spread like wildfire. Morale dipped lower and lower. The morale gains they'd made by bringing the Templar surplus into the redoubt vanished within hours.

By midafternoon, all of the meat they ould possibly salvage had been harvested and packed away. Simon posted guards, then assigned the men to the hunting party he planned to lead that night. He also gave orders for them to get to bed and rest up before the evening.

Simon sat in front of the computer and went over the topographical maps of the areas around the redoubt. Flying drones canvassed the valley where the deer massacre had occurred. He'd also sent out scouting teams on foot.

So far, no one had found the demons preying on the deer.

The door opened and Nathan entered the room. He joined Simon and surveyed the maps as well.

"Thought you were going to get some sleep, mate," Nathan said.

"I will."

"The clock's ticking. You're not going to have time for a lot of it if you don't start now."

"We need to know where to go if we're going hunting."

"If we don't find anything out here," Nathan said, "we can always go into London. A message is a message."

"I know. But I'm hoping that whatever demon is out here is just an isolated incident."

"Not bloody likely."

Simon heaved a sigh of disgust. "I know."

"The Burn is spreading farther, too."

That had been apparent from the drone recon, and from reports generated by scouts that moved in close to the city's outskirts.

"At best, we only have a few more months in this place," Nathan said. "It's time we started thinking about moving."

"We've already been considering that."

"We need to think more seriously, mate. Children and noncoms are hard to move. If we get trapped in the spring thaw, or if the Burn accelerates and turns the ground around us to mush, we're going to find the way even harder going."

"I know."

"If we wait till summer, we chance our water supply."

Simon knew that, too. The Burn affected too much of the groundwater.

"The biggest problem is finding somewhere to go," Simon said.

"You've got somewhere in mind?"

"Exeter." Simon tapped a key and a map of the city replaced the topographical images of the area around the redoubt.

"Why there?"

"It's centrally located, to a degree. At least we're not backed up against the English Channel and can be cut off. If we get attacked there, we can run in all directions. Also, there are fortifications there we can use. Military places as well as Exeter Cathedral and other buildings that could withstand an attack."

"Especially now that the Nodes are somewhat functional."

"There are tunnels beneath the city that we can use, too," Simon said. "To fight. To hide."

"Sounds good, mate, but it's a bloody long haul. And you try moving these people en masse, you're going to make an awfully tempting target."

"That's the downside." Simon sat up straighter. "I've been working some of the logistics with Wertham. What we'll have to do is move the people from here in stages. Send them out with Templar escort, leave them with Templar escort to protect them in case there's a need."

"The manpower we have is going to be spread pretty thin."

"That's the biggest problem. We need more people to make this happen. But it's the only chance we have. From Exeter, we can try for France if we can find enough boats. Or maybe even the United States if we can find a ship."

"There's no guarantee the North Atlantic Ocean is safe. There are stories that the demons have set up warrens along the coastline and attack any ships they find out in those waters. And there's supposed to be Hellgates that have opened up in the United States and France as well."

"Staying," Simon said, "isn't an option at this juncture. We're going to keep working on it."

"I know." Nathan clapped him on the shoulder reassuringly. "We'll get it figured out, mate. But you need to get some sleep."

"I will."

"Have you heard anything from Leah?"

The topic was a sore point. It had been over a week

since Simon had last seen her. She hadn't been out of his mind for more than five minutes at a stretch.

"No," Simon answered.

"You given any thought to checking up on her?"

"No," Simon lied. He'd thought about it, but he knew he couldn't. He had no idea even where to start looking.

"Well, maybe you should." Nathan hesitated. "What she did, taking that Node design, you and I would have done it, too."

Simon took a breath. "I know."

"In the end, mate, we're all just trying to survive."

Simon crouched in a corner of the tube station. He didn't know where he was or how he'd gotten there. The last thing he remembered was putting his head on his arms at his desk just to rest a moment. With all the signage around, as well as the rubble, the place looked familiar, but a lot of the underground areas in London did.

Darkness filled the low-ceilinged area. His helmet scanned his surroundings with night vision. Something *scraped* against the wall to his right.

Simon stood and took a better grip on his sword. He slid his shield free from his back and positioned it in front of him.

"Nathan," he called softly over the comm.

There was no reply.

"Scan for other Templar," Simon ordered the suit AI.

"Scanning," the suit AI replied.

The scrape sounded again, closer this time. And higher.

Simon glanced up at the ceiling. It was low enough that he could reach up and touch it. He felt something watching him.

"No Templar in area," the suit AI reported.

That didn't make sense. He wouldn't have come, wherever he was, alone. "Scan for all other life signs."

"Scanning."

Simon backed away from the scrape and tried to increase the night vision. Whatever it was, it somehow seemed to know exactly how far his night vision reached. It stayed just out of sight.

"No life signs in area," the suit AI stated.

"What about undead?"

"Select parameters."

Simon thought quickly. "Scan for decaying biological matter. Approximately ten pounds and up."

"Scanning." Then the suit AI sounded a warning almost immediately. "Unidentified object incoming."

Reacting to the unseen threat, Simon raised his shield. The webbing appeared out of the darkness, lit up by the night vision. The strands had two-inch squares. The webbing flared out in an eight-foot by eight-foot square that just raked the ceiling and the floor.

Simon knew he couldn't avoid the net. It came too fast, and it was too big. He pushed his shield forward, hoping to create some room as it closed round him. Instead, the net struck his shield, wrapped around him in a cocoon, and drew tight with a metallic hiss.

"Templar weapon," the suit AI said. "Extraction attempts useless."

Despite already knowing that, Simon struggled. The net tightened around him, trapping him. He couldn't believe he'd been caught so flat-footed.

Footsteps rang against the concrete floor. In the next moment, lights flared to life in the tube station and revealed an armored figure.

She was—or had been—a Templar. Judging from her features, revealed through her faceplate, she was about

Simon's age. Her brunette hair was pulled back and severe brows arched over her ice-blue eyes.

"Hello, Simon," she said in a low, seductive voice. "Or should I call you Lord Cross?"

"Miriam?" Simon said, recognizing the woman. He hadn't seen her since he had last been in the Templar Underground, over four years ago.

"I was." Miriam drew her sword and squatted in front of him. She rested the blade across her thighs. "And I am."

"Why did you do this?"

"Because I came hunting you."

For the first time, Simon noticed the greenish tint to Miriam's features. She'd always been more a handsome woman than beautiful, but the greenish cast to her skin made her look striking.

"Why?" Simon asked.

"My master wanted you."

"What master?"

The familiar rumble of a train suddenly filled the tube. Simon knew the sound, but he couldn't believe it. No trains had run since the night he'd escaped with survivors from the city.

"You'll see soon enough," Miriam said.

A train roared into the station and screeched to a halt. Sparks flew from the steel wheels as the brakes bit and took hold.

Simon struggled again, but the net grew so tight that it made it hard to breathe even with the armor.

"Warning," the suit AI said. "External pressure now dangerous. Suit integrity may not hold."

The train door kicked open automatically. Steam boiled from inside the cars. Miriam took hold of the net in one hand and lifted Simon from the ground. She walked toward the car.

"Where are you taking me?" Simon asked.

"Just wait," Miriam said. "It's a surprise." She stepped through the doors and dropped him in the middle of the car. She took a seat and opened an electronic reader as if she were a regular traveler.

Simon struggled again, but only got the warning once more. His mind raced as he tried to figure out how he'd ended up in the tube station, and how the train remained operable with all the power grids shut down.

It was madness.

"Then you're mad," Miriam said, as if she'd heard his unspoken conclusion. She gazed at him over the reader. "Have you given any thought to that?"

Unable to free himself, Simon lay back as the train hurtled through the tube.

FORTY-THREE

Shrieks pierced Simon's ears as the train's brakes locked down. Sparks sprayed high in the windows and sent flashes of light reflecting inside the car.

"Time to go." Miriam stood and reached down for Simon, catching a fistful of the net near his neck with her hooked fingers. She dragged him from the car as if he were a sack of potatoes. The action caused the net to squeeze more, and some of the strands cut into his armor.

"Warning. Armor integrity breached," the suit AI said.

The train doors shrieked open, and a huge splash of bright light flared into the car. Pain stabbed into Simon's eyes till the faceshield could polarize and counteract the illumination.

When he could bear the light again, barely, he stared out at his surroundings in surprise. Instead of a tube station, Miriam dragged Simon into an open field of burned grass and diseased trees. It was like no place Simon had ever before been.

Miriam tossed him forward effortlessly. He bounced and skidded across the ground, digging divots into the scorched earth as he hit. He rolled into a shallow lake and sank into the mud three feet below the scum-covered surface. Wicked, barbed plants stood above the lake and curled beneath it. They immediately whipped into motion, drawing back and surveying Simon.

"Danger," the suit AI said. "Flooding through suit breach."

Simon felt the water invading his armor at his waist. Instead of cool or cold as he'd expected, the hot water threatened to boil him. Pain climbed his midriff.

"Seal breach," Simon ordered.

"Attempting seal," the suit AI responded.

The water gurgled into the armor. The noise echoed in Simon's ears. The hot water continued to spread, filling up his chest cavity, then trickling into his helmet.

"Failure," the suit AI said. "Failure. Failure. Failure."

The barbed plants struck without warning. Needle-sharp points rapped against his faceplate. Fissures splintered across the surface, but it held for the most part. Beads of hot water formed along the cracks and dripped inside his helmet.

Panic rose inside Simon. He fought to hang on to his composure. Struggling, he managed to rock and roll enough to roll over in the lake. The movement only mired him more deeply in the mud. Then he saw that it was alive with thorny creatures equipped with questing mouths that latched on to his armor. His helmet continued to fill.

You're dreaming, he told himself. *You have to be.* Since he couldn't remember coming here, the tube station and this strange world all had to be figments from a nightmare.

But he couldn't wake.

Something dark and sinuous slithered out of the scummy shallows. It looked like a snake, but he quickly realized it was a tentacle of something much larger. The tentacle rooted under him, then wrapped round him and lifted him from the lake bottom.

"Do you know what this place is, Simon?" Miriam asked over the suit-comm.

"No." Simon had to turn his head to keep water from going down his throat or up his nose.

"This is one of the demon worlds. Not where they're from. They haven't shown me one of those yet. But this is one of those they've captured. This world has been Burned and remade."

The tentacle dragged Simon across the lake bed. For the first time he realized chunks and pieces of buildings lay at the bottom.

"This is what's going to happen to your world," Miriam taunted.

Simon spat water and tried to find room to breathe in the filling helmet. "It used to be your world, too."

"Not anymore."

"What happened to you?"

"I . . . became someone else. Someone that could survive in this world."

"How?"

"You ask too many questions."

Simon's focus returned immediately to his own survival when he saw what the tentacle was attached to. The silt-filled water proved hard to see through, but he saw the massive, bloated body seated in the middle of the lake.

The dark green creature possessed six tentacles. A single, malevolent eye measuring nearly three feet across stared at Simon from the center of its body.

"Identify demon," Simon whispered. He couldn't remember anything like the creature in the material the Templar library had held.

"Command failed," the suit AI replied.

"Can you identify the demon?"

"Query failed."

Simon bumped across the muddy lake bottom.

The lake water that half filled his helmet smelled foul and tasted worse. "What kind of demon has hold of me?"

"Parameters for question invalid."

"Why are the parameters invalid?"

"No creature holds you."

"The creature ahead of me."

"Nothing is there."

"Scan for demons."

"Scanning." A handful of seconds passed. "No demons."

Simon concentrated on the demon. However it blocked the suit AI's sensors, the demon did a complete job.

Something splashed into the water next to him. Holding his breath, he turned his face into the rising water inside his helmet.

A shimmering figure stood there. She was so transparent that she looked like she was made of glass. The shape told him at once that she was female. Her hair floated freely in the lake. A one-piece uniform covered her body. Then he recognized her profile.

"Leah," Simon spluttered.

She turned to face him. Her expression showed doubt and fear. "Simon?" He didn't know how she talked underwater.

The water inside his helmet made it impossible for him to keep watching her. He had to breathe. He turned his head, took a breath, and looked back for Leah. He was surprised to find her at his side.

"What are you doing here?" she asked.

Simon shook his head, unable to speak because of the water in his helmet. He wasn't going to be able to breathe inside the helmet much longer, either.

"This isn't real," Leah said. "None of it."

Simon thought that might have been interesting to debate if he hadn't been drowning.

"For all I know," Leah said, "you're not real."

The tentacle dragged Simon toward the demon. A gaping maw opened in the creature's body. A pink gullet lined with foot-long fangs took shape.

"Are you real?" Leah asked.

Simon turned his head and tried to answer, but it was too late. The water had risen so far inside his helmet he could no longer breathe or speak. He stared at her through the cracked faceplate.

Leah extended a large knife. She sawed at the tentacle. Black blood flooded the water in a spreading cloud. The tentacle writhed, then released Simon.

He knew it was too late. The water inside his helmet was drowning him. He struggled against the net. Leah dragged her knife along the armor. The net strands parted liked string. That wasn't supposed to happen, either.

Planting his feet against the muddy bottom of the lake, Simon propelled himself toward the surface. His hands worked at the helmet locks because he couldn't verbalize the order for the suit AI to disengage the armor. He managed to get the helmet off just before he reached the surface.

When his head broke the surface, he breathed in great draughts of air. He held the helmet in one hand. Treading water in the armor was almost impossible. If it hadn't been for the automatic flotation feature to ensure neutral buoyancy, he'd never have managed.

"You're still alive?" Miriam called from a small hill overlooking the lake.

Simon didn't answer. He spun around in the water and looked for Leah. Despite her unexplained ability to breathe and talk underwater, he still didn't know how much danger she was in.

"Simon."

He turned to Leah's voice and found her standing in the water just below the surface. She made no effort to swim, merely stood there as if she were on level ground.

Then she lifted his sword toward him. Somehow it had fallen loose during the underwater struggle. For a moment the image of her handing him the sword out of the water mesmerized him.

"Take it," she said.

Simon closed his fist around the sword's hilt an instant before a tentacle wrapped his leg and pulled him under. He managed to finish one last breath of air, then slid once more beneath the water.

Submerged, he manually blew the air from the buoyancy bladders the armor had automatically filled from his air supply. Bubbles erupted around him and boiled to the surface. Taking his sword in both hands, he reversed it and took a firm grip on the hilt. He sank like a stone to the bottom, then managed four quick strides to the demon nestled in the crater.

The demon's tentacles lashed at Simon and took hold of him. He didn't know where Leah had gone until she was suddenly beside him. Somehow, she managed to bat some of the tentacles aside.

As if sensing what Simon planned, the demon hoisted itself from its nest and tried to scuttle away. Simon leaped forward and put both boots on top of the demon's center body mass. He fired the boot anchors and felt them bite into the creature's flesh. Then he rammed the sword through the awful eye staring helplessly up at him.

Blood and green-tinted fluid flooded the water. Either the blood or the fluid—or, possibly, both—burned Simon's exposed face. The warm tingle quickly turned angry.

With a final twist of the sword, Simon withdrew his

boot anchors and yanked the blade free. A paroxysm shuddered through the demon. The tentacles whipsawed through the water and churned the silt from the lake bottom.

Holding his breath, Simon turned and ran toward the lake's edge. Even with the armor's amplified strength pushing him onward, the going was hard. When he got there, Miriam waited with her sword drawn.

FORTY-FOUR

Who's the woman?" Miriam demanded.

Sword in hand, Simon looked back over his shoulder. Leah strode from the lake in the one-piece black armor. She didn't wear her mask. Her hair hung wet and heavy. She didn't carry a weapon.

"She's my friend," Simon said.

Miriam smiled, and it was a ghastly caricature of the expression Simon had seen on her face in times past. "Then 'your friend' has come all this way to watch you die."

"No. I didn't come here to die, Miriam."

"Simon," Leah called.

Simon shifted so that he could keep an eye on both women.

"This isn't real," Leah told him. "None of it. You're dreaming. Or I'm dreaming."

"This isn't a dream." Simon stood his ground uneasily. "How did you get here?"

"I don't know. It doesn't matter."

"It does. The last thing you remember is that you went to sleep, right? Back in the redoubt?"

Simon shook his head. "This doesn't make sense. I'm here. I feel like I'm here. My sword feels real. That demon in the lake felt real."

"I know." Leah's voice was patient. "I've been going through this for days."

"Going through what?"

"I've been taken prisoner by the demons. They're holding me at the Apple store. They've got me in some kind of machine that—"

"Shut up!" Miriam snarled. She whipped a hand forward and a dagger glittered as it spun through the air toward Leah.

Simon reached for the deadly blade, but even his amplified reflexes were too slow. The dagger buried to the hilt in Leah's chest.

Curious, not seeming at all in pain or concerned, Leah glanced down at the knife protruding from her sternum. "This isn't real." She grasped the knife and pulled it from her flesh.

There was no blood, no wound.

She looked up at Simon. "You're dreaming. Do you see? But it's dangerous in here. While you're dreaming, the demons access your mind. You've got to wake up." She threw the knife at him.

Effortlessly now, Simon plucked the twirling knife from the air. It *tinked* against his armored palm.

Miriam drew a sword from her back and sliced the air. In response, the blade ignited and became wreathed in flames.

"I'm going to kill you, Simon."

Miriam started forward, and the heat from her sword baked into Simon's exposed flesh. "You can listen to your little harpy all you want to. She's just going to be the death of you."

"Simon, don't—" Whatever else Leah was going to say was lost when she abruptly faded from view.

Moving slowly, never stepping over his feet, so he remained balanced, Simon kept his sword in front of him. "Where is she?"

"Who?" Miriam's smile was sweet poison.

"What happened to her?"

"She was never here. Just a figment of your pitiful imagination." Miriam slashed with her sword, coming close to Simon but not making him yet defend himself. "Are you in love, Simon?"

Simon paced carefully. Miriam was good at swordplay. But this wasn't Miriam.

"You're not real, are you?" Simon asked.

In a blinding display of skill, Miriam exchanged a quick flurry of thrusts and cuts, and managed to slice into Simon's left thigh. Warm blood trickled down his thigh.

"How real do you think I am now, Simon?"

Without answering, Simon attacked. He used his height, longer reach, and superior strength to batter at her defenses. Metal rang and the clangor echoed over the lake.

Then ripples started out in the middle of the lake. Within seconds, tentacles clustered at the top of the water and came toward shore.

"You didn't think that was the only demon down there, did you?" Miriam struck at Simon's unprotected eyes and turned him so that his back was to the lake.

Unable to see how close the demons were, Simon tried to get the upper hand and turn Miriam again. She held him fast. When he retreated, hoping to give himself brief respite, she pursued so closely that he had no chance to turn. Sweat coursed down him. His muscled ached.

"You're tiring." Miriam smiled. "I'm not going to tire. Either I'm going to kill you or the demons will."

A tentacle plopped onto the shore. Curling and twisting, it searched for prey. Out of the water, it didn't move so effortlessly or gracefully.

"I'm sorry." Simon parried her strike, then parried again.

"For what? I won't let you bleed on me."

"For what I'm about to do." Simon had her rhythm now. Like the real Miriam, this one had a fault in her swordplay that occasionally came up. When she felt she had the upper hand, her bladework fell into a routine as she worked faster and faster.

"You're not going to—"

Simon parried her sword, but this time he lunged forward as well. It was a bold and dangerous move because he didn't completely have control over her weapon. The sword's flames braised his ribs. She held the weapon to him.

"Warning," the suit AI said. "Failure of defenses and armor imminent."

Simon ignored the suit AI and the pain baking into his side. He held her sword trapped, then dropped to one knee and hooked her under the opposite shoulder with his free arm. Holding on to her, aware of the tentacle only inches from his foot that slithered over the sand toward him, he whirled and threw Miriam in a judo move.

Cursing, Miriam flew through the air at the bulbous head of the demon in the lake. Tentacles caught her and drew her into the maw. She disappeared in a single gulp.

Before Simon could move, more tentacles whipped round his body and lifted him from his feet. He tried to use the sword, but tentacles quickly lashed his arm to his side. He squirmed and wriggled, but it did no good.

Simon.

Leah's voice echoed inside his head. Simon thought of her, locked somewhere in the belly of an infernal machine created by the demons. It was more than he could bear.

Unless that was part of the dream as well.

"Warning," the suit AI said. "Biometrics approaching dangerous levels."

Biometrics? In that instant, Simon felt his pounding heart and forced respiration. That felt like part of the dream, and made sense for him to feel that way, but it wasn't.

"Wake me." Simon struggled against the tentacles, unable to completely let go the dream.

"Caution: stimulant might cause cardiac stress."

"Wake me." The maw opened beneath Simon. "Wake me *now*!"

The tentacles released, and Simon dropped toward the waiting maw. He flailed his arms and legs to no avail. When he dropped into the cavernous opening, the demon's teeth and lips clamped closed behind him.

Simon awoke in darkness. For a moment he thought he was lost somewhere in the demon's gullet. His breath locked in his lungs as he flailed around him. Then he realized he was in bed. Cold sweat covered his flesh.

"Hey, mate, you okay?" Nathan peered over the side of the bed above. Sleep and fatigue thickened his voice.

"Yes." Knowing he wasn't going to be sleeping anymore, Simon sat up. "No."

Nathan cursed. "You're still asleep."

"Not anymore."

"You sound confused."

Simon waited a beat, feeling his heart slow. The sweat chilled him. "Have you been having nightmares?"

"What? You going to sing me a lullaby?"

"If you've been having nightmares, there's a reason for it."

"You're bloody right. It's called being at war with a vicious demon horde that's invaded our world. Something like that, mate? It'll give you nightmares straightaway."

"I dreamed about Leah."

"Knew you had your clock wound over her."

Simon ignored the comment. "She talked to me in the dream. Said she was trapped inside a demonic machine that's being used to invade our dreams."

"Okay, now you've got me awake."

"Good. We need to get moving."

"Doing what?"

"We're going to find out how many other people have been suffering nightmares." Simon stood and headed for the shower before climbing back into his armor.

FORTY-FIVE

Warren stood atop a building with his arms outspread and let the hot wind from the Burn wash over him. He breathed in the foul stench and felt his senses reel. Tonight felt different than any other he had spent in the city. Part of him knew that it was because tonight he was the hunter, not the hunted.

He spotted an owl sliding silently through the sky. Since London had gone dark and the noise level of mechanical things had dropped, some of the scavengers had moved into the metropolitan area to scavenge food. Other predators gathered to feast on them.

Effortlessly, Warren slid his mind from his body into that of the owl. Over the past few nights, he'd hunted throughout the city in a similar manner. The exercise had gotten easier and easier. His powers continued to grow, but he didn't know how much of that to attribute to constant practice or the desperation that resonated within him.

He'd even managed to take over some of the smaller demon things, but doing something like that always left him with a headache and a foul taste in his mouth for hours. Their minds and thoughts, even the simpler killers, were too strange, too darkly evil and malicious.

As the owl, he flapped his wings and gained altitude. He climbed through the cloudy night and spiraled for a moment over the building where his body stood. For a moment he was afraid of how vulnerable he was out in the open, but he trusted Daiyu and her followers to protect him. That had been another change that had taken place. Once they had seen the value he'd brought them, he'd taken comfort in their protection.

All of the Cabalists in her sept wanted the power that Warren wielded. Most of them had small things from demons, bits and pieces of flesh, horns, and bones that they had successfully grafted onto their bodies with Warren's help. Their powers had increased, and as they gained, the sept gained members as well. Daiyu's group now numbered a hundred strong. Twenty of them arrived with Warren tonight. He'd had to limit them to that number, and that had almost started several fights. They believed in him, and that felt good.

Warren, what are you doing?

Lilith's voice echoed inside Warren's head. For the past few days, his contact with her had been intermittent. He didn't know what she was doing, and he no longer tried to figure it out. She had her own agenda, and she'd ripped away his hiding place.

"I'm hunting." Warren felt a little defensive and he resented that.

You've got a group following you.

"Yes."

Finally, ambition rises within you.

Warren checked a scathing response. "I already had ambition. I wanted to stay alive."

You still want to stay alive.

"I can't do that on my terms anymore."

By hiding?

"Yes."

Your terms were wrong. You've been given power for a reason. You're going to be part of the great battles that stretch ahead of you from this moment on.

Warren wondered if the power she referred to was the silver hand she'd given him or if it was the powers he'd already manifested before the Hellgate had opened. He heeled over in the sky and sailed through the low-lying fog that masked the rooftops. Daiyu's Cabalists occupied rooftops, fire escapes, and alleys. They all waited on his orders.

I will have need of you soon.

For a cold instant, Warren thought about telling her he was no longer in thrall to her, that he intended to go his own way. Then he was afraid he'd thought that too loudly.

"All right."

Be safe until I call for you. You and I, we owe a debt to Merihim that needs paying. I know of a machine he's had the demons construct that means much to him. Soon we'll have to confront him.

That possibility left Warren chilled.

You want your revenge, too, don't you?

"Yes."

Good. I'll see you then.

Warren felt her absence as she pulled away from him. He forced the owl's wings to beat faster, till he screamed through the tall buildings in the East End. As he passed, he spotted gargoyles on some of the buildings, and some of the gargoyles spotted him as well.

Lookouts, he realized.

One of the winged demons sitting hunkered at a roof's edge leaped from the building, flapped his wings, and gave chase. With uncommon skill and grace, Warren controlled the owl and forced her to skim by the sides of buildings in his effort to escape the demon. The owl's wingtips brushed the side of the building.

The gargoyle overshot the corner. Before the creature changed directions, Warren flew in through an open window, across a room full of cubicles, and out a broken window on an adjoining wall. Outside, he dropped altitude and skirted low to the street.

He'd learned through experience that flying low left him vulnerable. Predatory birds hunted from the sky and used their keen sight to spot prey. Flying this low to the ground, he *was* prey.

Without a sound, he glided through the silent streets. A group of blood zombies feasted on a small group of scavengers they'd caught in an alley. The screams of the hapless victims as they were brought down were blood-curdling.

Warren felt badly for them. No one should have to die like that. But more than anything, he was glad he wasn't them. It was selfish, but he didn't feel ashamed of his feelings.

Three blocks farther on, Warren found his prey. The demon was one of the greater demons. Warren felt the power clinging to the shambling monstrosity and knew that he was Named. But he felt new, the way Shulgoth had when Warren had seen that demon in London's streets four years ago.

The demon was at least ten feet tall. Broad and long-bodied, his short legs lent him the appearance of an ape. Snakelike tentacles jutted from his head, overshadowing his low brow. Red-violet scales covered his massive body. His snout belonged on a raptor, long and cruelly curved.

Ah, you have grown ambitious.

Warren glided to a stop in an empty window three stories above the demon. His fluttering wings drew the demon's attention for just a moment, then the creature looked away as it strode without worry through the twisting street.

"You know him?" Warren watched the demon.

Yes.

"He feels newly ascended."

He is.

"How do you know him?"

You're not the only one who has ambitions. I've found out much since I've been in the city.

Warren had listened to stories over the past weeks, but none of them had mentioned Lilith.

I'm still not prepared to make my move. There are many who will not be happy that I survived.

Warren hated the fact that so many of his thoughts were open to her. "Who's the demon?"

Kareloth. He has ascended since coming through the Hellgate.

"How?"

The Templar still fight fiercely, as do the military units still hiding within London. They've killed a few of the demons. Others, as always, have died at each other's hands. There is always attrition. Demons are the first to hold grudges, and the last to rid themselves of them.

"How dangerous is Kareloth?"

Lilith's laughter mocked him. *Fearful?*

Warren took no insult. "I want to win. And to do that, I can't needlessly risk the lives of those that follow me. I have to give them victories, not defeats."

You're learning much.

Warren watched the demon walk toward a group of Darkspawn and carelessly bat them away from a cornered woman. Casually, Kareloth reached inside the car where the woman had taken shelter. He dragged her out, screaming for help, then ripped her into pieces, and dropped the bits into his mouth.

Are you going to give your warriors a victory?

"Yes," Warren said.

Good. You need to hang on to that nerve. We'll face Merihim soon.

Warren released the owl's mind and tumbled back to his body.

Back inside his own body, Warren felt a momentary wave of dizziness. He staggered, then it was past. He opened his eyes and looked at the rooftop.

Naomi gazed at him in concern. He waved her aside and turned to Daiyu.

"Have you found a demon?" Daiyu asked.

"I have. This one won't be easy, but we can bring it down."

"How powerful is it?"

"It's one of the Named."

If Daiyu was nervous over that, the emotion didn't show. Her face remained placid. After a moment, she nodded. "The rewards will be worth it."

"I think so."

Daiyu brought the walkie-talkie to her mouth and gave the orders.

"Are you sure we can take this thing?" Naomi asked.

Warren stood beside her at the mouth of an alley. He felt his power bubbling just under his skin, threatening to explode on its own if he didn't give it release.

"We have to," Warren said. "If we can take it down and

harvest the body parts, we'll be stronger." He paused as he watched Kareloth farther down the block. "To survive, we need to be stronger."

"You mean, *we* need to be stronger." Naomi smiled ruefully.

Warren nodded. "I mean that you, all of you, need to be stronger. The more we learn, the more the demons will hunt us."

"Are you ready?" Daiyu asked over the walkie-talkie headset Warren wore.

"Yes."

Daiyu hesitated. "I don't want to lose any of my people."

"I can't guarantee that. I can guarantee that whatever we take from Kareloth will enhance the abilities of everyone we successfully graft to."

Silence echoed in the walkie-talkie for a moment.

"All right," Daiyu said, "but don't walk away from this."

"I won't."

"If you do, I'll track you down and kill you."

"Not exactly the best incentive I could hope for," Warren said.

"Perhaps not, but I mean every word of that."

Warren didn't doubt her. He stayed within the shadows and waited till Kareloth reached the alley where he stood. He planned to let the demon walk by him, then attack without warning.

Instead, Kareloth hesitated. He came to a full stop and snuffled the air, snorting like a pig. Unerringly, the demon turned and smiled into the shadows that wreathed the alley.

"Human." Kareloth grinned. Saliva dripped from his

jaws. His lips ricked back to reveal sharp, serrated teeth still bloodstained from his earlier victim. "I know you, Warren Schimmer."

Panic flooded Warren as he stood pinned in the demon's gaze.

"Merihim sends his regards." Kareloth opened his mouth and breathed a great gout of flame.

FORTY-SIX

Leah fell through nightmares. She didn't know how many she visited—or created—because they all seemed to run into one another. They became a kaleidoscope of insanity that threatened to drink her down.

Every time she tried to gather her wits round her, to focus on what she knew to be true, the landscape of nightmares shifted and she'd be somewhere else. She most tried to cling to the memory of Simon Cross. She had touched his thoughts. She was sure of that.

But she didn't know if he'd believe she was truly there or would remember what she'd told him.

The maddening jumps continued. She ran beside a soldier who tried to enter an exploded building for one of his teammates. She felt his panic as he shoved through the falling timbers and tried to avoid the hottest flames. His suit protected him somewhat, but the heat threatened his swirling senses.

"You've got to get out of here," Leah told the man.

"Can't." The soldier caught hold of a sagging timber and shoved. A section of the wall fell away. "George is in here somewhere." He lifted his voice. "*George!*"

"It's too late."

"It's not too late. I'm not going to let it be too late. George is my mate. I told him I'd watch his back."

A Stalker demon crouched in one corner. The creature bunched its legs, getting ready to jump.

"Look out!" Leah clawed the SRAC machine pistol from her side and brought it to bear as the Stalker leaped. She shoved at the soldier with her free hand, but it passed through the man's body. In the next instant, the SRAC's bullets speared through the Stalker's body without a trace.

The Stalker hit the soldier and bowled him over, sending both of them sprawling onto a section of flaming carpet. The fire-retardant material of the soldier's suit protected him from catching fire, but the heat consumed him.

Leah felt the man's body burning. Pain raked angry claws through her flesh. She cried out in agony. Instinctively, she ran to the man and tried to pull him from the fire. He rolled and fought the Stalker, but Leah couldn't get a grip on him. Frustrated and helpless, she watched as the battle continued.

Then a section of the ceiling fell and dropped on them, hiding them from view.

"No!" Leah ran forward, stumbled on the debris, and fell.

When she got her feet under her again, she stood chest-deep in the dank water of a cave. The cold water felt greasy against her skin even through her armor. The stench of death, decay, and raw sewage made the air so thick and almost impossible to breathe.

Her suit's infrared system didn't penetrate the gloom far enough to see any walls. She listened intently, not wanting to move until she knew if something else was in the water with her.

Movement slithered below.

Leah stepped to the side and drew the sword sheathed between her shoulder blades. Since she'd never carried a sword, she knew that she wasn't herself in this incarnation. With a skill she'd never before possessed, she stood ready and waiting. For the first time, she realized that the HUD before her eyes had a 360-degree view of her surroundings.

In the next moment, three Templar surfaced in the murky water. All of them stood and drew swords. They ignored her and gazed around the cave. Simon wasn't among them.

"Have you seen anything?"

It took Leah a moment to realize the woman addressed her. "No. Not yet."

"Good. Maybe we escaped them." The Templar surged forward through the water. "Joseph, do you have any idea where we are? This cave system isn't on my HUD. We're still beneath the city, I can see that, but I don't know how we're supposed to get out."

"One thing's for certain," the third person, a man, stated, "we can't go back the way we got here. We'll be buried in demons."

Leah slogged along after them. There wasn't anything else she could do.

"There are a lot of cave systems and abandoned tunnels beneath London," Joseph said. "Mining and transportation created most of the tunnels."

"It was your idea to come here, mate," the other man accused.

"Knock it off, Nigel," the woman said. "We've got enough troubles without trying to assign blame for this mess we're in."

"Listen to you, Mai. What gives you the right to—"

She whirled on the other Templar and lifted her sword point to the bottom of his helm. "Lord Cross gave me the right to tell you what to think, you git. And unless you get with the program, I'm going to jettison you and let you find your own way out of here. Do you scan me?"

Nigel's blank faceplate remained blank and featureless. However, through whatever power that bound her to the experience—dream or real-time, Leah felt his fear and anger. They were divided equally for a moment, but he gave in to his fear.

"All right, Mai," Nigel said. "It'll be as you say."

"Good." Mai lowered her sword. She turned away from him and started slogging through the muck again.

Leah hurried and caught up to her. "You know Simon?"

Mai didn't break stride. "Of course I know him. This isn't time for silly questions."

"I need to get a message to him."

"Tell him when we get back."

"I don't know if I'll make it back."

"You aren't going to throw in the towel so quick, are you? Because if that's the way you—"

The lizard-demon struck without warning, rising from the dark depths and lunging at Mai. The Templar's augmented reflexes almost saved her as she threw herself to one side. The lizard-thing opened its mouth and popped out a barbed tongue that crossed ten feet of space in a nanosecond. Incredibly, the tongue penetrated the armor on the first attempt.

Mai jerked and writhed. Her panicked and pain-filled cries filled Leah's audio inside the armor. Leah ran forward and lifted the sword. She swung again and again, chopping through the lizard's tough hide. Ichors poured from the wounds, but the lizard pulled its struggling prey into the elongated mouth.

"Help me!" Leah cried. "She still has a chance!"

The Templar broke free from the paralysis that held them and rushed forward.

Leah tried to figure out where the lizard's brain was. She hoped that if she could pierce the brain or sever the spinal cord she might save the Templar.

"Warning!"

The voice came from inside the suit. Leah hadn't expected that. She still struggled to understand the 360-degree view the HUD afforded. Everything looked *wrong*.

"Warning! Second demon within range!"

Leah noticed the demon then. A second lizard had risen from the water and rushed at her. The scrawny legs were incredibly powerful. She turned to meet the new threat, but she knew she moved too late.

The demon opened wide its jaws. The black tongue uncoiled from inside the mouth and lashed forward.

Leah tried to move. The tongue hit her just left of center in her chest. If it missed her heart, and she wasn't certain, it was a near thing. She was surprised that there was no pain. Shock already flooded her system and started shutting her down.

She stumbled backward but managed to grab the tongue with one hand. The barbs bit into her flesh as the lizard snapped its head back and reeled her in. Then the jaws closed on her with crushing force and she—

—was suddenly somewhere else. She choked back a cry.

"Quiet," someone hissed. Then Leah felt her hand squeezed tightly. "Don't interrupt the Voice."

Leah sat cross-legged in a circle of people in a dark room. All of them ringed a strangely cut box that levitated in the center of the circle. Black curtains covered the windows, but the way the heavy material moved told her the windows were broken.

When Leah gazed at her companions, she realized they were Cabalists. Their robes and strange armor fashioned

from demon hide announced their identities as much as
the tattoos and demon body parts they had stitched into
their bodies. Most of the wounds looked infected.

From the information that Control passed along, the
Cabalists believed they enhanced their natural powers
and added others by grafting the demons' bodies to their
own. According to reports, they were at least partially
successful. But the grafts often didn't take. Most of the
time, infection set in and threatened the host body until
the grafts were undone.

Others, too stubborn or believing that the infection
would turn, died horrible deaths trying to adapt. Several
of the Cabalists around Leah looked sick and weak. Hollow eyes burned as they stared at the floating box.

"This is Ordonar's Box," a man near the floating object said. "Homer and Aristotle wrote of the Box, but
those writings have been concealed. They believed the
soul of a demon was trapped inside. The Greeks didn't
create the box. Ordonar was believed to have been a
priest in ancient Tibet, a holy man who acknowledged
that demons walked in this world."

The Box twisted and spun at a faster rate. At first, Leah
though it was brass, then she saw the reddish gleam and
thought it was more likely that it was copper. Strange sigils
stood out in bold relief on the sides.

"Although the ancients tried to understand the Box,"
the speaker went on, "none of its secrets were ever discovered. In time, when the Romans took over much of the
Greek culture, they also recovered the Box. It was brought
to England. A scholar here thought a crypt with similar
markings had been found. Before the Box arrived, the
scholar was found murdered. Some said it was the curse of
the crypt, which was never found."

Power grew in the room. Part of Leah knew what it

was. The force felt like an electrical surge buildup. Her skin became tight and dry. Her hair stood on end. Electrical sparks jumped on some of the Cabalists in the circle. Leah wanted to get up and run.

"Easy," the man next to Leah whispered. "The Voice knows what he's doing. Everything will be fine."

"While in England," the Voice went on, "the Box was also lost. Stories of assassins, pagans, and jealous officers followed the Box. No one knows what the truth is. In the early nineteenth century, explorers found the Box. Until now, it's resided in a museum. No one knew what it was. I do."

The Voice stood. He was a tall, lean man with the face of a wolf. He looked like a ska fan, dressed in jackboots, his head shaven, piercings over his face.

"Tonight, brothers and sisters, we open the Box and free the demon soul inside. It will try to escape our circle, but we won't allow that. We will hold on to it and make it do our bidding. Once we do that, our understanding of the demons and the power that we can wield will increase. We will all benefit."

No! Leah tried to speak and couldn't. *Demons don't have souls!* She knew that from the research she'd stolen from the Templar when she'd first gone to the Templar Underground with Simon. She didn't know what the Box contained, but she didn't see that it could be anything but evil.

And powerful. That scared her most of all.

"Now," the Voice said, "it's time to open the Box. Ready your shields. Don't allow it to escape."

Magenta shimmering filled the darkened room, glowing like a lava bubble.

Leah tried to free her hands. Both Cabalists on either side of her held on.

"No," the man hissed. "Stay strong. Believe. We can

bend the demons to our will. That's our destiny. It's what we've been working toward."

Leah couldn't move. Her body wasn't under her control.

The Voice spoke strange words that Leah couldn't understand. The Box spun faster. Blue lights flickered over the Box's copper surfaces. The Voice continued speaking. The words came louder and faster. Wind whipped free in the room. Blue lightning leaped from the Box.

One of the bolts struck the man next to Leah. Horrified, she watched as the man jerked and spasmed. Electricity flowed through her and locked her jaws and joints. Leah barely managed to hang on to her senses.

Abruptly, the Box stopped spinning. Lightning continued to sizzle from it, forming a direct connection to the Cabalists.

"Control it!" the Voice shouted. "Use your powers!"

Leah held on to the two men next to her. She had no choice. The electricity surging through her wouldn't allow her to release either of them. The man on her right frothed at the mouth.

Then the Box exploded. A bright blue flash filled the room and blinded Leah. When her vision returned, only partially, a demon stood in the center of the circle.

The demon had two faces set side by side. Both of them were hideous. Scales flared along the thick neck that hooked into a massive chest. Four arms, two to a side, stuck out from the demon's body. All of them held weapons. The legs were long in comparison to the rest of its body, and they were thick as tree trunks. A forest of horns crowned its head.

"Control me?" the demon snarled. "Fools!" He lifted one arm and laughed.

More lightning jumped from the mace in the demon's

hand. Leah felt the increased current wracking her body. The head of the man to her left suddenly exploded, scattering blood, brains, and bone—all of it cooked. Around the circle, more Cabalists suffered electrical beheading.

Then a deep, agonizing pain struck deeply within Leah's head. There was a great release, and she knew nothing more.

Exhausted and hurting, Leah regained consciousness back in the cube room. Vomit stained the floor. She put a hand to her head, checking to see that it was all still in one piece. The last sequence—whether dream or memory—had been too intense.

Then she grew aware someone watched her.

When she turned to look, the cube demon had returned. She put her back against the wall and drew her knees up to her chin.

"You're doing very well." The demon almost preened. "Better than expected. During the time you've been here, you've reached out to many of your fellow humans."

Leah didn't speak. She refused to let the thing know how much what she was going through was affecting her.

"Other humans have died," the demon said. "Some of those were ones that were taken after you. You have a remarkable resiliency. But, in the end, it will only make you live longer. You can't escape. You will die here. Until you do, you will continue to aid us."

Giving in to her anger, Leah hurled herself across the room. Even if she died in the attack, she couldn't be used against Simon or anyone else. Dying was worth that.

The demon caught her effortlessly. One hand seized her wrist and the other clamped down on her head. It picked her up and threw her into the steel wall hard enough to knock the breath from her.

Wheezing, trying desperately to get air back in her lungs, Leah held her hands over her head to open her rib cage.

"Foolish," the demon said. "You can't sacrifice yourself so easily. When the time comes, you'll die. But not until this. You no longer have a choice in the matter."

Leah willed herself to be calm as she tried to regulate her breathing. She watched the demon intently, but she didn't know when it left the cell. One moment it was there; in the next, it was gone.

Knowing that a door had to be in that end of the cell, Leah crawled over and examined the walls, floor, and ceiling. She found nothing. It was as if the demon had aligned its atoms with those of the wall and slid through.

When she turned back round, a box of food sat at the other end of the cell. Nothing had gotten by her, which meant that the demons entered and left her cell at will. She remained a prisoner.

FORTY-SEVEN

W arren lifted his hand and formed a shield before him. The demon's fiery breath crackled
and hissed as it struck the barrier. Flames
lapped at the edges as they curled around. Waves of heat
slammed into him, almost hot enough to parboil his
skin.

Naomi stood at his back, using him and his shield as
protection.

Daiyu and the Cabalists attacked the demon. Heavy
nets, reinforced with the energy they manipulated, dropped
from men inside rooms overhead. The nets popped and sizzled as they touched the demon's skin, like electrical cables
attached to opposite current. Quivering and shaking, the
nets looked like live things seeking to slide away from the
demon.

Kareloth struggled against the nets. He knotted all four
hands in the strands and pulled. Some of the nets broke,
and the energy residing within the ropes burned like fire-
works. The demon breathed out again. Flames licked at
the nets, but they were flame-resistant. They wouldn't be
able to withstand the attack for long, though.

Warren drew the spear from the magical duster. When
Kareloth saw the spear, his eyes widened.

"Where did you get that?" Kareloth demanded.

Afraid of getting hurt, knowing that the demon was dangerous as long as it was alive, Warren made no reply. He closed on Kareloth and drove the spear at the demon's heart.

Instead, Kareloth caught the spear and stopped it short of piercing his flesh. The contact turned the spear cherry red. Kareloth's hands, both of the left ones, charred and cracked. He roared with rage and shoved the spear backward.

Propelled by the demon's immense strength, Warren flew off his feet and back into the alley. He knocked Naomi down, and they tumbled in a sprawl. Only then did the agony from Warren's own burned hand reach through his fear and fill his mind.

His hand, his human hand, had cooked. Blisters formed immediately. Black crust covered his palm. He couldn't feel all the pain because the burns had killed the nerves. That was a small blessing. He also couldn't move his hand. Panic throttled his thinking for a moment.

"Let me help." Naomi rose to her knees, helped him to his, then took his hand in hers. Almost instantly some of the pain went away. The black crust grew less dense, and the blisters lessened.

Warren calmed.

"I need you." Naomi looked at him. "Help me. It's still more than I can do."

More in control of the animalistic fear that rattled through him, Warren concentrated on his hand. The healing sped up. In only a few seconds, his hand was once more whole. He flexed it, feeling everything again and finding the hand totally mobile.

Once more on his feet, Warren picked up the spear and turned back to the demon. Daiyu and the Cabalists attacked with fire and lightning, with swords and pistols that fired insects that dug into Kareloth's flesh. The demon roared with rage and fought the nets that held him. Other Cabalists held on to ropes and anchored the demon in one spot so he couldn't run.

Pustules and sores covered the demon's body from the Cabalist guns. The insects burrowed into the flesh and sapped strength as well as spurting toxins that sped through the central nervous systems. Before any of the demon's body was used to enhance Cabalist recipients, those harvested pieces would have to be thoroughly disinfected.

The nets continued to rip. A hole grew larger, and Kareloth thrust his two-faced head through. His right hands clawed at the nets and forced a shoulder through as well.

Warren wanted to stab the demon again, but he was hesitant. The pain from the earlier attempt remained fresh in his mind.

"When I get out of here," Kareloth bellowed, "I'm going to kill you. I tried to kill you quickly. Before, you were just a small favor for Merihim. Now, I owe you for the pain you've caused me."

Warren's first instinct was to run. He couldn't imagine going one-on-one with Kareloth. The Cabalists were hard-pressed to restrain the demon now, and that small edge they maintained was slipping away.

You can't run. He'll only follow. This is your only chance.

Focusing on the fear, Warren embraced it and let it feed the power that surged through him. He was no hero. He'd never be a hero. But he was a survivor. He'd faced his stepfather down when he was just a child. And he'd used the one power that had always been his.

"Kareloth," Warren said in a voice that only cracked a little.

The demon swiped his right hands at Warren. They were only three feet short. The nets hung halfway down the demon's chest. Once they plunged below that, they'd fall quickly.

"I know your name," Warren said. "You have to listen to me."

"I don't," Kareloth said. "I'm going to grind your bones to dust."

"Stop struggling. Now."

The nets finally gave way and dropped to the pavement. Kareloth managed one step forward . . . then stopped.

"Daiyu," Warren said, feeling as though his heart were about to explode. "Pull your people back."

Daiyu gave the order. With the demon free, they were only too happy to comply.

Kareloth lurched but couldn't take another step. His arms waved helplessly. Muscles bunched across his body as he strove to fight off Warren's hold over him.

"You're at my mercy." Warren lifted the spear in his metal hand. "I'm going to kill you, and you're not going to do anything to prevent it."

Fear glazed Kareloth's eyes. Both his faces quivered. "You . . . can't . . . do . . . this."

"I can." Warren felt the demon fighting against him. The demon felt immediately more tired, and weaker. Hefting the spear, Warren walked forward and drew it back. If there had been other demons around, his power wouldn't have worked so well. While he was controlling Kareloth, another demon could have killed him. But in this instance, his power and strategy worked.

Without another word, Warren threw the spear through the demon's heart. Once more, the obsidian spear burned cherry red. But this time Kareloth's chest blackened as it was consumed by the heat. In seconds, only the spear held him up.

When Warren retrieved the spear, Kareloth dropped to the pavement. All four of his eyes stared sightlessly.

Trying not to show how scared he still was, Warren walked over to the demon. Warren's knees quivered and almost buckled under him. He took a shuddering breath and fought not to throw up. It wasn't the scent of burned flesh that got to him. What bothered him most was how close he'd come to dying.

"The corpse will draw other predators," Daiyu said.

Warren nodded and kicked Kareloth in one of his faces. The demon didn't move.

"Harvest it," Warren ordered.

The Cabalists fell to the task with zest. Horns, eyes, hands, and sections of scaled hide all slid into bags. The demon's corpse diminished, shuddering as they took what they wanted.

Naomi drew her knife and moved in as well.

Warren watched them silently and tried to keep himself quiet and controlled. He couldn't help thinking that the Cabalists' bloodlust wasn't far removed from the demons.

But they were his people.

Later, back in Daiyu's lair, Kareloth's pieces were sorted out and distributed. Warren withdrew from them and found a room to himself. His fear and the energy he'd expended had taken their toll on him.

The room was dark. Night still remained, but not much of it.

Without undressing, he lay down in the bed. He was glad to be alone, but he also wished that Naomi would join him. However, he knew he wasn't going to ask her.

Before he could give the matter much thought, he drifted off to sleep.

"You spent all our money again!"

Hearing his stepfather's voice so clearly again woke Warren just as it had all those years ago. When he focused his eyes, he woke on that threadbare couch back in that Manchester flat all those years ago.

Martin DeYoung, his stepfather, sat in the open window and drank from a whiskey bottle. He was a powerful man who was slowly turning to fat. His black skin held a bluish tint. His shaved head gleamed in the streetlights. A short goatee framed his square chin. His nose had been broken so many times before that it was misshapen and gave him trouble breathing and sleeping. He wore khaki pants and a soccer shirt.

"I'm really close to breaking through," Tamara Schimmer protested.

Warren stared at his mother. She was Jewish and white, with pale skin, dark hair that hung in ringlets, and dark eyes that constantly looked bruised. She often forgot to eat and take care of herself because of her studies.

Get me out of here, Warren thought desperately. *This has already happened. I don't want to relive it again.* But he was trapped in the nightmare once more. His eight-year-old self buried his head in the pillow as he had all those years ago.

"I needed things," his mother continued.

Warren knew her argument wasn't going to work. It never did. There was no one in the world as right as Martin DeYoung was when he decided he was right.

"The money I've spent trying to get in touch with my

power isn't going to matter," his mother said. "Once I've achieved my mastery over the arcane—"

Warren knew bad things were going to happen. When Martin drank as heavily as he did now, bad things always happened. He'd had a bad day at the track, or on the ball games. He was constantly betting. Bookies and enforcers often looked for him. Warren had seen them.

"Mastery!" Martin's voice was so strong and unforgiving that Warren thought the windows might break. "You can't even manage a house, you cow! We live in filth!"

The social services people had sometimes told Warren's mom that, too. They'd threatened to take Warren away from her. Only she'd moved, leaving everything but her books on lore and magic. Those were the things she prized above all else. She'd studied those every moment she had.

Martin continued his rant. "I work hard all day—"

"You're a thief!" his mother interrupted. "Don't you go getting sanctimonious with me!"

Anger mottled Martin's face, turning it even darker.

"I know what you are!" his mother continued. "You and your friends just—"

When Martin stood, Warren bailed off the bed and climbed behind the couch. It was where he always hid anytime they had a fight. The couch wasn't much of a hiding place. Martin always found him and beat on him, but Warren had always tried to do something to save himself another round of pain.

"I needed that money!" Martin said. "I had it hid! You shouldn't have gone into my private stuff!"

"You live here!" his mother replied. "I put a roof over your head! What I took wouldn't even pay your rent!"

"You get this place free through social services 'cause

FORTY-EIGHT

W arren knew the dream usually ended quickly at this point. Although he didn't want to, he peered around the side of the couch because his eight-year-old self had all those years ago.

Martin took a large, short-barreled pistol from the back of his waistband. Light glinted on his gold watch and ring, and from the pistol's shiny silver barrel. Cursing, he trained the weapon on Warren's mother.

She didn't move. He'd aimed pistols at her enough over the months they'd been together that she no longer cared. He'd never once fired at her.

Martin rolled the hammer back. White flecks of spit showed on his blue-black lips. Then he squeezed the trigger.

Five thunderous roars filled the room.

Although he hadn't wanted to, Warren screamed in fear as his mother jerked and started bleeding from her chest, abdomen, and face. She was already dead, but his eight-year-old self hadn't known that then.

Drunk on the whiskey and his own sense of empowerment, Martin opened the weapon's cylinder and shook the empty casings onto the floor. He thumbed new bullets into the cylinder and stared at Warren.

"Now you're gonna get yours, you little ape!" Martin snarled. "I've been getting sick near to death looking at you, listening to your mother talk about her ideas about magic and you! I ain't gonna have to listen no more, though!" He snapped the cylinder closed and took aim.

Warren screamed, but he no longer heard his voice. Martin fired the pistol. The bullet struck Warren's right hip and knocked him down. Panic filled him when he saw all the blood coming from the hole in his side. He hurt, but he was numb, too.

Martin fired again, but the second shot cored the wall above Warren's head. A puff of white powder jetted from the plasterboard.

"No!" Warren screamed. He wanted to beg his step-father not to shoot him, to call the hospital for his mother, but he couldn't. He tried to talk, but he couldn't.

"Ain't gonna do you any good to beg," Martin said. "I'm gonna shoot you right in the head. I'll never have to see you in this life again." He took aim.

Warren looked at the man and let loose all of the hate he'd held back for months. His mother had said that she'd wanted him to get along with Martin. Warren had tried. He'd always tried to do what his mother had asked, even if it was something he hadn't wanted to do or didn't see the need to do.

"I hate you!" Warren screamed. Then in a calm, wish-ful voice, he said, "I wish you were dead."

A smile crawled across Martin's face. "I guess you got some backbone after all. I wouldn't have believed it if I hadn't seen it." He took aim.

Warren lay helpless on the floor.

Then, incredibly, Martin didn't fire. Instead, he turned the pistol back on himself. He begged and pleaded for help as he pressed the pistol barrel to his temple.

Then he pulled the trigger.

The crack echoed through the flat. Warren's nose filled with the scent of charred meat. He lay quietly on the floor, waiting to wake up in his bed. As he continued to lay there, he heard the shouts of neighbors. Someone banged on the door and demanded to know what was going on.

Martin's body spasmed. Incredibly, the dead man sat back up. In real life, Martin had hit the ground dead and hadn't moved a muscle. The police had taken his corpse away after a while. Counselors had told Warren that later.

That wasn't going to happen this time.

This time Martin leered at Warren, one side of his head blown open. Bloody meat and bone fragments clung to his cheek.

"Thought you killed me, didn't you?" Martin smoothed a hand across the side of his head. "Well, you're wrong. Whatever power you've got, mine's better."

This didn't happen! He's dead! A voice gibbered in fear at the back of Warren's mind. He tried to get up. Back then, he hadn't moved until the emergency services people had arrived. They'd carried him from the flat in a gurney.

Now, he rose to his feet, but his side felt like it was on fire.

When Martin moved his hand from his head, demon's scales showed there. Patches of his head were missing. A curved horn jutted up from his temple where the wound had been. When he reached for the pistol, he closed a demon's clawed hand around it.

Martin grinned. "This is how it should have ended, Warren." He took aim. "This is how it's gonna end tonight. And you're gonna be just as dead."

"No!" Warren whispered in a hoarse voice.

Before Martin could fire, a woman suddenly stepped into the room. Warren didn't recognize her. She was dark-haired and violet-eyed. She took in the situation at a glance, then launched a kick that caught Martin's wrist.

Bone snapped with a brittle sound. The pistol flew into the air, turning end over end.

The woman spun again, and this time she put a boot in the center of Martin's face. Flesh tore from his face and revealed a demon's features beneath. He fell backward and landed hard against the wall. The shelves containing Warren's mother's books fell to the floor.

Inhumanly fast, Martin caught himself and launched himself at the woman just as she plucked the pistol from the air. Then Martin hit her, and they went down across the broken recliner Warren's stepfather had brought home one day.

The pistol changed in the woman's hand. When the Martin demon tried to sink his teeth into her throat, she shoved the pistol between his jaws and pulled the trigger. The Martin demon's head exploded.

The woman grimaced and shoved the demon's corpse from her. She rolled to her feet and walked over to Warren.

"Hey, it's going to be all right," she told him. "You're going to be fine. That thing is dead. It's not going to bother you anymore." She held him to her for a moment to offer comfort.

"Who are you?" he asked. "This isn't the way it happened. You weren't there."

The woman pushed him back and looked at him. "You're not a child, are you? Not in real life?"

"No."

"Then all you have to do is wake up. Wake up and all of this will go away."

"What caused this? I've never had anything like this happen." Warren felt terrified. His thoughts were his own. Only Merihim and Lilith had invaded them.

"My name is Leah," she said. "I'm being held by the demons in some kind of machine. They're using me—and several others—to gain access to people's dreams. I don't know why. I've tried to reason it out. Maybe it's just a fear tactic. Maybe it's a way for the demons to monitor the humans left in the city. I've tried to stop doing this, but every time I close my eyes, I'm inside someone's head."

Warren looked at her and saw how tired she was.

"Where are you?" he asked.

"At the Apple store. At least, that's where I think I am. That's where I was taken captive."

Behind her, Martin started quivering again. She must have noticed the distressed look in his eyes, because she glanced over her shoulder and saw the thing's head starting to re-form. It looked like it was going to be more demonic than before.

Leah turned back to him. "You've got to go. Some people didn't live through these nightmares. You might be one of them."

"If that's true," Warren said as the fear rose inside him again, "then you saved my life tonight."

Leah gave him a wan smile. "Maybe. Maybe I only saved you from having a really bad dream."

Behind her, Martin lurched and jerked as he forced himself to his feet. He moved more slowly now. "I'm gonna get you," he growled in an inhuman voice. "I'm gonna get you both."

"Go," Leah said. "You need to get out of here."

"How?"

"Just wake up. That's all you have to do. Just wake up."

Warren woke in darkness, but he wasn't alone. Lilith, looking young and ravishing now, sat at the foot of his bed. Voices came from down the hall and let him know the Cabalists were still divvying the demon's body.

"I came as soon as I saw that you'd succumbed to the sleep trap," Lilith said.

Warren looked at her but said nothing.

"That woman," Lilith said, "probably saved your life when she interfered." She smiled. "Of course, she's also the reason Merihim's minions are able to reach inside your mind in the first place."

"What was that?" Warren asked. His voice sounded dry and weak.

"A weapon. I mentioned it earlier, but I didn't know Merihim had it working quite so well. It's become quite dangerous lately. Some of the humans die while trapped in their dreams. Others wake up and hurt still more people."

Warren sat up and held his throbbing head. The ache between his temples was worse than he'd remembered in years.

"I've been trying to find the machine," Lilith said, "but Merihim has hidden it."

"She told me it was at the Apple store."

Lilith examined his face. "Do you know where that is?"

"Yes."

"Then you have to go there."

Warren couldn't believe it. "No. That's the last place I want to go." But he thought about the woman and felt bad that she was trapped there. He consoled himself with the thought that she was already dead and only her memory was still in the machine. Or that she was just a construct dreamed up by the machine. But he would have known if she'd been lying. He felt certain about that. There'd been no indication that she'd been lying.

"Merihim will be there," Lilith said in a low voice. "You and I both owe him for what he's done to us."

Although he knew what Merihim had done to him, Warren had no idea what the demon had done to Lilith.

For her to carry a grudge for thousands of years, it had to have been something.

"It's time," Lilith said. "There must be a reckoning among all of us. You have an army now. Heal them. Make them powerful. And we will conquer Merihim once and for all."

Warren wasn't convinced.

"If you don't," Lilith said, "Merihim's creation will come for you in your sleep again. This time you might not escape so easily."

That gave Warren no choice. He didn't want to have to face another night that had Martin DeYoung and his mother's murder in it. Those nightmares were bad enough when he'd caused his stepfather's death through his suggestion. But to have to live through nightmares where Martin wouldn't die was too much.

Regretfully, Warren got up from bed and walked to the door. When he turned back to the bed to address Lilith, he discovered that she was gone. For a moment, he wondered if he'd dreamed her as well.

No, she whispered into his mind. *Go. You have much to do.*

Warren went.

FORTY-NINE

Lyra Darius was back in Temple Church as the Battle of All Hallows' Eve was just beginning after the Hellgate opened. Demons had attacked the convoy Lord Sumerisle had put together to get his granddaughter out of harm's way. After the vehicles and the demons had been destroyed, Lord Sumerisle had asked Lyra to escort Jessica to the Underground entrance beneath Temple Church. There would be people there, Lord Sumerisle had said, who would be able to care for her.

Out on the church grounds, demons had massed and attacked. The contingent of guards—other military people who worked with Lyra and whom Templar Lord Sumerisle had sent—had managed to hold off the creatures long enough for Lyra to get Jessica inside the church. They wouldn't have managed that without Keira Skyler and her Cabalists. All of them had worked together to save the young girl Lord Sumerisle believed would be a major force in the fight against the demons.

"What's going to happen to Grandfather?" Jessica asked. She was eight years old. Even though she'd been told about demons since childhood, she'd been confronted by monsters tonight. That had left her shaken.

She's just a child, Lyra thought as she went through the church doors. *Why would demons want to harm a child?* The whole idea sounded monstrous. But, she supposed, that was exactly the point after all, wasn't it?

"He's going to be fine," Lyra answered. But she thought, *He's going off to die.* When she'd heard what the Templar planned, and why, Lyra hadn't been able to feel it was all a waste. But the demons knew that the Templar were going to be their hardest battle. It would be better if they thought they were all dead.

Somewhere deep inside her heart, though, Lyra hoped the Templar succeeded.

"I saw them," Jessica said. "I saw them."

"I know." Lyra ran through the dark church with the child at her side. They were scarcely more than fifty feet from the stage where the entrance was supposed to be.

Outside in the church cemetery, gun blasts and frightened voices continued to echo. It sounded very much like the war that it was. Lightning flashed through the large stained-glass windows.

"Grandfather always told me about the demons," Jessica said. "I knew he wasn't lying. He's never lied to me."

Except for tonight, Lyra thought. *When he told you that he'd see you soon.*

"But I just didn't expect to see the demons," Jessica said.

"I know. Try not to think of that now. Come on. We're almost there."

One of the high stained-glass windows suddenly exploded inward. Bright, colorful glass spun across the church. A Reaper demon—huge and winged, man-shaped but clearly a demonic thing with horns, talons, and fangs—came through the window holding Keira Skyler.

The First Seer of the Cabalists looked incredibly demonic herself. Thick pieces of demons' horns stuck out on both sides of her head. Her skin was pale against the demon hide she wore as armor.

The Reaper demon bit into Keira's chest and pulled out her heart. It tossed the organ into its mouth and chewed as Keira slumped dead in his embrace. Then the demon turned its attention to Lyra and her young charge.

Lyra hauled Jessica to temporary safety behind one of the heavy pews. She pulled out her machine pistol and stared at the evil thing. Its ruby eyes focused on her. Hiding wasn't an option.

"Keep going, Jessica," Lyra encouraged the young girl. "Keep going!"

True to her heritage, Jessica bravely got her feet under her and ran toward the hidden entrance.

Lyra pointed the machine pistol and opened fire. The demon, almost three times her size, swung a hooked sword that cleaved through the pews and reduced them to splinters. Lyra kept firing, but it didn't seem to do any good. She hid behind a pillar as the Reaper charged after her.

It growled and swung the massive sword into the pillar, shattering it. Lyra kept firing and running, ducking the wicked blade as the demon swung it again and again.

Across the church, Jessica reached the hidden entrance and opened it. Lyra took solace in that, then one of the Reaper's wings lashed out and caught her, knocking her to the floor and almost robbing her of her senses.

"Lyra!"

Hearing the child's voice, the evident panic and worry, focused Lyra. She pulled her head together just as the Reaper yanked its blade from the stone floor and turned in Jessica's direction.

"Jessica!" Lyra screamed as she pulled a grenade from her hip. She activated it, and the blue glow stood out bright and sharp against the darkness inside the church.

"Lyra!" Jessica stood waiting in the tunnel leading to the Underground.

"Jessica! Get down!" Lyra heaved the grenade at the Reaper.

Jessica dived for cover just before the grenade exploded against the demon. Growling incoherently, the Reaper dropped to the floor like a felled redwood.

"Hit the switch!" Lyra ordered. Her right arm was injured. She cradled it as she limped toward the opening as fast as she could.

After a moment, Jessica found the switch and threw it. With a grinding noise, the section of flooring started closing at once. Jessica ran for it as best as she was able. There was just enough time to reach the opening—

—then something grabbed her ankle and yanked her from her feet. She fell hard against the floor and grabbed the lip of the opening. The Reaper had regained consciousness. It growled as it tried to haul her in.

Incredibly, Jessica grabbed hold of Lyra's wrists and tried to pull her into the opening.

"Go on!" Lyra ordered.

"I won't leave you!" Tears tracked down Jessica's scared and determined face.

"I *promised*!" Lyra shoved the girl back into the opening, and she fell out of sight. She plucked another grenade from her combat webbing and rolled over to face the Reaper. "For the living!" she'd said, remembering Lord Sumerisle's final salute. Then she'd banged the grenade to activate it.

"Lyra!" Jessica yelled.

When the event had actually taken place, Lyra had managed to kill the Reaper just in time. Tonight, though, the demon lashed out a big hand and knocked the grenade out of Lyra's grip.

"No!" Lyra yelled, not believing what had just happened. That hadn't ever occurred.

The Reaper grinned at Lyra, knowing she was almost helpless, and dove for the opening. Before Jessica could get back out of the way, the demon was upon her, scooping her up in one big hand.

"Jessica!" Lyra pushed herself to her feet, but she knew she'd arrive too late.

The demon's jaws distended as it lifted Jessica. Bravely, the little girl faced her end without a whimper, exhibiting all the steel that went into being a Sumerisle.

"No!" Lyra shouted. "This wasn't how it went!"

A figure leaped past Lyra. The familiar blacksuit the agents wore identified the person at once. The agent grabbed one of the demon's wings, planted feet against the Reaper's back, and shoved a machine pistol against the base of the creature's skull. A full-auto burst ripped into the demon's head.

Without a sound, the Reaper dropped Jessica and fell face forward.

Lyra limped up to Jessica and took the girl in an embrace.

The agent turned and faced Lyra, then ripped her mask off. Leah smiled tiredly at Lyra. "So this is your tie to the Templar."

Lyra held the girl. "Yes."

"No wonder you want Simon back in the Underground. That's Jessica Sumerisle, right?"

"Yes. But I don't understand what you're doing here. I'm dreaming. I have to be dreaming. This happened four years ago, and you weren't there."

"No." Leah shook her head. "I've been taken captive. The demons are using me to locate people—any people now—and fill their sleep with nightmares."

"We've had a huge outbreak of nightmares and sleep-walkers," Lyra said. "A few people have died in their sleep."

"You've got to come to the Apple store," Leah said. "That's where I'm being held. The demons have a ma-

chine there. I came looking for you tonight. I didn't know
if it would work. If you hadn't been sleeping, I guess it
wouldn't have."

"Can't you stop this?"

"I've tried." Leah shook her head sadly. "God knows
I've tried since I've been in here. There's nothing I can
do. And I'm not the only one. The machine has to be destroyed. You've got to—"

Panicked, breathing hard, Lyra woke up in her quarters
at the complex. She took a moment to gather herself.
Then she got out of bed, showered, and got dressed in her
blacksuit.

By the time she reached her door, she had a strike team
assembled and leaders awaiting her in her ready room.

FIFTY

Y ou know, mate," Nathan said, "this is possibly the craziest thing I've ever done."

Peering through the helicopter's cargo doors, Simon looked down at the city. Despite the tension of the moment and the stakes, he couldn't resist saying, "Doesn't even make my Top Ten."

"Yeah, well not all of us were born with a death wish."

"Does that count the demon-infested landing zone?" Danielle asked. "Because I think that should get it in the running."

"That doesn't count the demon-infested landing zone," Simon said. He checked the parachute harness one last time. "So I'll give you the Top Ten."

"Maybe they can put that on the headstone," Nathan said.

"Aren't you optimistic," Danielle chided. "Thinking there's going to be enough of you left to bury."

"They gotta put my memories somewhere," Nathan said.

Simon thought about Nathan for a moment. He had the baby on the way. Before they'd left the redoubt, Simon had told him to stay there. Nathan had refused.

"It's still not too late to turn around and go back," Simon said over a private link.

"The only way I'm turning around," Nathan told him, "is if you lead the way. Are you ready to do that?"

Leah's down there. "No."

"Then neither am I. Let's kick this in the arse and get it done."

A few minutes later, the helicopter pilot let them know they were on the final approach path. The craft sank lower and became a target for small flying demons at once. They couldn't catch the helicopter. It couldn't slow or it would become prey for the Blood Angels.

Simon looked at the Templar with him, then opened a channel to them and the Templar in the two other cargo helicopters. "Tonight we strike back for the first time. Let the demons know that we haven't been completely beaten. Let them know that they won't get this world without a fight." He paused. "For the living."

"For the living!" the Templar echoed.

The pilot cleared them for the drop.

Simon was the first through the door. He threw himself into the familiar starfish dive profile and watched the altitude drop away on his HUD.

"Initiate parachute," the suit AI called out.

Reaching across his chest, Simon hit the parachute release. The canopy belled above him. He grabbed the guidelines and tracked his descent onto the Apple store. Fifty-three Templar landed on the building's rooftop. Four missed and ended up in the street below.

Without a word, the Templar set up the rooftop charges while Simon and others climbed into rappelling lines. He checked his weapons a final time.

"Lord Cross," a female voice said over the comm-link.

The intrusion didn't come as a complete surprise. Simon had deliberately used a frequency he knew Leah had access to. He'd hoped that somewhere along the way they could connect up.

"Yes," Simon answered.

"We haven't met," the woman said. "My name is Lyra Darius. I'm a friend of Leah's."

Simon smiled. "I take it you're not out after an evening constitutional."

"No. I was in contact with Leah earlier tonight. I learned where she was. We've surrounded the building, and we're prepared to go in after her. Failing that, we're determined to blow it up."

"And kill Leah?" Simon didn't like thinking about that.

"If we must. I have to say, when I saw the helicopters and then those armored suits, I started to feel more optimistic about our chances."

"I didn't come here to kill Leah."

"Nor did I. I have hopes it won't come to that."

"It won't."

"How do you want to do this?"

Simon watched the Templar step back from the rooftop charges. "By now the demons have to know that we're here, so I thought we'd try the direct approach. See how much confusion we could stir up along the way."

"You're going through the roof."

That surprised Simon. "Yes."

"If we carried the armor you do, we might have tried that. We don't."

"We do," Simon said. "We're going inside, getting Leah and the others, doing as much damage as we can, and then we are going to get out of there."

"You're going to have the demons at your heels."

"Probably."

"It's a good thing we'll be set up in the streets ready to defend you."

"That sounds good."

"We also found a few of your stragglers that missed the

building. We'll take care of them until you're able to care for them again."

Simon smiled again. "If we make it through this, I'll stand you to a drink."

"I'll do the same. I've got a feeling that we're going to need it by then. Good luck."

Simon thanked her, then gave the order to blow the rooftop charges. The explosions rang out in quick syncopation. Plumes of dust jetted into the sky, and the roof came apart.

Before the Hellgate had been open, one of the Cabalists had been a city worker who had used HARP technology to clear some of the collapsed tunnels under London to make more routes possible. His name was Jernigan, and he was a wizard with the portable HARP trenching tool that they'd liberated from the city offices.

Almost sick with fear, Warren trailed the man as he carved a new passage from a utility tunnel that ran across the street. With the HARP carving the way, taking out all inorganic matter in seconds, they made good time.

After measuring the distance a third time, Warren knew they were under the Apple store. Since the woman had contacted him in his dreams, Warren had thought about her a lot, wondering what she was like. The plan to get her had come relatively quickly to mind.

Warren directed the Cabalist to take them up. That was harder because he had to cut the tunnel at a slope that took them up without making the incline too hard for them to climb.

The Cabalists followed somewhat eagerly. All of them now had something from Kareloth that enhanced their powers. They wanted to know how strong they'd be in a fight. None of them wanted to die, but they were willing to risk death.

Personally, the woman—Leah—was the one that drew Warren there. The nightmare he'd had about his step-father was different than anything he'd ever had before. He didn't want to repeat that.

Then there was Merihim. If this was something truly put together by the demon, as Lilith said it was, there was a debt owed that only blood could pay.

He followed the tunneler up the grade, finding it steep enough to be difficult. A moment later, the final layer between the floor and the store beyond evaporated. The way was clear.

Warren fully expected that they'd come up in the middle of the Darkspawn that had put the machine together. That didn't happen. The Cabalist group came up in the back of the building where merchandise was stored.

At the doors, Warren peered out and found that most of the demons had their attention locked on to the ceiling. They surrounded a large machine that was nearly as tall as the store's interior.

In the next instant, thunderous blasts echoed throughout the building. A large section of the roof tumbled down. Behind it, dangling from rappelling cords, eight Templar descended into the building. They opened up with their weapons at once.

Attacked from above, the Darkspawn quickly got hammered before they could set up into positions and free their own weapons. The Templar rappelled to the floor, drawing fire, but even as they got set up in defensive positions, another wave of Templar descended the rappelling lines.

Even so, the Darkspawn weren't giving up without a fight.

"We're going to be trapped between the Templar and the Darkspawn," Warren said.

"The Templar aren't our enemies," Daiyu said. "The demons are. If this is as important as you say it is, we have no choice. The Templar will only benefit our efforts."

Unless they kill us, Warren thought. His own experiences with the Templar hadn't been stellar. Still, he waded into the battle.

Simon was one of the first Templar on the floor. He saw the machine ahead of him, less than fifty feet away. It had been located almost in the center of the building. Now all they had to do was find Leah, destroy the machine, and get out alive.

If he hadn't been taking heavy fire from demon weapons, he might have almost been optimistic.

"Simon," Danielle called. "We've got Cabalists inside the building as well."

Simon accessed her HUD view and saw the Cabalists, their tattoos and dress identifying them at once. "Where did they come from?"

"A hole in the floor. They just cut their way in."

"Awfully convenient, don't you think?" Nathan asked sarcastically as he fired a rocket into a knot of Darkspawn grouped near the machine.

Simon thought about that. "Leah said she was walking through the heads of a lot of people. Her friend Lyra is here. I wasn't the only one she got a message out to."

"Maybe we should have baked a cake," Nathan said.

Simon readied his weapons. "You ready?"

"Yeah, mate. I'm ready. You lead and I got your six."

With his sword in one hand and the Spike Bolter in the other, Simon stepped out from cover and marched into the face of the Darkspawn. The Spike Bolter chewed into their ranks and knocked them down. Before they could run, he was among them and he swept the sword through them. Limbs, heads, and entrails quickly covered the floor. He holstered the pistol and gave himself over to the bladework.

Nathan mirrored him, working in tandem to everything he did. Between them, they became a destructive force.

A Darkspawn threw itself at Simon, hoping to catch him on his blind side. If he'd had a blind side, if the 360-degree view of the HUD hadn't been possible, the attempt might have succeeded. Instead, Simon met the effort with the crashing blow of his huge left hand and caved the demon's skull in. Then he caught the falling corpse and heaved it into more demons in front of him, temporarily clearing the way.

He took more of the ground, moving closer to the huge machine. Darkspawn fired from gantries that surrounded the mechanism.

In the next second, a roiling ball of fire from a Cabalist hit in the center of them and sent them flying. Most of them were in flames and probably dead before they hit the ground.

"Do you see a door on that thing?" Simon hacked more demons and kept moving forward.

"I do," Nathan said. "While I was dawdling around back here, I marked it."

Simon accessed Nathan's observations through the HUD and spotted the door. "Once we get inside," Simon said, "getting back out again could be difficult."

"In for a penny, in for a pound, mate. If Leah's in that thing, we're bringing her out. When you're ready, you just give the word."

"Ready," Simon said, thinking of Leah and everything she'd gone through.

"I was afraid you were going to say that."

Simon kicked, fought, blasted, and shoved his way toward the door. When he arrived, he found it was more like an airtight hatch that would be found in the Templar Underground.

Before he could open the hatch, a woman dropped out of the shadows and landed beside him. The demon's horns and the tail she wore marked her at once as a Cabalist. Tattoos covered every square inch of her skin. Her right hand glowed slightly, and when she hit Simon with it, he thought he'd been struck by a battering ram.

He reeled back against the gantry railing and barely hung on. Before he could recover, she twisted and kicked him in the face. He fell back against Nathan, throwing them both off balance for a moment.

"Get her," Nathan growled, and shoved Simon forward.

FIFTY-ONE

Anger welled up in Warren when he saw the Cabalist that attacked the Templar on the gantry. He recognized her as the one whom Merihim had picked over him. She still wore the hand that Merihim had given her.

"Warren," Naomi said.

"I see her," Warren replied. He knocked aside the Darkspawn he'd been battling, leaving it for Naomi. She covered it in a pool of fire that clung to the creature as it scrambled madly back toward its fellows.

With a single jump, Warren reached the gantry twenty feet up. When he touched down on the metal landing, she looked over at him. Savage glee lighted her face.

"Hello, weakling," she greeted.

Warren didn't say anything. She threw a ball of fire at him. He blocked it with a shield, then launched a fireball of his own. It struck her and burned her in several places. She cried out in rage, but began instantly healing.

"You can't hurt me," she told him. "Merihim has taught me more than he ever taught you." She hurled a lightning bolt at him.

Already in motion, Warren drew the obsidian spear and thrust the butt to the ground. The lightning strike hit the spear and went through it, grounding out against the gantry. Warren had already shielded himself from it, but he didn't know if the Templar would be protected.

Before the woman recovered, Warren thrust the spear through her skull and killed her. He levered her body over the side into the milling masses of combatants.

Looking back, he saw that the two Templar had entered the machine. Warren glanced back over the side, found Naomi, and telekinetically moved her to the gantry.

"We're going inside," he told her.

"All right."

Warren plunged through the doorway, thinking of the woman Leah.

Once inside the machine, Simon found that his comm no longer connected him to anyone outside. However, he could get in touch with Leah.

"Simon?" she asked, and the note of terror and doubt in her voice hurt him.

"I'm here." Simon stared down long rows of cubicles that looked like sleeping compartments in Tokyo train stations. They were miniature coffins with barely enough room inside for an individual. He tracked her signal to one of the compartments, then broke the lock and pulled the cubicle out.

Leah lay inside, arms crossed over her chest. She looked ill, but her eyes were open and she was responsive.

"Where am I?" she asked.

"Still inside the machine." Simon offered her his hand and she took it. Gently, he helped her to her feet. Thankfully, there were no demons in evidence, but the fighting continued outside. The noise of the battle echoed down the hallway.

When he turned to walk back out, a Cabalist blocked his way. He recognized him as the man he'd cut the hand off four years ago. The one that had been in league with the demon.

"Warren," Leah said hoarsely.

"You know him?" Simon asked.

"Yes. I visited him in his dreams. He was one of those, like you, that I was able to communicate with."

Simon held his defensive stance at the ready, standing in front of Leah to protect her. His sword glinted.

"Leah?" the Cabalist said.

"Yes," Leah replied.

"You're with the Templar?" Warren sounded as though he couldn't believe it.

Simon respected the man's spear. In the tight confines of the tunnel, the spear gave the Cabalist reach and speed.

"No," Leah answered. "But Simon and I know each other."

"I see." Warren sounded disappointed. He focused on Simon. "Four years ago, you cut off my hand."

"Four years ago, you were with a demon that was trying to kill us," Simon replied. "I've heard you haven't kept much better company since."

"He is tonight," Leah pointed out. "Maybe we could all have this discussion somewhere else. Where we might not get attacked by demons. And there are a lot of other people to get out of here."

"We'll talk later?" Simon asked.

Grudgingly, Warren nodded.

Then they started freeing the other people trapped in the machine.

For a moment, Warren thought they were free. Although the building still remained dangerous, the combined might of the Cabalists and Templar had driven the Darkspawn back.

The Templar took control of the people who'd been held captive in the machine. Only fourteen of them had been left alive. Seventeen other cubicles only held corpses of people who were only hours dead.

Simon Cross gave orders for the Templar to plant explosive charges on the machine. They worked quickly in tandem, slapping preshaped packages on the machine.

"Get your people clear," Simon told Warren. "When this goes off, the building probably won't be left standing."

Warren gave the orders, but he didn't leave the Templar. Naomi stayed with him.

Merihim appeared in a blasting wind that knocked everyone down. Even the Templar fell and skidded across the floor.

The demon stood eight feet tall before adding in the horns. He was massive and muscular. Red scales covered his body. His harsh, blunt face always reminded Warren of a lizard. Merihim wore blue-green armor and carried a green metal trident.

"Well, worm," Merihim addressed Warren, "I see you've decided to try your luck."

Heart pounding, fear filling him, Warren stood on shaking knees. He thought about heroes and how they were always witty during battles like this. But that wasn't him. He wasn't a hero or brave or witty.

"You shouldn't have come here," Merihim said. He drew back his trident and drove it toward Warren's chest.

A sword knocked the trident aside. Then Simon stepped in front of Warren. The Templar held his sword in both hands.

"If you want to kill him," Simon declared, "you're going to have to go through me."

Merihim smiled. "Very well." He gestured and Simon lifted from the ground, held in an invisible grip.

The Templar grabbed his Spike Bolter with his free

hand and opened fire. Wounds opened up on the demon. Merihim growled angrily.

In the next moment, two more Templar attacked the demon from behind. Merihim flailed at them with his trident. Warren blocked the swing with a shield he summoned.

Simon fought the power that held him and finally won. He didn't know if his freedom was caused by his own efforts or through that of Nathan, Danielle, Leah, and the Cabalists who had remained behind.

As soon as his feet hit the ground, Simon gripped his sword in both hands and ran forward. He never broke stride as he lunged to attack. The demon tried to bring his trident back around, but Warren blocked his efforts again with his shield.

With the demon's wide-open chest as a target, Simon sank his sword into Merihim's flesh. The palladium-edged blade sank deeply into the demon's body and grated off bone. Simon's weight and momentum knocked Merihim backward off his feet. He crashed to the floor and started struggling immediately. Simon held the sword fast, but the floor pushed it back at him.

"Watch him!" a woman's voice yelled. "He'll try to escape this place with his magic."

From the corner of his eye, Simon saw a beautiful, black-haired woman standing only a few feet away. He didn't know where she'd come from.

In the next minute, Warren shoved an obsidian spear through the demon's head. Merihim quivered and shook. With his dying last gasp he cursed them all.

"I'll see you again," the demon promised as his strength left him. "When I climb back out of the Well of Midnight, I'll come looking for you."

The black-haired woman walked over to Merihim and placed her hands on each side of his head. She mouthed words that Simon couldn't understand. Blue haze drifted up from Merihim, and she breathed it all in. When she finished, she showed a huge grin, then Merihim's body burst into flames.

Simon gave the orders to plant the charges one more time, and they got out of the building. He watched from across the street as the detonations occurred and shook the building down to the ground.

By then, more demons started to gather. They had no choice but to flee. Maybe the machine was destroyed, as was the demon that had midwifed it, but the Hellgate remained open and the Burn continued changing all of London.

EPILOGUE

W
hat are you going to do now?" Leah asked.

Simon stood with her atop one of the hills near the redoubt. The sun was setting in the west, and a beautiful panorama of color spread up from it.

"We're going to have to leave," he said. "There's no choice. The demons are spreading out from London. Sooner or later they'll find us."

"But you have the Node technology now."

"No. We have *some* of the Node technology. We don't know if it'll ever be strong enough to protect whole cities. Or even the survivors we've gathered. Until then, we're going to have to look out for ourselves and try to find other ways to defeat the demons."

"With the Truths the Goetia manuscript mentions?"

Simon nodded. "We're still working on those. This is still a battle we can win. It's just not going to happen overnight. We'll learn more about them. The demons have been fighting, doing the same things over and over again for millennia. We've just started, really." He looked at her. "What about you?"

"Lyra is interested in what you've found out about the Goetia manuscript. I expect I'll be helping teams sift through all the information out there that we can recover. Old books. Old manuscripts. And, occasionally, demons we can interrogate. If these so-called Truths are out there, we'll find them."

Simon took her shoulders in his big hands. "I'm going to miss you."

She smiled up at him. "You're not gone yet. And it's not like you're going to be at the other end of the world. I can make the trip, and you'll probably still need to talk to the Templar here from time to time."

He gathered her into his arms and kissed her. For a moment he let himself believe that the world was just the two of them, and that none of the problems they faced existed.

The illusion didn't last long. The Hellgate still stood proudly over London.

THE END

ABOUT THE AUTHOR

Mel Odom lives in Moore, Oklahoma, with his wife and children. He's written dozens of books, original as well as tie-ins to games, shows, and movies such as *Buffy the Vampire Slayer* and *Blade,* and received the Alex Award for his novel *The Rover.* His novel *Apocalypse Dawn* was runner-up for the Christie Award.

He also coaches Little League baseball and basketball, teaches writing classes, and writes reviews of movies, DVDs, books, and video games.

His Web page is www.melodom.com, but he blogs at www.melodom.blogspot.com. He can be reached at mel@melodom.net.